Praise for

THE CARDINAL SINS

"Father Greeley does a spirited job of humanizing the lives and work of Catholic priests, showing that they don't live in ivory towers. The sex scenes are handled with taste but will undoubtedly shock old-school Catholics." —*Publishers Weekly*

"*The Cardinal Sins* is a tightly paced, clear-focused novel. . . . The characters (especially the women) are appealing; the dirty doings underneath the cassocks are shocking without being unnecessarily lurid; and the ecclesiastical backgrounds (a senile, psychotic archbishop is one of the many vivid cameos) have an authentic feel." —*Kirkus Reviews*

"Some might not like what Greeley has to say. . . . What is important is that *The Cardinal Sins* is about people one can care about and issues that matter." —*The Washington Star*

"There is bitterness and anguish in this novel—grief over the possibilities unfulfilled and roads not taken; but there is also courage, honesty, and the healing touch of religion." —*The San Francisco Examiner*

"For all his criticisms of the Church, Greeley loves it and believes in it completely, and this shines through the entire book. One ends up feeling positively about it all. I had an urge to go find my rosary beads." —Michele Ross, *The Atlanta Journal*

"A spectacular . . . fascinating story, fraught with all kinds of suspense and building up to a terrific climax."

—*The Catholic Review*

"An American *Thorn Birds,* a contemporary *Keys of the Kingdom,* a multigenerational novel you will treasure."

—*Literary Guild Magazine*

"A deft and readable novel with something to say about American Catholicism, *The Cardinal Sins* is a kind of modern parable. . . . Greeley is clearly doing his priestly thing: telling a story to preach a lesson."

—*The Catholic Messenger*

"Andrew Greeley, Roman Catholic priest, sociologist, and author, has never shied away from turmoil or criticism when writing about the Catholic Church. He calls it as he sees it, and sometimes what he sees shocks many a reader. But he goes on telling us, and we go on reading."

—*Levittown Courier-Times*

"Artfully written. There are moments in the course of the story when the Church and individual priests, bishops, and laypeople are portrayed in ways that will bring a lump to your throat. There are many pages that could only have been written by one who loves the Church deeply."

—*Inland Register*

"As a woman I read this story of forbidden love with total fascination; as a writer, with total admiration."

—Cynthia Freeman, author of *Come Pour the Wine*

ALSO BY ANDREW M. GREELEY FROM TOM DOHERTY ASSOCIATES

BISHOP BLACKIE RYAN MYSTERIES

The Bishop and the Missing L Train

The Bishop and the Beggar Girl of St. Germain

The Bishop in the West Wing

The Bishop Goes to the University

The Bishop at the Lake

The Archbishop in Andalusia

NUALA ANNE MCGRAIL NOVELS

Irish Gold

Irish Lace

Irish Whiskey

Irish Mist

Irish Eyes

Irish Love

Irish Stew!

Irish Cream

Irish Crystal

Irish Linen

Irish Tiger

THE O'MALLEYS IN THE TWENTIETH CENTURY

A Midwinter's Tale

Younger Than Springtime

A Christmas Wedding

September Song

Second Spring

Golden Years

All About Women

Angel Fire

Angel Light

The Cardinal Sins

Contract with an Angel

Faithful Attraction

The Final Planet

Furthermore!: Memories of a Parish Priest

God Game

Jesus: A Meditation on His Stories and His Relationships with Women

Star Bright!

Summer at the Lake

White Smoke

Sacred Visions (editor with Michael Cassutt)

The Book of Love (editor with Mary G. Durkin)

Emerald Magic (editor)

ANDREW M. GREELEY

THE CARDINAL SINS

A TOM DOHERTY ASSOCIATES BOOK
New York

This is a work of fiction. All of the characters, organizations, and events portrayed in this novel are either products of the author's imagination or are used fictitiously.

THE CARDINAL SINS

Originally published in 1981 by Warner Books

A Forge Book
Published by Tom Doherty Associates, LLC
175 Fifth Avenue
New York, NY 10010

www.tor-forge.com

Forge® is a registered trademark of Tom Doherty Associates, LLC.

Library of Congress Cataloging-in-Publication Data

Greeley, Andrew M., 1928–
The cardinal sins / Andrew M. Greeley.
p. cm.
"A Tom Doherty Associates book."
ISBN-13: 978-0-7653-2291-3
ISBN-10: 0-7653-2291-9
1. Catholics—Fiction. I. Title.
PS3557.R358C37 2009
813'.54—dc22
2008046469

First Edition: March 2009

Printed in the United States of America

0 9 8 7 6 5 4 3 2 1

In memory of Hilda Lindley

Stern as death is love,
Relentless as the nether world is passion.
Its flames are a blazing fire;
Deep waters cannot quench love,
Nor floods sweep it away.

—Canticle of Solomon

A NOTE ABOUT THE CARDINAL SINS

The so-called cardinal (or "deadly" or "capital") sins are not sins at all but seven disorderly propensities in our personality that lead us to sinful behavior. Pride, covetousness, lust, anger, gluttony, envy, and sloth are sound and healthy human proclivities gone askew: self-respect, self-preservation, communion, personal freedom, self-expression, celebration, relaxation. The cardinal sins result not from fundamental evil but from fundamental goodness running out of control, from human love that is confused and frightened and not trusting enough of love. The cardinal sins have nothing to do, of course, with the members of the Sacred College, who, as we all know, commit hardly any sins.

Traditional Catholic spirituality has contended that all of us have a "dominant fault," the cardinal sin that is strongest in our personality (just as in medieval morality plays a different character paradigmatically represents each of the seven vices). If one were to seek the dominant fault of the four leading actors in this story, one might conclude that Kevin's weakness is pride, Patrick's covetousness, Ellen's anger (with an occasional dash of gluttony), and Maureen's sloth (or "acedia," as it is sometimes called). They are all troubled—as are the rest of us—by not a little lust and envy.

—A.M.G.

AUTHOR'S NOTE

Unfortunately there is no real-life counterpart of Patrick Cardinal Donahue. Despite all his flaws and faults he is a much more effective leader than many of our current crop of crimson-clad princes of the Church. The student of the history of the Sacred College will perceive, I am sure, that many less worthy than he have worn the sacred scarlet during the last millennium.

He is a product of my imagination, a "what-if" character like everyone else in the book (save for those not marked with an asterisk in the Cast of Ecclesiastical Characters, which follows). Also imaginary are the events in the archdiocese of Chicago after 1965.

The book, then, is story, not history or biography or (perhaps sadly) autobiography. It is nonetheless true.

ANDREW M. GREELEY

Chicago
Spring 1981

CAST OF ECCLESIASTICAL CHARACTERS

MONSIGNOR ADOLPHO, Spanish curialist*

SEBASTIANO BAGGIO, head of the Congregation of Bishops, moderate papal candidate

GIOVANNI BENELLI, papal chief of staff, later Archbishop of Florence

FATHER CARTER, American Jesuit teaching in Rome*

AGOSTINO CASAROLI, Vatican official dealing with Eastern Europe, later secretary of state

RAFFAELLO CRESPI, apostolic delegate*

RICHARD CUSHING, Archbishop of Boston

PATRICK HENRY DONAHUE, seventh Archbishop of Chicago*

PERICLE FELICI, general secretary of Vatican Council, leader of Curial conservatives

MARCEL FLAMBEAU, Archbishop of Luxembourg*

JOHN KROL, Archbishop of Philadelphia

HANS KÜNG, Swiss theologian

ALBINO LUCIANI, SALVATORE PAPPALARDO, GIOVANNI

*Denotes fictional character.

COLOMBO, UGO POLETTI, CORRADO URSI, Italian archbishops, "compromise" papal candidates

ANTONIO MARTINELLI, Archbishop of Perugia* (from Piacenza)

ALBERT GREGORY MEYER, fifth Archbishop of Chicago

DERMOT MCCARTHY, Irish curialist*

JOHN COURTNEY MURRAY, American theologian and expert on religious liberty

DANIEL O'NEIL, sixth Archbishop of Chicago*

ALFREDO OTTAVIANI, aged reactionary curialist

SERGIO PIGNEDOLI, moderate papal candidate

JOHN QUINN, Chicago canon lawyer

OPILIO ROSSI, SYLVIO ODDI, conservative curialists (from Piacenza)

GIUSEPPE SIRI, Archbishop of Genoa, conservative candidate for papacy

SAMUEL STRITCH, fourth Archbishop of Chicago

LEO JOSEF SUENENS, Archbishop of Mechelen-Brussels

JEAN VILLOT, papal secretary of state

KAROL WOJTYLA, Prince Archbishop of Cracow

JOHN WRIGHT, Bishop of Pittsburgh (later Cardinal)

BOOK I

The Forties

CHAPTER ONE

1948

Patrick Donahue had been my closest friend since as long as I could remember. We were inseparable all through grammar school and our three years at Jesuit High. He'd been a little guy, much shorter than I, until we were freshmen. Then he shot up and out almost overnight. Grown-ups thought he was adorable when he was little; now they were charmed by his poise and his mature courtesy. Older girls once said he was "so cute" with his towhead, long eyelashes, and silver-blue eyes. Now that he was seventeen, women of all ages thought he was magnificent.

Two years before, at fifteen, Pat was tongue-tied and embarrassed with girls; now he seemed to have nothing else but girls on his mind, even when they were only well-developed freshmen like my "cousin" Maureen Cunningham.

It was said by everyone in those days that Pat looked like Guy Madison, a comment that will make sense only if you can remember those days or if you watch very late television movies. Guy Madison or not, his laugh was contagious, and his sense of fun made him the center of any group of which he was a part.

Pat was not as good a student as I, and not a leader, either. He was—and it is important that I note this—much more devout than I. It was an erratic kind of devotion, marked by closed retreats, sustained periods of daily mass and rosary recitation, complicated reforms of his moral life, and then dramatic relapses into drinking and girl-chasing: the Irish approach to spirituality, my father assured me, disapproving of my more even and casual approach to the deity.

Early on a Saturday morning in the humid July of 1948, Pat was walking next to me, talking about my cousin Maureen, when a gray Packard rolled over in the ditch across the road from us and exploded. Pat's courage and quick reaction saved their lives. I stood there glued in the summer dust, waiting for an orange ball of flame and smoke to devour the car. Still, I got the credit.

I had been walking down the hill behind the village on my way to church. Pat was climbing up the hill, his handsome face and cheery smile undimmed by a night of merriment on the beach. He offered to walk back down to church with me, mostly, I think, because if we came home from church together, my mother and father might not ask any questions about how he had spent the night. I should have been angry with him; he was my guest, and I was responsible for his spiritual and physical welfare. But Pat's laughter and high spirits, especially in those days, made it hard to be angry at him.

"Not much in the way of serious necking," he said, grinning complacently. "Not even enough to keep me from Communion at mass."

"Beer after twelve breaks your fast," I said primly.

"You already sound like a monsignor." Pat walloped me on the back in great humor. "Kevin, they're going to ordain you a monsignor."

"At least a bishop," I said. "Maybe even a cardinal."

"Kevin Cardinal Brennan." He laughed. "I like the sound of it. Make me a papal knight or something?"

The asphalt on the road was soft from the heat. I dreaded the walk back after mass. It was going to be another miserably hot day. "And Maureen a papal dame. Dame Mo. I like the sound of that!"

"She *is* some dame." Pat shook his head appreciatively. "I know she's your cousin, but for a freshman she's got the hottest lips on the beach."

"Not really a cousin," I pointed out. "Our fathers have been law partners for so long that we call each other 'Cousin.' So those hot lips aren't off limits to me, either."

"That'd be the day. Kevin Brennan, the pillar of piety, necking all night on the beach."

The thought of Mo's lips pressed against mine was far more appealing than I was willing to admit. "Where is Maureen? Too hung over to walk up the hill? Or just too spoiled?"

Pat shrugged his shoulders. "Marty Delaney is going to drive them back up in his Packard. I wanted the exercise. Told them you would be angry if I didn't stay in condition for the basketball season."

"It's your scholarship, not mine."

My reminder sailed by him unnoticed. Pat needed the scholarship to go to college. The Brennans were wealthy enough that money would never be a worry for any of us. I suspected Pat thought it was unfair. I thought it unfair that he possessed ten times as much charm as I did.

Before we could say anything more, the Delaney Packard roared around the final curve separating the hill from the village. Marty must have been driving sixty miles an hour. He would have made the turn with a few inches to spare if old Doc Crawford's Buick, on its way to the yacht club, hadn't turned the corner from the opposite direction. Delaney swerved—instinctively, I suppose—to avoid the big red car, skidded toward the side of the road where we were walking, then back across the slippery asphalt and into the ditch. The Packard rolled over like a turtle at the end of a stick, its wheels spinning helplessly in the air.

Pat raced toward the car. "Let's get them out of there," he shouted.

My feet felt as if they were cemented in the ground. I finally trudged after him, each stride taking an eternity.

Inside the car, people were screaming. Pat wrenched the door open. "Give me a hand, Kevin," he yelled to me.

We pulled Marty Delaney out from the driver's seat. His face was a mask of blood. Sue Hanlon was next to him, unconscious, her dress torn and her slim legs twisted beneath her at an unnatural angle. I helped the battered but conscious Delaney to the side of the ditch as Pat gently set Sue in the dust.

We were dragging Joan Ryan and Joe Heeney from the back seat when the fuel tank blew. The force of the explosion knocked all of us into the ditch. Joan's thin dress caught fire, and she wailed hysterically as the flames leaped to her long, blond hair. Joe lay silently by the side of the road. For a moment I thought we were all going to die. Then Pat knocked Joan down and rolled her over in the dust, extinguishing the fire, and I carried Sue to the safety of the road. I stood there dumbly while Joan, her hysteria spent and her freckled face streaked with dirt and soot, and Pat dragged the two boys away from the crackling flames.

Doc Crawford, who had managed to stop his car only a few yards from the accident, was suddenly next to me, trying to get Sue out of my arms. I struggled for a while and then put her down on the grass. I sat next to her while Doc probed and grunted and shook his head. Acrid smoke from the burning automobile tore at my nostrils and stung my eyes.

The State Police ambulance arrived after what seemed like hours. Ted Smith, the police lieutenant, and Father O'Rourke, the alcoholic pastor of our village church, stood next to the smoldering wreck, shaking their heads.

"If we had been a few seconds later," Pat was breathing heavily, "they all would have gone up in smoke." His face and hair were black, his white shirt and slacks ripped and dirty.

"And us with them," I said. Only then did I realize that Maureen had not been in the car.

"None of them have a right to be alive," said the lieutenant in a nasal, rural-Wisconsin drawl. "Damn fool kids, drinking all night and then doing sixty miles an hour in a twenty-mile-an-hour zone. Lucky you were here, Kevin."

"You saved their lives and maybe their souls, Kevin," added the haggard old priest, rolling up a soiled purple stole. "If they'd died without the last rites, after what they were doing on the beach, they would have gone straight to hell."

"How do you know?" I demanded. "Anyway, it was Pat who saved them."

They didn't seem to hear me. I saw a spasm of pain cross Pat's face.

"Two of them look like they're goners, the girl especially," said Ted, fingering his trim, Tom Dewey mustache. "If they make it, Kevin, it's all your doing."

Still in a daze, I walked back to our house, at the top of the hill, vomited the knots out of my stomach, and went to my room to sleep away the rest of the day.

"They're all going to be fine except the Hanlon girl," my mother said when she woke me for supper, her red hair glowing in the rays of the afternoon sun. "Sue Hanlon will probably be crippled for the rest of her life."

For years I saw Sue's legs, twisted beneath her, in my dreams.

Now I can't distinguish them from the butchered legs of another woman who also haunts my dreams.

Pat returned to our summer house at the lake the last week in August, after the excitement about the accident had died down. One afternoon he blew a softball game against some of the local kids; he was the tying run coming in from third, and he tried to skirt around a half-pint catcher instead of knocking him down.

I sulked at supper that night, angry at him for losing the softball game, although Pat, as usual, joked with the rest of the family. After supper, he asked if he could borrow the Studebaker to see what was going on in town. I knew, of course, that he wanted to go pick up Maureen on the property next to ours. Mrs. Cunningham thought Pat was a charming young man and raised no objections to her daughter's roaming around southern Wisconsin with the son of a sanitation worker.

Silently I gave him the keys.

"You want to come?" he asked tentatively, his face turning the bashful pink that so charmed the ladies. "We could find Cunningham and Foley."

Ellen Foley, to whom I was assigned for the week by Maureen and Pat, was the runt of the litter. Maureen had taken the poor thing under her wing, and I had got her by default.

"Forget it," I said sullenly. I settled in a rocking chair on our open front porch, which overlooked the village and the lake. My grandfather and Maureen's had bought several square miles in the hills behind the lake before the First World War, preferring the quiet and privacy to what my father called the "resort slums" along the beach.

In the years spent recovering from the Depression my father had been tempted to sell his section of the land. Finally, just before he went into the service, Tom Cunningham assured him there would be enough money in the law firm to take care of our family while he was away. Dad returned from nearly four years of service with white hair, a chest full of medals, and an eagle on his shoulder, only to find that the law firm had sagged. Tom was more interested in his beautiful little girl than in running the firm. Dad, now "the Colonel," permitted himself only the comment that such was the fruit of marrying late in life, and threw himself into the practice the same way he had led charges at Cassino and Bastogne.

Three years later we were affluent beyond anyone's dreams. The Cunninghams, without doing much work, were trailing close behind us. Dad was talking about building a swimming pool at the lake and a winter house in Florida; neither he nor my mother suffered any compunctions about spending money. In those years everyone's expectations rose and expanded like a hot-air balloon. There was never going to be another Depression. The sky was the limit.

In our neighborhood in Chicago, though, "postwar" created a split that, in 1948, seemed permanent. The Cunninghams and the Brennans had seemed only a little ahead of the Donahues and the Foleys during the common suffering of the earlier years, but now we were rich, and Pat's father was still a sanitation worker—a garbage man—and Ellen's father was a poor Irish cop.

I watched the lake beneath me turn crimson in the sunset, motorboat wakes slicing across it, colored sails lazily drooping in the still air, cars slipping around the shore roads to Friday-evening cocktail and dinner parties. I was worried about Pat Donahue. Unless we won the city championship next year, he probably would not get a scholarship to Notre Dame. If he had girls on his mind during the season, as he did this summer, he could blow it.

My father slipped into the rocking chair next to me. "Beautiful view, isn't it, Champ?"

I grunted agreement. My father didn't know what to make of me. I'd been a winsome little punk when he went off to war. He'd come home to find his wife as beautiful as ever, his younger kids wide-eyed with joy, and his oldest a mysterious, calculating fourteen-year-old. As he put it later, "A tall, lean gallowglass with a grim face, thick red hair, and hard green eyes." To make matters worse, I promptly told him I was going to be a priest.

"This reminds me of a lot of places in Italy and Switzerland," he said thoughtfully. He rarely shared memories of the war with us. "A few times I thought I'd never see it again."

I didn't say anything.

"Hard one to lose today," he went on, tentatively.

"Pickup game," I said noncommittally.

"You like to win them all, though," he mused.

"Can't imagine where I got it, Colonel," I said dryly.

His eyes were twinkling in the fading light. "Maybe winning isn't as important to Pat as it is to you."

"I was thinking the same thing," I replied. "So when Pat comes back with the car and the girls, I'll forget about it."

He slapped my knee and wandered off in the darkness looking for my mother, trailing a rich smell of Turkish tobacco in the night air.

When the Studebaker lumbered up the driveway with Pat and Maureen Cunningham in the front seat, I cut through Pat's apology and got in the back of the car with Ellen Foley. She looked, I thought, like a frightened, ponytailed third-grader caught disobeying the instructions of a patrol boy.

Pat drove down the hill to the village with elaborate care.

Maureen taunted him that it was my car and there was no reason to be careful.

"Sure, Pat," I said tartly, "pile it up. It's covered by the company insurance policy. Mo's father will probably get you off with involuntary manslaughter; Father O'Rourke will anoint us, if he's sober enough; and we can play poker with Sue Hanlon in the hospital."

"You should have gone into the seminary three years ago," Mo said, dismissing me. "Then you'd be in a place where everyone keeps all the rules all the time."

"And I wouldn't have to put up with spoiled only children whose fathers think they can do no wrong," I answered.

We drove to the Sugar Bowl in silence. I sensed reproach from the small person next to me.

The Sugar Bowl was an ice-cream joint with a jukebox, very bright lights, the smell of sour milk, and wooden tables that may well have predated the Civil War. All the male heads, and most of the female ones, turned when Maureen entered. She sensed all the attention and loved it.

Maureen was gorgeous: perfect white complexion, long black hair, the figure of a model, reckless wit, teasing dark eyes. She was any teenage male's dream of The Woman. When we saw *State Fair* at the beginning of the summer, we all agreed that Mo was better-looking than Jeanne Crain.

Maureen maneuvered herself into the booth so that Pat would have to sit next to her. Her bare knee brushed lightly against mine. "Are your folks going to the Labor Day dance at the club?" she asked me, effectively cutting out the two nonmembers who sat with us.

Flustered by the unexpected contact, I turned to the waitress and gave her our order: two banana splits, one chocolate sundae, and one chocolate malt for my "date."

In control again, I answered Maureen's question.

"I doubt it. You know how my mother objects to drunkenness. We'll probably have a hot-dog roast at the pond. My father cleaned up the place so we can swim in it."

"Oh, good, that sounds like fun," Maureen said. "We'll have to go there one day."

"Another setting for one of your immoral swimsuits?" I asked, trying to sound disapproving.

"I don't notice you looking away when I show up," she said acidly. "For someone who's going to be a priest, you stare as much as anyone else."

The jukebox finished "It Might as Well Be Spring" and turned to jitterbug music. "Come on, Pat," said Mo, grabbing his hand, "let's dance. Kevin the Creep can explain to Ellen why I'm the only one who dares to make fun of him."

I watched them dance. Two tall, handsome young people superbly coordinated, in full possession of their supple bodies—a black-haired magic princess and a blond, fair knight. The stuff of which romantic dreams are made.

"Why did you send him home today?"

I looked for the voice that sounded like distant bells chiming and discovered that it had come from Ellen. It was the first time all evening she had spoken directly to me.

"I didn't send him home. I went home before him."

Her eyes were wide and soft and remarkably clear. "I don't mean that. I mean when you were coaching at third. You had a tie. Why not hold him at third and wait for the next batter? You were grandstanding as much as he was."

"We were building up steam," I said. "If he'd scored, we might have got five or six more runs."

Her eyes continued to watch me unblinkingly. "Tim Curran is the best hitter on the team. Chances were better that he'd drive Pat in than that Pat would knock over the catcher." Her pert, sunburned nose wrinkled slightly.

"Girls don't know anything about baseball," I said lamely, immediately vexed with myself for falling back on such an unfair put-down.

"He didn't want to win enough, and you wanted to win too much," she said, her voice decisive. "Anyway," she added, placating me, "I think it's nice the way you take care of him." Her eyes fell away from my face.

"When you grow up, Ellen Foley, you may be dangerous."

Her face colored to the roots of her pale ponytail. I watched her sip her chocolate malt. There was something neatly delectable about her smooth throat, clear complexion, and determined chin.

"Is there anything strange about the way I'm drinking this, Kevin Brennan?" she asked, her huge eyes regarding me clinically.

"With merriment I watch, and awe,/Ethereal Titania sip her magic straw."

The words tumbled out before I could stop them. Her lips turned up in a smile. "Maureen said you were sweet about twice a year."

"Now you can hold your breath waiting for the second time." My fingers, as impulsive as my tongue, reached for her hand on the table. She pulled it back quickly as I touched it. It felt as though an electric current leaped back and forth between us.

"A good thing that you and your quick tongue are going to the seminary," she said.

We were saved from saying any more by the arrival of Tim Curran, his eyes glowing with the light of two beers.

"Hi, Chief," he greeted me. "Hi, Small Fry." He patted Ellen on the head as if she were a puppy dog. "Mind if I sit while those two neck out there?"

"They won't notice any of us when they come back," Ellen said. "What new schemes for the Black Raider?"

Tim brushed a lock of curly hair out of his eyes. "I'm working on a really great scheme for October," he began eagerly. "Kevin, here, is too old for such things, but I say, hell, why grow up? Isn't that right, Kevin?"

She was only a runt, but she was my runt for the evening. I didn't like Tim's smiling at her like a devil-may-care IRA gunman. "We all have to grow up," I said darkly.

"What's the October scheme?" Ellen said, ignoring my disapproval.

"I can't tell you yet, but it will be better than when old man Honnikar came into his delicatessen and found that someone had rearranged all his shelves."

"Or the McGinitys when they returned home and found their living-room furniture in the dining room and vice versa," Ellen added.

"You're too young to remember that," I reprimanded her.

She shook her head defiantly and finished the last dregs of the malt. "I'm not too young to remember that you were the one who put the life-size Sacred Heart statue on the toilet seat in Sister Pauline's bathroom."

My face, which, come to think of it, had been warm for some time, got warmer. "It was Tim's idea."

"And Kevin will never tell anyone how he managed to get into the convent with the statue."

"It was easy. I just—" I checked myself because I realized I was trying to impress Ellen Foley with my skills as a member of the Black Raider's band.

"Almost spilled the beans," Tim said, grinning owlishly.

"You must have the goods on him, Small Fry." He nudged my shoulder. "There's still some beer left in the village that would be a shame to waste. See you both later." He left, slipping through the crowd on the dance floor as if he were indeed the mysterious, invisible Black Raider of our childhood.

"He's the nicest," Ellen said admiringly.

"He drinks too much beer," I replied.

Fortunately for me, Mo and Pat, breathless and exultant, chose that moment to return to the table. I was undoubtedly about to make a fool of myself.

⁂

The next morning, as I brought the breakfast dishes to my mother in the kitchen, she said, "Wasn't that the Foley girl in the car last night?"

"Mothers don't miss much," I said, putting the dishes into the sink and taking a towel to the silverware.

"That's what they get paid for," she said. "She's become a very lovely thing, hasn't she?"

"I didn't notice."

"No?" She was thoughtfully rinsing out a glass. "Maybe you should look a little harder."

"Like Dad, my tastes do not run to small women."

"If you're like your father, you're indiscriminate in what you admire as long as it looks good in a swimsuit."

"I haven't seen Ellen in one yet, but I don't expect it will affect my blood pressure."

"I worry about girls like her. Her mother makes her a slave, taking care of all those little children, as though Ellen is the one to blame for the size of the family. She'll grow up and get married and won't know how to be anything but a drudge. I'm surprised Kate Foley let her off for a few weeks up here."

"Ellen was sick last month. The doctor thought it might be a mild case of polio. Mo says it was exhaustion. Anyway, don't worry about her. She's as smart as they come."

My mother's eyes widened. "You noticed her intelligence and not her figure, Kevin? Maybe you *do* belong in a seminary."

We both laughed.

"What do you young people want out of life?" she asked, being very careful to sound casual and not to look at me directly.

"We all want contradictions," I replied with equally elaborate indifference. "Pat wants to be powerful and popular. Maureen wants to be a painter, but she also loves to dabble in politics. Ellen—I'm not sure about what goes on in that head, but I think she wants to be a writer and have a family. They're innocents. Me—I just want to be a priest."

CHAPTER TWO

1948

Pat Donahue was afraid. His throat was dry; his hands were wet. The deeper they walked into the dank, humid woods, the more uncertain he became. She moved ahead of him, swaying slightly, dodging now and then to avoid snagging the peasant skirt and blouse chosen out of deference to Sunday. She did not look back at him as they picked their way down the worn old path.

They came to a clearing. Could she hear the pounding in his head?

She turned toward him with an inviting smile. "This used to be a summerhouse where my grandparents came to drink tea and lemonade. The Colonel had it cleaned up and painted at the same time he fixed up the pond. Considerate of him, wasn't it?"

He followed her up the three creaking steps into the tiny, latticed, octagonal enclosure. It was dark and musky inside, thick with the smell of fresh paint, as isolated from the rest of the world as a desert island. She turned toward him again, her eyes glittering with expectation. He took her into his arms roughly and began to kiss her lips. She pressed her body against his, then eased her head away.

"Not bad at all, Pat, not bad at all. I like the way you kiss." She laughed at him.

He started to kiss her again. This time he was more patient and careful. Their lips explored each other, probing, searching, hunting. She let him dominate, yielding herself to his strength.

He wrestled her to the floor of the summerhouse. His hands went under the dress, up her thighs. His touch was gentle despite the fever in his blood. Tenderly he caressed, probed. She gave herself to his explorations, sighing softly with pleasure.

With some assistance from her, he partially undressed her. She was passive in his arms, breathing heavily. He would do it. She wasn't expecting that. You were supposed to stop short. He would teach her a lesson.

She fought him, then gave up, as if resigned to losing her virginity.

His passion changed suddenly to fear and revulsion. He drew away and turned from the sight of her half-naked body. "We'd better go find Kevin and Ellen," he said weakly.

She climbed slowly to her feet. "Mustn't keep Kevin waiting," she said, her voice unsteady as she dressed.

They walked out of the stuffy summerhouse into the cool shade of the clearing. Pat felt cheated. Would going all the way really make it any better?

He wanted to apologize for what he had done. She was pretending not to mind. "We're going to have to do this again. It sure beats playing pinochle," he said, trying to sound as if it were something he did every day.

"What did you say?" I asked Ellen absently.

If she was impatient with my inattention, her soft eyes didn't show it.

"I said we're not going to do what they're doing, are we?"

"What are they doing?" My mother's observation about her

figure didn't seem very accurate, though the loose white shorts and blouse she wore didn't provide many hints.

"Everything short of intercourse, I imagine," she replied evenly.

"I'm not so sure that it will be 'everything,' " I said. "Do you want that?"

"No." She wouldn't look at me. "Do you?"

"Not with someone just out of the cradle."

There was no answering taunt. I dismissed her from my mind. Pat and Maureen were the problem. I prayed to God, not all that sure he would care about Pat and Mo if I stopped worrying about them.

It was the first time I'd seen the pond since Dad had cleaned it up. About thirty-five yards long, it rose from a natural spring and flowed in a brook down toward the lake. In a hollow between two hills, probably carved by a minor glacier, the pond was surrounded on all sides by very old weeping willows. Except in dry times, the water flowed through it too quickly for mosquitoes and other insects to breed. The rocks that formed its natural basin were eroding slowly, and the slab of granite that was the natural dam at the end of it wouldn't last, my father said. Then it would have to be turned into a mostly artificial pool. Until then we would enjoy it as a swimming hole, deep enough at the dam end so that you could dive into it.

It was a hot, humid day, the kind of Middle Western Sunday afternoon that only summer-worshipers like me can stand. An inviting sheet of silver, the pond always seemed mysterious to me. I imagined it inhabited by water spirits, some dark like the willows when the sun no longer shone on them, some light like the jewels that seemed to dance on the water. I stared at the pond and wondered about Maureen and Pat. Heavenly Father, please protect them. . . .

"It's so beautiful," said Ellen, beside me. "What a shame we didn't wear our swimsuits."

I was angry at this little nuisance, a tiny cat meowing outside a window. "You don't need clothes to swim here," I said roughly, reaching for the top button of her blouse.

Even now I don't quite understand what happened. Though I told myself I would stop after the first button, I was trapped, as she was, in the grip of powers beyond control or understanding.

My finger pressed the button so hard it cracked. Her expression did not change. Her eyes were still clear and cool. I went to the next button and the one after it, calmly, leisurely, as though falling into a trance. I told myself as I pushed away her blouse that all I wanted to do was see her in her underwear. We would swim in our underwear.

Yet there was a flow to my movements as inevitable as that of the water trickling over the rock dam behind her. My hands went to the straps of her bra as if someone else were moving them. It was a ridiculously elaborate garment for a child, but I managed to unhook it with ease.

My mother was right. Ellen Foley was indeed a woman. Her breasts, pale white, were flawless. She was a diminutive but superbly carved idol.

She did not move a muscle as I stripped her; there was only a quick gasp of breath and then a rush of conflicting emotions across her face as my fingers pulled the elastic waistband of her panties down.

I held one of her hands and stared at the fullness of her beauty. I felt no desire, indeed did not even think of desire. Yet it was much more than an aesthetic admiration. What I felt for Ellen Foley was infinitely beyond physical desire.

She slipped her hand out of mine, picked up her clothes, and arranged them neatly on a rock. Then she began to unbutton my shirt.

I was a mixture of shame, joy, pain, exaltation, enslavement, freedom. When, kneeling before me as I had before her, she removed my shorts, I felt the same sting of embarrassment and pleasure I had seen on her face. She piled up my clothes in a neat stack next to hers and took both my hands in her own, her breasts shivering as she moved.

We stood there, more one than two, for a long time. Neither of us said a word, both of us smiling. Then I lowered her gently to the warm waters of the pond. She let the water spill over her body, sank beneath the surface, and then rose to float next to the rock, beckoning me to join her. I dived in, and we swam together, at first slowly and solemnly. Then, after she dunked my head, we began to play, chasing each other as though this were the final act of a ballet choreographed by the unseen power whose instrument we were.

Afterward, we sat on the rock, our bodies drying in the sun. We did not touch each other; we didn't have to. I'm sure it was Ellen who kept the interlude magical and mysterious. Naked, she was elegantly graceful, more modest in her delicate self-possession than when clothed. She was incapable of vulgarity. She was as graceful as the stirring of ripples on the pond.

Finally I broke the silence. "We'd better get back. Maureen is probably using us as an excuse to escape from my predatory friend."

She smiled and pushed my clothes toward me. For the first time I became conscious of how beautiful her smile was.

Minutes after we dressed, Pat and Maureen arrived, he whistling, she looking uneasy and tense.

"What were you two doing?" Maureen demanded archly, noting Ellen's wet hair.

"Talking about gods and books and other things," I said.

Four more times that humid August, oblivious of Harry Truman and Alger Hiss, Ellen and I went to the pool and enacted our solemn, silent ritual. The last time, with thunderclouds slowly forming in the afternoon sky, Ellen materialized quietly on our porch in her inevitable oversize white blouse and shorts. Already in a trance, I rose and followed her back into the woods. On the rock, after we had worn ourselves out with swimming, we began to touch each other's bodies, as though we were touching the sacred vessels in an ancient sanctuary. Then I put my arms around Ellen and she nestled her head against my chest. It lasted an eternity.

On the Sunday night of the Labor Day weekend, there was the traditional huge bonfire in the village. Crates, cartons, paper, broken furniture—anything combustible was heaped high in the public park at the shore of the lake and set aflame.

This year it was a cool weekend. I watched the dancing fire and thought melancholy thoughts about the end of summer, and about growing older. The reflection of the fire turned the faces of the young people watching it strange and mysterious colors; they were like Halloween ghosts dancing before they descended back into hell.

Tim Curran, his enthusiasm supercharged by beer, was beating fiercely on his uke. Pat led the crowd, singing at the top of his rich tenor voice. Mo, with a sweater casually worn over her halter, clung to him as if he were about to leave for war. I did not sing. I was in no mood for "Buttons and Bows." Ellen and I stood silently apart from the others, hypnotized by the fire.

"Pat leads the fun and you lead everything else," she said in her Wise Old Woman tones.

"Shut up," I said gently. "You'll spoil the mood."

"The bonfire," Ellen said, disobeying my order. "Reminds you of the fire in the car, doesn't it? But you shouldn't be sad about it, Kevin. You saved their lives." She took my hand and moved closer to me.

"Pat saved their lives," I insisted.

"Pat and you both saved their lives," she said, like a schoolmarm correcting a dull student.

I put my arm around her and held her tightly.

CHAPTER THREE

1949

Maureen filled my glass with lukewarm champagne. Tonight she was fifteen going on thirty, her mood bubbling like the sparkling wine. Pleased with my careful inspection by the glow of candlelight, she drew herself up to her full five feet nine inches, only a few inches shorter than I.

"To 1949, Cousin Kevin!" she said, toasting me as well as the year.

Outside, the lightning crisscrossed the sky and the rain beat against the windows.

"To the end of the Berlin blockade, and to Harry S. Truman's second term," I responded, as gravely as I could.

"Oh, hell"—she stamped her foot impatiently—"don't be so goddamn serious. Let's drink to what you really want for the new year: a city championship and a good start in the seminary." She swallowed half the champagne in her goblet.

I cautiously sipped from my glass. My parents, exploring the possibilities of a Florida home and following a characteristic, last-minute impulse, had rented an old house at the edge of a swamp. They had gone to a New Year's Eve party at the hotel, leaving me as baby-sitter in charge of the little kids and Maureen. The former did what they were told, though my fourteen-year-old sister, Mary Ann, stayed up until eleven-thirty. Then, sleepy-eyed, she had tiptoed off to bed—only a year and a half younger than Maureen and yet a generation behind her. Mo and I had the house to ourselves. When the clock over the fireplace had chimed twelve, we had opened the bottle of champagne she had smuggled in that afternoon.

"Happy 1949 to you, Cousin Mo, and may it bring you whatever you're looking for." She frowned at me and filled her glass again, nervously stubbing out her cigarette.

"Hey, Christian," I said, "why are you stealing all the firewater?" We had seen *Treasure of the Sierra Madre* that afternoon for the third time. Its expressions were now part of our vocabulary.

"So the seminarian likes my magic drink," she said, pouring champagne into my glass. "Well, let's drink to our friends. To Pat Donahue; may he get his Notre Dame scholarship and his first good lay."

"Maureen!" I pretended to be shocked.

"Oh, screw it, Kevin," she shot back. "Pat is like most jocks. He's got to prove that he's a man over and over again." Then her anger faded as had the Florida sunshine earlier in the day. "Okay, Kevin, I withdraw the second half. To Pat's scholarship and the city championship that goes with it." She was smiling again. Her loveliness, emphasized by light-brown slacks and sweater, was irresistible. I sipped to her toast and kissed her.

"Happy New Year, Maureen," I said, hoping my rapid breathing didn't show.

"Hey, that's not bad for a baby-sitter," she exclaimed. "Sit down while I get some pretzels and put on a record. If you want me, just whistle." That was from *To Have and Have Not,* which we had seen the day before.

I did as I was told. My last New Year's Eve before entering

the seminary, alone in candlelight with a beautiful girl in a Florida storm, and the champagne was making my head spin even faster.

"Are you really going to take City, Kev?" she asked, placing the pretzels in front of me and joining me on the couch, which groaned in aged protest. I remembered all the things the retreat masters had said about eating late at night with a girl. Well, whatever I did could be confessed, though that attitude was sinful in itself. "It depends on Pat. When he's on, he's the best shot in the Catholic League. When he's off, we're just another team. Leo is the only real threat, and we ran all over them last time. If Pat gets twenty-eight points again when we play them in March, it'll be a walkaway." I was now guzzling the champagne as eagerly as she was.

Mo was thoughtful. "He's an awfully nice boy, Kev. Even when he's playing his Joe Stud game, he's afraid to hurt people." She leaned her head on my shoulder and sighed. "When I'm with you, I start getting responsible for people just like you do. Anyway, let's drink a toast to poor Ellen. . . . Well, I'll be damned. You drank all the champagne."

"I did not!" I said. "You had two glasses for every one that—"

Her black eyes flashed. "Ha, you've been counting. Let me tell you, Mr. Babysitter, you're not so smart. Would you believe there's another bottle in the kitchen? I smuggled one in yesterday when no one was looking. And you're just soused enough now that you won't stop me from opening it."

With that, she made off for the kitchen, returning a moment later with the fresh bottle.

"To Ellen," I said dreamily when she had popped the cork and filled both our glasses. "What do we want for Ellen?"

One of the candles had burned out, and I could barely see

Mo's frown in the light of the other. Finally she said, "I guess I want her to get away from her horrible family. She's their cheap help, only worse. Even cheap help gets some time off. She wants to be a writer. Did she tell you that?"

I hesitated. "There's a lot to her."

My remark seemed to satisfy Maureen. She put her glass on the table, snuggled close, and kissed me. This time it was a slow, lingering invitation. "Damn it, Kevin," she exploded, "I'm not trying to seduce you to keep you out of the seminary. It's New Year's Eve, and I want some affection."

Her lips were everything Pat said they were: warm, sweet, skillful. Not off limits at all, Patrick.

I slipped my fingers under her sweater and touched her sleek belly. The record player started "The Tennessee Waltz." She sighed again, almost a groan, as I touched the fabric of her bra. I thought of Ellen's breasts and stopped. I rearranged her sweater so it neatly touched the waist of her tailored slacks.

We both sat up, silent, embarrassed. "Cousin Kevin," she said thickly, "you do take your baby-sitting responsibilities seriously . . . and you're a much better kisser than I thought you would be. Here, have a pretzel."

There was still half of the second bottle of champagne left. She poured herself another drink, motioned toward my glass, and shook her head in disappointment when I put my hand over it.

Somehow she managed to get to the other end of the couch. "I don't want to fight God, but would you mind telling me again why? Why do you want to spend the rest of your life locked up in a rectory, cut off from everyone else? Doesn't that seem a waste of your life?" The second candle was growing dim.

"It's not cut off at all. The priests in the rectory are with us at the most important times in our lives. Father Conroy walks the streets of the neighborhood every day. He knows all of us and most of our problems. You can go to him when you need help, and sometimes he comes to you when you need a kick in the . . . in the rear." She giggled and poured yet another drink. "They are the Church. With all the money everyone's making, Catholics are going to change, and the Church is going to have to keep up with them. People are moving from our neighborhoods to the suburbs. It's going to be an exciting time to be a priest." My voice ebbed away. I wondered if the alcohol in my blood made my explanation even more obscure than it usually was. "I don't know whether this makes any sense at all, Mo."

There was no reply for a moment. Then, "So much the better for God, so much the worse for me. You were born a priest, Kevin. I just hope you're around when I need one, and that you're as gentle as a priest as you are at . . . at other things."

We were silent a long time, both of us alone with our drink-confused thoughts. The last candle burned out. Maureen was sound asleep, her head on the tattered arm of the couch. She was a little girl again, not much older than Mary Ann. I poured the few ounces of remaining champagne down the sink and threw the empty bottles into the trash can behind the house. The rain was a slow drizzle; the air was heavy with humidity and the smell of flowers. I opened the rickety window of the parlor to get rid of the smell of champagne and cigarettes and flushed the ashes from Maureen's ashtray down the toilet. She was not supposed to smoke, though I doubt my parents were fooled. I even remembered to turn off the long-silent phonograph.

I tried to wake her, but she only buried her head in the side of the couch, so, taking a deep breath, I picked her up and carried her to the bedroom she shared with Mary Ann.

Mary Ann was in her usual deep sleep. She wouldn't hear the

judgment call on the Final Day. I barely made it to the other twin bed, and that only because I got an extra burst of strength from the thought of trying to explain myself if I dropped Maureen.

I laid her on the bed, took off her shoes, and pulled the spread over her. Was there anything else?

I kissed her forehead, said a prayer that life might be good to her, and tiptoed out. I had to feel my way down the corridor to my own room. My brothers, Mike and Joe, were sleeping even more soundly than Mary Ann.

At breakfast the next morning, I wondered how my head could be so big and how much I should confess of what had happened. Mom said, "Are you feeling all right, Kevin? Maureen seems to have come down with a touch of the stomach flu."

Ah, stomach flu—what a variety of ailments it covers.

"I'm okay, Mom. You don't think I'd do anything with Mo that would make me catch what she has, do you?"

Mom sighed. "No, darling. I can't imagine that happening."

Pat's shot floated toward the basket, a perfect arc. It slid around the rim, hung tentatively for a moment, and then, as though an unseen hand reached up, it popped out and banged against the board. Willewski, the big forward from Leo, cleared the board and rifled a pass to one of their guards. I raced back toward our basket, but the guard's pass beat me. Two on one. I went for the center. He passed off to the forward. The shot swished, and we were down to the Lions by fourteen points. Wearily, I made the time-out sign to the referee.

I was close to vomiting. My legs were flabby, my chest hurt, and my throat was constricted. The coach wouldn't talk to us. He never did when we started to blow a game.

We were going down before the machinelike precision of Leo's Lions, a superbly coached team with depth on their bench. We had beaten them in the St. George's tournament at Christmas because Pat got twenty-eight points. Now it was halfway through the third quarter, and he had six. The hostile crowd derisively chanted "Buckets, buckets" every time he got the ball. The whole season was going down the drain. What was wrong with Pat? When his hand was hot, he could hit on twelve shots in a row. When he was cold . . .

"I don't know what's wrong, Kevin," he said, his chest heaving as rapidly as mine. "It just won't go through the rim."

A week of adulation in the Chicago papers, interviews with the press, talk of the Notre Dame scholarship, the assistant coach from South Bend in the stands, and Pat choked. It didn't matter when a passing guard like me choked; no one could tell the difference, except maybe the Leo coach. When the hotshot gunner choked, the whole crowd knew it.

"Don't worry, you'll get the eye back." I patted his rump. "Come on, we're just letting them have an edge so it will be a big finish. Tim, you move in. If they keep two men on Pat, you'll be in the open and we'll feed it back to you."

The wiry Black Raider nodded, saving his precious breath. He was not much of a shot, but he never stopped trying.

The whistle blew. I brought the ball down, passing off to Larry Ryan, our undersize center. He fed the ball to Tim, who whipped it back to me. I fired it in to Pat, who was moving toward the basket. He rimmed another. Luckily it bounced back to me on the freethrow line, and I sank an easy swisher. Down twelve.

"Full-court press," I shouted, though we didn't have the strength to keep up the press for more than a few moments. I stole the ball from Leo's guard after a sloppy throw-in and fed it to Pat, who was standing near the basket. He should have passed back to me for the lay-up, but he shot mechanically. The ball banked off the board and went sloppily through the hoop. Down ten. The crowd began to cheer us on.

Whatever demons had tied Pat's hands were exorcised by that garbage shot. He hit seven in a row, missed the eighth, and sank the rebound. Leo was hot, too. Willewski matched Pat almost basket for basket, but we inched closer and closer. A minute to go and we were four points down. I was fouled driving toward the basket. The referee called a one-shot free throw; I argued with him that I'd been shooting and should have two. He just laughed at me.

Oblivious of the roar of the crowd, I sank the free throw.

Leo went into a stall. Tim Curran, beyond exhaustion, desperately lunged at the ball after Willewski had passed it to their center. He got a piece of it and bounced it in my direction. I raced toward the basket looking for Pat. He wasn't there. Two on one. I passed off to Tim, getting set for the rebound. His shot went through without touching the rim. No rebound. Tim had scored only five points the whole game up to then, but this one basket put us two points away from winning. Leo called time. They huddled with their coach, working out a play to kill the twenty-five seconds that remained. Our coach stayed on the bench because he had no idea what to tell us.

"Where were you?" I demanded harshly.

Pat was bent at the waist, gasping for breath. "I can't keep it up," he said.

"Sure you can. We're going to steal the ball again and you're going to run for the basket if you're bleeding to death."

Leo's in-bounds pass was perfect. Calm and cool, they whipped the ball around the forecourt, ignoring our frantic efforts to keep up with them. At ten seconds I knew I had to foul to stop the clock. I went after Willewski just as he caught a pass.

I hit the ball and knocked it out of his hands. Incredibly, there was no whistle from the ref. Maybe it wasn't a foul.

Two on one again. Four or five seconds, my chance to be a hero. I thought about percentages and passed off to Pat. He missed the shot, and Willewski, who came out of nowhere, and I went up for the ball. He fouled me as I tipped the ball toward a motionless and dispirited Pat. Pat sank the shot just as the buzzer sounded. We'd won City.

Much later, after the locker room was empty, I sat on a bench, my stomach still in a knot, heart still pounding. Mr. Martin, a young Jesuit scholastic who hung around with the athletes, was the only person in the room with me.

"Was he grandstanding, Kevin?" he asked.

I looked up at him. "You can bet on it, Mr. Martin—he wasn't."

"Why was he cold for so long?" The young man's thin face was pinched with disbelief.

"He was cold because he was cold," I said bluntly, reaching for a sock. "I don't figure Pat Donahue out. I just pass to him."

"And tip back rebounds from his missed shots," said the scholastic with more perception than I thought he had.

I pulled a T-shirt over my head. "That's why I'm going to the seminary, Mr. Martin. I won't have to rebound for Pat Donahue anymore."

A lot I knew.

❋

The sand was soft and cool against Ellen's bare feet. The water of the lake lapping against the beach occasionally nibbled her toes. Mrs. Cunningham herself had called to get permission for her to come this weekend. Even so, Ellen's mother was against it. There was too much to be done around the house. Two of the small kids were sick, she reminded Ellen, and Margaret Cunningham was a snob. Besides, how come, if they were good Catholics, they had only one child? Ellen's father, who occasionally defended her, insisted she be allowed to go. She got on the bus for the lake, determined to have a good time.

"So you don't think Jeanne Crain is a good actress?" she said to Pat, inhaling the mixture of gasoline, barbecue smoke, suntan oil, and mosquito spray that was summer-resort smell.

He squeezed her shoulder and laughed. "She doesn't have to be, Ellen. She didn't do anything tonight except look pretty."

Ellen stoutly defended her heroine. "She had to do more than look pretty in Pinky."

Pat laughed again, though not disrespectfully. He listened to her opinions about movies carefully and discussed them seriously. They couldn't talk about books, because he didn't read them. "Sure, Pinky *was better than* Letter to Three Wives, *but Jeanne-babe doesn't look like a Negro to me."*

She was glad he didn't say "nigger," an immoral word—or so the sisters at St. Dominic said. "You can have Negro blood in you and not look like one," she insisted. "Some scholars say twenty percent of those with Negro ancestors are able to pass as white." She thought that was the figure Sister Caroline had quoted.

"If I were a Negro and could pass, I would," Pat said very seriously. "I don't know how they put up with it. It's bad enough . . ." He didn't finish the sentence.

"I bet you'll love Notre Dame," Ellen said, bringing the conversation back to a safer topic.

"I don't know," he said, swallowing from his beer bottle. It was his fourth bottle of beer. "From what I hear, it sounds almost as much of a prison as the place Kevin's going to next year. Where will you go?"

"I guess I'll go to St. Anne's nursing school," she said tentatively.

"May as well become a nun yourself," he said, blowing foam from his lips, "as get mixed up with those German nuns. . . . Wait here a minute. I'm going across the road to get two more beers."

She thought of the peace of convent life. After all the noise at home, it would be a relief. She had two more years to decide. Her parents said she had to be a nurse so she could earn money to pay back all she owed them for her education.

Pat was silent, buried within himself, when he returned, a beer bottle in either hand. "What's the matter, Pat? What did they say to you?" Ellen asked.

"Nothing," he said sullenly.

"Don't 'nothing' me," she snapped. "They said something in there to hurt you, and I want to know what it is."

He patted her hand. "What a smart woman you are, little Ellen," he said. "All right. One of them, a guy from the country club who went to Notre Dame, said that the school was going downhill when it took garbage men."

"Oh, Pat, don't pay any attention to what those drunks say. You're just as good as they are. Better."

"I'm not so sure about that," he said dully, stroking her hair with one of his big hands. "Here, have a sip of this. It won't hurt."

She had never drunk beer before. To her guilty surprise, it tasted good. She didn't give it back. Sister Caroline said alcoholism wasn't hereditary.

"You have ideas on everything, Ellen," he said gently. "Why are people so hateful?"

She considered carefully. "Mostly envy, I guess," she said. "No one hates me very much, so I guess I have nothing to envy. If you weren't famous for winning the city championship, that man would never say anything to you."

Pat finished the bottle. "I'd like to stuff their goddamn scholar-

ship up their—I'll show them. Someday I'll show them all. Then we'll have the last laugh, Ellen, you and I."

She sipped her beer very slowly. On second thought, not nearly as good as malted milks, really.

They began walking, leaving behind the village with its gaudy lights reflecting on the smooth, black waters of the lake. The warm glow of the lakeshore homes cast splotches of gold and orange on the silent black mirror. Behind the village and up on the hill were the houses of the rich people, the Brennans and the Cunninghams, and people like them.

They were now near the wooded beach of the state park. During the daytime the beach swarmed with visitors. At night the park was closed, and you weren't supposed to be inside it. The highway, which was South Shore Drive, ran between the hills and the park. Ellen and Pat had climbed over the fence in silence. The park rangers were more interested in keeping out people who came from the highway than in kids who climbed over the beach fence.

"You're a wonderful person, Ellen," Pat said suddenly, breaking the peace that had settled on them.

"Thank you, Pat," she said simply.

He took her in his strong arms and kissed her passionately. I like being kissed this way, she reflected dreamily.

Then he changed. He snatched the beer bottle from her hand, hurled it into the lake, and pulled her to the sand. She was too surprised to resist, too frightened to plead. He pulled her dress up savagely and pressed his hand over her rigid body. She screamed and tried to wrench herself away.

"No one will hear you here," he shouted at her and pinned her to the sand with one massive hand. She gave up, whimpering in surrender while he fondled her.

Her tears broke the spell of his violence. He released her and staggered drunkenly toward the edge of the water. Ellen grabbed her purse and fled into the woods, dodging in terror the suddenly looming monsters that haunted the dark trees. She stumbled blindly over bushes and branches, cutting her feet, and finally tumbled headlong into the dirt after colliding with a park bench. Breathing like a frightened rabbit, she heard him coming. She scrambled to her feet and rushed through the dark again. Finally, her body soaking with perspiration and her lungs aching, she collapsed at the side of the highway. Her fingers dug into the sandy soil. "Oh, God, please help me," she pleaded. There was no answer from the starry summer sky. She willed calm into her body.

The forest behind her was quiet, as soundless as the stars. Without warning she was caught in a beam of light. It swept over her like a death ray and was gone in a whirl of noise. She rolled into the ditch by the side of the road. Her teeth were chattering, her arms and legs shaking. She huddled there sobbing while another beam swept over her head and another car roared by.

Once more she willed her shaking frame to be still. She must walk up the hill a mile and a half to the Cunningham house. In her purse were the sandals she had taken off when they began their walk on the beach. She put them on. Her feet hurt, cut by her frantic dash through the park. Her shins were bleeding from the collision with the park bench. She realized she would have to hide her injuries from Maureen's mother and make up a story about the torn and rumpled dress.

Lights shone on the trees ahead of her. Like a hunted animal, she scurried into the ditch. Only after the big Packard passed her did she recognize it. Mr. Brennan. Had the Brennans seen her hobbling up the hill with torn feet, bloody shins, and a tattered dress? Would they tell Kevin?

Pat lunged into the water, ripping the surface of the lake apart. God forgive me . . . please, please, forgive me.

He had searched in the park for Ellen, wanting to beg her forgiveness. He adored her. He had not wanted to frighten her. Then he had run back to the lake, torn off his clothes, and dived into the water, hoping to wipe out the filth of his sin. He was now near the middle, beginning to tire, the beer taking its toll. I don't care. I'll drown. No one will miss me. I promised on retreat last September. The priest made me promise before he gave me absolution.

He was slipping under the water. His lungs were filling. It hurt as though they were on fire. He instinctively struggled to the surface again, felt a smooth wall against his grasping hand, clawed at it, and found a rope. He hung on, a last link with life. Why not let go?

He decided to live.

The rope was an anchor from a good-size sailboat moored deep in the lake. His chest heaving up and down, he eased toward the boat. There was a light on on it, and there were voices. Just catch my breath and go back to shore.

A man and woman were on the boat. Not young, not old, they were partially undressed and relaxed in a casual embrace. He couldn't hear their words. More temptation. He should leave before he saw anything that would make him filthier than he already was.

He did not swim away. He was fascinated by the relaxed and leisurely posture of the couple. How could something that was fever-producing poison in him be so sedate for them? The woman laughed, a low, soft laugh of pleasure. His stomach turned in disgust.

Careful to make no noise, Pat slipped away from the anchor and swam toward the state-park beach. Much later, he lay there naked and exhausted, gasping for breath. He thought of Ellen's terrified sobs and of the woman's pleased laugh. He rolled over on his back and looked up at the stars. What time was it? The lights were off in the village. Two, maybe three o'clock in the morning. He groaned in despair. If only God would strike him dead.

Then the strange light came, a soft bowl of light, rising up from the waters of the lake, floating slowly down the beach. It circled around him, then enveloped him. Time stood still. Peace, joy, forgiveness, love, flooded into the depths of his being. The light warmed him. It cleansed and renewed him. Ellen was in the light; the woman on the boat; Maureen, too. All the women in the world were there with him, nursing, healing, loving him.

Then they merged into one woman in a white and gold gown. She told him what he had to do if he were to be free of the damnation that was fighting for his soul.

The gray, nervous spiritual director from Quigley Seminary warned me that it would be necessary to give up my high-school companions. "Male and female," he added, with heavy emphasis on the last word. I was now going to travel a different path from theirs. I must eliminate them from my life; I must sever all my "attachments" to them. The longer I put it off, the harder it would be.

Quigley compromised its principles by admitting me directly into the fifth year of its program because my father had called his old friend from army days, the vice-chancellor of the diocese. Most "specials" had to go back to second year and do high school over.

After a year at Quigley I would go on to the seven years of the major seminary at Mundelein, just north of Chicago, and be ordained, "God willing," my father said, doubtless echoing his military crony. The rector was permitted to save some of his dignity by insisting that I take a summer course in New Testament Greek, which they had not taught at Jesuit.

So I had spent the summer riding the streetcar to the dirty Gothic spires of Quigley—seminarians weren't permitted to drive cars—and making the transition to seminarian existence. It was a grim, unbearably hot two months. I missed the lake and my friends. I kept telling myself, as I studied St. John's terrible Greek and plowed through Charles Dickens on my own, that I'd soon get over the pain in my gut.

Maureen called me the week before Labor Day, just as I got back into our hot, empty house from my last class.

"Hi, stranger. Would you do an old flame a favor?"

The sound of her voice made most of the pain vanish. "Depends on the flame," I said, trying not to give a hint of the broad smile on my face.

"You're not going to stay in town *this* weekend, are you? We won't steal your vocation in three days."

"I'm driving up there in about a half hour. What's the favor?"

"Take Ellen Foley to the movies on Thursday night and the country-club dance on Friday."

"What's the matter with Pat?" I asked, my conscience now taking up cudgels against my joy at hearing Mo's voice.

"Oh, he's gone off to Mayslake to pray over his vision thing. Besides, he and Ellen had a bit of a tiff. You know how physical Pat gets."

My fist clenched, and my fingers went white on the phone receiver. "What 'vision thing'?" I said.

She gave a derisive laugh. "Poor, crazy Pat thinks he's seen the Blessed Mother and she told him what he's supposed to do with his life. Anyway, will you take Ellen off my hands for me? I don't think she's a threat to anyone's goddamn vocation."

If she could have heard the noisy thumping of my heart, she might have thought more of Ellen's sex appeal. "Do you want me to drive her up?" I said, astonished at my own recklessness.

"That was a quick change. No, that bitch of a mother of hers—ugh, how I hate that unctuous woman—won't let her come up till Wednesday night."

After I hung up I realized that "unctuous" was an adjective that Maureen had never used before. We were all getting older.

So on Thursday night I was sitting across from Ellen at the Sugar Bowl, watching her systematically demolish another malt and listening to her compare the hero of *All the King's Men*, which we had just seen, with the hero of Cozzens's *Guard of Honor*.

She was even prettier than I had remembered, with an animated smile, flashing eyes, and a quick, decisive voice. Ellen was discovering her body and her mind, and liking both.

"Can I ask a favor, Kevin?" she said shyly, lowering her eyes to the glass in front of her. The jukebox beat out "Riders in the Sky."

"Ask a hundred, pretty lady," I said.

A strand of her now short blond hair fell across her forehead. She brushed it away impatiently. "Well, it's not part of your deal with Maureen about me"—a tinge of color moved slowly across her forehead—"and you can say no if you want. Would you teach me to water-ski tomorrow . . . please?"

I put my index finger under her chin and tilted her head back up. "I'll pick you up at nine-thirty. And don't you ever think that I wasn't enthusiastic about that deal."

Then we were both embarrassed, remembering the link between us about which we would never speak.

There was no magic by ten-thirty the next morning. I was angry at Ellen, and she hated me.

"I'm worn out," she wailed at me. "Please let me back in the boat."

She was more than worn out. She was a limp, soggy little

mouse who infuriatingly would not or could not follow instructions. "You're a quitter!" I shouted at her. "If you're willing to admit you're a quitter, I'll let you back in the boat. Otherwise you stay out there and keep trying."

She splashed water at me with the palm of her hand. "You're an arrogant, insensitive snob!" she screamed. "Put down the ladder so I can get in."

I ignored her insult and her plea. "Keep the damn rope between your skis, the tips out of the water, knees close together. Don't panic when you find yourself moving." Her coordination wasn't all that bad. The rush of the water, the pull of the boat, the roar of the motor, scared her.

Next to me, Nick McAuliff, a seminarian who had joined me that day at the lake, was laughing. He'd been laughing ever since I had told Ellen, "Get the, uh, lower part of your body down over the skis." She had raged at me, "It's not a sin to say 'ass,' you stupid prude!"

I eased the cranky old red Higgins around, stretching the tow rope taut, shifted into gear, and slammed the throttle forward. I was so angry I gave it too much power. The rope would surely snap out of her hands.

"She's up!" Nick shouted.

I stole a look. The soggy little mouse had turned into a graceful bird. Ellen wasn't the kind to huddle behind the boat once she was up. After a time she soared out across the lumbering wake, dug her knees into the wind, and cut back across, screaming at the top of her voice in sheer animal joy.

She hung on for almost a full turn around the lake, then, overconfident on the wake of a huge Chris Craft, spun an elegant somersault through space and splashed her pretty ass hard against the water. She was still laughing when we got the boat alongside her.

Three times she tried to climb the ladder, and three times

she splashed back into the water, her laughter bubbling up as soon as she broke water. "Let's have the dance out here," she sputtered.

I reached down over the side of the boat, grabbed her under the shoulders, and pulled her up. Our bodies touched briefly as I set her on the deck. I felt a spasm of desire so fierce it almost knocked me over.

"You weigh more than last summer," I said.

"Four and a half pounds," she laughed merrily. "Most of which I lost out there in the water."

I wrapped her in a towel, patted her approvingly, as I would someone who had hit a home run, and deposited her in the back seat of the boat.

"You see how Kevin treats the girls now that he's going into the seminary," she said to Nick through purple lips and chattering teeth. "He does this to a girl the morning of the biggest dance of the summer so she'll be a wreck and he won't have to dance with her."

"You're both crazy," said Nick McAuliff.

Ellen was anything but a wreck that night. Her hair was delicately waved. High heels and a lemon dress with very thin shoulder straps added five or six years to her age. I was a boy out with a young woman. Beneath her dress I could feel the contours of her supple body. Sounds of "Some Enchanted Evening" guided our drifting bodies. My mother and father danced by us.

"Your taste in women is very good this year, Champ," my father said.

"Darling, you're absolutely gorgeous," Mom said to Ellen.

Ellen accepted their praise with natural grace. I drew her close. She was a good dancer.

"I want to say two things, Kevin," Ellen said, a mother superior ordering the community life.

"Say a hundred."

"Only two. The first is that I think you will be a wonderful priest, and I'll pray that you'll persevere during the hard times."

Oh, my God, "persevere." Nunnish talk on a dance floor.

"And the second thing?" I said lightly.

She burrowed her pale blond head into my chest. "The second thing, Kevin Brennan, is that I want to thank you for being so kind to me these two summers. I know you're kind to everyone, but mostly because you feel responsible. I . . ." The words were rushing out now like air escaping from a punctured tire. "I think you don't feel responsible for me at all. You are good to me because you like me, and . . . and . . . well, I'm just very grateful for *that.*"

Two of my fingers caressed a tiny spot on her back. "I do like you, Ellen Foley. But you've got it wrong. You're the one who's been good to me."

Later, when I kissed her good night, she frowned. "Should seminarians kiss that way?"

"Not to kiss you that way would be a mortal sin," I assured her. And just to prove it, I kissed her again.

You travel through life carrying the wounds of your past, the spiritual director told me. As I fell into a contented sleep that night, I knew that Ellen Foley, the fey water sprite whose creamy breasts I had reverently touched at the forest pond, would be a wound I would carry for a long time.

I tried to control my temper. "Pat, this is the nuttiest thing you've ever done. You don't have a vocation."

He was angry, too. A tiny muscle was twitching in his throat.

His hands were tightly knotted. "How the hell do you know what I've got and haven't got? You think you're the only one who can be a priest in the whole goddamn parish!"

It was the Wednesday night after Labor Day. Pat and I were talking in the sun room of our rambling old house on Mason Avenue. The lake was abandoned; the neighborhood was getting ready for school. Quigley Seminary began at nine the next morning—half a day for everyone but "specials," who would be expected to spend the whole day. Pat held in his hand the letter of recommendation from our pastor. He wanted my father to call the vice-chancellor. He had, after all, taken the same courses, and his grades were almost as good as mine. My father obligingly left the room to exercise his clout.

"What about your Notre Dame ride?" I demanded.

"Screw the ride," he said. "My immortal soul is more important than basketball."

"You can save your soul in other ways," I argued.

"Some people can't," he fired back, the color going out of his face. "I can't. The Blessed Mother told me that being a priest is the only way I can save my soul." His finely chiseled features were drawn taut, his clear blue eyes grimly determined. "And Father Placid says I certainly have a vocation. It would be a mortal sin not to respond to it."

"Your family?" I said, trying another tack.

"They're furious at me, just like you. I don't care. I have to do what God wants me to do. Please, Kevin, I need your help."

It was hard to stay angry at Pat, he was so sincere. "Of course I'll help," I said. "It will be great to have you with me."

He was so relieved by my approval that he didn't notice how hollow my words sounded.

After he left I stared dumbly at the mums blooming in our front yard. The sun, setting earlier each day, hinted of the coming of winter cold. It cast a crazy quilt of soft light on the lawn. Should I tell the rector about Pat's craziness? At Quigley they didn't like people who took Father Placid's kind of holiness too seriously. I decided against it. It was their business to find out, not my job to tell them, that he didn't belong in the seminary. Or the priesthood.

Maureen put the final word on the summer of 1949 when I met her striding briskly on very high heels into eleven-o'clock mass on Sunday.

"Tipping the rebounds isn't over yet, is it, Cousin Kevin?" Her large eyes danced with mischief.

Poor Maureen. She would have to pay a much higher cost for Patrick's "vocation" than I ever would.

BOOK II

The Fifties

CHAPTER FOUR

1953

"Godammit, Kevin, don't try to be so self-effacing." Maureen crushed out her cigarette. "You want to go to Rome so badly you can already taste the pasta."

I tried not to look at Ellen Foley, who was sitting near Maureen. Instead I looked out through the French windows on the just-fallen snow, crystal clean in the moonlight on the Cunninghams' garden. Their new home in River Forest, a block away from the house of a famous Italian gangster, was a palace, though my mother was right when she said it was a tasteless and vulgar palace. The only saving graces were the glorious sunbursts in the parlor and in the dining room, rose and yellow and gold celebrations of light from Mo's art classes.

"I've been to Rome with the family, and I'm sure I'll go again," I said, trying to control my voice. "There's no reason why I have to study my theology there."

"Bullshit," she snapped, downing an extra-large sip of cognac. "You're ambitious and you want to be a bishop. If Pat goes to Rome, he'll be a bishop instead of you." Her harsh laugh was already blurred by the effects of the Château Lafite served with dinner.

"I don't want to be a bishop," I said wearily. "And since they built the new North American College on the Janiculum, it really isn't a school for future bishops anymore, just a large American seminary."

"Kevin doesn't want to be a bishop," Ellen Foley said softly, her round, unblinking, gray eyes watching every change in my facial expression. "He just wants to win. Are you going to win, Kevin?"

"I don't know," I said, and sighed. Three and a half long years since I had spoken with Ellen Foley.

Our winter vacation in those days was at the end of January. Cardinal Mundelein had been convinced that his seminary, a sprawling collection of red-brick Georgian buildings in Lake Country, was a sylvan paradise. He couldn't imagine why seminarians would want to go home for Christmas. Though Mundelein had been dead for almost a decade and a half, we were still doing things in the archdiocese the way he had done them. The seminary authorities were happy with the arrangement because they didn't want us around our parishes when our college-age friends were home for Christmas vacation. It never occurred to them that there were midyear vacations for the laity, too.

I was breaking several rules by talking to two lovely young women, astonishingly feminine in their tight-waisted, full-skirted, "new look" dresses—just the kind of enticement against which Father Meisterhorst, our spiritual director, warned us for three weeks before every vacation began.

Sophomores in college, the two of them were breathtakingly lovely. After four months of the seminary, where the only women were nuns and seminarians' sisters on the three visiting Sundays—two hours each time—any girl looked lovely. You began to imagine that you heard the click of high heels on the empty concrete walks.

Ellen was suddenly the more beautiful of the two. She still seemed fragile, but now her pale face managed to convey quick intelligence despite its serene immobility. I stirred uneasily.

"Of course you'll win," Maureen exploded, cupping her hand around Ellen's cigarette to light another of her own—two elegantly plumed birds pecking at each other. "You get better marks, you're more popular with the other seminarians, and you're a natural leader."

"It doesn't necessarily follow. Both the Jesuits and the diocesan faculty like Pat. He's witty and charming. They think I'm too somber and"—the wine had loosened my tongue so that I said something I instantly regretted—"too smart and too rich. I caught hell for going to Rome with the family before my summer assignment at the orphanage last year."

It was dumb to admit something like that just to stir up feminine sympathy. Even though I was popular with my classmates—the first "special" ever to be elected president of the Quigley graduating class—I was not a favorite, to put it mildly, of the seminary authorities. I kept all the rules, did all the work, said all the prayers. But the authorities didn't like the family money. Pat was given the best appointive jobs, including his present one as head prefect. He governed with a hearty laugh, a winning smile, and a quick joke. I was a minor functionary, the master of games, responsible for athletic schedules, to whom Pat turned for advice on such major issues as whether to ask on a bitter-cold day for "inside smoking"—permission to smoke in the recreation room for the half hour that smoking was allowed after each meal.

"That is the most stupid thing I've ever heard," said Mo. "Oh, damn it, Kevin, sit down. Ellen and I aren't going to rape you." She waved us toward an elaborate antique couch that was tastelessly out of place in the plant room. "Is the Church ever going to wake up to the fact that this is the twentieth century? Do all of us have to leave before they change? Why should they envy you because your family has a few dollars?"

"The Church is changing," I said as I chose a chair across the room, as far away as I could get. "Look at the new Easter Liturgy."

"Kevin Brennan, only a seminarian could think that young people give a good goddamn about the Easter Liturgy," Maureen said angrily, rising from the couch to turn on the inevitable record player.

"How do you and Pat feel about the rivalry the seminary has imposed on you?" said Ellen, her soft voice almost a whisper. Unlike Manhattanville, where Maureen hobnobbed with the East Coast aristocracy, St. Anne's School of Nursing did not, in those days, produce rebellious young women.

"We don't talk about it," I mumbled.

"Why not?" Ellen persisted.

"Because we're men, and men don't know how to handle difficulties in friendship the way women do."

"You know, it doesn't really matter whether they like you, Kevin," Ellen continued. "And it doesn't really matter whether you win over Pat."

"You're right, Ellen. It's only a foolish game."

If I lost the race with Pat to Rome, the seminary was to be endured four more years, an inane and rigid life with every second budgeted from five-twenty-five in the morning until nine-forty-five at night and every move watched for signs that we might be "disobedient"—since obedience, not zeal or charity, was the most important of priestly virtues. The stern seminary discipline was poor preparation for the diocesan priesthood in the twentieth century. They used to say our rector was one of the best minds of the eighteenth century. And the rote memorization of Latin textbooks, which we barely understood, was certainly not useful training for work among a laity that was becoming college-educated and upper-middle-class.

Because we were in the seminary, we were excused from serving in the Korean War, which dragged on after we went to Mundelein. Larry Ryan, our pint-size center at Jesuit, was killed during the retreat from the Yalu River, and my conscience drove me to the point of leaving Mundelein and enlisting. My father gave me hell, arguing that I had to make up my mind which set of obligations were important in my life. Then the battle line stabilized, and I was not needed to defend democracy on the outskirts of Seoul.

Eisenhower was president, the seminary was split down the middle on the subject of Joe McCarthy, and the country was settling in for the long sleep of the fifties. It seemed Pius XII had been pope forever, and Cardinal Stritch, our archbishop, also forever.

⁂

"What in hell is the matter with your friend Donahue?" Tony O'Malley, a gregarious, red-faced seminarian asked me one cool spring evening as we were walking around the lake.

"What do you mean?" I said, instantly on the defensive.

"What's he running for?" Tony went on.

"What does it matter?" We crossed the bridge over the malodorous stream that previous generations of seminarians had cruelly named Stritch Creek after the Archbishop.

Tony was now uneasy. "No one says it to you, because you guys grew up together, but around here *they're* the enemy, and he's on *their* side all the time. He defends them, butters them up. And a lot of us think that he spies on us for them."

"I doubt it," I said evenly. "Pat just likes to be liked."

"By *them,*" Tony replied, "not by *us.*"

I remained silent, waiting O'Malley out.

"Some of us think he's trying to beat you out for Rome," he said softly, not looking at me.

"He can have it if he wants it."

"You're the one who ought to go." Tony was a lawyer pleading a case. "They've always sent the class leader; they've always prepared him beforehand by two years of special Italian. You're the class leader, and they're giving you the Italian course. But Pat seems to be buttering up any faculty types who don't like you."

" 'Always' is three years," I said. It was only after the construction of the new college in Rome that Cardinal Mundelein's policy of sending all his young men to his own seminary was violated, one of the few Mundelein policies that Cardinal Stritch could work up the energy to change.

"Haven't you noticed the way he butters up that damn fool Vandy?" O'Malley went on.

Professor Harold F. X. Vandenberghe, S.J., was a nearly senile Jesuit philosophy teacher who put us to sleep four afternoons a week. We had to listen to him while sitting on the stiff chairs of the big lecture hall decorated with fake Renaissance nude (male) paintings. Someone had conned Cardinal Mundelein into believing they were Paolo Veronese originals. Vandy never once looked at us during a lecture, apparently obsessed by the shape of the evergreens outside the window. His lectures were an endless monotone Latin commentary about the difference between Thomas Aquinas and Francisco Suárez. He was on the side of the latter.

"So?" I said, beginning to lose my patience with both O'Malley and Pat.

"So, you know how the faculty keeps alive the fiction that

Vandy can spot talent. Donahue has his eye on the Janiculum Hill, and you're the only one in the whole building who doesn't know it." O'Malley looked at me sharply. "And what about this thing between him and Stan Kokoleck?" he asked. "They keep talking about 'particular friendships,' but the rules don't seem to apply to Donahue. If he's not sucking Koko, it's not because Mac isn't looking the other way."

The word "homosexuality" was unspoken in the seminary in those days. We pretended it didn't exist. There was not much of it that was overt. If you lock up a couple of hundred lonely young men, "attachments" can get to be a problem, especially when the seminary superiors and faculty have a penchant for favoritism toward handsome students like Pat Donahue.

"I can tell you to forget that," I said, hoping I sounded confident. "If there's one thing that Pat is not, it's"—I hesitated for the word—"that kind. There are a lot of girls on the West Side who can testify to it."

A couple of days later Pat cornered me and proposed that we meet in the gym during the evening recreation period to plan the basketball tournament that was still six weeks away. His job as head prefect gave him keys and the authority to be in the gym when no one else was allowed there. It was only when he turned on the lights in the small office in the gym that I realized my rebound-tipping days were back again.

"I'm going out of my mind, Kev," he said in a choked voice. "I need help. It's bad enough losing him. I can't stand seeing him with anyone else."

One corner of my mind noticed the snow melting outside in the winter's first big, grimy thaw. The pool of water forming in front of the gym was my link to reality.

"What do you mean?" I asked, stalling for time.

"I, uh . . ." He paused in embarrassment. "Well, I was with Koko during the vacation and I guess I had a bit too much to drink, and I . . . uh, oh, God . . . I got rough with him and, well, he doesn't like me anymore. He says he likes Marty Fitzpatrick."

"Two sick little creeps," I snapped.

"Koko's not a creep," he said, pleading with me. "He's sensitive and understanding, and I can't last here without his help. I've got to have him back."

The temptation to ask him whether he was going to take Koko to Rome with him swirled through my head. Instead I asked, "What have you and Stanley been doing, Pat? If I'm supposed to help, I'd better know."

"It's not sinful," he said, a wan, crumpled hero slumped over a cherrywood desk in a tiny cement-block room from which the smell of male sweat would never be exorcised. "It really isn't. At least it's not something with a girl."

"Worse," I said sharply.

"No, it isn't, not really, not if you understand the way we feel about each other. If it wasn't for Koko, I'd have to leave. It's so lonely up here." He was sobbing now. "I miss my parents and my brothers."

My anger was beginning to turn to pity. Maybe, after all, it was the seminary's fault. Everyone got a little strange inside the damn place.

"What do you want me to do?" I asked.

"Talk to Koko. Tell him I'm sorry I hit him. Tell him he's got to stop being friends with Marty. I'll lose my mind if I keep seeing him with Marty."

"Pull yourself together, Pat. Go to confession; forget the past."

"I *can't* go to confession. They'll make me leave if they find out." He was trying to gain control of himself, his handsome face ravaged with despair.

"Get a special confessor. The rules say you can have one. They'll let you do anything you want. Only you've got to stop."

Pat nodded. "I know it has to stop, Kev. I wanted to ask you for help months ago. Just talk to Koko for me and I'll do anything you say."

We left the gym and walked back through the slush toward the residence hall. The mist was turning into fog. Pat asked cheerfully about the vacation and about the Cunninghams' new house. Not five minutes after his "confession" to me, he was demanding details of my encounter with Mo and Ellen.

I watched Marty and Koko for a day. They were more than just "friends." I told Father Meisterhorst, the ancient Jesuit spiritual director, in his holy-card-decorated office, that I had to report, as a matter of conscience, my worry about the relationship between Martin Fitzpatrick and Stanley Kokoleck. The Jesuit cocked an eye at me. "Ah, are you sure, my son, that you know what you're talking about?"

"Yes, Father, I do indeed know what I'm talking about."

The two were not in class the following morning. When I went back from the classroom hall to the residence building, they were already gone. As Pat and I hurried over to the dining hall for lunch, we speculated on what had happened. Pat seemed remarkably unperturbed.

A week later he greeted me with a big smile as we came out of Vandy's class together. (You always walked with the person you encountered at the door—another protection against "particular friendships.") "It was great to talk to you the other night, Kevin," he said. "I'm a hundred percent better already."

My rebound-tipping wasn't over for the year.

In the middle of April, while spring was trying unsuccessfully to be born, I was walking by myself on a dull Thursday morning—no class on Thursday, because that was the way they did it in Rome—along the lower road between the artificial "Lourdes grotto" and the dirty lake. You weren't supposed to walk by yourself—I suppose because you might have dirty thoughts while you walked, or maybe just because you might have thoughts, something the seminary seemed to frown upon.

I sat on a bench underneath the jetty that reached out into the lake while I tried to sort out the Rome problem. I heard the sound of two men walking above me. There was something in the tone of their voices that made me vaguely uneasy. One was Tony O'Malley.

"Twice a week?" said the other voice. "Why?"

"He's got a girl on the line in the town of Mundelein," said O'Malley. "They took Koko away from him, so now he's trying to go the other way."

"Are you sure?" The other voice was obviously impressed by O'Malley's confidence, but wanted proof.

"Jerry, the barber, told me he saw Donahue pick her up in front of the drive-in where she works. She's a junior at Libertyville High School. Jerry says Donahue shows up about ten-thirty on Tuesdays and Thursdays and they go off in her jalopy."

"Why did he tell you?" It was Ted Froelich, one of our straight and more sensible types.

"I don't know. The point is that he did, and we can't let a guy like that represent Chicago in Rome. We've got to tip Mac off. Watch Donahue's room tonight if you don't believe me. Then you can tell Mac next Tuesday."

The voices drifted away.

I remained on the bench, my body and mind paralyzed. Patrick Donahue didn't belong in the seminary. Now I would be rid of him, permanently. I didn't have to do a thing. I would win the contest for Rome by default.

The girl drove cautiously down the road into the seminary grounds, avoiding the single police car that patrolled the area nightly. She parked beneath the powerhouse, slid across the front seat, and hugged him.

He gave her a distracted kiss on the forehead, slipped out of the car, and dodged through the trees toward the residence hall. Getting back into the building was the most dangerous part.

He crept toward the doorway in front of the building; he'd left the door open, certain that it would remain that way. No one used this doorway, and not even Mac knew there was a key to open it. He slipped down the corridor, illuminated only by the vigil lights at the other end. Now it was merely a quick, silent rush up two flights of stairs and he would be back in his room. He thanked God that Cardinal Mundelein had provided each seminarian with his own room. The most dangerous moment came as he rounded the top of one flight of stairs and began to climb the second. Mac would be able to see him if he should happen to open the door of his suite.

There were always a few seconds of delicious terror when he made that dangerous turn. He loved the excitement of his game almost more than he did the body of the girl.

Mac wasn't there. With a mixture of exultation and relief he leaped up the last flight of stairs and rushed recklessly the last few steps to the safety of his room, a thrill not unlike that of the last few moments before possessing the girl. As he shoved the door open he wondered about experimenting with her next time. There were some variations he'd read about last summer. . . .

Halfway to his bed, he recoiled. Someone was sitting at his desk.

⁂

I hurried out of the semidark chapel after night prayers, hoping to take a shower before lights-out, at nine-forty-five. Mundelein was probably the only seminary in the world with the luxury of private bathrooms.

When I saw Ted Froelich walk down the corridor and knock on Mac's door, I bounded up the stairs to the third floor and raced to Pat's room. I knocked on the door, first lightly, then loudly. No response. I opened it and peered in. Darkness. I flicked on the light and then quickly turned it off. He had not even messed up his bed, much less left a dummy under the covers.

If Mac found an empty bed, he would sit there and wait until Pat came back.

I peeled off my cassock and clothes, found Pat's pajamas behind the door in his bathroom, put them on, and crawled into his bed. I covered my head with a pillow, as though I were drowning out the sound of the outside world.

I barely heard the door open. I didn't move. Was the pillow in place?

For one scary moment I thought I might have to mimic Pat's voice. I kept my eyes tightly closed. Mac's heavy breathing moved inside the room to the edge of the dresser, which marked the opening of the sleeping alcove. I sensed a dim light—a penlight, maybe. Carefully I opened one eye. Mac was moving the light slowly over the foot of the bed, making sure that the outlines under the blanket were truly those of human feet. The light went off. Soundlessly he glided toward the slightly open door and slipped out. Soft soles. The door closed with a faint click.

Very sleek.

I waited a long time. Eventually I got up; carefully made the bed, as best I could in the dark; hung up Pat's pajamas; and put on my clothes.

I sat on the hardwood chair by his metal desk. Not many books on the shelves. No intellectual, my friend Pat. The room turned cold as the heat diminished in the building. It would start warming again just as three nerve-shattering clangs of the bell awoke us at five-twenty-five. I debated giving up my vigil and retreating to the coziness of my bed. I'd persuaded the good nun in charge of our floor to provide me with two extra blankets—only a technical rule violation.

Then I heard shoes on the terrazzo floor of the corridor—not the soft soles that Mac wore. I held my breath as they came closer. I'd look pretty silly sitting at Pat's desk if it was a member of the seminary staff.

The door swung open and someone entered, his breathing heavy. In the dim light of the corridor I saw his face just before he closed the door. So that was the way a man looked after sexual satisfaction.

"Have a nice time, Patrick?" I asked.

He seemed to fold in on himself, swaying drunkenly toward the desk. He huddled over it, both hands on its flat, cold surface, his head bowed between his shoulders. "What . . ." He gasped for breath.

"One of your friends found out about the girl and tipped Mac off. He came looking for you. I happened to be in your bed. You're safe *this* time."

He sank to the floor, his head resting on the desk. "How . . ."

"Never mind," I said. "I found out. You didn't cover your trail very well."

"You shouldn't have, Kevin." His voice was hoarse. "Don't ever risk your vocation for me. I'm not worth it."

"Maybe I just get my kicks from keeping you out of trouble."

I paused at the doorway, looked cautiously up and down the corridor. My room was only half a dozen steps away. I wanted to say something more to him but couldn't find the words. I slipped out into the dim corridor.

Pat never mentioned our late-night maneuver. Froelich didn't come back to the seminary the following year, eased out, I imagine, on the grounds that he was an habitual liar. He entered another seminary, however, and is now a bishop in Kansas.

Three weeks later the competition came to an end.

McNulty signaled me as we walked in silent single file out of chapel after dinner. "Come to my office," he said curtly.

I went to his stuffy, cigar-reeking office and waited about twenty minutes—enough to make me tense and uneasy, which is what he had in mind.

Mac was a slender man, about my size and maybe only twelve years older than I—a young priest by my standards today. He had thin, receding blond hair and a big, high nose that made him look just a little like an aloof beagle. (He's still a priest, a moderately successful pastor. And I still don't like him.)

"You're proud, Brennan, proud," he said, pouncing on me as soon as he came into the room. I knew I had lost; in one terrible moment I even suspected that I was to be dismissed from the seminary as the only way they could justify what they were going to do. I learned many years later that Vandy and a few other Jesuits had wanted to do just that, and that Mac had talked them down.

"I guess I'll have to work on it," I said noncommittally.

"You should be going to Rome, you should. . . . But we can't send someone as puffed up as you. Mr. Donahue isn't as smart as you are, and doesn't have as much influence with the other men as you do, but you are cold and arrogant. You are inept with people—"

"Then why do I have influence with the others?" I cut in, wanting to score at least one point before I was dismembered.

Mac was leaning back in his chair, watching me solemnly. "If you are going to argue with me, we can end this conversation now," he said.

"No, Father," I said respectfully, "of course I don't want to argue. I'm just trying to understand."

He appeared mollified. "Your problem is you think you're better than everyone else because your family has so much money."

"We were not so well off when my father was away in the service," I interrupted, confident that the appeal to patriotism would disconcert him.

"Unfortunately you didn't learn enough from that lesson. You have four more years here to learn that money doesn't make you superior to the rest of us."

"Yes, Father," I said dutifully. "I'll try." I wanted to scream my contempt for him so that the whole seminary could hear it.

"Rome isn't everything," he continued. "You can look on these next four years as a penance time, a time of atonement, a time of reflecting on the unimportance of money."

"Yes, Father," I said, and then couldn't resist adding, "though I like this seminary, and I really don't think that four years here is a penance."

"You are a very smart young man, Mr. Brennan," he said uncertainly. "I'm not sure whether you're taking this disappointment well or whether you're playing a game with me."

"There's a third possibility, Father," I said imprudently. "Maybe I'm not really disappointed."

⁂

Pat was waiting at the door, his face anxious and gray.

I shook his hand. "Congratulations," I said. "I'll sell you an Italian dictionary."

The spasm that crossed his face was one of pain, not joy.

"I won't go, Kev," he whispered. "They should send you. If I turn them down . . . My family needs my help at home."

He meant it, every word of it. He also knew what I would say in response.

"You'll be no more help to your family here than in Rome. They're not going to send me, anyway. No reason to give it up for someone else. Of course you'll go."

He could have insisted. They would have sent me. He knew that, and I knew it. There in the corridor our paths began to diverge. Somehow I was no longer the winner.

CHAPTER FIVE

1955

I couldn't get the pinpoint lights in Pat Donahue's eyes out of my mind. Were they there before he went to Rome? What was the fear lurking beneath the suave, mature Romanita he had acquired these last two years? Why did he seem especially anxious when he talked to me? The wit and the charm were as winning as ever, and he had a string of funny and disrespectful Vatican stories. Yet his merriment seemed more forced than it used to be. What had happened to him in Rome?

Our battered pickup truck, borrowed from the Clearwater Lake villa where I was staying with my classmate Nick McAuliff, chugged up the manicured drive to the Tansey "summer cottage." I banished Pat from my mind as best I could as we turned into the driveway. Four women were sitting on the front porch, quietly reading, as though they were clients at an overly expensive old people's home—which is what the Tansey place looked like. My mother was frowning over *The Quiet American;* Mary Tansey was grimly plowing through *Andersonville,* her peaked little face drawn in a scowl even tighter than her normal angry grimace at the indignities of life. Maureen, radiantly lovely, was lazing through *The Man in the Gray Flannel Suit,* and Georgina Carrey, a dark-haired, well-endowed woman seven or eight years older than Maureen, glanced indifferently at the Eagle River *Weekly Gazette.* All were in stages of undress suggesting either beachwear or sleepwear, though in Mrs. Carrey's case I suspected an innate desire to wear as few clothes as possible. The remnants of a late-morning breakfast were scattered around the linen-covered table—toast crusts, empty orange-juice glasses, and a couple of half-filled coffeepots amid the silver service.

The ample and perfectly groomed lawn of the Tansey house stretched toward the edge of the cliff. Below, the blue waters of Lake Minocqua seemed to glitter deceptively, giving little hint of how much colder this lake was than our little lake at the other end of the state.

"Too late, Kevin," Maureen announced, kissing me assiduously and making my face feel warm. (I could see that Nick would have a field day when we got back to the villa.) "The golfers got an early start." Mo had an Audrey Hepburn pixie haircut, the impact of *Roman Holiday* still very much with us.

My mother awarded me a more maternal sign of affection; Mary Tansey barely noticed my existence; and Georgina Carrey gave me a careful, evaluative stare before going back to the *Gazette.* I introduced Nick, who had been assigned to accompany me from the villa to where my parents were staying. It was not exactly a rule that you had to bring a classmate along. It was just a wise thing to do if you expected to get another day off.

Nick accepted coffee; I poured myself some tea. The golfers—Arnold Tansey; the Colonel; Pat Donahue; Mo's boyfriend, one Burke Haggarty from Boston; and John Carrey—had left early. I was sure that Arnold, a rock-hard former Notre Dame football star who was one of the 154 millionaires in the United States that year, wanted to start early, and that was that.

The Tanseys were responsible for the pilgrimage to northern Wisconsin. They had met Pat on a trip to Rome, and were, naturally enough, charmed. They had paid the fare for him to come back for two weeks at the end of July. He had arrived like a conquering hero, oozing Roman urbanity. Since my father was Tansey's lawyer, Mom and he were invited along, as were Maureen and Burke, the latter representing some sort of political connection. John and Georgina Carrey were already there with their young son; I was not told what the connection was between the Carreys and the Tanseys, though they were both from the same rich parish on the South Side of Chicago.

"What was the movie last night?" my mother asked me, closing Graham Greene with a shiver of distaste.

"*On the Waterfront* last night, *Roman Holiday* the night before that, and *High Noon* tomorrow night."

"What do you think of Audrey Hepburn?" Mo demanded.

"The haircut looks better on you than it does on her," I replied.

"Hmm . . ." she sniffed. "Is that all you do up here—watch movies and play golf?"

"It gives us a chance to catch up on the movies we missed at the seminary."

"Why do they lock you up here for half the summer?" Mo asked, kicking her chaise lounge in disapproval.

"Because they want to protect them from the dangers of the world, Maureen," said my mother, who did not approve one bit of the seminary system. "By which they mean people like you, who wear swimsuits that are no better than lingerie. We can't have future priests knowing about things like that, can we?"

"That's not a thing priests ought to think about," Georgina Carrey said piously. "They get in enough trouble with their drinking as it is."

I had the feeling that she said this because she believed she ought to say something and not because she believed it. Mary Tansey, a woman cut out of cardboard, patiently continued to work on *Andersonville.*

"While we're waiting for the golf jocks to return," Mo said, "let's try the lake. It's cold enough to wipe any temptations out of your head. Come on, Nick."

I said something about that not being very likely, but after we rode down the lift and plunged into the lake I was inclined to agree with her. Even Mo, in a molded two-tone strapless suit, was no threat in water under sixty degrees. We hurried out and dried off on the brand-new pier, basking in the hot sunlight and reveling in the tangy smell of the pines.

"Odd bunch," I said as the three of us stretched out on the pier.

"Idle-rich capitalists oppressing us proletarians," said Nick. "Hell, I bet they have heat in their house at night, which is more than they have at the villa."

One quick look was enough to persuade Mo that she could trust Nick. "Georgina is a tease; Mary is a creep; Arnold is a blockhead; John doesn't really exist. Thank goodness for your mother and father, Kevin." She leaned back contentedly on her towel. "What do you think of Burke?"

"Nice enough for Boston Irish," I lied. Burke Haggarty was a handsome, empty jerk, made no more intelligent because he spoke of "cahs" when he meant "cars."

She sat up and leaned toward me. "He took me out to the Kennedy compound last month. I played touch football with them. They're fun people. When Jack runs for president in 1960, Burke is going to inherit Jack's seat in the Senate. It's all decided." Her naked shoulders moved up and down rapidly as she breathed enthusiasm.

"I don't think a Catholic can be elected president," Nick said carefully.

"Jack Kennedy can," Maureen said with confidence. "Hey, look who's coming. If she flirts with Burke once more, I'll pull her eyes out!" She hummed "Whatever Lola Wants, Lola Gets" as Georgina Carrey got out of the lift and swayed in our direction. In a boned, strapless suit with a back that plunged as low as it could, Georgina made Mo look chaste.

"May I join you?" Georgina said in her husky voice.

"Why not?" Mo said unenthusiastically. She turned to me. "Hey, what do you think of the Roman? Has he got class or has he got class?"

"I'm impressed," I admitted. "He's certainly acquired a lot of polish hanging around with those Italian aristocrats. They'll probably make him a bishop."

"Makes us look like peasants," said Nick with a touch of bitterness, his round, freckled face distinctly unhappy. "I'm not sure I like to have crown princes at our bucolic summer retreat."

Mo raised an eyebrow. "The crowd's not pleased with the hero? Come on, Kev, you ought to be able to do something about that."

"Clerical envy is a deadly thing," I said, trying to apply some suntan lotion to my back. "We all like Pat, yet it's a long way from Clearwater Lake to the Via Veneto."

Mo plunged on. "He seems to have a very different life than you guys, a lot more freedom."

"He doesn't get up at five-twenty-five." Nick continued to stare at the lake, his voice tight. "He doesn't have to spend an hour and a half praying before he walks a half mile for breakfast; he doesn't have three short smoking periods each day; he doesn't live like he's in a Navy boot camp; he doesn't spend half of his waking hours staring at four empty walls; and he doesn't get exiled from the city for all but a few weeks every year. We're prisoners, and he's soaking up culture and Romanita."

"It's not that bad," I mumbled, staring across the lake, letting the pine trees come back into focus. Georgina Carrey showed no signs of heading for the water. The suit was for display, not for swimming.

"Pat is Pat, and we all love him," Nick said. "How can you be mad at him, even if you know he's running for pope? It's only that I've spent five years surviving this damn, stupid system, and I'm envious of someone who has escaped it."

"So you admit that you hate the system?" Mo said, sitting up in triumph.

"That's why classmates become so close," I said, now that the truth was out of the bag. "We've spent a long time against a common enemy, a Georgian museum piece spread over a couple of hundred acres of northern Illinois hills that tries to turn out priests like a sausage factory turns out salami."

"And succeeds," Nick added bitterly. "Just to make sure that we don't get a chance to find out what life is like, it sends us to this frigid place for most of the summer to isolate us even more."

"Pat Donahue was very nice to us when we were in Rome with the Tanseys," Georgina said vacuously. "He even got us into the catacombs underneath St. Peter's."

"A really titillating place, from all I hear," said Mo, eyes sparkling with mischief.

"Maybe they're having lunch upstairs by now," I suggested, and started for the lift.

When we returned, they were indeed having lunch, though the meal began like a wake. Arnold Tansey, a massive man with muscles like lampposts, a bald head lined with a fringe of black hair, and a jaw like a sledgehammer, was sulking. Such characters were pigeons for the Colonel on the golf course. Tansey had made his money in the construction business he inherited from his father after the war. He was a single-minded, bull-headed man with little intelligence but with the forcefulness of a Sherman tank. At forty-five he was a millionaire with no children, a wife he ignored, and the absolute conviction that he knew everything. For all of that, though, there was a certain attractiveness in his bluff simplicity, especially when contrasted with the bland, bespectacled inoffensiveness of John Carrey, whose money had been made, I gathered, in auto parts.

The women had donned shifts and shirtwaists for lunch—all but Maureen, whose terry cover-up defied the Tansey custom of formal lunch.

"I see Chicago got a new mayor while I was away," said Pat, cheerfully trying to break the ice.

"Dick Daley won't last more than one term," said Arnold Tansey, rising to the bait. "Martin Kennelly was a fine mayor, a decent businessman. Dick Daley is a prisoner of the unions. He and Bill Lee think they're going to run the town. When the AFL and the CIO merge this winter, Chicago will be the first city to have a labor government. Dick Daley and George Meany are planning to take over the country. They'll run Walter Reuther for president; you watch. The business community must fight back to stop a takeover. They think they can do it next year because of the President's heart attack. We've got to unite behind Senator Goldwater to stop them."

"Always thought Senator Daley was a socialist," said my father. "Like his father, Big Mike, before him."

"You just watch," said Arnold confidently. "New Deal socialism is going to run this country right into the ground. We've got to go back to the oldtime business virtues."

"Like 1933," Pat said. My mother and Mo both snickered behind their tuna salad, which had been served on flawless china by two servants.

"Why don't you tell us more about Senator Kennedy," Mo said to her young man.

Burke Haggarty was already on his second beer. He yawned, boredom in his pale-blue eyes, disdain in the tilt of his needle-sharp nose. "Jack is a superb politician," he drawled, "quite good at the game. Though, to tell you the truth, I think Bobby, with whom I went to Harvard"—he said *Ha*-vuhd—"by the way, is much better even than Jack. A delightful instinct for the jugular. We're going to revolutionize American politics."

Haggarty was ten or fifteen pounds overweight, his eyes had the glaze of the habitual drinker, and his silver-tipped black hair somehow managed to look untidy despite constant grooming. Oh, God, Mo, not him, not for all the seats in the United States Senate.

"The Colonel may just be able to deliver Cook County for him," Pat said, digging into the Smithfield ham.

"A Catholic can never be elected president," said Arnold Tansey.

"The hell he can't," I said hotly, taking my eyes off Georgina Carrey's torso long enough to get into the fight. "I don't like to have to win with a *Ha*-vuhd *ba*-stuhd, but we're going to win before the sixties are over."

"I hope you're right, young man," Tansey said grudgingly. "I see you have your father's fire."

"No, his mother's fire and his father's good looks," said Pat.

Once the laughter died away, Georgina Carrey made her contribution to the conversation. "Would you please pass the ham, Arnold?" she asked, as though it were an invitation to an assignation.

After lunch, Pat drove with us in the pickup truck back to the villa. We were going to play tennis and then get ready for a "splash" that night, a wild satirical revue, based on *Showboat,* to which the families of the seminarians who were in the area were invited, a concession that would never have been made back at Mundelein.

"So, tell us about Rome," Nick said as we picked our way carefully down the dirt road through the pine trees that linked the Tansey house with the state highway.

"It's a wonderful opportunity," Pat began. "Our teachers have the best minds in the Church, our fellow students are from all over the world, we study in the heart of Christendom, and we're in Rome during the time of the greatest, most forward-looking pontificate in several centuries. Pius the Twelfth is certainly a saint."

"Even though he dealt with Hitler and Mussolini?" I said with pretended innocence.

"Come on, now, Kev," Pat said smoothly as we bumped off the dirt road onto the highway. "That's not really fair."

The boyish charm was now practiced and disciplined; the quick words flowed in complete sentences; the warm smile appeared not a moment too soon nor a moment too late. Only the eyes still showed fear. Odd, I'd been dimly aware of the fear all along; now for the first time I saw it clearly.

"I envy you the freedom," said Nick, his lean body tense with the anger we all felt toward the rigid seminary system. "You live in one of the world's most urbane cities; we live in Lake County. You spend your summers wandering around Europe; we go to Clearwater Lake, for the love of God."

Pat laughed easily. "It's not that much different, really, Nick. Besides, think of all the temptations in a city like Rome."

"At Mundelein," Nick said, "we could use a little more temptation."

"Speaking of temptation," Pat said, "that Carrey woman has quite a build, hasn't she? I wonder what the villa crowd will think of her?"

"I don't know," said Nick. "I'll take your friend Maureen any day."

"You're going to have to get in line for that happy privilege," Pat said. "And it's a long line, though I'd gladly give you precedence over that Boston snob."

"You guys always seem to have beautiful women around you," Nick said. "Whatever happened to that little blonde you taught to water-ski, Kevin? Remember her?"

"Vaguely," I said.

"She graduated from St. Anne's last June," Pat said promptly. "She's working in the psychiatric department at Loretto Hospital."

"Made peace with her, huh?" I said resentfully.

"Yes, I made peace with her. . . . She's dating Tim Curran, you know."

"The last of the Black Raider's band," I said.

"He's stopped drinking. He's working in the shoe department in Marshall Field's and going to night school. Wants to be a lawyer."

"Is he doing all that for Ellen?"

"I don't think so. I think she came after the, uh, 'conversion.' Anyway, I'm afraid that Tim's become very serious. The old comedian is gone."

I told myself that if anyone could keep the comic in Tim Curran alive, it was Ellen Foley.

After the "splash" that night, there was a "haustus," an ice-cream party, on the wooden porch outside the assembly hall at the villa. A full August moon glowed on Clearwater Lake.

"Will you get in trouble if I'm seen talking to you?" Maureen asked, devouring a vast dish of chocolate-chip ice cream.

"I'll get all kinds of points for good taste, Mo. What do you think of our villa? Cardinal Mundelein built it for us just like he built everything else, a wooden camp on the side of a lake to temper the spirits of his plebes during the sinful summer months."

"Bitter, bitter," she said, her warm smile and generous eyes making me glow inside. "I think it's a nice place, and I think you actually enjoy it. You get your reading and your exercise and your fun and an occasional glance at figures like Georgina Carrey's. What more does a young priest-to-be want out of life?"

"More than that, I can tell you," I said.

She was wearing a white dress with the sleeves pushed up, with a thin sweater wrapped around her shoulders to fend off the northern-Wisconsin cold. "You're a romantic, Kevin, even more than I am. An innocent romantic." She crossed her arms as though the chill of innocent romanticism had momentarily become worse than the night air. "I sure hope your Church doesn't let you down."

"It probably will," I said glumly.

"Did you lose to him this afternoon?" she asked, tilting her head.

"Beat him six-two, six-love," I said morosely. "Only it's no fun. Pat has learned how to be a gracious loser."

"And you haven't learned to be a gracious winner?" she grinned.

"That'll be the day," I conceded, and laughed with her.

The Colonel arrived just then with more chocolate-chip ice cream. "Jerome Kern has cause for action for what you fellows did to *Showboat,*" he said.

Huddling under several layers of blankets in the dorm that night, I prayed for the Black Raider and his lady. And then, as an afterthought, I prayed that God would exorcise the fear from Pat Donahue's eyes.

Two days later Maureen and Pat took a canoe out on Lake Minocqua. The temperature had climbed back into the eighties, and the sky was cloudless. They skimmed over the water and beached on the shore of the opposite side at a spot where there were no housing developments.

"The forest primeval," said Maureen, stretching to get the kinks out of her muscles.

"Not quite," he corrected her. "The jack pines are all gone. The lumber companies got them at the beginning of the century."

"It's a lot nicer than our lake," she said, peeling off the shirt she was wearing over her swimsuit, then plunging into the chilly waters.

"I'm going to poke around in the woods," Pat said. "Don't take any chances."

He was more relaxed than he had been the first two days of his return. Maureen's breezy irreverence seemed to put him at ease.

He found a thin trail and walked back into the woods for about ten minutes, until he stumbled into an old jack pine that the loggers had missed, so wide that he could get his arms only around a third of it. Strange that they'd passed it up, because an overgrown logging trail was nearby. He heard voices coming down the trail and jumped back into the underbrush, not wanting to be caught trespassing.

Hiding behind the tree, he saw that the voices belonged to Arnold Tansey and Georgina Carrey. He almost stepped out of the woods to greet them, then hesitated. They were a long way from home.

As he hesitated, Tansey took the woman in his arms and kissed her. She seemed to struggle, but could not escape from his viselike grip. Pat enjoyed watching the pseudorape. She had teased Pat since the first time they'd met in Rome, pretending at a phony piety but bombarding him with unmistakable hints.

Soon Georgina's protests stopped, and she became an active participant. Pat stayed to the end. Then, feeling guilty, he crept back through the forest to the lake. Maureen was stretched out in the sun, dozing peacefully.

It was such a long time since he had petted with her. How innocent it had been, compared to the furious demons eating at him now.

Later, as they paddled back across the lake, he couldn't get the image of Georgina's body, arching up to blend with Tansey's, out of his mind.

⁂

The next day the Colonel and Pat thoroughly beat Tansey and Burke at golf. The host was not pleased. He sulked through the ride home. Rather than endure a cocktail hour of continued silent recrimination, Pat found a lawn chair in the sunlight near the edge of the bluff and "rested his eyes." It was a warm, stodgy summer afternoon. He dreamed that he and Maureen were marooned on a desert island. The island became an arctic ice pack.

He woke up shivering. The weather had changed. There was a distant roll of thunder and a quick sparkle of lightning. Rain was already falling across the lake, and whitecaps were frothing, pushed by a chill wind.

He reached for his sweater and stood up. Just as he turned toward the house, he saw a canoe tip over on the lake.

It was a green one that had been carrying two ten-year-olds, a boy and a girl. Their heads appeared from beneath the canoe like bits of driftwood. Pat watched as though it were a silent horror movie. The canoe began to spin in the water as their panicky efforts to right it merely overturned it again. They were more than fifty yards offshore; afraid to swim, perhaps; or maybe they didn't know how. As he watched, his feet mired in the thick lawn, a swimmer appeared at the foot of the bluff, stroking against the rising waves. He didn't have to take a second look to know that it was Maureen.

He raced back to the house. Kevin, who had managed to get away from the villa again, was on the porch, reading the paper.

"Mo's saving some kids on the lake," Pat shouted. "Get help!"

Without waiting for an answer, Pat ran back to the edge of the bluff, decided that the lift was too slow, and plunged down the tangled, brushy path through the pine trees. By the time he got there, the rain was beating against the tiny beach. The little girl from the canoe was already on the slippery pier, sobbing hysterically. The storm had dropped a curtain of water, obscuring everything but the waves that were smashing against the pier.

Then the curtain lifted for a moment. He saw the overturned canoe rocking unattended in the waves. A head broke the surface. Short, black hair. It disappeared again. Mo dived in search of the little boy. Pat kicked off his shoes and was about to dive in when she surfaced again, holding something this time. She started to swim toward shore.

He dived in and swam to meet her. He took the child from her arms as the rain swirled around them. Maureen was gasping for breath, her shoulders heaving. The child didn't seem to be breathing. As Pat pushed the boy onto the pier, the Colonel materialized out of the mist and began artificial respiration. Mrs. Brennan swept the sobbing girl into her arms. The Tanseys milled around, shouting above the wind and the thunder.

The boy was breathing again—choking, wheezing, rasping, but definitely breathing.

Maureen wasn't on the pier. Where had she gone? Pat found her, and Kevin, in the boat house, sitting on the floor, her head against an old bench. She was sobbing.

"He's all right," Kevin was saying as he put his arms around her. "He's all right. You don't think the little brat would dare to resist the Colonel's first aid, do you?"

There was a laugh somewhere in the sobs.

"It's all right, Mo. It's all right. You saved them both," Kevin said.

Gradually the sobbing stopped, and she relaxed in his arms.

Pat walked quietly away feeling like someone who had stumbled into a married couple's bedroom by mistake.

As he climbed up the hill, watching the rainbow the shower had left behind, his fingers clenched and unclenched. The dark furies that had assailed him since he had come home were growing more vicious. Hatred, desire, loneliness, struggled for dominance within him. Kevin, Maureen, Ellen: the most important people in the world to him didn't care about him.

The next morning he pleaded an upset stomach to escape from golf. The demon inside him was growing more violent and more demanding. He heard the cars pull away one by one. It was the servants' day off. Only he and Georgina were left in the house. She was still in her bedroom, not having appeared for breakfast.

He told himself he was going down to the beach to swim. He put on swimming trunks and walked out of his room as if in a trance. Resolutely he took two steps toward the stairway and the beach. Then his feet reversed themselves and he walked down the corridor to her room. His temples were throbbing.

He pushed the door open. Her room was trimmed in lace, and sun streamed through transparent curtains. She lay on her bed in a loosely belted, thin white robe.

"Get out," she said.

He locked the door. "You've been asking for this since we met in Rome."

"I'll tell my husband," she said unconvincingly.

"I don't think so." He exulted in his masculinity as he peeled off his trunks. "I saw you with Tansey. I don't think you want John to know that you're a punchboard."

"Bastard," she said with a snarl.

He took her brutally. As he expected, she loved it.

Back in his room he sobbed in disgust and self-hatred and murmured an act of contrition.

A few days later Pat was on his way back to Rome. The Tanseys and the Carreys closed down the house and returned to their neighborhood, St. Praxides, with its country club and the "only decent golf course in the Middle West." My parents went back to our lake, where the temperature was at least ten degrees higher. Maureen returned to Chicago, since her parents were spending little time at the lake these days. Burke Haggarty, on the point of expiring from boredom, saved his life by flying home to Boston and the Cape.

Before Pat left, he and I walked down the villa road toward the railroad stop and the hamlet of Clearwater Lake—a general store with a public telephone from which we could call our families in Chicago. Only in an emergency were we permitted to make a call from the villa. The baseball team was practicing on one side of the road; the golf course, on the other side, was crowded. Great vanilla-ice-cream clouds floated across the sky. The imperious warning of a train whistle urged us toward the track.

We walked silently along the road.

"Damn it, Kev, there's just one thing wrong with Rome," Pat

said, jamming his hands into his carefully fitted white slacks. "I love it, but I miss the guys from Mundelein. And I miss you. You ought to be there, too. It's not right that they started sending two people to Rome the year after us."

"I gather they didn't want to have the contest again," I said, as embarrassed as he was.

"It wasn't a contest as far as we were concerned." His fair face was animated. "*They* made the contest; we didn't."

"Yeah."

The Northwestern train lumbered into view, surprisingly on time. Villa authorities had suggested to Pat that it would be discreet to go home on the train instead of with the Tanseys.

He squared his shoulders, took a deep breath, and held out his hand. "Still, I miss you, Kev. It's only two more years. I hope they send you to Rome for graduate school."

I shook hands with him, putting as much warmth into the handshake as he did. "Not very likely. Anyway, I've had enough school."

He hesitated, as though he wanted to say something else. The tiny dots of fear reappeared in his eyes. Instead, he shook hands again.

The train stopped. We walked quickly to the steps and climbed up, and I handed him his elegant red duffel bag. "Give my best to your family," I said.

"Oh . . . yeah. I'll spend a day or two with them before I go back to Rome."

A week with the Tanseys, a day or two with his parents. And I was the only seminarian to bid him good-bye.

He found a window seat on my side of the car and waved as the yellow and green train huffed and puffed and moved slowly away. I watched it until all I could see was a trace of diesel exhaust in the distance.

The villa season inched slowly toward its end, on August 15. I was anxious to get back to the seminary. Only two more years and the battle with the system would be over. I could begin my life as a priest and do the things I wanted to do since the first days I'd watched the priests in our parish as a little boy.

On August 8, just a week before the closing date, Father Desmon, the battered old Jesuit who presided over the villa, called me out of line as we filed out of mass. There was a call in the office from my mother, he told me. His anxious face looked ever more careworn, his misshapen glasses drooping over his nose.

I was frightened. Too many of my classmates learned of death in the family in the same way. Dad? One of the kids?

Mom wasted no words. "The Cunningham house in River Forest burned down last night."

"Mo?" I screamed.

"She wasn't home." Mom's voice was uneven, distraught. "The Cunninghams both died of smoke inhalation. Dead on arrival at St. Anne's. Ellen was there when. . . . Oh, Kevin, you've got to come back for the funeral, day after tomorrow. Maureen needs you."

Need me or not, they weren't going to get me. I explained carefully to Father Desmon that Tom Cunningham and my father had been partners for twenty-five years, that their fathers before them had been partners, that the Cunninghams had taken care of us during the war, that Mo was like a sister to us.

He shook his head miserably. "If it were up to me, Kevin," he said, his sad eyes downcast, "I'd put you on the train in five minutes. Unfortunately, I don't make the rules. You know what the rector would say if he found out. If we let one person go in for personal reasons, we'll have to let everyone go. I'm sorry. I really am."

And he really was, poor man. I called my mother back.

She yielded to one of her rare moments of uncharitableness when I told her. "Heartless sons of bitches," she said softly. "They don't know what Jesus was talking about."

Mom was right. Nevertheless, I stayed at the villa.

Maureen did not die in the fire, because she got home at three in the morning from a date—a wild drinking party, I would later learn—and discovered the fire engines in front of her blazing home. Mom said Maureen blamed herself for her parents' death because she thought if she were home she would have smelled the smoke from the fire, caused by her father's falling asleep with a lighted cigarette in his hand.

"The poor child would be dead herself," my mother insisted, absolving Maureen of any guilt.

Mo would not absolve herself. I'd read enough psychology books that summer to know that indulged children most resent their parents and feel most guilty when their parents die.

I went to visit Maureen the day I returned from the villa. I found her at the side of the new swimming pool behind the Cunningham summer home, a beer can in her hand and two empties on the tile next to her chair. She was watching a point in the hazy sky far above the willow trees on the other side of the pool. As always, there was a record player going somewhere. It sounded like "Rock Around the Clock"—hardly mourning music.

"Hi, Mo," I began tentatively.

"Kevin, Kevin, Kevin!" she exclaimed, knocking over her deck chair in her haste to embrace me and cry on my shoulder.

"Sorry I wasn't here before," I said, groping for better words.

"Better today than before." She was wearing a white bikini, the fashion finally having made it to our lake, though only to private pools. Maureen was no longer a fresh and blossoming girl but rather a lithe and elegant woman. "I need a strong and unthreatening shoulder today." The weeping slowly ebbed, and she disengaged herself from me. "Bet you wouldn't hold Ellen Foley in a bikini that long." She grinned wickedly as she dried her tears with a stray piece of Kleenex.

"Ellen Foley is too modest to display that much of herself to the wandering eye," I replied, glad that we were back on familiar turf.

"Same old Kevin," she said, laughing, wiping away the last tear, and reclining on her chair again. "Tell me about yourself. We had no private time at Eagle River."

I sat down on a deck chair that I rescued from the other side of the pool. "Not much to tell. Growing in wisdom and virtue and waiting to show up under some pastor's Christmas tree. Anyway, you're the subject today."

"Well, I'm going back to that shit hole in Purchase in a few weeks and endure those idiot snobs from the East and count the days till I graduate. After that"—she shrugged her lovely shoulders—"I don't know, Kev. I've got a pool my parents never used"—she gestured at the pool—"more money than I can ever spend, and nothing to live for. Did you ever find that challenge for me that you prayed for a while back?"

"Don't feel guilty about your parents," I pleaded.

"Guilty?" She cocked an eye at me. "Hell, I don't feel guilty, Kev. They were barely alive, anyway. Don't tell me they've gone to heaven. How can people with so little vitality go anywhere? How they ever worked up enough passion to conceive me I'll never know."

I listened silently.

"Anyway, they certainly won't go to hell. I say the Memorare to the Blessed Mother every morning and the Rosary every night. Maybe God's got a kind of limbo for people who don't have enough fire to either sin or be virtuous. They'd enjoy a place like that." She twisted uneasily in her chair. "Me—I'm going to hell, Kevin. I know it already. I'm shallow and wicked with gifts that I'm going to waste. I'll live a few more years, and then it's suffering, or maybe just nothingness. Anyway, I'm not sure the change will be all that great."

Her madonna face was an implacable mask.

"No, you won't," I said, hoping to break her out of the despair. "Just tell St. Peter at the gate that you know my father. He's got clout everywhere."

She laughed, got out of her chair, and dived into the pool. A dozen laps later she climbed out, draping a towel around her shoulders. "Thanks for getting me out of my black mood. I'll get you a beer, dear cousin."

When she came back with the frosty bottle of Heineken's, she was serious again. "You think there's hope for me?" she asked.

"God will find you as irresistible as everyone else does, especially in a bikini."

"Oh, hell. He can peek at me naked in the shower any time He wants," she said, grinning. "Do you suppose He does that, Kevin? Does He like our bodies? He must, I suppose, because He's responsible for them."

I almost gave her a warning about humanizing God, but somehow managed not to. "If He should turn out to be She, She might be jealous of your body, Mo."

When I returned to our house, my mother was on the front porch, peering at me over her reading glasses. "Words of consolation?" she asked.

"Half an hour of laughs," I said disconsolately. "There was an answer Mo needed, but I didn't have it."

"You may make a good priest, after all," she said, turning back to her mystery story.

I worried about Maureen's despair just the same. What do you say to a person who doesn't think she's going to get to heaven? For that they had provided no answer at the seminary, only the assertion that it was an unforgivable sin.

The next Friday evening, I was in Chicago, driving down Austin Boulevard after I'd made a raid on an Oak Park bookstore to buy out their collection of psychology books. I saw a familiar figure with light-blond hair standing patiently at a bus stop. She was wearing a short-sleeve blouse and a flaring print skirt. I backed up my new Chevy convertible, which was banned at the seminary and at the villa but not in the city, not till I was ordained, anyway.

"Waiting for a pickup, lady?" I asked.

Her face became stern, then relaxed. "I'm sorry, Kevin," she said, climbing into the car. "I'm not used to being accosted."

"I don't know why not. You look gorgeous. Where can I take you? To the hospital?"

"No, I'm going to Loyola for class," she said nervously. "It's a long way. Why don't you drop me at the El."

My heart was pounding. Lord, she was a knockout. "Not on your life. What are you taking—biology?"

She blushed. "Literature, would you believe?"

"I thought you were going to be a nurse?"

"Can't nurses write?" she said with a quick spark of anger.

So, with maturity comes fire, too.

"You always dress up that way for class? Or is it none of my business whether you have a big date with Tim Curran afterward?"

She smiled. "Of course it's your business. Tim is a dear. He's working till nine, but he'll meet me after class."

I turned down Chicago Avenue, not paying much attention to the traffic. I caught a glimpse of her solemn gray eyes, which were regarding me with something like adoration. Oh, God.

"You were wonderful with Maureen," Ellen said. "She told me what you said to her. Kevin, you gave her life back to her."

I felt very warm, and monumentally self-satisfied.

Fingers touched my hand lightly. "The parish that gets you, Father Kevin, is going to be very fortunate."

Despite Pat Donahue and Burke Haggarty and Georgina Carrey and Arnold Tansey, the world seemed a much better place.

"Did you ever notice the strange look in Pat's eyes?" I said impulsively.

"Sure." Her delicate face was solemn again.

"What's he afraid of?" I shifted into gear and crossed Cicero Avenue, wishing that the ride to Loyola would last all night.

"Well, you, whenever he's with you. And others, depending."

"Why?"

"He wants people to like him."

"We all want that." I kept my eye on the car in front of me.

"Not that way," she insisted. "Not that desperately. Anyway, you may as well forget it, Kevin. You won't ever be able to make his fear go away."

I pulled the car over at Rush and Pearson streets by a no-parking sign. The dirty gray Gothic of Quigley Seminary, across the street from the somber, dark brick of Loyola's Lewis Towers, reminded me I shouldn't be in a car with a pretty girl.

"You improve with age, Kevin," she said.

"Not just an angry fanatic or a self-righteous prig?"

"You pretend to be those things because you'd be defenseless if people knew how soft and gentle you really are." Her lips brushed mine, and I thought the world had caught fire. "You're almost as tough as a dish of melting ice cream."

She slipped quickly out of the car, closing the door and taking a step toward the Towers. Then her shoulders squared and she turned back to the car.

"Melting chocolate ice cream." She laughed and winked.

Despite the disapproving spires of Quigley, I watched her until her trim little backside disappeared among the crowds of young people swarming into Loyola.

But it was not Ellen who haunted my dreams at Mundelein that fall. Rather, it was Pat Donahue, and the tiny dots of fear I had seen in his eyes.

CHAPTER SIX

1958

"Father, there's a girl at the door who says she knows you," Harry Fagan bellowed, in an only partly successful effort to drown out the "Volare" being played by the nineteen mildly coordinated musical instruments of the "Melody Knights" of Jesuit High School.

"Tell her I'll see her tomorrow, before the game," I shouted back. The Jesuit High band was more enthusiastic than it had been in my day, but less skilled. The five hundred or so adolescents crowding into our parish hall didn't care. To have the Melody Knights at your High Club dance was, for some unaccountable reason, high prestige. Lou Carmody, a bright-eyed Jesuit scholastic, was delighted to bring them to our dance, and I was for the moment a "neat new priest" by the standards of the local teenagers.

"She said her name was Ellen," Harry shouted again, his bald head glistening in the dim artificial light.

"I'll see her now," I said, trying to weave a path through the surging masses of adolescents, boys leaning against walls and pillars, girls dancing with one another.

"Remember our rule about nonmembers," Harry yelled after me. A young priest at St. Praxides had not one but hundreds of pastors. Every lay person in the parish thought it was his obligation to establish standards of behavior for the young cleric so fortunate as to be accepted into his community of the newly affluent. Even those who knew who my father was could not quite get over the assumption that all priests came from the poorer classes.

Some adults who did not have teenage children would poke their heads into the High Club dance to check up on me. Leonard Kaspar, our impeccably groomed head usher, put in an appearance for a few minutes at every dance, his handsome face and pencil mustache registering stunned disapproval of what was going on. "Doesn't the pastor want them dressed in suit coats and ties, and the girls wearing skirts?" he said with distaste as he saw the hoards of adolescents in sweatshirts and Bermuda shorts.

"Talk to him about it, *Mister* Kaspar," I snapped, turning away, confident that for the present I had the votes of the parents of teenagers against a reform that would empty the hall.

Ellen was waiting by the admissions desk at the foot of the stairs leading to our low-ceilinged basement parish hall. "No membership ID, Father," she said, a flicker of a grin at her mouth.

"No teenagers get in without membership cards," said Georgina Carrey decisively. Georgina volunteered a great deal of time to St. Praxides, in order, I suspected, to keep a watchful eye on her teenage son. "We can't make exceptions, Father." Her hands were set in solemn warning on her ample hips.

The mistake was understandable. Ellen, in plaid Bermuda shorts and a white blouse under the required slightly dirty trench coat, her hair gathered in a ponytail and her face showing no trace of makeup, was once again the third-grader in the back of my long-forgotten Studebaker.

"Driver's license," Ellen said, holding up the card diffidently.

"Georgina," I said, "this is Ellen Foley. She will look like a teenager for the next twenty years. Actually she's a registered nurse with a psychiatric specialty."

Georgina hesitated, not sure whether to believe me, caught sight of Ellen's minute diamond engagement ring, and turned gracious. "I'm sorry," she said, radiating all of her not-inconsiderable charm.

We escaped from Georgina back into the adolescent din. "Oh, Father Kevin," Ellen said enthusiastically, "how wonderful. You'll be able to be a teenager all of your life."

I was hot, tired, and tense. "Did you come to visit, or do you want to talk?"

Her wide, gray eyes turned serious. "I've wanted to talk for days. Tim gave me his car tonight and said I'd better get it out of my system."

My heart sank. I was afraid she was going to talk about my saying the wedding mass. Tim, so solemn and serious at my ordination, had asked me to officiate.

Monsignor Rafferty, my pastor, would not let me off on Saturday to take a wedding somewhere else. "I'll make an exception, son, only for members of your immediate family. Brothers and sisters, not cousins," he had said.

"Can you wait until I chase the natives home?" I asked Ellen.

"I've got all night. No rush," she said.

I summoned Monica Kelly, the skinny little leader of the sophomores whose tight golden curls made her distinctive in a crowd of female adolescents. I introduced Ellen.

"Hi," Monica said briskly. "What high school do you go to?"

"Sienna," said Ellen, not batting an eye.

I went back to my High Club chores, ejecting drunks, breaking up fights, sweeping up the remains of broken Coke bottles, and defending the property of St. Praxides from depredations that would on the morrow offend the Monsignor, Sister Superior, the chief engineer, the head usher, the president of the Altar Guild, and a number of other functionaries interested in the elimination of teenagers. I loved every minute of it. Teenagers were one of the reasons I became a priest.

I learned one attitude in the seminary that was essential to success at St. Praxides: cynicism. The Church was not going to change. Leadership was going to remain in the hands of men like Monsignor Rafferty for as long as I lived. If you wanted to do anything for the people—and I did—you had to learn how to placate and manipulate men like him. For someone with my training it was not hard to know what to do. You kept your mouth shut, told them as little as possible about what you were doing, did as much as you could get away with behind their backs, and hoped they wouldn't find out.

Leo Mark Rafferty did not want a lot of noisy teenagers on the property on Friday nights. In fact, he didn't want anyone at all on the property if he could avoid it, save on Sunday morning, and then with collection envelopes in hand. However, he was in no position to disagree with Georgina Carrey, whose wealth awed him. As long as she wanted a High Club for her fourteen-year-old "John Junior," there was going to be one.

We finished cleaning up at eleven-thirty, sent the sweepers home, paid off the Melody Knights, bid a final farewell to Georgina, her waiflike son, and her husband, and sat down at a table to talk, both of us with a Coke bottle in our hand and munching cookies from a plate Ellen had managed to hide from the Ostrogoths.

"That woman try to seduce you yet?" she said, lighting a cigarette.

"No, but she will."

"So long as you know that." She stubbed out the cigarette after one puff.

"I won't give in," I promised.

"Never a doubt. Your tastes are different." She looked at the cookie she was nibbling. Still a chocolate addict, though the calories had yet to have any effect.

"What's on your mind, Ellen? I see the worry in the back of those gray eyes."

The eyes turned slowly toward me.

"Mo. She shouldn't marry him," she said simply.

"I had a hunch she shouldn't," I said. "He's more than ten years older than she is and looks like an alcoholic playboy."

"I think," said my somber friend, "she's getting married because I'm getting married, and she's afraid if Ellen has got a man, the supply may be running down."

"You think it's one more of Mo's impulses?"

"Ever since her parents died, she's been crazy. Oh, Father Kevin, you've got to stop her."

"Unless you want me to call you 'Nurse Ellen,' you cut that stuff out," I said.

Her smile lit up the room again. "All right. And by the way, what is that man with purple buttons doing pacing up and down at the door watching us as if I'm a woman of ill repute?"

"That's not a man," I said with a sigh, "it's a monsignor. Excuse me."

I walked back to the door of the silent hall. Leo Mark Rafferty, who looked like an angry, overweight dwarf even when he was happy, was distinctly not happy now.

"Just what do you think you're doing, young man?" he demanded, his red face turning even redder.

"Talking to a young woman," I said nonchalantly. Inspired

by Ellen's presence, I was going to depart from respectful opportunism. Not even a curate—the lowest form of life in the Church—can be safely humiliated in the presence of a woman who loves him.

"Do you think that's proper behavior?" The color in his face deepened, and his cheeks puffed up as if he were going to explode.

"She's a close friend of my family and is engaged to one of my classmates. She wants to talk to me about a problem of a mutual friend."

"Let her make an appointment at a decent time of the day. Now, dismiss her and get back to the rectory. You know that there's an eleven-o'clock rule in this diocese."

"I'll tell you what, Monsignor," I said calmly. "You call the Vicar-General tomorrow morning and ask him whether a priest counseling someone in the school hall after a dance is breaking the eleven-o'clock rule. Also tell him that you want me transferred. I don't give a good goddamn what you do. I'm staying here as long as it is necessary to deal with this problem."

Leo Mark's color was now a surprised and ghastly white. He backpedaled abruptly, as though someone had opened a furnace door.

"Oh, I didn't know it was important, Kevin. By all means, take as long as you want. Uh, make some coffee if you'd like."

As he scurried off, I knew I'd found his weak link, and blessed the Lord for sending Ellen.

"Kevin wins another," she said, grinning at me.

"Don't bet on it," I said, taking a cookie off the top of a second pile she'd somehow found. "Now, about Mo."

"Talk her out of it."

I sighed and put my cookie back on the plate. "Could I talk you and Tim out of marrying?" I asked.

"Of course not," she said. "We're in love."

"Don't you think Maureen would say the same thing?"

"Are Tim and I as blind as she is?" she sighed, shoving away the cookie plate.

I felt very tired and very old. "Look, Ellen, I'm so new at the parish-priest business that I don't even have the prayers after Low Mass memorized yet. About the only thing I've learned is that when young people think they're in love, you can't talk them into or out of anything."

"Won't you even talk to Maureen?" she pleaded.

"If she wants to talk to me . . . if she's trying to find someone to encourage her in a decision she's already made to get out, then I'll certainly do that. Your psychiatric training should tell you that's all I can do and should do."

She frowned. "You're a priest, not a psychiatrist."

"If Maureen is guilty about her parents' dying in the fire and wants to expiate it by destroying herself, there's nothing you or I can do about it."

"You won't do anything?" she asked.

"If I think of anything I can do, you can depend on it that I will."

"I guess I knew that's what you would say." She stood up and buttoned her trench coat. "I'd better go home."

I would have enjoyed talking to her in that gloomy and echoing parish hall until the sun rose.

I set my alarm for five-forty-five. Monsignor had punished me for the High Club by giving me the earliest mass on Saturday mornings. I went back to bed after mass, only to be awakened in fifteen minutes by a phone call from Pat Donahue.

"Hi, Kev." He was disgustingly cheery for a Saturday morning. "Got a minute?"

I sat wearily in the chair next to my phone. "Shoot."

Our friendship seemed back on track since he returned from Rome. We were both working hard and liked our work. In our shared commitment to the priesthood we'd found, I thought, a basis for a "mature relationship"—a phrase I'd picked up from the psychology books. He was still diffident with me, but the pinpoints of fear appeared only rarely.

"Well, I . . . I know how much Mo and Ellen mean to you."

"They mean a lot, but I still can't say their wedding masses."

"Would you mind if I said them, then?"

"Good God, no, Pat. Why would I mind? Give it all the Roman elegance. They deserve it."

His good humor returned. "Thanks, Kev, I appreciate it. I wanted to make sure. See you next Thursday, if you can make it."

After he hung up I stared balefully at the phone. Then said to hell with it and went back to bed.

The following Thursday I spent the afternoon of my day off on a shaky folding chair in the cramped, dimly lit basement of a church at North Avenue and Paulina, listening to a lecture about the Church's obligations to the inner city. The audience was the Catholic Action Clergy, a substantial chunk of the liberal priests of the diocese who were still loyal followers of Monsignor Reynold Hillenbrad, a charismatic if undiplomatic seminary rector banished by Cardinal Stritch to a parish a few years before I showed up at Mundelein. Most of the intellectual and organizational ferment going on in the diocese at that time was being stirred up by the followers of "Hilly." Cardinal Stritch was sufficiently permissive—or perhaps sufficiently lazy—to let these activities flourish, confirming the generally held conviction that if Hilly had been diplomatic with the pastors of the city and the Jesuit faculty at Mundelein, nothing would have happened to him. The Cardinal discovered that it took more effort to defend him than to replace him, and off he went. His younger followers were much more devious.

I was not part of the Catholic Action crowd. There was too much work in the parish, and Monsignor Rafferty discouraged his priests from participating in "those damn outside activities." I was at this meeting because the featured speaker was Pat Donahue.

Pat, handsome and glowing, was at the door of the basement, shaking hands with everyone who came in. "Hey, great, Kev," he exclaimed when he saw me. "Wonderful of you to come. Hope I don't let you down."

Pat was enjoying an enormous success at Forty Holy Martyrs Church, on the near South Side. The chemistry between him and the inner-city Negroes was magic. Hundreds of Negroes came to his convert class each semester. He had baptized more than two hundred converts already, most of them parents who chose Forty Holy Martyrs School for their children instead of the decrepit and disorderly local public schools. I had listened to one of Pat's "instructions" to his class of converts and was impressed by his simple, direct, and effective style.

"The boy is really a winner," his pastor, old Hugh Mulcahey, said to me in a stage whisper after the class. It was more than my pastor had ever said about me.

Most of the audience in the church basement that afternoon expected Pat to talk about the techniques used to convert Negroes to Catholicism, the chief device being a requirement that the parents of non-Catholic kids in the parochial school take instructions. Instead Pat talked about the "social and human environment" of the inner city. It was a masterful performance, subtly adjusted to the mentality and disposition of his liberal-leaning clerical audience.

He told vivid stories about the impact of poverty and injustice on the family lives of Negroes in his parish; he described the dangers of life in "high-rise slums"; he painted a bleak picture of the dangerous temptations that faced the most virtuous young Negroes. He argued that the Church must respond to the human and social, as well as to the religious, needs of the Negro community. (The word "black" wasn't fashionable then.)

He didn't patronize the "citizens," as did most priests in "the work"; in fact, he didn't even use the term "citizen," a clerical code word for "Negro." He issued a stirring call to action.

"We've got to become the Church of the poor," he said, launching his dynamic peroration. "We have an enormous opportunity in the inner city to educate, to liberate, to preach; we must become identified in the minds of the Negro people with their cause. We put too much of our money and too many of our people into rich suburban parishes where there are few human problems and little need for the Church. Every young priest ought to serve in an inner-city parish. We should stop building schools and churches and rectories and gyms for the rich, and build houses for the poor."

There was thunderous applause, and I applauded with the rest. It was churlish of me to wonder if Pat's two-hundred-dollar custom-tailored suit and expensive French cuff links were compatible with his message of poverty, and to wonder where, on his seventy-five-dollar-a-month salary, he found the money even to buy such a suit. If Pat had generous friends, that was his business.

Two weeks later Leo Mark appeared at the door of my room. "There's a young woman in the office downstairs who says she's your sister," he mumbled.

"I suspect maybe she is," I replied, thinking I was beginning to get the measure of the man. "Did she say her name was Mary Ann? Brown, curly hair and green eyes and freckles like mine? Nice figure, kind of the sturdy girl-athlete type?"

He nodded, not quite sure what to say.

"Better go see her, then," I said, buttoning up the cassock I'd taken off my desk chair and slipping by him. (You didn't appear in the rectory office without a cassock at St. Praxides, even if it was your sister.)

"Hi, Priest," Mary Ann said as I walked into the office. She was wearing the mandatory trench coat and Bermuda shorts.

"Monsignor said you were claiming to be my sister."

"What kind of creep is he?" She pecked at my cheek. "And what kind of rectory is this?" She gestured distastefully at the elaborate Danish-modern furniture and the stern, formal portraits of the three twentieth-century Piuses—X, XI, and XII.

"A carefully designed one, I'll have you know. I couldn't even buy a lamp for my desk without having the interior decorator select it."

"They had an interior decorator?" she said incredulously. "I thought this kind of thing only happened by accident."

"What's up?" I was tired and I wanted to get to bed. Communion calls on foot tomorrow morning. The pastor said I didn't need a car, and the older curate never ventured to lend me his. "Everything all right at home?"

"Oh, it's not that," she said, with a wave of her hand. "It's Ellen. You've got to stop that marriage."

"Why?" I said, my chest tightening. "They seem so well matched."

"Both quiet, serious, thoughtful people?" she said sardonically. "Brother, I don't know what went on between you and Ellen, but if you understand her at all, you know she's smart and witty and has a wild streak inside her."

"I'm not unaware of it."

"Look, I've got nothing against your friend Tim, but he's all seriousness now. He never laughs or does anything playful, like he used to. He hasn't had a happy thought in five years. Ellen doesn't need that. It will kill her. She'll have a lot of kids in a hurry and go right back to the drudgery her mother condemned her to the day she was born."

Ellen and Mary Ann were close friends. Both had remained in the Chicago area for college. My sister's diagnosis was undoubtedly correct. There was no room for my fey little water elf in Tim Curran's carefully calculated life.

"There are only two weeks left, and besides, I can't stop the marriage. I'm not God, and I don't want to play God in her life."

My sister watched me as though I were a clinical specimen under her microscope. "You know, you're an interesting kind of priest, Brother," she said slowly. "Strong on enthusiasm and energy, short on compassion and kindness."

"Maybe I'll acquire some compassion with the years."

She was contrite. "I'm sorry for being a bitch. But you must care about what's happening to Ellen. I mean, you just can't let her throw her life away."

"I don't know that marrying Tim is throwing her life away," I argued. "And anyway, she wouldn't listen to me."

"Yes, she would," Mary Ann insisted. "You couldn't stop Mo, but you could call Ellen tomorrow morning and blow the whistle on that wedding."

I hesitated. "Even if I could, it wouldn't be right to meddle in her life."

My sister acknowledged with a sigh that she knew I'd say that. Her mission was a failure. She left the rectory to drive back to the West Side.

My throat was dry as I walked slowly up the stairs to my

room. The pastor's door swung shut just as I reached the head of the stairs. Waiting up to make sure the young priest didn't try to sneak out.

⁂

Both Ellen and Mo were married on schedule, with pious letters from me substituting for my presence. Mo went off to Boston with her new husband, reportedly furious at me for not coming to the wedding.

A lot else happened that spring and summer. Charles De Gaulle became head of the French government again, Robert Welch founded the John Birch Society, and Cardinal Stritch died in Rome. Pius XII, near death himself, rebuffed the Curia's attempt to send Leo Binz to Chicago and insisted on the "scripture man," as he called him, the second name on the terna, Milwaukee's scripture scholar, Archbishop Albert Gregory Meyer. In early October, Pius died. He was succeeded on October 25 by Angelo Giuseppe Roncalli.

Pat was with us in the parlor at St. Praxides when the CBS television report came from Rome. It was not carried "live" then, because we didn't have satellites yet, but still the rich voice of Winston Burdette told us that the new Pope was the seventy-seven-year-old patriarch of Venice.

"Oh, my God," said Pat in dismay. "They must have been deadlocked. Roncalli is a second-string diplomat; he's never done anything in his life. This is a disaster," he said then to Leo Mark, who was honored to have a bona fide Roman in his parlor at the time of a papal election.

Then came the remarkably robust voice of Papa Roncalli, giving his blessing—*Urbi et orbi*—to the city and the world. A little more than a week short of twenty years later, the cardinals would elect another pope. Three of the men who had chosen

Roncalli—Wyszynski, Leger, and Siri—would be in the Sacred College. So would Pat Donahue.

But on that golden October morning on the South Side of Chicago, Pat could only shake his head in dismay.

"A transition pope; we'll have another conclave soon," he said, his hands jammed ruefully in his pockets.

On January 25, 1959, Pope John announced the Second Vatican Council.

CHAPTER SEVEN

1959

I remember the precise moment when I decided Leonard Kaspar, our head usher, was robbing the Sunday collection at St. Praxides. It was the October in which the Chicago White Sox had survived to the World Series for the first time since 1919—and lost, of course. Pat, Nick McAuliff, and I were sitting in the pastor's room listening to *The Sound of Music* on Leo Mark's six-hundred-dollar hi-fi, which he never used. Leo Mark was on vacation, so I'd skipped my usual tour of duty with the bowling league and had supper with my friends. Pat was deeply concerned about John XXIII and his recent encyclical on the Latin Liturgy, which apparently forbade even discussion of the possibility of the Mass in English.

"It will be a mess as long as he's in power," Pat lamented over his second martini, an indulgence that we were forbidden by our five-year pledge but that was not denied Pat, as the system never bethought itself to demand the same pledge from North American College alumni. "Roncalli is strictly a third-rater. Everyone agrees that the Roman Synod is a disaster. God knows what the Council will be like. My friend Tonio Martinelli wrote me the other day to say it probably would never meet."

"Does he really think we won't even talk about an English Liturgy?" Nick demanded.

"He probably doesn't care." Pat looked reluctantly at his empty glass. "The draft was written by an old friend of his. Tonio, who approves of preserving Latin, of course, says that is the way the Church is run these days. Favors for old friends."

"The Colonel would understand that," I said.

"Maybe your parishioners can get along in Latin," Pat said with a grim frown. "But on Thirty-fifth Street, mass might just as well be in Sanskrit."

We listened to the music, trying to forget about a Church that insisted on the Latin Mass for those who lived on Thirty-fifth Street.

Halfway through "Edelweiss," I saw it. I guess it was Leo Mark's hi-fi. Leonard Kaspar had one just like it. I remembered asking the monsignor, when he proudly announced at the supper table that "Len"—("Mr. Kaspar" to the curates, of course)—had decided to buy a system just like his, how a man who had a middle-level clerical position at Tansey Industries could afford such an expensive system.

"That's an improper question, young man," Leo had said. "You should concern yourself with administering to the people of St. Praxides instead of estimating their income. Besides, Mrs. Kaspar and Mrs. Tansey are sisters."

The response was irrelevant. Arnold Tansey wasn't giving money away to anyone.

My reverie was interrupted by the telephone. It was Georgina Carrey, asking breathlessly about the orchestra that was to play at the Altar Society's spring luncheon. Even if the pastor was out of town, something had to be decided. Did I know where he could be reached?

"He never tells us where he's going, Georgina," I said wearily, "or when he will be back. Maybe Mr. Kaspar knows."

"Oh, Leonard and Martha are in Florida," she said with little interest. "I'm sure the Monsignor isn't with them."

"How can the parish survive without its pastor and head usher?" I asked. "Anyway, I'll see what I can do about it tomorrow."

"Who was that?" Pat asked, grinning. "You sounded quite solicitous. A woman, I bet."

"Not your type," I said. "Too pious. Goes to church every day."

"We can still catch a flick," said Nick, uninterested in the women of the parish.

"I've got some work to do," I said. "You guys go ahead."

I walked with them to Pat's sleek new Falcon, parked behind the rectory. The car was against the rules, too, but apparently no one had told the Roman trainees that they couldn't own one for five years after ordination.

"God, the place is lit up like a Christmas tree," said Pat, waving his hands at the massive St. Praxides "plant." "What's going on?"

"Normal autumn night in quasi-suburbia," I said. "Choir practicing in church, religious education for public-school kids in the hall, grammar-school basketball practice in the gym, CFM preparations in one rectory office, Marty Herlihy's preconfirmation classes for adults in another office, the bridge tournament in the library, St. Vincent DePaul Society worrying about our nonexistent poor in the rectory basement, and I don't know what's in the auxiliary meeting rooms in the basement of the hall. Nothing much. Kind of a routine evening."

Pat shook his head, his hands on his hips in dismay. "Was that what you were ordained for, Kevin? Is that what preaching the Gospel means in this neighborhood?"

"I don't know," I said honestly. "It's all fun, though, and most of it doesn't need any help. As you can see, I'm not at any of them. Hell, they paid for the buildings. If they want to use them for bridge and basketball, it's their business."

Pat sighed. "There I go again. Sounding like a fanatic. I'm sorry, Kev, you're right. I guess it's part of being a young priest." He grinned deprecatingly. "I mean, to think that what you do is the only important thing anyone can do."

I hurried back to my room when the car pulled away, took an envelope out of my file, and focused the high-intensity light on the slips of paper inside it. Leo Mark was a chronic "poor mouth." Expenses, he insisted, were going up, and revenue was not increasing to match it. His annual report was a masterpiece of vagueness and obscurity. Gradually, however, I managed to get enough of a feel for expenses to know that he had grounds to worry. St. Praxides was just barely staying out of the red.

The Monsignor wouldn't ask for more money, because that would necessitate a detailed financial report to the parish. It would be, he told me haughtily, the first step to sharing financial control. Another reason for his hesitation might be that he couldn't figure out what was wrong with the parish finances, and was afraid to be shown up as an incompetent in a neighborhood of high-power businessmen and professionals in whom the pose of financial skill was evidence of, and an occasional substitute for, masculinity.

I added up the collections from the first four Sunday masses for the last three months. Curates regularly counted these collections in the rectory basement, though my keeping tabs on the totals in order to follow the parish finances was not part of the job.

For several months I'd also been steaming open the sealed deposit slips from the bank on Monday mornings and making a record of the parish's weekly contributions to the American banking system. I was permitted to bank the money, and then to stop at the cleaner's to pick up the pastor's freshly pressed suits, but not to make out the deposit slips, a responsibility delegated to the much more trustworthy Leonard Kaspar.

Our deposit was usually around $2400, and the collection from the first four masses accounted for some $1400 of that. The church was almost empty at seven-A.M. mass, less than half filled at the eight, and crowded at the nine, but mostly with kids, whose contributions were small. We were nowhere near crowded at the ten-o'clock high mass. More than half of the parishioners, including virtually all of the affluent ones, came to the last two. Yet we were getting only about a thousand dollars from them. I rearranged the numbers on a sheet of paper. Five hundred of that thousand was in checks. Only five hundred dollars in cash from almost two thousand people?

Kaspar took the last two collections back to his house after the final mass, counted the money, and then returned to the rectory late Sunday afternoon to make out the bank slip and lock the collection in our archaic safe. The pastor said that there was no danger of theft, since only a few people knew that Kaspar counted the money in his own house. Now I knew why, whenever he was on vacation, he'd fly home for the Sunday masses, a sign of dedication that the pastor had publicly praised at the Christmas midnight mass.

I walked down the hall to the room of the only curate who was younger than I. "Marty," I said, "would you come to my room for a minute? I've got something to show you."

Marty Herlihy was a short, intense young man with burning eyes, fair hair, and a remarkable capacity to spend long hours on his knees in prayer. He was both more relaxed and more charitable than I. If the evidence convinced him, I had a case.

I told him what I suspected and watched his eyes widen in disbelief that was close to anger. Then I showed him the figures.

"Good heavens, Kevin," he said softly, "this could have been going on for years."

"And will go on for years unless we stop it," I said bluntly.

He nodded. "The pastor will never believe you. My brother is at the Chancery—"

"I don't want to go that route unless we have to," I said. "The first thing is to get evidence."

"How can we prove it?" he asked, rubbing his chin. "I mean, even if it is true, how can we convince the Monsignor?"

"It's easy. We just add up the collection envelopes from the last two masses. Subtract what he reports for those two masses from the envelope total and we have the minimum that he's taken."

He frowned. He seemed reluctant to comprehend what I was saying. "Kaspar mixes the envelopes. How are you going to tell which ones are from the last two masses?"

"No problem. When we're counting the money from the first four masses, we make a small mark on the back of each envelope. The next morning, we separate the unmarked envelopes and total them."

"And that leaves out the cash that's thrown in the basket without an envelope. It's a conservative estimate of the theft," he said.

"Precisely."

There was a moment of silence. "You enjoy this, Kevin, don't you?" he said, not making a judgment, only asking a question.

I took advantage of the pastor's absence to call Ellen Curran and make a date for supper at her and Tim's apartment.

The Ellen who greeted me at the door of the shabby apartment had a bad complexion, and had put on weight. Her hair was stringy and had lost its luster. Worst of all, the light was gone from her big, gray eyes. She managed to smile, but it cost her an effort. "Kevin"—at least her handshake was warm—"it's wonderful to see you. Parish work seems to agree with you. Doesn't it, Tim? Maybe we should all be priests."

Tim's smile was broad and unforced, a faint touch of the old Raider, but he was thin, tired, and nervous. Going to night school and holding down a job was taking its toll on him. He rubbed his hands together repeatedly as though trying to dry them. "Gosh, Father Kevin, it's been such a long time. Your first mass was the last time, wasn't it? Come in, sit down, meet our daughter. She's a real beauty."

Caroline was all of that, a lively, flirtatious bundle of six-month-old energy squirming in my lap. "She's a special little girl," I said approvingly.

"She *is* a winsome little bitch," Ellen said fondly. "Doesn't believe in sleeping at night, though."

"You shouldn't use that language about our daughter, El," Tim reproved her softly. "It's not appropriate for a Christian mother."

Not a flicker of reaction from Ellen. It was as though she didn't hear it. "She has her mother's gray eyes," I said, struggling to bridge the dangerous silence. "I bet she's already figured me out."

"And she's going to have a little brother in the spring," said Tim proudly. "A fine Catholic family—two children in two years."

"And ten in ten years," said Ellen without emotion. "Anyway, you can compare her with Mo's daughter, Sheila, when you see her next month."

Before we could discuss the Haggartys, the Curran heiress, much to her parents' humiliation, spit a fair amount of her last meal on my jacket. She seemed vastly amused as her mother and father scurried to repair the damage. She also adamantly refused to give up her place in my arms.

There was nothing to drink before dinner, since Tim no longer believed in drinking, though he was willing to make an exception for Ellen and me in the case of the white wine I'd brought to drink with our Friday-night fish.

"I don't remember your being a teetotaler in the old days," I said, laughing, trying to cover my own awkwardness. The apartment smelled of overcooked food. The furniture was secondhand, the carpet threadbare. "There was a time when it looked as if you were going to dispose of every six-pack on the West Side."

Tim leaned over, rubbing his hands. "I didn't think in those days about the terrible waste of money that goes into drink. I just can't justify it." His shoulders were pathetically thin and frail. Timmy, I thought, whatever happened to the old spark?

"Have you seen any good movies lately, Kevin?" Ellen said, abruptly changing the subject.

"You should call him Father Kevin, honey." Again the soft reproof. "He *is* a priest, you know."

Again no reaction to the reprimand. "You two talk about old times, and I'll see if our perch object to being cooked," Ellen said. "Father Kevin, if that little imp gives you any trouble, just put her back in her crib. She'll scream, but it's good for her lungs."

As she left for the kitchen, she brushed her fingers against Tim's cheek and neck. "Don't let him eat too many crackers, darling, and spoil his appetite."

Tim beamed happily and began to discuss our championship season at Jesuit High. The cheese and crackers were not much of a threat to my appetite. The former was rock hard, having just been taken out of the refrigerator, and the latter were dry and stale.

Nor were the perch and potatoes much better, both having been overdone, mostly because the volatile Caroline had staged a temper tantrum at a critical moment in their preparation. The wine at least dulled the pain. We ate in the kitchen; there was no dining room. Tim did his best to help with serving the food, and though he managed only to get in the way, he was thanked dutifully for his assistance. We talked about Khrushchev and Castro at the United Nations, and Tim expressed the opinion that the United States ought to get out. The Currans both agreed that Maureen had been right, and that John Kennedy could win the nomination the following year.

Mostly we talked about Tim's plans once he finished law school and passed the bar. "We're going to buy a house in River Forest and a summer home at the lake near your family, and Ellen is going to be the best-dressed woman in the parish," he said. "She's got the taste for it, and someday she'll have the money."

"More important," I said, "she's got a family that adores her, despite the princess's temper tantrums."

I would have said it a thousand more times for the gratitude that ignited her gray eyes. "That's what I tell him, Father Kevin. I don't care about anything else."

Tim patted her hand. "We'll get you the other things, too, honey."

"What kind of work do you want to do after you get out, Tim?"

"I hope to go into a law firm that's politically connected," he said, his thin face looking even thinner in its earnestness. "Maybe we can reform Chicago politics. I mean, for every honest lawyer, like your father, there are twenty crooks."

"Better say a hundred," I said, and laughed. I couldn't imagine anything for which Tim was less qualified.

We were interrupted by the phone. Tim answered it, and came back dejected. He had to work the next day, despite plans to paint the kitchen.

"Still," he said, "we need the money more than we need a kitchen without those brown splotches, don't we, honey? Next time Father Kevin comes, we'll have a shiny new kitchen."

I left early, pleading the six-thirty mass and the need to say the Breviary. I'd said the Breviary and had the eight-forty-five mass. There was nothing to talk about with them.

Tim asked respectfully for my blessing on his family. Ellen fetched the quietly sleeping Caroline. Mother and father knelt, hand in hand. I blessed them all, praying that God the Father, the Son, and the Holy Ghost would do for them what I could not do. In response to this invocation, Caroline began to cry.

At the door Tim put his arm around his wife's waist and said, "Grand to see you again, Father Kevin. A real honor to have you in the house. Promise it won't be so long next time."

"It won't be," I lied. Ellen's sad expression told me that she knew better.

⁂

"The worst part of it," I told my mother on the telephone the next day, "is that she knows she's made a bad choice. There were tears in her eyes as I left. If she can fool herself into thinking that it's going to be all right—"

"Why do you have to see everything in such moralistic terms?" my mother demanded with more impatience than she usually displayed toward her firstborn. "It might work out yet. Give them some time."

"It didn't look like it was working out last night," I countered.

"It's a bad stage in their marriage, darling. One baby and another one coming. I'm sure they love each other."

"She feels sorry for him."

"That's part of loving. Ellen is a very determined woman. She won't quit easily. When they have some time and some freedom from troubles, just watch their marriage pick up."

I was skeptical. "What can I do?"

"Be a good friend; see them often; take them out to dinner; cheer them up. Don't be grim and serious with them, as hard as that may be."

It was sound advice, and I had every intention of following it. Yet I kept putting off a phone call to the Currans.

The following Wednesday afternoon, with the door to my study shut so that the pastor's sister, who was also the housekeeper, could not spy on us, Marty and I added the figures from the Sunday envelopes on a battered old adding machine.

I pushed the "total" button and pulled back the handle of the machine. "Fifteen hundred dollars," I said. "Just from the envelopes. That doesn't count the checks not in envelopes or the loose cash."

"At least another five hundred," he mused aloud, his voice tight.

"A thousand dollars a Sunday, fifty thousand dollars a year, for how many years?" I said, clenching my fist.

"It's worth flying home on Sunday to count, isn't it? Makes you a very dedicated layman." Marty was now angrier than I was. "What do we do?"

"We do the same thing every Sunday till Christmas. We also do it on Christmas, to see how much he's taking then. We go to Leo with it. If he doesn't believe us—and I bet he won't—we'll threaten to go to your brother."

"I'm all right, Kev, because of my brother. But if it gets

around town that you did this to Leo Mark, you'll never be forgiven. You know what a respected pastor he is."

"If this story gets out, he won't be," I said. "Anyway, I don't give a damn what they say about me."

The "missionaries" came the first two weeks in November, two towering, grim-visaged men in blue religious habits and black cloaks who thundered on about sin and death and hell from the pulpit on Sunday morning and every night of the week, stirring up past guilt, unnerving sensitive consciences, and turning cold every marriage bed in the community from fear of "sins of the flesh" and "race suicide." Two of the curates were shipped off the first week to make room for them. The other two went the second week. Marty arranged for the first week off and I for the second, so one of us could keep an eye on the Sunday envelopes.

The first week was a surrealistic horror. The men were the first victims. Oddly enough, they were more likely than women to wonder whether they had mentioned in full detail all their sins in every confession they'd made during their entire lives. Each night after the sermons and each morning through the masses, I sweated it out in the confessional box, trying to persuade the haunted men of the parish that God was not a prosecuting attorney. It was especially difficult because the missionaries were reputed to be holy men and wise, far holier and wiser than the young, red-haired curate who was a bit of a radical anyhow.

Though our male parishioners were almost all successful business and professional men, their religious training left a powerful residue of superstition and magic in their approach to sin and God. Just what the missionaries needed.

"A lot of bad confessions out there," said one of the missionaries, a man with long, white hair who got drunk every night in the rectory. "I heard one man tonight who hasn't made a good confession for fifty years. Think of all the sacrilege." He tossed off a glass of bourbon, neat.

I sipped my Pepsi. "Seems a shame to cheat God of all the fun he would have had punishing a guy like that," I said.

"It seems to me," said the missionary, "that when you find a parish filled with bad confessions, it is a reflection on the priests who serve there."

Leo turned white. I was pretty sure they wouldn't be back again.

"On the curates, not the pastor," I said, rising to answer the ringing telephone. "They're the ones who've been hearing bad confessions for fifty years."

It was Monica Kelly. "Are those guys creeps or something, Father?" she demanded. "Pete tells me he can't kiss me good night anymore or his lips will be roasted by burning coals for all eternity. Hey, Father—Pete isn't that good a kisser."

Pete was the president of the High Club, and Monica's current boy friend.

"Pass the word to the kids, Monica, that they shouldn't believe anything those two say, especially when they tell you that if you love God you've got to be a nun or a priest. Tell them that only Father Herlihy and I are infallible, like the Pope. Understand?"

"Yes, Father," she said dubiously. "They've got our boys scared."

"Tell your boys to come by after school tomorrow, at five. I'll see them in the library. You girls stay away. I'll take care of you next night. Understand?"

"Okay, I'll spread it around. Kissing really isn't sinful, is it, Father? I mean, if you don't do it too long?"

"Monica, you could kiss Pete for twenty years and it wouldn't even be a venial sin."

She giggled. "You'd better believe it."

Pat offered to drive me to the airport to catch the plane to New York. It saved dragging Mary Ann or the Colonel all the way out to the South Side.

He seemed uneasy.

"Kevin, I owe you more favors than I can pay back in a lifetime. I'm trying to pay back a few of them with what I'm going to say. It may not sound that way to you, though." He paused lamely.

"Shoot."

"Well, some of the people in your parish who know we're friends have asked me to talk to you . . . about your attitude. They're upset about it, and they thought I could help."

"The Kaspars and the Tanseys and the Carreys," I said, knowing suddenly where the cuff links and the new car in which we were driving came from.

"Yes, especially Len Kaspar, who has been very good to us down in the parish. He's underwritten the expenses of all our instruction classes this winter. And he doesn't have nearly as much money as Arnold or John, either."

"How nice of him," I said with a sarcasm that Pat could not possibly appreciate. Our money paying for convert instructions and for Pat's car.

"If you want me to stop . . ."

"Keep shooting."

He ran his hand through his hair, winced, and stopped for a red light on Sixty-seventh Street. "It's a pretty broad indictment. I'm not making any judgments."

"I know you're not."

"They think you don't have any respect for Leo Mark, that you're contemptuous of the well-established parishioners, that you're pushing radical liturgical innovations, that you preach too much about racial justice, and that you'd like to take over the parish and run it your own way."

"Guilty on all counts," I said. "Go tell them I said that, and that I intend to continue just what I'm doing."

We pulled up by the United Airlines entrance at Midway. I got out of the Olds and grabbed my bag from the back seat. "This is a present from Kaspar?" I pointed at the car.

"Yes, it is. My old car broke down, and I didn't have enough money. . . ."

"I thought so." I slammed the door and strode into the terminal.

⁂

I rode the train up to Boston to see Maureen before I flew home from New York and my vacation.

Sheila was a lovely little girl, though as placid as Caroline was active. After being properly inspected, she was handed without protest to a matronly nanny and carried off to some quiet part of the house where an unlikely temper tantrum would not disturb adult conversation. Her mother was also a contrast to Caroline's mother—trim, smart, smoothly girdled in a fashionable two-piece dress. Tense with excitement from the quickening political campaign, Mo sat at her antique table in her chic Back Bay apartment as though already rehearsing to be a Washington hostess.

"We're going to do it, Kevin." She hit the table with her fist, just barely keeping her fur-trimmed cuff out of the bean soup. "Jack Kennedy is going to be nominated and then elected.

Burke is going to win the assembly race by the biggest majority in history, two years from now. When there's the special election to fill Jack's seat, he's going to be the new United States Senator from Massachusetts."

"And you'll move to Washington. How's Burke holding up on the campaign trail?"

She frowned. "He's not the best campaigner in the world. Of course, there are high standards in this state, what with Jack and Bobby. What counts is what he does after he's elected."

I didn't ask how much he was drinking, though I wanted to. "You campaign like the Kennedy women?"

"Sure. It's great fun." She beamed proudly. "Some of the men say I'm even better than Jean and Eunice, and Lord knows it's not hard to be better than Jackie."

"And what do you say?"

"I tell them I'm good at it because I'm from Chicago. That stops them. Is Mayor Daley really going to deliver Chicago for Jack? Some of the advance men say he's concerned about an anti-Catholic backlash."

"In Cook County?" I laughed. "Of course Daley is going to deliver Chicago—when he's sure that Jack Kennedy isn't a loser. We don't back losers in Chicago if we can avoid it. My father says that Daley is as Catholic as the Pope, maybe more so. Of course he'll support Kennedy."

"Speaking of the Pope," she said, her angelic face leaping from one animated expression to another, her fingers nervously playing with her soup spoon. "What's with my friend, the Pope from the West Side? He's not the letter-writing kind."

"Busy remaking the Church and warning about the incompetencies of *Papa* Roncalli," I said, watching her closely. "My guess is that he's on his way up. I'll say one thing, though: he's mended all his fences with his classmates since he came back from Rome. He's one of the gang again, no trace of the erratic basketball player with the hot hand turning cold."

"Replacing you as the leader, Kevin?" she said, arching that lovely eyebrow.

"I peaked out in that role at nineteen."

Elbows on the table, hands on her chin, Maureen leaned toward me. "Do you think he wants to be a bishop? He was in his element at the Cape when he was here this summer." She shoved her chair back impatiently and began to pace like a mountain lion in a cage. "You should have seen him turn on the charm out at Hyannis. The Kennedys are used to smooth-talking priests. A few smiles, some boyish laughter, and a couple of jokes, and he even had Rose eating out of his hand. He really enjoys it. He loves being with the rich and the powerful."

"Who wouldn't?"

She was not listening to me. "I love Patrick dearly, but he's not much good at resisting temptation. Money, power, pleasure—they activate his dark demons. Either he works out those demons with his poor parishioners or he's going to destroy himself."

"Dark demons? I'm afraid I don't know—"

"Damn it, Kevin, we've all got them. Pat is at a turning point in his life. He's halfway into corruption now. . . . Don't give me that look. He *is.* If you don't stop him, he's going to give up on his poor and go for power. Then we'll all have trouble, he worse than any of us."

"I think you're exaggerating."

As if she had tired of speaking of Pat Donahue, she abruptly changed the subject. "How is Ellen? Her letters don't tell me anything."

"She's pregnant again, and I suppose that doesn't help—"

"Won't happen to me for a good long time, let me tell you," she said, interrupting me.

"And though they're very loving with each other, something seems to be missing," I said.

"Would you believe sex?" She sat down again and stabbed at her mashed potatoes. "Oh, Ellen doesn't say, but I can tell. She's a romantic dreamer, and they're both innocents. I mean, really innocent. They don't know a thing about sex. After Tim Curran got her cute little ass undressed, I bet he didn't have the faintest idea what to do next."

"I wouldn't know," I said. "I think with time it will work out for them. All they need is a few breaks."

"Don't we all," she said bitterly, pushing her plate away and reaching for the wineglass.

At JFK Airport, waiting for the flight back to Chicago, I thought to myself that there were a lot of things that could go wrong in a marriage besides sex. On the way home I concentrated on the simpler task of doing in Leonard Kaspar.

Only in the car going back to the rectory did I remember that I'd forgotten to bless Sheila Haggarty when I left her mother's apartment in Boston. The poor tyke probably needed all the blessings she could get.

CHAPTER EIGHT

1959

A major winter storm system had moved into Chicago. The faces of the pedestrians hurrying along Michigan Avenue were pinched and anxious. They did not bother to look up at the massive new Hancock tower rising like a steel and glass Tower of Babel into the darkening clouds. The airports were closed, both Midway and the newly operational O'Hare. Len Kaspar would be unable to get back to Chicago from Florida. I was sure we would have him. His scheme was daring but ultimately clumsy. Only a dullard like Leo would be taken in. And there was no reason why Leo's successor would not be a dullard, too.

We survived our first three masses without a head usher. At ten, as the choir was tuning up, the sun broke through the clouds.

The final mass began at twelve-fifteen, and Len Kaspar still wasn't at his station by the main entrance of the church.

"The boss is having kittens about who's going to count the money," said Marty. "All we need do is volunteer."

"Let's not rush. If we appear too eager, Leo will smell a rat. We don't want to blow it."

At five after one Leonard Kaspar appeared, suave and unconcerned. He apologized to the pastor, explained about the weather, and modestly received the pastor's enthusiastic praise for dedicated service.

Later in the afternoon my father and I were in his study, watching the snow melt in the fading sunlight on our front lawn.

"Incredible," he said, puffing furiously on his aromatic pipe, "absolutely incredible. What a marvelous lawyer you would have made, Kevin. Though, mind you, I'm sure you make an even more marvelous priest." He added the latter comment in hasty embarrassment.

"Prosecutor, where do we stand?" I said.

He frowned and ruffled his white hair.

"Your evidence is thin, Champ. You have grounds for suspecting that money was stolen in the months you've kept records. For the previous nine years all you have is conjecture. A jury would probably convict on the evidence you have, if you could get it to a jury. Your big problem would be a directed verdict of not guilty on grounds of insufficient evidence. The police would be cooperative if you go to them, but then it's out of your hands. It could turn into a very messy public scandal that would hurt the parish and the Church. Probably kill your pastor, which I don't think you really want."

"So we threaten Kaspar, recover whatever we can, and then shut up?" I was pacing up and down nervously.

"Right," he said. "If Tansey is involved, you're fighting one very tough man—and I'm in a potential conflict of interest."

"Can we break Tansey?"

"Yes, I suppose so. No man is unbreakable. The scandal would touch him, and he's proud that he's clean as a whistle."

The Colonel called me the following afternoon, "Kaspar's Florida real-estate investments are worth two million dollars. He's got enough money to retire from larceny tomorrow and never feel the pinch."

"The bastard," I snapped.

"The land isn't very liquid right now, with the economy in a slowdown. He could get a loan on it, though, without any trouble. If anyone offers you two hundred thousand, settle, and quickly, Champ."

I'd just finished the girls' volleyball schedule when Marty Herlihy burst into the room.

"I counted the envelope from Sunday," he said eagerly. "He took twelve hundred dollars yesterday. How long do we let it go on?"

"Till he makes a mistake," I said calmly. "We'll get it back. He's got a lot of real estate in Florida."

"What if he won't pay?"

"He'll pay," I said. "All we have to do is threaten to tip off the Internal Revenue Service."

"That's blackmail." Marty's eyes were wide with shock.

"That's getting our money back," I said, returning to the volleyball schedule.

Christmas was a nightmare at St. Praxides: twelve hours of confessions, many of the parishioners still battling the neuroses the missionaries had stirred up; then the midnight Mass, which went on until two o'clock. Forty-five minutes were consumed by a rambling sermon in which the monsignor thanked everyone in the parish for his cooperation—everyone, that is, but his curates and the infant Jesus. We were up at six A.M. to help with Communion at the morning masses and to count the money from the Christmas collection. Each Christmas was viewed by the pastor as a kind of referendum in which the people of the parish voted their support for his administration. If the collection increased, he concluded that he was a man approved. If it should hold constant or fall back, then he had somehow failed. Each year he went into a pre-Christmas funk because he was convinced that he would get the no-confidence verdict.

Of course, he never did.

Len Kaspar counted only the last mass that day.

At three o'clock in the afternoon we all met in the rectory basement and, while other Christian families were eating dinner, arrived at the grand total. Leo Mark looked as if he were about to have a heart attack as he jotted the numbers read to him by Len Kaspar—sleek, tan, and dapper in a new suit.

Leo Mark added them up once, shook his head in disbelief, added them again, and then turned ruddy with joy. "Six thousand dollars—up twenty-five hundred dollars since last year," he exclaimed.

"Congratulations, Monsignor!" Len was equally happy. "The people came through for you again."

It was my turn to take the money to the bank. We couldn't risk leaving it in the parish safe overnight. Some poor bank attendant was giving up his Christmas dinner waiting for our deposit. As a special exception, the young curate in charge of the deposit was allowed the use of the monsignorial Cadillac, since the alternative was hiking through the snow for a mile and a half with the money slung over his shoulder.

The next day Marty reported the results of his research. "Christmas spirit must have affected Kaspar. He stole only five hundred dollars yesterday."

"Barely enough to pay for that tailor-made suit," I said.

The Sunday after New Year's I was assigned the ten A.M. high mass. I could sleep until nine, as my first duty was to assist with

Communion at nine-thirty. It bothered the Monsignor, but he was never able, despite considerable effort, to figure out a reason for the ten-o'clock man to be up on Sunday before nine. I didn't normally sleep late, but whenever I said the ten, I slept late as a matter of principle.

I was groggy at nine-forty-five when Marty came off the altar. God punishing me, I suppose. Outside, in the still, cold air, the white smoke from the neighborhood chimneys pointed skyward, like Indian campfires on the prairie.

"He's not here," Marty said breathlessly.

"Who's not here?" I spilled the small Hosts into a ciborium.

"Kaspar. He's in Florida again. He called. There's another storm, and he won't be in until late afternoon. He assured Leo Mark that he'll count the money tonight."

"And?" I fit the gold cap on the top of the ciborium.

"And Leo Mark is in a tizzy. If we don't get the money counted by three, it will throw off the whole schedule. Vague hints that we may have to do it."

"We'll have to count it ourselves." The pastor snapped his gold watch case shut and rose from the table. The two older curates were excused. The Monsignor, Marty, and I charged down to the knotty-pine meeting room in the basement and began to slit envelopes.

My hand was trembling.

At three we were finished. "Two thousand thirty-five dollars," I announced as I arranged the little bundles of green paper on the table, "including the checks."

"Down from last Sunday," said the pastor. "People on winter vacation. They don't realize that their good fortune causes the Church to suffer."

"I mean for the last two masses," I said blandly. Marty was pale; his fingers worked in strange little patterns on the table.

"That's a mistake," said the pastor. "You must have mixed in the first masses."

I lifted a money bag onto the table. "Nope. Here's the first four masses." I poured the little green bundles and the uneven stack of checks out onto the table as though the bag were a holiday cornucopia.

Leo counted every stack, totaled the checks once again on the dilapidated adding machine, then counted the cash yet again.

"There must be some mistake," he said, his face ashen. "There's over three thousand dollars here, and this is an off Sunday."

"It's also the first Sunday in how many years—ten?—that Len Kaspar has not counted the last two masses," I said, inspecting the label on the air conditioner in one of the windows of the meeting room.

"That's an outrageous statement," Leo Mark Rafferty said heavily. His heart was not in it. He had heard the stories about trusted parishioners who had turned thief.

"Look at these records, Monsignor." I pulled out the sheets from the last four months. "Note that our bank deposits always indicate that the collections at the last two masses are less than those at the first four. I couldn't figure it out myself. I think we have an explanation now."

He was so overwhelmed that he didn't ask me where I got the figures.

"We might dig out the envelopes from the last couple of Sundays," Marty said, reciting his lines on cue. "I haven't filed them, and we could see if the envelope totals confirm what seems to be happening."

"What will my friends say when they find out?" Leo stammered. "My reputation as an administrator will be ruined. We must keep it a secret." The pastor's body was quivering now. "We'll never get it back. I'll just dismiss him as head usher, and . . . we won't tell anyone. We can't let it get out."

"We won't recover it all," I said, "but we'll get some of it. I think we can keep it a secret. But if there's no attempt at restitution, I'd be in favor of turning it over to Chancery and the state's attorney. I'd feel bound in conscience, wouldn't you, Marty?"

Marty nodded.

Leo Mark began to cough. I was afraid he was going to choke to death. Then Leonard Kaspar, in a tan cashmere coat and a paisley scarf, bounded down the steps. "What's going on here?" he asked with false heartiness.

"I'm dismissing you as head usher as of this moment," said the pastor, buttoning up his cassock in an effort to recover his dignity.

Though the pencil mustache quivered, Kaspar kept his cool. "The first Sunday I miss in twelve years, Monsignor, and you fire me?" He sounded hurt.

Mrs. Kaspar followed him in, bundled up in her mink. She was younger and prettier than Mary Tansey. Like her sister, she was cut out of cardboard.

"A thousand dollars more in the collection when *we* count it," I said, glad the confrontation was coming.

He turned on me furiously. "You smart-assed young punk. What the hell are you implying?"

"I'm implying, Mr. Kaspar, that something has been wrong with the last two collections for a long time. I've got records here for four months." I shoved them across the table. "In that period of time the parish seems to have lost eighteen thousand dollars."

"Are you going to let this arrogant bastard defame me?" Kaspar said, turning to the pastor. "It's a fluke. Next Sunday it'll be back to normal."

The hard look on Martha Kaspar's face clinched it; she was into it up to her perfectly matched pearls.

"If it is a fluke, then I'll owe you an apology," I said coldly. "*We're* counting next Sunday, aren't we, Monsignor?"

Leo was torn. He was afraid of Kaspar's wrath, afraid of scandal, afraid of his reputation. But, strangely enough, he was even more afraid of me.

"Yes, Kevin," he said meekly.

Kaspar snatched the sheets from the table, tore them up, and threw them at me. "Your figures are a crock of shit, Brennan. They don't mean a fucking thing."

"I've got copies of them upstairs," I said, "and it's *Father* Brennan to you."

"Come on, Martha." He grabbed his wife's gloved hand. "We don't have to put up with this!"

"We've got projections back for a decade," I said, making most of it up, "and you owe this parish at least a half million dollars. I guess you're going to have to sell some of your Florida land. We'll give you ten days; otherwise the state's attorney and the Internal Revenue Service are going to hear all about it."

For the first time, fear crumpled his smooth face. He started to say something, but his wife tugged at his arm. They turned and walked up the stairs and out into the falling snow.

Leo's face was buried in his hands. "What will happen, Kevin?" he asked, now a docile old man.

"Depends on whether they get Tansey into the act. Don't worry, Boss." I put my hand on his shoulder reassuringly. "We can't lose."

Back in my room, in the brown leather easy chair, I called the Colonel and reported success. My father replied that he would notify Tansey the next day that he was withdrawing as his counsel. "Never did like the hardhead, anyhow," he observed.

I liked the win, but I didn't like the aftermath. I thought of the pastor's sobs, Kaspar's quivering mustache, his wife's hating face, Marty's thin lips. I wished there were someone to talk to.

Impulsively I grabbed the telephone book, looked up "Curran" on West Jackson Boulevard, and began to dial. I'd dialed five of the seven numbers before I hung up.

⁂

Tuesday afternoon the pastor came to my room.

"Kevin, uh . . . your friend Pat Donahue is on the phone. Mr. Tansey wants him to talk to me about our problem."

"Son of a bitch."

"Kevin, please. He stressed that he wasn't taking sides, just trying to work things out in a Christian way. Should we see him? He says he can come tonight."

"Sure. Why not?"

I was furious at Pat. We may have needed an honest broker. We didn't need him.

After supper that night Pat drove up to the rectory in yet another new Oldsmobile. For services rendered, from Arnold Tansey.

Marty Herlihy, Leo Mark Rafferty, Patrick Donahue, and I sat around the pastor's study, sipping Irish Mist, the five-year pledge no longer remembered.

"Mind you, gentlemen," Pat said smoothly, "I don't approve of what has happened. On the contrary, I consider it despicable. Like you, I want to protect the Church from scandal. So does Mr. Tansey. He has undertaken to guarantee a payment of fifty thousand dollars a year over the next two years, in return for which he will want your word that this whole matter will be forgotten. Would that be agreeable, Monsignor?"

"Well, that's very generous of Arnold," said the pastor, rubbing his hands together. "I think that we'd certainly—"

"Our figures show half a million," I said bluntly.

Pat stirred uneasily, setting aside his glass. "Mr. Tansey does not believe that this can be proven; nor does he believe that there is the kind of evidence that can be used in a court of law. He does not condone what has been done, as you may well imagine, yet he wants to see that the Church does not suffer because of these losses. He cannot, of course, assume responsibility for the entire loss."

"Then let Mr. Kaspar assume responsibility for the entire loss," I insisted. "Let him sell some of his Florida land. Mr. Tansey is aware, I suppose, of what an IRS audit might reveal about his relatives?"

Pat's high color faded. "He is well aware of that, Kevin, though he thinks the Church would want to avoid the publicity that such an investigation would cause."

"But not quite as much as he would," I countered. "What about the Florida land?"

Pat wet his lips. "The land is in Mrs. Kaspar's name. Neither Mr. Tansey nor Mrs. Tansey thinks that Mrs. Kaspar ought to be punished for something of which she was unaware."

"Bullshit!" I yelled.

"Should I tell Mr. Tansey that his offer is unsatisfactory?" Pat looked nervously from me to Leo and back. The son of a bitch; the goddamn sellout son of a bitch.

"Well, I. . . . Don't you think, Kevin . . ." Leo pleaded.

"Call him," I said, "and tell him that I said three hundred fifty thousand dollars."

"I can't do that." Pat had all his color back and more.

"You goddamn well better do it, or *I'll* call him."

Pat went to the pastor's office. I heard him talking softly.

"Mr. Tansey is on the phone." He said it as though it were the Pope himself. "He is very upset about what was done to the parish. He is now inclined to raise his offer to two hundred fifty thousand dollars."

"Done," I said coldly.

"Pardon?" Pat's mouth hung open.

"Done," I said, emptying my snifter of Irish Mist and filling it again.

"Fifty thousand over five years?"

"Eighty-three over three years."

Pat returned to the phone.

"Mr. Tansey finds that suitable," he said, smiling. "Before he hangs up, he wants me to say that he assumes that he is dealing with gentlemen and that this is a gentleman's agreement, a kind of oral handshake."

"We are as much gentlemen as he is," I said.

Pat came back into the parlor. "It's all set. The first check will come next week."

"Does he want to back-date it for last year's taxes?" I said bitterly.

It was as still as a tomb for a moment.

"I'd better be going," Pat said uneasily.

"See you, Pat." I didn't shake his hand.

The woman wore a heavy red robe when she opened the door. A Christmas present, no doubt. He had fought off temptation for almost five years. Now he was caught in its grip much as she would soon be caught in his.

She smiled with satisfaction. She knew what he wanted. Her hands went to the belt of the robe. Outside there was ice; here there would be a few moments of warmth. The robe fell from her shoulders.

Thursday evening Pat was waiting for me in my room, twisting his fingers.

"I owe you an apology," he said uneasily.

"Forget it," I said. "It's hard even now for me to believe what happened."

"I was certain—"

"Rich people are no different from poor people, Pat, unless you become dependent on them. Then one becomes corrupt."

"Easy for you to say," he said bitterly.

"I know, Patrick, I know."

"I need their help to keep the instruction program going, and our parochial school. Mulcahey is a nice man, but incompetent."

"I'm going to help run this parish from now on. We'll set up a parish-to-parish fund to help your work. Will that do?"

Some of his vivacity returned. "God, that's generous, Kevin. I don't deserve it."

"Regardless. Your parish does."

The tiny dots of fear did not go from his eyes. He stood up and extended his hand. "We'll be working together again, just like the old days."

I shook hands with him. "Just like the old days."

BOOK III

THE SIXTIES

CHAPTER NINE

1961

It was a warm April evening. The Peace Corps had just been created. Khrushchev was making noises about Berlin. John Kennedy was in the White House, and John XXIII was in the Apostolic Palace. The ice floes were melting; the thaw was upon us.

Marty Herlihy stuck his head into the pseudo-knotty-pine room where I was writing some long-overdue letters.

"Hey, Kevin, phone call."

"I'll call back, Marty. Take a message."

Marty shook his head. "The tone says he needs to talk now."

"Give you a name?"

"Tim Curran. Ring any bells?"

"Warning bells."

I picked up the phone in the money-counting room—still the most important in the rectory, as far as Monsignor was concerned.

"I hear you have a son to keep the princess company. I hope the family is well," I said.

"Uh, oh, great, thanks, Father Kevin." His thin voice sounded despondent. "Ellen is a little tired, and I'm busy studying for the bar exam in August. But I think the worst is over."

"Give my best to Ellen," I said. Brendan Curran had been in

the world for almost a year, but I had promptly put his existence out of my mind. The old neighborhood and most of those in it were now part of the past.

"You've got to come see them both . . . after the bar." He sounded unspeakably weary. "Caroline's a walking wonder."

That's all they needed—a two-year-old who could terrorize her baby brother.

"I hear he's got his mother's eyes," I said. Mary Ann and her boyfriend, Steve McNeil, were the godparents. Pat had baptized him.

"Yes, Father, we really love him." He sounded as if the love required enormous effort. "Uh, Father, I'd like to ask you a question. I mean, kind of private . . . if you don't mind."

"Uh-huh," I said noncommittally.

"It's about birth control. You see, Ellen is worn out, and the doctor said it would be better if we didn't have another baby for a couple of years. We've been married for three years, and she's been pregnant eighteen months of the time, and . . . Father Kevin, it isn't easy."

What's the point in having a wife if you get so little enjoyment out of her? I knew the rest of the conversation by heart.

"Have you tried rhythm? Ellen's a nurse, and I'm sure . . ." There was the priest, always sounding like a pompous dolt in a conversation like this.

"Yes, well . . . I mean, Ellen's periods are regular, but it doesn't seem to work for us."

I wondered how close they had tried to cut it. "I know it's rough." I tried my latest psychological skill, "nondirective" or "client-centered" counseling.

"Ellen wants to use this new pill thing." He finally had the courage to bring it out in the open. "She says the Church is going to change, and there's no point in us waiting until 1965 or something for the change. Is there going to be a change, Father? I mean, I don't want to commit a mortal sin or anything like that."

"I don't think there's any reason to anticipate a change, Tim," I said guardedly. If one partner in a marriage insisted on contraception, I was ready to give the other absolution in the confessional. Maybe I could stretch that to include this kind of case. Oh, God, I told myself, how I wish I could.

"What I want to know is, would it be a mortal sin for us if Ellen used this pill?" There was agony in his plea.

"I'm sure Ellen wouldn't want to do anything that she had decided in her conscience is sinful," I said carefully. "She should heed her conscience." The parish safe seemed to glare at me for my departure from orthodoxy.

"But we've got to listen to the Church in forming our conscience, don't we?" he said dubiously. Maybe he was too tired to see the way out I was providing him.

"I'm sure Ellen has always listened to the Church," I said desperately.

"I guess you're right, Father Kevin. I knew we couldn't do it. I just wanted to make sure."

I started to make another try, and then gave it up. Tim was not yet ready to assume the burden of making his own moral decisions. In another year there would be a third small Curran. Then they'd use the pill regardless of the Church. Later they would have conscience trouble, try rhythm again, and have a couple of more children before they were thirty-five. There were a hundred families just like them in St. Praxides.

"I wish I could help, Tim," I said feebly.

"You've been a big help, Father." I could hear the despair of a man who had been in a cave so long he would never recognize the light again. "Pray for us, please."

I sat there next to the coin counter as though I were in a hospital waiting room after someone had died.

On the way upstairs I stopped by Leo Mark's room.

"Anything doing?" I asked.

He looked up nervously. His eyesight was weakening, and the changes in the Church were shaking his confidence.

"Yes, Kev," he mumbled, looking for a piece of paper. "Gina Carrey called and wondered if you would bring over the canceled checks from the inner-city project. She wants to make a report to the board tomorrow night. Here they are. . . . Would it be too much trouble?"

"No problem," I said.

Georgina Carrey was a difficult—not to say "a dangerous"—woman. Soon after we had caught Kaspar, the monsignor had asked me to bring a stack of invitations for a Woman's Guild meeting to the Carrey house. His requests were always polite and cautious these days. I honored most of them, to sustain his morale.

John Carrey had been away, it turned out, on one of his numerous business trips, and John Junior was already in bed. Georgina was dressed in a black hostess gown that was somewhere between a dress and lingerie, but a lot closer to the latter. I managed to suppress a look of surprise.

"Can we talk a few minutes, Father?" she had asked anxiously.

She was then nearing her middle thirties. Her dark hair fell with artificial neglect about her shoulders. She had a very handsome, if somewhat horsey, face.

As Georgina rambled on about the "visions" she was having at night—serpents and angels and that sort of thing—I considered the situation. I was tougher than she. She would no more be able to dominate me in bed than she would any place else. It would be fun to bend her to my will. My fists clenched, and my heart pounded faster. Why not? Teach her a lesson she'd never forget about teasing men, I rationalized.

"John is a marvelous man," she had whispered hoarsely, the thin belt on her gown slipping aside and revealing garter, nylon, and thigh. "But he just doesn't seem to be interested in my spiritual problems. He travels so much."

She waved her hand desperately, vulnerable and defenseless. The opulent couch on which she reclined would make a superb bed. I imagined the delicious taste of her skin against my lips. Wasn't it time for me to experience the sensation of enjoying a woman? Then I thought of Ellen and realized I was being tempted. I relaxed my clenched fists.

"Maybe you ought to have a long talk with John and persuade him to curtail his travels," I said, rising from the deep chair in which I had been trapped. "I'd be glad to suggest such a talk, if you think it would help."

She had stood up, gathering the gown into more or less proper array. "If you think so, Father. I'm so grateful for your sympathy." Then she hesitated. "I'm sorry for wasting your time."

That had not been my last encounter with Georgina. Now, two years later, I found myself getting into my car—or rather the parish car that Leo Mark had purchased for me—on my way to the Carrey house. I remembered that I had been saved from temptation not by my own virtue or intelligence but by a quick image of a woman whom I had condemned to another pregnancy. My stomach turned over in self-loathing.

I took a deep breath, pushed the button that opened the garage, and backed out into the April night. I blotted out all thoughts about Ellen as I drove through the streets of the neighborhood. And I forced myself to consider the decision I might face soon. Joe Herlihy, Marty's older brother, worked at the Chancery. His information was that two people were going to be sent to Rome in the summer for three years of canon law and to work on the staff of the Second Vatican Council. My name was on the list.

I had been in that position before and was not eager to be there again, especially since, according to Joe, Pat Donahue was on the list, too.

The Second Vatican Council would be the most important Catholic event for centuries. I wanted the chance to be there. Still, I didn't want to leave St. Praxides, now that we had everything running smoothly.

Pat's work at Forty Holy Martyrs had gained him national attention. He had been written up in three Catholic magazines and was giving retreats, lectures, and days of recollection all over the Middle West. Maybe he deserved the extra time in Rome. Maybe we would go together, a possibility that was not altogether attractive.

I knew my name was on the list because Cardinal Meyer liked me. Once, he took me aside after a funeral mass and told me he had read some of my memos for the Chicago Marriage Education Office and had found them interesting. The big Dutchman from Milwaukee was awkward at small talk but somehow, nevertheless, easy to talk to. He asked intelligent questions and listened carefully. His parting remark—"I want to see more such work"—was a compliment rather than a command.

In front of the Carrey house I wondered what the Dutchman would think of Georgina Carrey. I pulled the door knocker, heard the gong inside, and waited for Georgina. As always, John was away, and John Junior was out with his friends.

I dumped the shoe box of canceled checks from the inner-city project on her couch.

"Don't know what the hurry is, Gina," I said, pecking at her cheek. "But you command and I obey."

She was wearing black slacks, a white blouse, expensive jewelry, and too much perfume.

"I wanted to talk to you," she said, her eyes cold and her face hard.

I sat on the edge of the couch. "Talk, lovely lady, talk."

"I'm pregnant," she said.

"Wonderful. Congratulations!"

"You damn fool!" she blurted. "I haven't slept with John in five years."

"How far along?" I asked automatically.

"Oh . . . not very far. Probably five weeks."

"Are you going to have the child?"

Her jaw sagged. She looked much older than her thirty-five years. "A priest suggesting abortion?" she said in horror.

"Not suggesting anything," I said, "just asking. I have to know the details if you want my help."

"I'm not getting an abortion," she said decisively.

"Are you going to get a divorce and marry the man?"

I felt very little sympathy for her.

"He won't marry me," she said, her eyes filling.

"Well, then, you'd better get John into bed as soon as he comes home from this trip, and keep him there for a while."

Her face twisted with venom. "You want me to deceive John? What kind of advice is that for a priest to give a woman?"

"John will probably be so happy to be on the receiving end of some affection for a change that he wouldn't mind being deceived even if he knew."

"All that cut-and-dried, is it?" she asked bitterly, going to the bar at the other side of the room.

"You have to make some decisions," I went on. "Somewhere in that lovely body of yours there is an impulse to try again at motherhood. Otherwise you'd have an abortion, good Catholic or not.

You don't know how John will react if he's faced with incontrovertible evidence that you've been sleeping with someone else. Either you jump back into his bed or you run the risk of having to work for a living, which you might not especially like."

She picked up a large Waterford crystal glass and poured it full of gin. "You enjoy seeing me humiliated," she said wearily.

"Not especially," I lied.

She sat across the coffee table from me. "Do you want a drink?" she asked absently. "Sorry I didn't ask."

"No thanks. Can you get back into John's bed?"

She sniffed as though I were an idiot. "Of course."

"When does he come home?"

Her shoulders slumped. "In a couple of hours."

"Then I'd better leave you alone. You'll doubtless have some preparations to make." I rose to leave.

She walked to the door with me. "Someday I may want to thank you for being such a miserable bastard," she said coldly.

I put my arm around her and drew her to me. I kissed her forehead. A pleasant, tender lethargy seeped through my veins. *Temptation again*, warned a voice in the distant recesses of my brain.

"Thank you, Father," she said in a faint voice, and then added an echo: "Pray for me."

In June the appointments were announced: Patrick H. Donahue from assistant at Forty Holy Martyrs to graduate study in Rome. I called Pat to congratulate him. He was pleased to hear from me and said that the appointment came as a complete surprise.

The usual Roman response. They must learn it the first day of class.

The Council would be an extraordinary event, I told him. We were entering a new era. He was noncommittal about that. Would I have supper with him the next night? He would be alone at the rectory and wanted to talk about it.

However much the poverty at Forty Holy Martyrs, the food was good and the cook excellent. I produced a bottle of Barolo as we sat at the table in the high-ceilinged, faded old dining room.

Pat grinned. "Don't tell me you're going to break the rule again and drink some of it."

"The occasion calls for it." He opened the bottle and poured some for both of us. *"Ad multos annos,"* I said, toasting him.

"God, Kevin, I wish there had been more time these last three years." He looked tired and worn. His face was lined; his eyes were weary. "Have you seen Ellen and Tim lately?" he asked abruptly.

"No," I said, sorry that he had broken the brief mood. "How are they?"

"Not very well, I'm afraid. Ellen's pregnant again. Tim is studying till he's red-eyed. Their apartment smells of diapers. Ellen looks awful, overweight and blotchy, and the babies cry all the time. She's terribly bitter. Won't go to church. You can imagine what her turning against the Church does to poor Tim."

"We make a damn good scapegoat," I said. "Maybe because we work so hard at it."

"I've done what I can," Pat said, filling my wineglass and passing me the platter of roast beef. "Ellen won't listen to me. I think it might be better if Tim just let her work through her anger." He smiled deprecatingly. "Sorry if I sound like a psychologist—I've read a few books, too—but he can't leave her alone. He figures he's responsible for her soul. The two of them never had a chance. . . ." His voice trailed off for a moment. "Would you give it a whirl?" he asked suddenly.

"Me?" I said in astonishment. "Why should they listen to me? I haven't had time for them in over a year. Ellen would throw me out of the house."

"No, she wouldn't. Anyway, think about it. Poor Ellen," he said sadly, "she looks and acts more like her mother every day."

"I'll think about it," I promised. "Now, let's talk about more simple subjects, like Rome."

Another uneasy frown creased Pat's forehead. "I don't know whether to accept it or not. The Chancellor gave me a week to think it over."

I wolfed down the potatoes. "Why not take it?"

"I don't want to leave the work," he said, waving his hand. "I don't want to be cooped up in a chancery handling marriage cases for the rest of my life. And besides, I've been to Rome. Four years is enough time to spend there."

"You'll go."

"I suppose I will," he admitted, "though with mixed emotions. I wonder why they didn't send you."

"Because I'm indispensable for the salvation of the soul of Leo Mark Rafferty, because I don't know Italian, and because I'm not bishop material. I can think of a dozen other reasons, but those will do."

"I'm sure you were on the list," he murmured.

"I know I was, but I doubt that I was number two on the list, or that they really wanted me in Rome. If they did, they could easily have sent me. They haven't hesitated about two graduate students before."

"There's a priest shortage now," he said, wanting to be convinced, but hesitant.

"Look, Pat. Remember me? Kevin Brennan? The last of the

great political operators? Three generations of Chicago Irish pols in my background? The tamer of Leo Mark Rafferty? If I wanted something from the folks at the Chancery, I'd go down there and ask. And I'd get it. Or I'd have my father pull strings. Have you forgotten that the Colonel knows everyone?"

Pat looked relieved. "So long as you're happy."

⁂

In late August there was a call from the Cardinal's secretary. He wanted to see me at two-thirty that afternoon. Yes, of course I could make it. As though there really were a choice.

For all the ornate oak paneling and red carpet in his office, Albert Meyer was still an easy man to talk to.

"No more memos from you, Kevin?" he began.

"Busy summer, Your Eminence," I replied.

He flicked an eyebrow and reached for a cigar. "Smoke?" he asked.

"I'll take one for my father, if I may."

He laughed and gave me the cigar. "I've met your father, of course. A remarkable man. Didn't mention you until I said that I knew he had a son who was a priest." The eyebrow flicked up again.

"One black sheep in every family."

"Not even gray," said the Cardinal, who for all his reputation for being humorless liked to fence with words as much as I did. "In any case, some people wanted to send you to Rome this spring; others didn't. I intervened and settled the matter. You would be wasted in canon law. I want you to go to graduate school in America. You would like to study psychology, I presume."

I wished the roller coaster would stop so I could collect my thoughts.

"Yes, I would like that," I said, adjusting my mode of expression to his—plain, matter-of-fact.

"I thought as much. Rome would be inappropriate for such study. You could remain at St. Praxides and go to graduate school at the university."

"Yes, I could." The roller coaster was going faster.

He made a small note on a piece of paper. "All right, Kevin. I'll see to it. I'm convinced that in the years ahead a bishop will need trained social scientists on his staff. You may assume that you are preparing for such work. We'll make the tuition arrangements with the university."

"My family . . ." I began. The sleek red leather armrest of my chair was turning wet under my clammy fingers. I wished I did smoke cigars, so I could do something with my trembling hands.

"No," he said, interrupting, "this is our responsibility." He rose from his chair. "Keep me informed, Kevin. Send me anything I ought to read, either your own work or other people's." His massive hand closed around mine, and then I was walking down the stairs toward Wabash Avenue, hardly aware that I had left his office. Albert Gregory Meyer had turned my life upside down in twelve minutes and—I looked closely at my watch—twenty-nine seconds.

I didn't tell anyone, not even my family, until the announcement appeared in *New World,* our diocesan paper. A very low-key transition into a new life.

Pat called a week after the announcement in *New World.* I expected congratulations.

"I need help, Kevin," he said, anguish in his voice.

I could see another rebound coming my way. "Name it," I said.

"Can we talk . . . I mean on the phone? Is it safe?" He sounded terrified.

"We have well-trained housekeepers, Pat," I said impatiently. "Let's have it."

"I've had some trouble with a woman."

"What kind of trouble?"

"I, uh . . . I got her pregnant and, well, she's going to write to the Cardinal about it."

"Just before you leave for Rome," I said.

"That's right. Just before I leave for Rome. I can't stop her. It will be a private letter. Her husband won't find out. I wonder if you could talk to her for me."

A warning alarm went off in my brain. "Why should I talk to her?" I asked.

"She respects you. It's Georgina Carrey," he added, almost as an afterthought.

I should have known. "I'll have a go at it. Don't stop packing." I hung up.

I sat in my chair, watching the sun sink beneath the walls of St. Praxides' school. A hot, humid summer evening. If I didn't stop her, Georgina would do him in. He'd be an obscure pastor somewhere in the Southwest for the rest of his life—if he managed to stay in the priesthood at all.

I put on my Roman collar and headed for the garage.

Georgina, in a free-flowing green sundress, sat at her desk by the open French window.

"You look good pregnant," I said. "You should be that way more often."

"According to your damn psychology, I *want* to be that way," she said flatly, favoring me with the briefest of glances.

I sat on the arm of an easy chair by the desk. "Don't do it, Georgina."

Her face twisted into an ugly mask. "I'll destroy him. I'll make it impossible for him to be a priest anywhere in the world. He lied to me; he cheated me. I'll see him in hell before I let him go to Rome." Her fists were knotted into tight balls; her back was rigid with fury.

"Settle down," I ordered. "How come so angry now? You weren't that way in the spring."

She collapsed into her chair, her hatred spent. "He doesn't return my phone calls, won't see me, won't come here for dinner. He doesn't care about me."

Poor, stupid Pat. A few elementary courtesies and Georgina would have taken it all in stride.

"You know what Pat is, Georgina. You should have expected this when you got involved with him. Fidelity from Pat Donahue? Don't be silly."

"I'll crush him," she said, her eyes once more tense with hatred. "He's a cheap little worm."

"Because you were dumb once is no reason to be dumb again. You don't think you can keep that letter secret, do you?" I didn't know whether she could or could not, but I had to play my only card. "The word will leak out, then where will you be?"

"I don't care," she said sullenly.

"Yes, you do. You've been successful in seducing John?"

"Of course."

"I bet he likes having you to cuddle up with again. Doesn't he?"

I could see the hatred turning from Pat to me. Well, fair enough. Her pride forced an answer. "Certainly."

"I bet you even like it now and then. Anyway, you've got your son and your unborn child, and a nice life. It's not worth throwing everything away on revenge that will go sour as soon as you taste it."

Her hands knotted again on the green fabric of her dress as I talked; then they unknotted, became limp and passive. "I hate you, Kevin Brennan. I despise you, and I never want to see you again." Now there were two executioners' faces in that resplendent mirror.

I stood up. "In that case, Gina, you're going to have to move out of the neighborhood. I'm not leaving my parish."

I walked out into the sticky night.

The Carreys moved to Lake Forest a few weeks before the birth of their daughter, Patricia, a blond child of whom John Carrey was especially proud.

Pat and I walked through the forest preserve. It was deserted on this Tuesday morning in summertime, though beer cans and rubbish from the last weekend left no doubt about the nearness of humankind.

"Not like the lake in the old days, is it?" said Pat ruefully. "You must miss it in August."

"I'll get up there at the end of the month, after the High Club picnic."

"I guess the forest is to me what the lake is to you." He ran his fingers through his hair. "I'm glad you've got time to talk. You must be busy getting ready for graduate school."

"Not too busy."

"It was a day like this when we saved the kids in Delaney's car. Remember?"

"You saved them, and it was a Sunday, earlier and much hotter."

"I don't know what happens to me, Kevin." He jammed his

hands into his pockets and frowned. "It isn't biological, not until the end, anyway. This terrible . . . I don't know what to call it . . . not tension exactly, but force . . . seems to take over. I can't stop myself."

"I'm a beginning graduate student in psychology, not a therapist, Pat."

We stopped in a sunlit meadow. "I know that. And I'm grateful for your help with Georgina . . . I can't believe I'm going to be a father."

"For all practical purposes, you're not." I started to walk again.

"I'm glad I'm going to Rome. It will give me a new start." He walked down the path after me, his tan slacks and open-neck shirt marking him as an outdoorsman blessed with both fashion sense and a solid checkbook.

"Maybe you ought not to go."

His eyebrows arched in surprise. "Why not? You're set for graduate school. You couldn't take my place."

"I guess I'm convinced now of what you said when the appointment came last spring. You'd be better off spending your life in the inner city instead of the inner circle."

"I'm afraid I don't understand."

"We've all got our demons, Pat." I was quoting Maureen almost verbatim. "If you go on to Rome, you're almost certainly going to have access to power. Part of you wants it; part of you doesn't. I think the part of you that doesn't is the real Pat."

"Afraid I'll be corrupted if I go to Rome—power, wealth, pleasure, the whole business?" He grinned engagingly, expecting I would deny it.

"Yes." I didn't have to look at his eyes to know that the fear was back. "Tell Meyer that for reasons of your spiritual life you prefer to stay at Forty Holy Martyrs. He won't think any less of you. More, probably."

"I ought to get away from Georgina, don't you think?"

"I've told you what I think."

He laughed uneasily and slapped my back. "Good old Kevin. Always honest, always blunt. You're probably right. You know, even to think seriously about staying at Martyrs makes me feel happier. I'll agonize over it for a couple of days and let you know."

He left for Rome three weeks later without talking to me again.

⁂

The same afternoon after my walk with Pat, I beat Calvin Ohira for the first time at his pistol range. Ohira was a third-generation Japanese American from Nebraska, as Methodist as I was Catholic, who ran a very elegant karate school on Ninety-fifth Street. It was a perfect place to run off tensions. I won a black belt but was never able to beat Calvin.

One day he'd taken a large key—his "magic key," he called it—from his drawer and led me into the basement, where, in a soundproof and padded room, he had a pistol range. "Must be ready if we're invaded again by Orientals," he'd said, grinning, covering his bitterness over the relocation camps of the 1940s.

The Colonel, war hero or not, did not tolerate guns, so of course they fascinated me. I got to be pretty good with a .38, although Calvin still outshot me. But on that Tuesday I routed him.

"I'd hate to be the one you're imagining in front of that target," he said.

"Never can tell when you're going to need it," I said. I was nervous as I put the revolver back in its case.

I would need the karate and the gun only once in my life, on a tiny island off the coast of Naples. Then I would need it badly.

October 2

Dear Ellen,

This will be even more confused and disorderly than my other letters. I'm always ashamed to put my notes in an envelope. You type so neatly and think so clearly and my letters are a mess like everything else in my life.

I don't even know how I'm going to tell you what's happened. I should phone or come home to see you. I'm too proud, though, to admit what a fool I've been.

It serves me right. While you were being pure and good, I was necking and petting and then screwing every attractive boy who came along. I tried to stop, oh, God, how I tried to stop. I'd go to confession, promise not to do it again, pray to the Blessed Mother for help, and then meet a good-looking man and it would all go down the drain.

I thought I knew everything there was to know about men. I figured I could have anyone I wanted who was worth having—well, leave Kevin out.

I really did love Burke. That's the humiliating thing. Me, the old sophisticate, got taken in. He's witty and bright and fun to be with, and very much part of the Irish aristocracy around here. I enjoyed being with him. I liked the summers on the Cape.

His drinking worried me. I said to myself that I'd have no trouble settling him down, and he did try to give it up. Then, when he was buried in the primary last year and the Kennedys dropped him (though they still took his money), he went back on the bottle, sometimes staying away from his law office for three or four days at a time. I knew I had married a weak man, a rich spoiled charming baby. I was determined to make the best of it—for Sheila, I told myself, though the truth is, I didn't want anyone to know what a dumb thing I'd done.

The sex was never much, even in the beginning. I suppose no

one will believe it, but I was chaste with him before we were married, mostly (to tell the truth) because he never tried very hard except for a few cursory passes. Obviously, we did better enough after marriage to produce Sheila. Occasionally, when he had a lot of drink in him, he'd even be kind of good.

I was prepared to live with that, too. Sex, I told myself, was overrated; Lord knows, despite my frantic efforts as a kid, it usually didn't turn out all that great, however much I've been addicted to the thrill and the danger.

All of this is a long way around. I'll have to tell you the horror story now. In the middle of August I took a weekend off from the house at the Cape. It wasn't exciting, anyway, since we'd slipped off the invitation list for the Kennedy compound. One of my classmates from Purchase married a Brahmin whose family has been here longer than the Cabots. They summer up on the North Shore where only the WASPS from the 18th century are normally allowed. She was having a regional class reunion. Burke said he would take care of Sheila and, anyway, Nanny was there.

A day with the real aristocrats was all I could take. They made Burke look like a paragon of vitality and masculinity. So I drove back to Hyannis on Saturday night.

The lights were on all over the house. Sheila was in her playpen, dirty, hungry, and screaming. Nanny was nowhere around. (I found out later that Burke had given her the day off.) There were people laughing and yelling upstairs. In our bedroom I found Burke, another man his age, and two teenagers—a boy and a girl. They were drunk and doing things to one another that kept most of their available orifices occupied.

When I came in Burke invited me to join the fun and games. I refused and he called me a lot of names, blamed me for his drinking, said I was frigid.

Well, there's no reason to say any more, is there? I collected Sheila, put her in the car, and drove to a motel. The next day I went back to Boston and, Sunday or not, called a lawyer. On Monday I rented a house in Newburyport, where there's a great art school. Burke called me to apologize. I wouldn't talk to him.

I don't want anything from the divorce, only Sheila and the things I brought to the marriage. I've seen the parish priest in Newburyport about an annulment. He isn't very optimistic. Bisexuals, he says, are not the same as homosexuals.

Burke a faggot? I think so, mostly anyway. Not enough for the Church, though. Anyway, I'm not all that interested in doing the marriage bit again.

I pray for Burke every night when I pray for my parents. He's as dead to me as they are. I thought at first that maybe I had let him down. Now I know that the only one I've let down is me.

I'll probably keep on doing that.

Love,
Mo

P.S. Love to Tim. Let me know as soon as you get the results of the bar.

October 5

Dear Mo,

I love you, I love you, I love you.

I'd like to kill Burke.

If I believed in God anymore, I'd say God damn him.

It will be all right, Mo, I know it will be all right.

I'm sick (yep, third one coming) and I'm tired, and worst of all, I'm crying for you. Please call me so we can cry together.

Ellen

And, damn you, stick with the painting this time!

During my first semester in graduate school I read John Noonan's book *Contraception* and joined the ranks of priests who were changing their minds about birth control. It was too late for Ellen Foley Curran, however. Mary Ann, getting ready for her wedding, mentioned at Christmas that Ellen was expecting a child in March.

"Three before her twenty-eighth birthday," my sister said. "How many will she have by the time she's forty?"

"A shame," I said, dully staring at the pile of Christmas wrappings at the foot of the Brennan tree. "How are they taking it?"

"She goes on taking care of the kids. He studies until two in the morning. They don't talk to each other much. They don't fight, though. They still love each other, only they don't have any time."

"I thought he took the bar exam last summer?"

"Flunked," Mary Ann said glumly. "Dad thinks he'll never pass it. Some kind of emotional hang-up."

Merry Christmas, Ellen.

CHAPTER TEN

1963–1964

"When is Pat coming home from Rome for his vacation?" my mother asked as I climbed out of the pool.

I put on my terrycloth jacket. It was cold for early August. I needed a vacation so badly that I didn't much care.

"The end of the week, I guess. Why?"

She looked up from the letter she was reading. Her red hair was now liberally laced with snow.

"Maureen is going to Europe," she said pensively. "She's going to study painting in Rome. Says she wants a new life for herself."

"Not going to marry the boy from Newburyport?" I asked, feeling the guilty hole in the pit of my stomach that always appeared when we talked about Maureen Cunningham Haggarty.

My mother shook her head. "I told you how devout he and his family are. Maureen was finally turned down by the Boston marriage tribunal on her annulment."

"Bastards," I muttered. Two years of work in social psychology had convinced me that the narrowness of the Church's annulment policy was unconscionable. Half the people in the country who got married were psychologically incapable of contracting a union that reflected the love between Christ and the

Church, which is what a sacramental and hence indissoluble marriage was supposed to be. There would be a change when we caught up with modern psychology. We would be granting annulments the way Nevada grants divorces. Too late for Maureen and her Tom Murray.

"Can Pat do something for her in Rome?" my mother asked in a conspiratorial tone.

"He'll know where to grease the palms," I said. "Let's see what he says next week."

Every month, while I struggled with graduate school and with keeping St. Praxides afloat, I would get a long, wide-eyed letter from Pat. He was decidedly high on the new Pope, Paul VI, "the greatest churchman of the century," and ecstatic about the Second Vatican Council. "The next session will change the course of Catholic history," he'd written. The letters were rich with details that would never appear in the newspapers: what Cardinal Suenens said to Paul VI the morning after the election; the hostile reaction of Cardinal McIntyre to black bishops; the comment of one African with a double doctorate to the reactionary old man from Los Angeles that he would not ride on the back of the bus no matter what the Cardinal thought of "niggers."

For all the juicy tidbits, though, there was a fuzziness in Pat's reports. He did not seem to grasp that there were differences of opinion between the progressive northern-European cardinals and his own Roman friends and patrons.

"If you were Tom Murray's parish priest, would you have told him to break the engagement with Mo?" my mother asked, her eyes as gentle as mine are supposed to be harsh.

"Trying to trace the son's changing ideology?" I said, and laughed. "I don't know Tom Murray; you and Dad were high on him. If Mo is in love with him, he must be okay."

"Temporizing," said my mother, "just like your father, and

you're not even a lawyer. Yes, Mo is head over heels, and now the Church says she can't have him."

I watched a speck of blue appear between two clouds and then quickly scurry away. The wind rattled the trees around the pool.

"He ought to marry her anyhow," I said. "The Church is going to change on annulments. Maureen is free to marry, even if the Boston tribunal doesn't think so. They just might have to wait a few years to get it blessed in church." My voice took on a bitter edge. "If he's not ready to run a few risks, he doesn't deserve her."

"Risks with his immortal soul?" asked my mother, raising an eyebrow at the last two words.

"A good confessor could have reassured him on that," I said angrily.

"You could have told them that," my mother said, her tone a mixture of bafflement and disappointment.

I stood up. "I wasn't asked. Want a beer?"

She shook her head. "Don't wake up Mary Ann. She's so tired."

Mary Ann, who was expecting a child in another two months, was the picture of health and contentment. Mother was more worried about the first grandchild than Mary Ann was.

I heard a telephone ring and thought about answering it, but before I could get to the kitchen, it stopped. Mary Ann must be awake. Probably Steve calling from his office in Chicago. He and Dad would arrive in the evening for a long weekend. I took two cans of beer out of the refrigerator and gave one to my brother Mike, who was poring over an anatomy book.

Mary Ann came into the room, in shorts and a maternity blouse. Her face was parchment white, her eyes enormous. She walked as if in a trance.

"Are you all right?" Mike said. He was instantly on his feet, the bright medical student, half-fearing, half-hoping that there would be a baby to deliver.

"What? Oh . . . yes, Mike," she murmured, sinking into the couch. Outside the wind howled ominously.

Terror clutched at my throat. I had seen the look before.

"Who's dead, Mary Ann?" I said, hardly recognizing my own voice.

"Tim Curran," she said, as though she couldn't believe her own words. "He died an hour and a half ago. That was Father Conroy. Ellen asked him to call me. Tim died at St. Anne's—her hospital—a . . . brain embolism?" She looked at Mike, not sure the word was right.

In the depths of my soul a voice told me that I had killed him just as surely as I had doomed Maureen to the loss of her beloved Tom Murray.

"All that hard work and worry," said Mary Ann, reaching for tears that would not yet come. "All those children, the strain, the tension—"

"Embolisms are not caused by stress," I said, cutting her short. "He would have died even if he'd been rich and single."

"That's right," Mike said quickly. "There's nothing anyone can do about them."

"I'm sure that will be a big help to Ellen," Mary Ann said bitterly as at last the tears began to flow.

August 10

Dear Ellen,

I suppose you thought you'd never hear from me again. Like the old bad penny, Mo returns. Anyway, I'm in Rome, of all places. I've had it with Chicago, Boston, Newburyport—whatever. I've rented myself an apartment here; Sheila goes to English language nursery school, and I take art lessons. I'm going to be serious about the painting this time; I really mean it. The teacher in Newburyport was good, then along came Tom Murray and I went through the love thing again, and messed it up again. It wasn't quite the same: he was surely heterosexual and didn't drink; his weakness was religion, which, it turns out, is almost as bad as liking little boys. He loved me, the family loved me, the Boston matrimonial tribunal did not. They dropped me like a hot whore when the monsignors said I was a "no, no." He's dating someone else now, I hear.

If I sound bitter, I'm sorry. I did love him. Not like Burke. It was honest love.

Rome is nice, though terribly hot. I went searching for Pat Donahue after I settled in. He's very much the young-cleric-on-the-make around Rome. One of the older families, the Martinellis, have kind of adopted him like the Tanseys did in Chicago. They have lots of money and lots of contacts in the Vatican. They show off Pat at all their decadent Roman parties—right out of La Dolce Vita except the women aren't as pretty—the clean-cut, freshly scrubbed American cleric with the perfectly tailored cassock and the broad shoulders.

Pat would sell his grandmother's soul to get ahead in the Church. He doesn't like to see people suffer, is serious about the social justice thing, and really believes that God has called him. He chops his life up into tiny compartments, and doesn't let them interfere with each other.

I was out walking with him the other day and he had a smile and a happy word for everyone on the street. The locals hate the clergy because of the old papal states thing, and the clergy hate them back. Most priests try to smile at people, and they're likely to get spit on. Everyone smiles back at Pat. He's more handsome than ever, too—despite all the pasta. Speaking of which, I'm on another diet. Can't let my figure go this early in life.

Pat is not a bad guy, not really. I mean, he has tunnel vision and will use anyone he needs to get ahead, but he doesn't have a mean bone in his body and is kind and sincere whenever it doesn't hurt his career. Buttering up the Martinelli family (the Monsignor is an obvious fag and his lay cousin, Alfredo Delucia, a lecher), lecturing piously to me about the Catholic history of Rome, and being a sweetheart with Sheila—none of this seems inconsistent at all, somehow.

Hell, who am I to talk?

My best to Tim. Hope all is well.

Love,
Mo

Connelly's Funeral Home was jammed with young men and women coming to pay their last respects to Tim Curran and secretly rejoicing in their hearts that it was he and not they. The building smelled of strong perfume and decaying flowers.

"I'd forgotten what Irish wakes were like," said a subdued Pat Donahue, just a few hours off the plane from Rome. "They don't have them in the Old Country anymore, you know," he added, sounding like a travelogue commentator. "God, I'm glad to be home."

Ellen stood apart from Tim's family. According to Mary Ann and Steve, who had been at the wake the first night, his parents, needing someone to blame, blamed Ellen. Her own family wasn't there, never having forgiven her for the marriage and the loss of income.

Ellen was fat, and not merely from her pregnancy, which seemed to be in about its fifth month. The calories in her chocolate cookies and candy had finally caught up. Her face was bloated, her hair lusterless. Even from a distance, though, her eyes were still luminous. I felt wretched.

"How is she going to live?" Pat asked as we waited patiently, preferring not to use our Roman collars to get to the head of the line. Around us everyone was chatting merrily. The wake was a social occasion, not a moment of which ought to be wasted, not even those that were spent waiting in line to assure the widow that you were "sorry for her trouble."

I shrugged silently, searching for words that would not come. Ellen's eyes were like beacons up close, grimly searching the dark and cold emptiness of space. Despite her heaviness, she looked incredibly young in her ill-fitting black dress—an overweight teenager.

"It's only the beginning of his life, Ellen," I said, taking her hand tentatively. It felt like a piece of dry driftwood.

The beacons swerved on me. She pulled her driftwood hand away. "You *would* say something like that."

Oh, oh, it's going to be bad, I thought.

"I'm surprised, Father Brennan, that you found time to come to his wake. I'm sure Tim would be delighted to know you were here."

"I'm sorry, Ellen."

"I bet you are. You're always sorry, aren't you, Father? Sorry you couldn't come to his wedding, sorry you couldn't baptize his children, sorry you couldn't talk to him about his problems, sorry you couldn't have dinner with him, sorry you couldn't visit his home. Not as nearly as nice a home as your rich friends', was it, Father?" There was not a trace of hysteria or grief in her voice. Her facial expression did not change. The indictment was all the more powerful because it was so calm. Connelly's was suddenly silent. I was glad my parents weren't there.

"I'm sorry, Ellen," I said.

"What's happened to Kevin Brennan's quickness with words?" she said, taunting me. "Don't tell me you have nothing clever to say?"

"Nothing."

"Do you know how much he loved you?" she went on, her eyes now burning with anger. "The sun rose and set on Kevin Brennan. He even read those incoherent psychological articles you write for your damned scholarly journals. He quoted you as though you were the Bible. He yearned for just a word of approval from you. You never gave it—not a single word. He was just the kid who scored a basket or got a hit when you needed it. You didn't care whether he lived or died. Now he's dead. And you don't really care about that either, do you?"

There was nothing to do but wait it out. I saw her two older children, a boy and a girl, both with Ellen's wide gray eyes and pert nose. The girl even had a ponytail. They watched me, eyes solemn, not knowing what was going on, but frightened.

"Yes, I do, Ellen."

"No, you don't. And don't bother coming to his funeral tomorrow, even if you do have time. Tim Curran had to live without you; let him be put back in the ground without you."

"I'll pray for both of you, Ellen," I said softly.

"Save your prayers," she replied, her lips a thin, bitter line. "Neither of us needs them."

As I left Connelly's, I saw Ellen sobbing in Pat's arms.

September 15

Dear Ellen,

Oh, my God, I just heard. What can I say? I'm so sorry. I had a novena of masses said at the Paulist Church. Called them on the phone. I wish I was with you. I wish I could do something. Anything.

My poor wonderful darling Ellen. You'll be all right. I know you will. It will take time, but God will protect you.

One more thing. I know you're angry at Kevin. Forgive him. Please do.

I don't give a damn about Kevin. He's so thick it won't bother him much. Forgive him for *your* sake, not his.

Write me. Please.

Love,
Mo

Pat and I were having a drink in my room at St. Praxides, Marty and Leo Mark having long since gone to bed.

"Well," he said, taking a long draught of his martini, "you were right, Kevin. I probably should have stayed at Forty Holy Martyrs. The temptations to corruption are all over the place. I think I'm fending them off, though I wish you could be around to hit me over the head when I need it."

"Women?"

He winked at me. "Thank God, no. I think I've got that licked, though the streets are filled with gorgeous girls. It helps having Maureen around. Her candor is even rougher than yours." His face crinkled in his most appealing grin.

"So, what's the problem?"

"Power, money, the ability to do things—most of which are admirable. The Council is a fascinating political game. You'd be great at it. For me it's like a drug. I don't want to get addicted. The people, well, they're smart and urbane. But . . . I don't know quite how to say it . . . effete, bloodless. Some of the bishops don't seem to have any hormones at all. Which, God knows, is not my problem." He grinned again.

"Still making up your mind?"

"Whether I want in on the ecclesiastical power game? Yes, I'm still trying to make up my mind. It's a game where you can do a lot of good."

"And it might do you a lot of harm."

He poured another drink for himself, and nodded. "You're

probably right. . . . Say, have you seen my daughter? Isn't she a beauty?"

I needed another drink, too. A big one. "Patrick, you're not— "

"Don't worry, Kevin. I won't tell you how I saw her, but it had nothing to do with Gina. I'm really proud of that little tyke. Not yet two years old and talking like she was six."

"You're crazy, Pat. Why take chances? Why torment yourself? Do you want to be Georgina's husband?"

"God, no," he said, and shuddered. "But I *am* Patsy's father. I haven't done much good in the world, but she's something fine I'll leave behind."

I reduced substantially the level of my second drink. "You could destroy everything. Your life, hers, the Carreys'."

"I've only seen her once, Kevin," he said. "I probably won't do it again for a long time, if ever. Still, I'm proud of her. I wanted to share my pride with you." For the first time this trip there was the fear again in his eyes. "I'm sorry if you're offended."

"Not offended, terrified," I said.

⁂

In November, John Kennedy died in the streets of Dallas. The Pope, the President, and Tim Curran.

Life went on. A week after the President's death, Steven Kevin McNeil, a redhead with the traditional hard, green eyes, entered the world. On Christmas Day, Timothy Curran, Jr., appeared, joining Brendan and Caroline and a year-and-a-half-old girl whose name I'd never heard.

In Rome the bishops overwhelmingly voted for a vernacular Liturgy, some thirty-seven years before Pat Donahue thought we would be ready for it, and the forces of change seemed completely in charge of the Council, despite Pope Paul's apparent reluctance to give them his total support. Both the documents on religious liberties and on the Jews were postponed. Albert Gregory Meyer, now one of the ten Council presidents, had a powerful impact through his statements, written for the most part by two brilliant, progressive scripture scholars—Frank McCool and Barnabas Ahern. The Cardinal's success in Rome made him popular in Chicago, much to his surprise. He was worried about the outcome of the Council. "They don't play fair," he said to me during a brief visit in his office. I had told him of the offer to me to stay on at the institute after my dissertation, an offer that he quickly approved of. "They twist the apparatus of the Council to suit their own purposes. They're just not fair." He offered me a cigar, forgetting again that my vices were spiritual.

On the first Sunday of the following Lent, all the altars in the archdiocese were turned around to face the people for the first time in a millennium and a half. And the Mass was said in English. Pastors braced for a storm of protest. The storm never came.

Ellen said little at the party. She went because one of her friends said that she needed a night out. It was hard to tell the former priests with their wives from the priests and seminarians with dates. Once, she called an ex-priest's wife "Sister," thinking she was a nun, a mistake that was easy to make, since most of the women looked like nuns, save for one or two quiet and attractive women who turned out actually to be nuns.

She thought to herself that if she were a priest who left the priesthood, she would want to have nothing to do with the Church. Yet all they talked at the party was ecclesiastical gossip: who would replace Spellman in New York; what the new Archbishop of Philadelphia was like; what Michael Novak and Daniel Callahan had said.

There was too much drinking; there were too many dirty jokes; there was too much sexual innuendo. She hated the Church because of what it had done to her. And these fools, playing at the edge of life, turned the Church into a sick joke. She thought of Sister Caroline and wondered if that good woman was now wearing a polyester pantsuit. She shivered slightly.

A young man named Tim Prindeville, accompanied by a tall, angular, and much older woman, was talking about Pat Donahue, a subject that interested all of them.

"Pat's sucking half the cardinals in the Curia," the man said flatly. "Just watch. He's going to be Archbishop here someday. Then we'll all be in trouble."

"And no woman in Chicago will be safe," said Ellen's own date. "Pat's never been able to keep his pants zipped."

She stopped listening. She felt as though she were not even in the room, an outsider watching from a great distance. She felt that way often now.

Her date tried clumsily to fondle her at the end of the evening. She pushed him away. He shoved her roughly against the door of her apartment and tore open her blouse. She yielded, letting him amuse himself

"Open the door so I can come in," he said, finally. "I won't do anything more."

"Not if I have to stand here all night," she replied unemotionally.

Finally he gave up and left. She sat a long time at the window of her apartment. The house was quiet; the children were all sound asleep. The night was cold, and the stars were very far away.

My father leaned back in the enormous high-back chair in his office and sighed as he took a hefty swig of the Jameson's twenty-four-year-old special reserve. He was pushing sixty now, but seemed no older than when he had come back from Germany.

"You'll graduate in June," he said expansively. "That's pretty fast for a doctorate, isn't it?"

"I'm what they call a mature student," I said. "Strongly motivated to get it over with, no family to worry about, and funded by the Church. It isn't all that tough." The Jameson's was like liquid thunder. I wondered how many clients were favored with it.

"Then what?" he asked.

"I don't know. More research. People are interested in my notions about local community and human development. Stay on at St. Praxides. Wait till the Council is over and the Big Dutchman decides what he wants me to do." I shrugged.

"Happy?" He was playing with a letter opener on his desk.

"Sure," I said. "Why wouldn't I be?"

He hesitated, pushed the letter opener aside, and began to play with a crisp, letter-size envelope. "Champ, we don't normally ask favors of you."

I grinned, trying to break the ice. "I figure I owe you a few."

He grinned back. "You may not figure you owe us this one." Then he plunged ahead. "We had a family meeting last Sunday at dinner. You were tied up with the teenagers at—"

"Yes," I said guiltily. "Sorry I missed it."

"Well, we decided that Ellen needs help." His mild eyes were watching me intently.

"Help?"

"Right. She's on welfare, you know." I didn't. "There wasn't any insurance money; her family won't forgive her for marrying Tim, and his family will only help if she gives them the children. She's got to get back to nursing part-time to regain her self-respect. She'll need a housekeeper for the children and money for clothes—all kinds of things. Well, we figured that if we don't assist her, no one else will. So"—he pushed the envelope across the desk toward me—"so we're going to give her this."

I drained the Jameson's and picked up the envelope. It wasn't sealed. Inside was a check to Ellen Foley Curran for twelve thousand five hundred dollars. I put the check back in the envelope and carefully returned it to his desk.

"She won't take it," I said, wishing I were in a safe place, like the Sahara during a sandstorm.

"It was a unanimous decision," he went on, paying no attention to my comment, "and one quickly arrived at. The figure is a compromise. Your mother and Mary Ann wanted it to be fifteen thousand dollars; I thought Ellen was unlikely to take anything more than ten thousand dollars." He spread his hands on the desk. "Your mother and I have always believed in compromising on family differences."

"She won't take anything," I insisted.

"But you raise no objection to our . . . concern for Ellen? If you do, we could go back to the drawing board."

"Objection?" I said brusquely. "No, of course not. It makes me proud to be part of the family. But Ellen won't take a penny. You know Irish pride."

He exhaled slowly. "That is why we're asking you to handle the tough part. You persuade her to take it."

I looked out the window at the new office building going up across the street from my father's office. The jackhammers were drumming away. The late-March snow had stopped. "You must have heard about what she said at the wake," I said, not wanting to look at him.

"That's why we want you to bring this to her," he said firmly. "By now she'll be so guilty for that explosion she'll figure she owes you a favor."

No wonder he was one of the most successful attorneys in Chicago.

I pressed the doorbell for the third time. Maybe no one was home, I thought hopefully. Then the familiar voice, faint and listless, in the little box next to the bell. "Who is it?"

I took a deep breath. "Kevin."

There was a long pause; then the buzzer sounded. I didn't think I would even get by that obstacle.

The building smelled of stale cabbage. The walls of the stairway had been painted beige sometime before the Great Depression. There were some black kids playing quietly on the second-floor landing. On the third floor, a door was open for me.

I expected the apartment would be a mess—crying kids, smelly diapers, unkempt carpets and furniture. But it was neat, spotlessly clean, cheerfully decorated, and bright from the sunlight streaming in through the kitchen window. Brendan and Caroline smiled politely and went back to quiet play with a pile of toys. Maria was asleep in a crib, and Timmy sucked at a bottle in his mother's lap.

The only mess in the house was their mother—overweight and untidy in ill-fitting clothes and stocking feet, a carton of cigarettes on the tiny camp table next to her chair, a stack of paperback books near her on the floor, a dish of candy close at hand on the coffee table.

She was an old woman already, her figure gone, her hands stained with nicotine, her eyes tired, her voice listless, her movements slow and heavy.

"How is it going, Ellen?" I asked, wishing I had a better opener. The envelope in my inside pocket was already burning a hole in my jacket.

"I don't take back a word I said at the wake."

"I hardly expected you would," I said. "I thought maybe we could go beyond them."

She continued to rock little Timmy with utmost gentleness while she tore me apart. "Would it ever enter your insensitive, complacent head that I loved Tim? No, of course not. You don't know what love is. Sure we didn't have much of a marriage, but that wasn't his fault. I loved him, loved him with all the love I have. I never made him happy, never gave him any peace, and practically never gave him any pleasure, either. You and all the goddamn priests and nuns filled him with so much fear and guilt that he was afraid to love." She spoke in an emotionless monotone, as though there were no feeling left. "You said we couldn't screw unless we got married, and so we got married, and neither one of us knew much about screwing or anything else. I got pregnant practically on my wedding night. I can count on my fingers the number of times we made love during the last two years of our marriage. Yet we loved each other. Damn your self-righteous green eyes, we loved each other. And now he's dead, and we'll never be able to love again."

I was beginning to readjust my opinion of the Colonel's cunning. However, I didn't try to interrupt. Let her get it all out. The books she was reading were "women's gothics," not a solid piece of literature in the whole stack—my Ellen, who wanted to be a writer and who had read all of Dickens and Scott before her sophomore year in high school.

"You've got every right to be angry, Ellen," I said.

"Don't patronize me, you miserable son of a bitch." Still no affect in her voice. "Could you imagine in your celibate locker-room world that a woman might have passions and desires that aren't taken care of by having four children in five years, that there might be things a woman would like to do besides changing diapers?"

I interrupted, mostly on instinct. "'Celibate locker-room world.' Nice turn of phrase."

Two points of color appeared in the hollow of her cheeks. "Kevin always gets the last word," she snapped. Outside in the narrow alley kids were shouting as they played basketball.

I stood up. "Now you've got it, Ellen," I said. "I didn't win the fight at the wake, because it would have looked bad for a priest to do that in front of so many people, so I've come here to have that last word. I'm not going to let an overweight frump go through life telling everyone that she won an argument with Kevin Brennan."

"'Overweight frump'! Who the hell do you think—"

"Shut up and listen to the truth," I shouted, "because I'm the only one who's likely to tell it to you. You're a fat, self-pitying, neurotic woman, eating and smoking yourself into an early grave. The only interests you have in life are cheap soap operas"—I was guessing, but it seemed like a good guess—"and cheaper novels. It won't bring Tim back from the dead, it won't help these kids grow up, and it won't help you. Poor Ellen, the long-suffering, pitiable drudge. You're a God-damned fool, and I use all three words advisedly."

She followed me with those terrible gray eyes as I strode about the room screaming at her.

"What am I supposed to do?" she screamed back at me.

"You're supposed to stop smoking these." I threw the cigarette carton into a wastebasket in the corner of the room. "Stop eating these." The candy followed the cigarettes. "Get rid of these." I kicked over the pile of trashy novels. "And lose twenty pounds."

She rose from her chair, moved slowly to the vacant crib next to the one occupied by the undisturbed Maria, tenderly laid Timmy in it, and came back to her own chair. "More likely thirty," she said. "And then, Father? What am I supposed to do then?"

"Then you go back to work at St. Anne's or Loretto. Use your talents and training to regain your self-respect. And, while you're at it, find yourself a man."

"I had a man; I don't want another." She was fighting tears.

"Whether you want one or not, you'd better get one," I shouted. "Your kids need a father, you need a husband, and there must be millions of men in the world who need someone like you." I was running out of steam. I tried to regain it. "But for the love of God stop feeling sorry for yourself. You know what, Ellen? No one gives a damn about your self-pity, so get rid of it."

"Is there anything about me that doesn't need changing, Kevin?" she said, looking at the floor.

"Yeah, you can keep your gray eyes just the way they are when you're angry with me."

She looked up, a very slight upward turn to her lips. "I bet you came here all the way from the university to pay me that halfhearted compliment."

Then I remembered why I had come. The fire in me went out. I sat down on the sofa.

"Is that all, Kevin?" she said patiently.

"Oh, God, Ellen, I've made a mess of it. I'm sorry. No, that's not all. That's not why I came." I groped for an opening. "Uh . . . I need a favor."

A somewhat larger upturn of the lips. A long way from a smile, though. "Why didn't you say so? What is it?"

Run for daylight, Kevin Brennan. "The Colonel . . . doesn't ask me for much. He wanted me to do something, and I . . . well, I need your help."

Her brows narrowed.

I took the envelope out of my pocket and extended it toward her. "You've got to promise that you won't tear it up."

"Don't be childish, Kevin. Of course I won't tear it up," she said impatiently.

She took the envelope, opened it, looked at the check, and threw both the envelope and the check on the floor.

"I don't want your family's charity!"

I retrieved the envelope and the check, put the check back into the envelope, and placed it on the stained coffee table.

"Would you take our love, then?"

She winced, as though I had put a knife through her breast. "Why, Kevin?" she said, fighting the tears again.

"They had a family meeting last week. I wasn't there," I added hastily, so she wouldn't think it was my idea. "But I agreed as soon as I heard—"

"And probably kicked yourself for not thinking about it first."

"I think I once knew a girl who needled me that way." I plunged ahead. "They figure you need to get back to work part-time and that means housekeepers and clothes and lots of other things. Everyone loves you"—I rushed on, oblivious of the rapidly changing expressions of pain on her face—"so there it is."

"I couldn't get a part-time job at Loretto. They need full-time psych nurses," she argued, seeing the trap begin to close.

"You don't think the Colonel would leave something like that to chance, do you? Of course they'll take you back part-time."

"What are the conditions? What do I have to do?"

"If it were up to me, it'd be rough. A certain number of days' work, a certain number of pounds lost each month, a certain number of good books to exorcise that trash. Fortunately for you, my family is easier than I would be. No conditions. The check will come every year until we're satisfied you don't need it anymore."

"It's a loan?" she said, seeing the life preserver in the water and trying to reach for it.

"Nope, we're not in the lending business. We give presents to those we love." I stood up and walked toward the door. Her shoulders sagged; her body slumped wearily. She looked at the envelope as if it had been deposited on her coffee table by a flying saucer.

"I don't want to have to choose, Kevin," she said, her voice choked with pain.

"For or against life?" I said, my hand on the doorknob.

She nodded.

"Well, your friends have done a very cruel thing to you. We're forcing you to make that choice." I opened the door.

She was still staring at the envelope when I walked out into the hall.

CHAPTER ELEVEN

1965

July 12

Dear Ellen,

I'm back in Rome after a creepy Sunday afternoon up near Tivoli—the mountain region where effete Roman aristocrats have been going on hot Sundays since Romulus and Remus. It's all trees, cool shade, light winds, and no Roman smog. The perfect setting for a pleasure palace like the Casa Martinelli.

The women were all dreadfully handsome with fine facial bones that would make you cry with envy. The men looked like Rudolf Valentino imitations. The afternoon was all languid sighs and light little laughs and cynical comments about the financial doings of various powerful curialists.

Our hosts were Monsignor Martinelli, Pat's patron and a certified faggot, and his mother, the Principessa Martinelli, who is I suppose in her early fifties but looks fifteen years younger. She has two beautiful "maids," whom she nonchalantly caresses as they run back and forth with the espresso and the liqueurs. They matched the two gorgeous young clerics in Monsignor Martinelli's entourage. All in all, with other assorted characters, you have the house of the Borgias, except that the Martinellis view the Borgias as parvenus. The marble arches and breezy balconies of the villa were built when the Borgias were still tilling land in Spain.

No one seems in the least upset about the perversity of the place. As the Principessa said to me in her modulated tones, Cardinal Rodrigo Martinelli, the founder of the clan back in the 1400s, built the villa in two wings, one for his *bambini* and one for his *bambinae.* And she didn't mean children either.

"We're the only straights in the place," I whispered to Pat. "Shush," he said. "They're a very old family, and of all the nobility the ones most loyal to the Pope."

Then Tonio—the Monsignor—joined us, bowing again over my hand, though his hard brown eyes were more on Pat than on me, and saying "Our mountain retreat is a perfect setting for your wild beauty, signora." His cruel, thin lips managed a rather nice smile.

Later, as we eased our way down the mountain road in the darkness, Pat's reaction was strongly defensive. "They're much more experienced and sophisticated than we are, Mo," he told me. "They're more cynical and more relaxed. Sex isn't important in the Curia the way it was in the last century when some of the men who became popes had children. Most of us keep our vows. No mistresses and no little boys."

"Maybe," I said, "but Tonio is still a faggot—and he wants to own you."

"He does not!" he shouted at me. He became very angry at me for a moment. "And besides, Maureen, I don't like you thinking I'm going to get ahead in the Church by giving blow jobs to monsignors."

I apologized, told him I didn't question either his chastity or his heterosexuality. But I'm still worried. Pat thinks he's smart and can use Martinelli, maybe even be a friend and not be trapped. I'd just as soon cuddle up with a crocodile.

You're the psychiatric nurse. Please advise.

Sheila is getting over the summer flu. I hope your kids are well and the job is all you want it to be.

Love,
Mo

July 30

Dear Mo,

I'll advise, since you asked.

Keep Pat away from those creeps! He's still a naive kid from the West Side.

I loved your description of their villa. I'd like to see Kevin Brennan in that Tivoli setting. I bet he'd react to the Martinellis with the one emotion they can't tolerate—open contempt. The Brennans—even Mary Ann, whom I love dearly—are not given to the sensual cardinal sins like you and me and Patrick and the people at the Casa Martinelli. In the Irish tradition, they concentrate on pride and hatred and anger and revenge.

Come to think of it, I'm probably in both camps.

The kids are fine. Hope Sheila's better. I'm tired and lonely. Thanks for the prayers. They can't hurt.

Love,
Ellen

"None of them have anything against your Jews," said the bearded Franciscan in a soft Wexford brogue, nodding his head toward the purple stream of bishops flowing out of the portal of San Pietro. "The problem with the document on anti-Semitism is your Christian Arabs."

I had been in Rome only a week. The sky behind St. Peter's was crystal blue. The dome itself shimmered almost white in the crisp morning sunlight. The bishops of the Roman Catholic

Church, in multicolored splendor, were moving through the piazza and into buses and cars.

"You mean," I said hotly, putting down my teacup so I wouldn't spill it, "that the Pope is dragging his feet on the declaration for political reasons?"

"Denouncing anti-Semitism," Maureen said listlessly, "doesn't get him any votes and puts the Arab Christians on the spot." She rose from her chair.

"I'm getting some more espresso."

I watched her as she went into the café. Her body was better suited for extra pounds than Ellen's, and she was carrying many fewer of them. If your tastes went in the direction of full-bodied women, you might even think the extra weight was an improvement. The weariness in her eyes was not an improvement, though.

"Tell me, Father Kevin," said Dermot McCarthy, "would your man, the Dutchman, support the declaration? My boss is after wondering."

"He would defer to Spellman, who is the cardinal from the American Jewish Committee on that issue." I was not going to tell the all-knowing Dermot McCarthy that "my man," Meyer, and I had spent most of our only conversation in Rome discussing the October weather in Chicago.

"The Curia will let you have the one on the Jews, Father Kevin," sighed Dermot, "after they've mucked it up a bit. But they don't like the religious-liberty one at all. If you start giving people freedom of belief outside the Church, sure the first thing you know they're going to start expecting it inside, and then where will we be?"

"The whole crowd will fight on that one to the bitter end," I insisted.

He cocked his eye. "Will they, now? Well, you can depend

on it: the Curia won't make the mistake again for a long time of appointing bishops like that in America."

Maureen came back to the table with coffee for Dermot and tea for me as well as her espresso.

Dermot's fork played with a piece of creamy pastry. "Well, I'll tell you one thing," he said softly. "They're going to give you lads a run for your money." Again the St. Francis smile, and he was up from his chair and striding down the street, walking rapidly back in the direction of the Vatican.

"Don't trust that phony Irish charm, Kevin," Maureen said. "Sometimes I think he can't distinguish between what's actually going on and what he imagines is going on." She played with a strand of her closely cropped black hair. She looked tired.

"Mo, what can we do for you? Even if Tom did marry, the annulment—"

She caught me short. "What's in it for you, Kevin? What do you do for kicks? You surely can't enjoy this nutty power game here? What pleasure is there for you in worrying about my marriage mess, or Pat's love affairs, or Ellen's lonely widowhood, or whatever you want to call it? I bet that's what you do in the parish all the time. And all that work for a degree? Why do you bother? Why do you bother with me? You know I'm a lost cause."

I finished my pastry and was working my way through Dermot's. "You're not a lost cause, Mo, and I like bothering with you. The tired look in your eyes tears at my heart. As for why—maybe a little psychology is dangerous. A boy grows up while his supercompetent father is away taking care of the country. He learns to take care of his mother and the little kids; then he spends the rest of his life taking care of people. Gets good at it, some of the time."

"My God, Kevin," she said in horror, "is that what your vocation is all about? Why don't you get out?"

"Why should I? I like taking care of people."

She picked up her espresso cup, then put it back on its tiny saucer untouched. "You're happy, even with that explanation?"

"Why not?"

She leaned across the table and kissed me, in the shadow of St. Peter's, ignoring the scandal that might be caused. "That's for being sweet and worrying about me. And don't fret about Tom Murray. He's a prig. I don't know what I ever saw in him."

I was late getting back to the Villanova House where I was staying and went to bed almost immediately. I dreamed not about Maureen but about Ellen. I was at Loretto Hospital once again, just as I had been in reality a short time after handing Ellen that envelope. In my dream she was going after me with a knife. The roar of a Vespa outside my window woke me up before she could emasculate me.

It had been two months since that confrontation, and I still felt humiliated by it. I had been visiting poor Mary Tansey. Cardboard woman or not, she didn't deserve lung cancer. A parishioner from St. Prax was in the psychiatric unit. I debated whether to stop by his room. I was more afraid of not seeing Ellen than I was of seeing her.

My uncertainty was settled quickly. Ellen stood at the central nursing station, clipboard in hand, surrounded by a group of nurses and attendants.

"Hi," I said tentatively when her entourage was coolly and competently dismissed.

"Good afternoon, Father," she said. "Mr. McClutchey is in 417 if you want to see him. He's doing nicely."

"You look as if you're doing nicely, too," I said. "More than halfway back to playing weight. Read any good books lately?"

There was a stony silence. Her lips turned white. Her eyes hardened.

"I'm sorry," I said. "Dumb thing. I was afraid I'd see you and I wouldn't know what to say. Blew it again."

"You certainly did," she said coldly. "And please bear in mind that however much I may have to be grateful for your family's generosity, I do not have to put up with any inspection from you."

Ellen had turned away and clicked angrily down the smooth floor of the corridor. I went to see Joe McClutchey. Ellen wasn't there when I passed the nursing station on the way out.

After I awoke from my nap I took a shower—nonfunctioning Italian shower nozzles prove the existence of purgatory—and drifted down to the common room at the end of the American corridor of the Villanova. John Quinn, a Chicago "peritus," or expert in canon law, had provided two bottles of Jameson's. Praising his virtues to myself, since there was no one else in the room, I poured more than a little of it over ice taken from an ice maker that Quinn had also provided. There were only two ice makers in Rome at the time; the other was in the Chicago House, a gift from the always considerate Quinn to his cardinal.

"Would that be Jameson's you have there?" said a precise, elegant male voice. "Damn it, Kevin, are there only two of us with such superb taste in this whole city?"

John Courtney Murray was a tall, cool, incandescent spirit, six feet four at least. Bald, he wore thick glasses and had a matchless mastery of literary style. Murray had been forbidden many years before to write any further on the subject of the Church's support for religious liberty. He was banned from the first session of the Second Vatican Council and then invited by Cardinal Spellman, of all people, to be an expert at the remaining sessions. Now he was drafting a document on his favorite subject that might well create a revolution in Catholic thinking on freedom.

We sat on the hardback chairs and sipped our ambrosia.

"Need I tell you, Kevin," Murray said, "that it will be a disaster of monumental proportions if the religious-liberty declaration does not go through? Can you imagine in this era the Church's implying that in a Catholic state it is quite acceptable to persecute religious minorities?" He drained his drink, which I noted was not polluted by ice.

"Now," he continued, "I would not be surprised if those opposed to religious liberty try to exploit Father Donahue, who I am led to believe is a friend of yours. He is an excellent young man, charming, efficient, and intelligent. But he's no match for their trickery. We will all have to be vigilant in our areas of information. Might I assume we can count on you?"

"I'll take care of him," I said grimly.

October 1

Dear Ellen,

I've got another big party tonight, but I want to get this letter off to you before I start the final preparations. I don't know what to do about Pat. His family has disowned him. I'm sure you know what that's like! It started when he didn't spend much time with them during the Forty Holy Martyrs years. They expected him to be home every Sunday afternoon for supper. His mother must have planned showing him off every week all through the seminary years. Well, he didn't come home much; the parish kept him busy; he got involved with the people who were giving him money to keep the place going—like the Tanseys, God rest her, and the Carreys. I think he always found his family pretty dull. I'm not making excuses for him. Still, they didn't understand what he was doing, and didn't like him being in a Negro parish. Then they were angry that he didn't hang around the house during his vacation two summers ago. The letter from his mother yesterday was a real heart-wringer—they never hear from him, he'd let them down, betrayed them, was more interested in his career than in his family. I'm afraid they're right, but it's mostly their fault, isn't it? Their idea of a successful priest is one who does exactly what Father Conroy did at our parish twenty years ago—and comes home to Mama on Sunday afternoon.

Sometimes he says he'd like to give it all up, go back to Forty Holy Martyrs and spend Sundays with his family. If he had just a little more courage and a little less ambition he'd follow that instinct and be a very happy priest.

I'm not going to tell him that. It's up to him to make his own decision.

Hey, that sounds like Kevin, doesn't it? Maybe Kevin is contagious. Anyway, I had coffee with Kevin this morning. I know you hate him and you know I think you shouldn't hate him, so I won't say too much.

I bet you want to know how he strikes me now that he's the same age as Our Lord was when he died on the cross. It's kind of hard to answer. He's worse, and in a funny way better.

I mean, he's even more the cynical, ruthless, hard-eyed fighter than he's ever been. You have to peel off a lot of layers to get down to what Kevin Brennan feels. Yet . . . yet . . . that gentle soft streak is still there and maybe more obvious. You remember how sad his green eyes can get.

Pat wants to be a bishop. I want to do something useful with my life. You want to be a writer—I don't care what you say. What does Kevin want? I don't know.

You should make peace with him. You know you're going to do it eventually. Why not get it over with?

Now to the bash.

Love,
Mo

Like all Maureen's parties, this one was a brilliant success. Pat marveled that she could feign such interest in the issues of the Council when she really did not care about them. Her half-finished paintings, distributed casually about the old palazzo off the Piazza Farnese, did not seem any closer to getting finished from week to week. Maureen was neglecting her art lessons for conciliar politics.

Pat felt guilty about that. The paintings seemed to display some talent. One of his Italian friends, Fredo DeLucca, a cousin of Antonio Martinelli's, said that though it was a modest talent, it was worth developing.

Dermot McCarthy was just across the room, and as charming as ever. He was in serious conversation with the thin, blond wife of an English reporter. McCarthy, Franciscan robes and all, paid the women a lot of attention at Mo's soirees. You could never be sure what Dermot was up to. If he were the woman's husband, he could not be more solicitous of her. She was bored with Rome and much too easily charmed by the smooth-talking Irishman.

Maureen was willing to devote her time and energy to Pat's career. They were old friends met again after a long time, in a glittering but heartless city. They had seen much of each other while Maureen was selecting her apartment, hiring a nanny for Sheila, and finding a teacher. He did not ask her to have these soirees; she seemed to sense that he needed a place besides the Chicago House to see and be seen. The phlegmatic Meyer was not given to Roman social life, and his quiet presence chased brilliance and wit away.

The Romans seemed remarkably tolerant of every human arrangement. The American journalists gave no sign that they saw anything suspicious about a young minutante *and a rich patroness. Occasionally Pat tried to explain that they had grown up together, anxious that no one would misunderstand.*

Now Kevin was in Rome. Indeed, he was exchanging monosyllables with Antonio in the other room, looking vaguely displeased, as he often did.

Pat brought a plate of salami to the other room, passing Hans Küng, who was engaged in deep conversation with another theologian. One of the reasons for soirees like this, Pat had explained to Maureen, was to bring together members of opposing factions so that they could learn to know and respect one another. The ministry of reconciliation to which the Pope was so profoundly committed was everyone's responsibility.

The room was crowded with important journalists, the men who were, for better or worse, shaping world reaction to the Council. Maureen's parties were famous all over Rome. It was a perfect situation to exercise influence on world thinking. Pat was pleased with his opportunity.

Kevin was listening to Monsignor Martinelli now, Pat noticed. Towering over the dapper curialist by a good two thirds of a foot, Kevin seemed unimpressed. That was a shame. Both were pragmatists; both sought compromise solutions; both understood human behavior. He wished Kevin would pay more attention to the way he dressed. Off-the-rack black suits and turtleneck sweaters might be appropriate at the university, but hardly at a fashionable party in the heart of Rome.

"Your friend is telling me very interesting things about the psychology of Americans," said Tonio, his even white teeth glistening in a quick smile. "We have so much to learn. He truly ought to be a peritus at the Council. Perhaps Cardinal Meyer could arrange it for the next session, no?"

"He thinks it'll be the next Council before the Church is ready for psychologists," said Kevin.

"Could you join Maureen and me for lunch tomorrow at Sabatini's?" Pat asked suddenly. And, in an aside to Tonio, "We grew up together, you know, Monsignor, and have not yet had time to talk about all our friends."

"Of course." Tonio moved his hands in a gesture of tolerant urbanity. "We'll see if Felici can release the poor Council fathers ten minutes early so you can get your order in before the rush."

"Lunch? Why not?" said Kevin, though he didn't seem especially happy at the prospect.

Pat moved away. The apartment was crowded now, more than seventy-five guests, all of them "important."

The English reporter's blond wife was not quite drunk, still talking to Dermot McCarthy, who was discreetly holding her so that she was not quite leaning against him. Dermot lit the woman's cigarette. There was no doubt about the invitation in her eye. Dermot neither accepted nor rejected it. It seemed rather that the invitation was filed away for future reference, and perhaps future use, when it might be worth using.

Eventually the apartment was empty save for the sleeping Sheila, the last of the servants, and Pat and Maureen. Pat was putting away a few half-full bottles that had been salvaged from the party while Maureen reclined on the low, gray eighteenth-century couch, relaxing.

"Can't help it, I just love these things. I could so easily be a character in a Fellini movie. What do you think, Patrick?"

He closed the door of the liquor cabinet. "It's the elegance of the conversation that's the most delightful part, I'd say."

She fumbled for her cigarettes. "What did you think about Kevin?" she said, changing the subject suddenly.

He considered carefully. "Maybe he's still suffering jet fatigue, but he seems to be more sullen than ever. Doesn't miss a thing, though, does he?" He bent over and lit her cigarette, and thought of

Dermot and the English girl. "Did you notice him watching Fiona and her Franciscan friend?"

Mo smiled. "He treats Dermot as if he's a laboratory specimen. And Dermot, who doesn't usually miss much, either, is unaware of it."

The closeness of Maureen's bare shoulder shook him. He lit a cigarette of his own, hoping to steady his nerves. He felt light-headed. Too much Campari and soda. He ought to leave at once.

"Does Kevin see through himself?" he asked lightly, fighting to hide the tenseness that was taking possession of his body.

Maureen yawned and stretched sleepily. "Oh, yes, I think that's why he smiles so little. There's no escape for poor Kevin."

The movement of her body unnerved him. "I asked him to have lunch with us tomorrow at Sabatini's."

"Fine with me." She rose and walked toward the door. "You better get back to the Via Sardegna. Doesn't that Cardinal of yours make a bed check?"

"There's something I have to do first," he said, conscious of the smoothness of her shoulders and back, of the scent that drifted from her, of her breasts inviting his touch.

At the doorway of the apartment now, she turned to him, uneasy at the tone of his voice.

"What do you mean, Pat? Why do you look so funny? Oh . . . please, don't."

He muffled her startled scream with his mouth, pressed her body against his.

She fought him, struggling to escape from his grip.

He pulled her down on the sofa and ripped her dress, stripping her to the waist. He wanted to stop. Principle began to reassert itself. His fingers slipped away from her breasts. He breathed deeply. Yes, now he could stop. Oh, my God, she'll never forgive me. I must apologize and run. Never see her again. Find a monastery. He was no longer touching flesh, only black lace, much less dangerous.

Then she put her arms around his back and drew him down on top of her.

Their love was violent and reckless. They clung to each other long afterward, the perspiration of their bodies blending and binding them together. Neither of them spoke.

My taxi was caught up in the loud, fetid noonday rush hour. I cursed the stupidity of a culture that created four rush hours instead of two. My anger, however, didn't get me from the Piazza Hungaria in Parioli across the river to Trastevere any more quickly. My driver, with dramatic expostulations and even more dramatic gestures, fought his way up from the Tiber to the late-medieval church of Santa Maria, in Trastevere. I was already twenty minutes late. The lovely Romanesque building with its exquisite mosaics did not appease me; nor did Pat's manifest anxiety as he rose from the table in front of Sabatini's.

"Do you want to eat inside, Kevin?" he asked. "Or would you—"

"This is fine," I said mechanically. "Sorry to be late. Traffic."

"Makes Chicago look good, doesn't it?" He seemed more relaxed now that I was at the table. He poured a glass of Frascati for me. It looked like another afternoon for a siesta.

"Did Monsignor Martinelli get you out ten minutes early?" I asked, signaling the waiter for butter. My nerves were still in a shambles from the ride across Rome.

"As a matter of fact, we did get out a few minutes early. I suppose it was just a coincidence. I hope you and Tonio got to know each other last night."

"I think he would find it very difficult to understand someone like me," I said cautiously.

"Did you find Fredo DeLucca interesting?" Pat's eyes were hooded.

"A perverse Rudolph Valentino with sadomasochistic tendencies," I said.

A wave of color swept Pat's face. "That's terribly harsh, Kevin."

"I guess it is," I said. "These old Roman families set my teeth on edge. I don't know why."

"He's one of the most respected of Roman journalists. *La Voce* is a very influential paper, read by everyone in the Curia. Fredo has a distinguished audience."

I resisted the words forming in my head about the sexual predilections of Fredo's readers. Instead I said, "I suppose Mo is caught in the same traffic jam I was in."

"Oh, yes, probably. . . ." He paused and then rushed on. "It's really about her I wanted to talk, Kevin. I don't know what you think about Mo having those parties for me. I mean, she wants to do it, thinks she's helping my career." He grinned. "As though I was going to do anything but sit in the Chancery answering telephones for the rest of my life. Anyway, I decided I'd better tell you that there was nothing going on between Mo and me."

"My God, Pat," I said truthfully, "I never thought anything of the kind."

"Well, you know that we were kind of involved back in high school."

"Puppy love," I sniffed. "And sixteen years ago. No, seventeen."

He nodded. "There are so damn many rumors in this city. I thought I'd better tell you that I'd straightened myself out, and that I am very grateful for your help."

It sounded so formal. His eyes were restless, the old fear returning momentarily, as though he were hoping I would give him a vote of confidence. Suddenly a thought crossed my mind. I wondered if it was possible that Pat had a crush on *me.* Was I now Koko? I'd been around too many curial homosexuals lately, I told myself, switching off the absurd idea. I obliged with the vote of confidence.

"I never doubted it, Pat, but it's nice to know. Anyone makes a comment about you and Mo, I'll poke him in the mouth."

"Do you ever see Patsy?" he asked suddenly.

"The Carreys brought her to Mary Tansey's funeral mass," I said.

"What's she like now?" He leaned forward eagerly.

"A very pretty, blue-eyed, blond four-year-old," I replied carefully.

He sat back in his chair, nodding, and sipped his wine.

Then Maureen pulled up in a cab, her pale-green mini-dress revealing a generous segment of flank as she climbed out the narrow door. She was radiantly lovely.

Over the pasta they both demanded to know more about Ellen.

"I don't know very much," I said honestly enough. "For a while she seemed in a bad way. But she's gone back to work now and has shed about fifteen pounds."

"She must be positively svelte," said Maureen enviously.

"I'm not an expert, but maybe ten pounds more has to go," I said, remembering vividly how Ellen had raised my ante. "Anyway, she seems to be pulling her life together. We Irish tend to mourn for a year and then get on with life."

"I wrote her a long letter last Christmas," said Pat. "It seems to have had some effect."

"Must have," I said, hiding my sense of irony.

"Let's send her a card from here," said Mo, brightening at the thought.

So we wrote foolish things on a card and addressed it to Ellen. I volunteered to put it in the post-office box in Parioli.

After lunch we shared a taxi back to the intersection of the Via Veneto and the Via Sardegna. Pat, a little unsteady because of the wine, walked the short blocks down to the Chicago House. Maureen and I took a leisurely walk back toward the Trevi Fountain.

"Am I too hard on Pat?" I asked her abruptly, relaxed by the wine and the pleasant sensation of walking down the Via Veneto with a pretty woman whose legs caused heads to turn at every table on the street.

She regarded me with amusement. "Oh, Kevin, you're impossible. Of course you're not too hard on him." She took my hand. "You've sized up this city better in two weeks than he has in three and a half years. But don't be deceived by Pat's naïveté, darling. He works very hard and very effectively and does get some of the American viewpoint across. They use him outrageously, but you just watch Pat come up winners."

I told Mo about my fears that Martinelli would use Pat in a last-ditch effort to win a symbolic victory on religious liberty.

She nodded thoughtfully. "Pat could be persuaded that he's going to save the day and wind up doing something disastrous to himself. I'll keep my ears open. I suppose"—her eyes flashed wickedly at me and she squeezed my hand—"you'll know what to do if there's trouble."

"I might figure something out," I said sheepishly. I also filed another fact in my brain: Mo didn't care about who won the religious-liberty conflict. She didn't care much about the institutional Church. She cared only about keeping Patrick Donahue out of trouble.

Pat knelt before the altar in the tiny chapel in the Chicago House. He wanted to weep, but tears would not come. He was filled with pain.

I didn't want to do it. I almost stopped. She needed me more than I needed . . . I'm sorry. Oh, God, I'm so sorry . . . after all these years. I thought I had it beaten. I knew *I had it beaten. Then . . . Forgive me; forgive me; please, forgive me.*

The solitary sanctuary light flickered.

I won't do it again. Give me strength. I want to serve You. I know I can do good for the Church. I gave up marriage so I could help the Church. Your mother told me to at the lake the night she came to me.

There was a faint noise in the back of the chapel. Albert Meyer come to say his prayers. What if he knew? Patrick shuddered slightly. The Italian priest had given him absolution a few hours before—routinely, mechanically, as though priestly fornicators were not an unusual type of penitent.

Pat focused his eyes back on the tabernacle, still on the altar despite the liturgical changes. Did God care? Was he listening?

I am *sorry. I really am. I'm sorry I lied to Kevin, too. I'm sorry for all the evil things I've done. Give me another chance, just one more chance. Please. I'll never let it happen again.*

He sensed approbation, forgiveness, a chance for a new beginning. He would have wept then if it were not for the Cardinal, kneeling a few pews behind him. As he left the chapel, carefully blessing himself with holy water and feeling like a man reborn, he realized that Meyer was so lost in prayer that he would not have noticed tears.

⁂

John Murray was waiting at the entrance to the Villanova House. He waved me into the common room.

"There's a vague rumor," he said, "that the Curia is going to try to get Cardinal Cushing to propose to the Holy Father, in the name of a hundred American bishops, that the present document be withdrawn for the good of the Church and be replaced by something old-fashioned and harmless. It would be a devastating blow because it would give the Ottaviani group a chance to lean on the Pope to take the whole thing off the agenda. Poor Cush wouldn't know what he was doing, but he's been used that way before."

"What's in it for Ottaviani?" I asked, not quite understanding how the somber and reactionary head of the Holy Office could be a friend of a liberal like John Quinn, the canon lawyer from Chicago.

A native of Trastevere, Ottaviani was nearly blind as a result of an eye disease that was rampant among the Roman poor when he was a child. He was reputed to have the *malocchio,* evil eye. Many curialists were superstitious enough to be afraid of his stare.

"Ottaviani is not a bad man. To the right of the Emperor Justinian, mind you, but a man of conviction, unlike a lot of the others." He carefully polished his thick glasses. "He really believes error has no rights."

I thought that a nice guy who really believed that error had no rights was even more dangerous than a vicious guy who believed the same thing. "The game is addictive," I said, and sighed.

"It is." Murray replaced the glasses on his aristocratic nose. "Everyone in Rome chooses up sides."

Maureen tossed her packages on the bed and peeked into the room to see if Sheila was napping. The little girl was awake, grim and sad as always. Maureen kissed her, and the girl hugged back, intensely. Sheila needs me, Mo thought. Can I ever give her enough?

She called the nanny to dress Sheila for her evening meal, accus-

ing herself of being a bad mother because she had servants to do such things.

She unwrapped the packages of underwear and arranged the flimsy garments neatly on her dresser. If you're going to have a man in the house, you should be ready to give him a nice view of the scenery. She laughed happily. Pat had a lot to learn about the niceties of lovemaking. He was strong and passionate, however. She had forgotten how nice it was to have a strong and passionate man make love to you. Her body was pleasantly sore from the previous evening's encounter. Would he come again tonight? No, he would probably have to worry his conscience a bit.

She went into the parlor and lit a cigarette. The Church was going to change on celibacy, anyway. Why should they wait?

She walked slowly back to her bedroom, unbuttoning her dress. God probably didn't give a damn either way. He had made them both with important parts of their personalities missing. She would take care of Pat, keep him from making a fool of himself and the Church. He would be a cardinal someday, and, damn it, she'd see to it he'd be a good cardinal.

She threw her slip on the bed and padded into the kitchen to pour herself a large glass of Frascati. Ignoring Italian custom, she tossed several ice cubes into the glass and returned to her bedroom.

She considered her plans very carefully as she turned on the hot water in the tub. What would you think, Kevin dearest, if you knew my challenge is to try to make your friend Pat Donahue a cardinal? She dropped her underwear on the bathroom floor and tested the water with her fingers. Damn Italians don't know how to make plumbing work. She adjusted the cold knob.

She eased her body into the tub and sipped the frosted glass of wine with satisfaction. The affair would be inconvenient. Pat would want to break away. That was all right. A few more nights with him and he would be so addicted to her he would never wander far. She sighed happily. The only problem was Kevin. If he ever found out . . . She frowned. I love you, too, darling Kevin, but you're my enemy. She turned on the hot water again. It was dark in the bathroom. Nights came so early to Rome in October.

CHAPTER TWELVE

1965

I had gone through the Near East at a leisurely pace: Lebanon, Syria, Jordan, Jerusalem. In late November, with only ten days left to the third session, I was sitting in the Jerusalem Intercontinental, looking down at the lights of the Holy City and listening to rock music played by an orchestra of Arabs who were trying to look like the Beatles.

I began to read the Paris edition of the New York *Times.* The headline read "Rumor of American Retreat on Religious Liberty." Israel Shenker's article reported behind-the-scenes moves by some American bishops to "defuse" the explosive religious-liberty issue by substituting a draft that would be acceptable to Curial conservatives.

I made up my mind that very moment. It was a Thursday. The Council was in recess until Monday morning. I would catch the early Sunday plane and be back in Rome by Sunday afternoon.

At Lod Airport on Sunday I saw John Carrey. I tried to duck him, but he wouldn't let me go. So good to see me. Georgina was traveling with him now. Her attitude toward travel had changed dramatically after Patsy's birth. No, they were flying directly to New York. No time to stop in Rome. Maybe next trip. I breathed a sigh of relief. We would be on different flights.

John dragged me over to the departure lounge to say hello to Georgina. She was thinner, paler, and looked much older, though she still would attract attention in most of the airports of the world. She was polite and reserved. Her eyes were filled with hatred. Someday she would get her revenge, or at least have a try at it. I was glad Patsy wasn't my daughter.

November 10

Dear Mo,

I must write you tonight. I have two bits of good news that I must share with someone. They've made me Director of Psychiatric Nursing at the hospital. It will mean more money, more work, more prestige, and more time off the floor of the Unit, which is fine with me. It also means that I'm a success and that is terribly important. I've done one of the things I set out to do when the Brennans gave me their money.

The other bit isn't so important. No, I take it back. It's *more* important. Yesterday I weighed exactly what I did when I was nineteen. That's been harder than the job. I've had to concentrate on caring what I look like, when a lot of the time I don't. I tried on some of my old clothes and they fit. I'm so happy about getting my body back I'm going to celebrate with a malted milk tomorrow!

I know now that I can do it alone. Soon I will stop taking the money from the Brennans and try to find some way to pay them back. Not the money—that they won't take and don't need—but the love.

It's not over yet. I'm not yet me . . . how terribly psychiatric that sounds . . . but I'm on my way. In another year or two I'm going to start looking for a man, not because I feel I have to have one, but because it would be nice to have one.

I've read over copies of some of the hysterical letters I've sent you since Tim died. What a wonderful friend you are, Mo, for putting up with my being a cry baby. Now you're going to have to put up with me being a complacent self-analytic prig. I'll try to get over that, too.

I do wish I were in Rome for all the excitement. I feel sorry for Pat. You're right that Pat could find happiness and salvation—whatever that is—at Holy Martyrs and at Sunday supper with his family. He'd also find peace with some good woman (not you!). I don't think he'll take either of these courses and I worry about your involvement with him.

That last sentence is inexcusably priggish. Forgive me. I'm leaving it in, though.

I feel guilty about Kevin. He was in the Unit last summer and I acted like a little fool. I do hate him terribly. It's childish, but at least I can be honest about it now. I hate him because I wanted him to leave the priesthood and marry me. Maybe I still do. I blame the Church for ruining my marriage to Tim—and I don't think that's unreasonable—and I blame it for not letting me have Kevin. I hate Kevin for letting the Church stand in our way.

Isn't that a good enough reason for hating anyone?

Or for loving him so much that it hurts to think about him? Especially since I know that if he were a husband and not a celibate priest, he never would have been able to do for me what he did—to make me come alive again.

Despite all this self-analysis, which comes from hanging around shrinks every day, I haven't quite sorted it all out. I'm not sure I want to.

Keep on praying for me. I'm not praying for myself, or at least I'm telling myself I'm not praying.

Love you.

EL

The plane was late taking off and even later landing in Rome. It was almost dark when the airport coach finally pulled into the Stazione Termini. Coming out of the station, I heard a familiar voice.

"Ah, 'tis yourself coming back for the final fireworks, is it?"

There was Dermot McCarthy, as sleekly handsome a curly-haired black Irishman as you could imagine. He had been in Naples at a conference the day before, he assured me, and had come back on the *rapido.*

"Your man Pat Donahue is cutting a fine figure around here these days," he said with a broad smile.

"Is he, now?" I said, keeping my voice neutral.

"Indeed he is. I'm after hearing from some of my friends in the English press that there's going to be a big article on him in one of their Sunday papers next week on how he played a major role in the solution to the religious-liberty controversy."

"I didn't know it had been solved."

"Well, it has not been solved *yet,* if you take my meaning." He winked at me as we got to the curb, where a mob of Italians were fighting one another for taxis. "But I've reason to believe that it's going to be solved tomorrow morning with a very dramatic intervention from one of your American cardinals."

My stomach did a flip. "Never count on an American cardinal," I said, "especially not one who turns unpredictable as the night wears on."

He laughed merrily. "Ah, now, Father Kevin, you're the cute one. I'm also told that the author of the story is going to give a very nice account of the American divorcee who is Father Pat's patron. Won't that be fine, now?"

"I'm sure she'll appreciate the publicity," I said.

" 'Tis become a powerful close relationship, it has," he said. "But then, that's the way of things, I suppose."

⁂

Maureen frantically dialed the number again. The nun at Villanova answered wearily. No, Padre Brennan had not yet come back. Yes, he was returning today, but no, he had not come yet. Yes, of course, she would give him the message. How was the name spelled? Yes, yes, of course. H-A-G-G . . .

Maureen hung up. Good God, Kevin, where are you? We've got another rebound for you to tip.

She drew her robe more tightly around her shivering body. There was plenty of heat in the apartment. The cold was inside her.

Something terrible was going to happen tonight at Polesi's restaurant. Dear God, how could anyone be as dumb as Pat? That horrible little faggot Martinelli is using him as a tool in some monstrous plot. Poor, dumb Pat thinks he's going to save the Church.

They'd made love after lunch, quietly, soothingly, tenderly, while the nanny had taken Sheila for a ride in the countryside. Pat and Sheila had become very good friends. Her daughter seemed happier than ever before. Pat, amazingly, was wonderful with children. Mo had fallen asleep after their lovemaking and then was stirred awake by the sound of Pat dressing.

"Leaving so soon?" she said, yawning.

"I've got an important dinner engagement tonight," he said. Then he added "With a cardinal." He spoke softly, as though it were a secret. Such a naïve man. And such wonderfully strong arms.

"Which one?" she asked, instantly alert.

"Richard Cardinal Cushing," he said, buttoning his shirt.

"I didn't know you knew him well enough to get taken out to dinner."

"I don't know him all that well," Pat admitted, pulling on trousers over his strong, well-shaped legs. "This is a very important dinner we're going to have at Polesi's."

Automatically she noted the name of the restaurant. "Not very elegant for a cardinal," she murmured.

"Critical dinners don't take place in the obvious places," he said, outrageously pleased with himself and his secret.

"Religious liberty?" she said, trying to sound conspiratorial.

He just winked, kissed her lightly, and slipped out of the apartment.

"God damn it, Kevin Brennan, where are you?" The sound of her voice in the empty apartment startled her.

"Please, dear God, help me," she prayed, wondering if God bothered to listen to the prayers of sacrilegious fornicators.

⁂

I called Maureen's apartment. The line was busy. I waited, ignoring the Italians outside who were making threatening gestures because I was monopolizing the phone booth. I tried again. This time the line rang. Mo answered and I forced the *gettone* down the slot. "Kevin," I said into the phone. "How are you, Mo?"

She was almost in tears. "Did you get my message at Casa Villanova?" she said.

"No, I'm calling from the lobby of the Grand Hotel. Just got off the airport bus."

"Would you worry if you knew that Pat was having a tête-à-tête with Cardinal Cushing at Polesi's?"

"I'd be terrified. Was this sudden?"

"He's been working on something secret for days. I think it's about religious liberty. Kevin, stop him from . . . from I don't know what, but stop him."

"Is that the place across from the Chiesa Nuova?"

"Right." Her voice was firm and confident again. "In the old Borgia place, Piazza Sforza Caesarini."

"If you don't hear from me by eleven, you go to bed and sleep. You can count on it by then that we've won."

I hung up and then remembered I needed another *gettone* to call. I ducked out of the booth, waited in line at the concierge's desk to purchase it, accepted his contemptuous glance that said I wasn't registered there, and went back to the phones.

They were all occupied, and there was a striking young Roman woman waiting for an open booth, tapping her delicate little foot on the carpet. A door opened, and I rushed in ahead of her. She called me some very unpleasant names in Italian and then fled from the alcove when I turned my glare on her.

The phone at the Villanova rang interminably. The offended *portiero* finally answered it, implying by his curt *"Pronto"* that only a fool would call at five-thirty on Sunday afternoon.

There was another long wait until John Murray muttered his *"Pronto"* at the other end of the line.

"Kevin Brennan. Pat Donahue is having dinner with the Cush at Polesi's tonight. They're trying to put the fix on religious liberty tomorrow morning. Get over there and head Pat off at the pass."

"Right," Murray said crisply.

"The restaurant is in the Piazza Sforza."

"I know," he said. "Thanks, Kevin." The line went dead.

I held the door open for the young woman, whose brown Sophia Loren eyes were dancing in anger. I bowed most politely and apologized in broken Italian for my rudeness. At first she was monumentally chilly, but red hair has a way of thawing the feminine heart. She finally smiled and accepted my regrets with a pretty wave of her hand.

I retreated to a bar on the Corso Vittorio Emanuele, the kind of place that made you think it was 1935 and that Greta Garbo would come in any moment. I drank a very quick whiskey straight up, and then another.

Across the street there were only a few patrons at the tables covered with red-checked tablecloths in front of the Borgia house. At one of them I saw two men in cassocks, one with gray hair glinting in the streetlights. Pat was probably delivering the text of the religious-liberty document Martinelli wanted substituted.

I cursed Pat for being naïve, and the Cush for being a lovable victim whenever he roamed away from the security of Boston. I also cursed my American allies for not showing up.

The curses worked. A taxi pulled up across the street. Five men zeroed in on the table. There was much boisterous laughter. I thought I recognized the vast shape of Bishop John Wright, of Pittsburgh, and the tall, thin frame of John Murray. I got into one of the cabs and rode out to Parioli, feeling worn and grim.

I read the newspapers until just before the eleven-o'clock deadline when the good sisters locked the door. Then I went to the crowded common room. Murray and George Higgins, a social-action monsignor from Chicago, walked in smiling broadly. Murray gave me a very large "okay" sign.

The intervention of Cardinal Cushing was canceled at the request of the Eminenza, Felici said hurriedly in the midst of many more elegant announcements.

The Curia had still won, though. At the last business session of the Council before adjournment, one of the Council presidents announced that voting on the two declarations, scheduled to begin momentarily, had been postponed to the next session.

There was a roar of dismay from the Council fathers. Meyer pounded the resident's table so hard that it shook. He swept by a startled Ottaviani, almost knocking that poor old man down with the speed of his movement. Ottaviani would later assure American friends—honestly enough, it turned out—that the dramatic Curial coup had caught him completely by surprise, just as it had them.

I fled the Aula of St. Peter's, sick to my stomach in disgust at the Church and at the Pope. The man was a disaster. He had no courage when it came to times of crisis. He'd blow all the big ones.

The next day, Mo drove me to Fiumicino Airport, again wearing her pale-green minidress. We kissed chastely at the airport.

"Same question, Kevin," she whispered in my ear as we parted. "What's in it for you?"

"Same answer," I said. "Besides, I get to kiss pretty women occasionally."

"You won the battle but lost the war," she said sorrowfully.

"Meyer doesn't think so. He thinks the fuss they stirred up afterward scared the Pope more than the Curia people did. We've paved the way. The declarations will go through at the final session next year."

"I hope you're right," said Maureen. "You know, Pat's singing Meyer's praises now, says he's the greatest of modern churchmen."

I squeezed her arm and got in the passport-control line. "He's right, Mo."

The Big Dutchman didn't live to taste victory. He was dead within a few months, of brain cancer.

And as far as the Archdiocese of Chicago was concerned, I was dead, too.

Patrick Donahue, however, was very much alive.

CHAPTER THIRTEEN

1966–1967

Patrick Donahue insisted that I come to dinner at the Archbishop's mansion early in March of 1966. "A little reunion of the Romans," he insisted. I didn't see how I fit into the "Roman" category. The new boss was Daniel Cardinal O'Neil, overly friendly and loquacious.

"Glad to see you, Kevin," he said, thumping my back heartily. He was a tall, thin scarecrow of a man with a fringe of brown hair around a gaunt head. "Always admired your father's legal work," he added.

He had some little comment for all the guests, indicating that he knew our backgrounds—all very impressive until you realized that his beaming Chancellor, Pat Donahue, had undoubtedly briefed him before we came in.

O'Neil put us at ease, mixing and serving the drinks himself. The booze was first-rate, as was the elaborate dinner served afterward. The conversation was neither serious nor deep, mostly ecclesiastical gossip and story-telling. As the red wine began to flow and the steaks were served, no one much cared.

I had one Jameson and a single glass of the white wine. I was fascinated by the man, much as the fly is fascinated by the spider. He was a hurricane of words, swirling, pounding, reeling, spinning, utterly unpredictable save in one respect: the subject was almost invariably himself.

"What's that pastor of yours like, Larry?" he asked one of the very young "Romans." "Drink a lot?"

The newly ordained man hesitated, giving O'Neil the answer he needed. "Not really, Eccellenza. He was a military chaplain, you know. Rather a stern disciplinarian."

"Never was a chaplain myself." The Archbishop swallowed a huge bite of steak. "Had a lot of experience with them, though, when I was working in the secretariat, right next door to Monsignor Montini, our present pope. Spent some time in Berlin after the war. Flew into Tempelhof on the first DC-6 to land there after the surrender. Helped them organize the Berlin airlift. Rome played an important part in that, you know. Never did get out. It'll all have to wait for my memoirs, I suppose." Finished, he knocked off a full goblet of wine.

I took a sharp look at the Archbishop. There were no DC-6s in Europe until several years after the war. When the airlift began, in 1948, O'Neil was already Chancellor in Paterson, New Jersey.

"Enjoy your time in Rome, Kevin?"

"I was glad to see the religious-liberty declaration passed, finally, during the fourth session," I said. "It means a lot to this country."

"If I could only tell you the full story about how hard we had to fight to get that through," he went on, spearing another steak from the big platter in front of him. "Would you believe that some of those Roman scoundrels tried to get poor Cushing to propose an alternative draft at the end of the third session? Had to fight like hell to stop it. I made a couple of calls the night before to get some of the Cush's friends to talk him out of it. A near thing, let me tell you."

Did he know that I was the one who had called Murray? Unlikely. So he had heard the story about how Cushing was headed off at the pass and had simply made himself the hero of it.

Pat kept right on eating his steak, not batting an eye.

I decided to experiment.

"Well, certainly those of you who got the petition to the Pope that afternoon, after the Curia blocked the voting at the third session, turned the tide."

Pat's eyebrows went up as though I had just arrived from Mars. O'Neil had not lifted a finger that day. Indeed, he had been conveniently unavailable when Cardinal Meyer looked for him to get his name on the petition.

O'Neil nonetheless rose to my bait. "That was a near thing, too, Kevin, let me tell you." Another goblet was emptied. "If I had not pushed that petition, they would have won. We sure did a lot of work in those few hours. I could tell by the look on the Pope's face that he was pleased. Gave him just the muscle he needed to turn the tide. Why, he once said to me . . ."

I was listening no longer. My mind was numb.

Pat didn't seem very happy with me when he shook my hand at the door of the archepiscopal mansion. "He's really a fine churchman, Kevin," he said, his eyes pleading.

"Bullshit," I said.

March 5, 1967

Dear Mo,

I've found the man. He's perfect . . . well, not really, but he'll do very nicely. He's a psychiatrist and—can you imagine what my family will say—he's Jewish.

He's tall (well, compared to me anyway), has curly brown hair tinged with gray, a thin refined face—he looks like an Old

Testament ascetic without a beard. And he has gentle, gentle brown eyes.

I don't care whether he marries me or not. I'll put it more strongly. I won't marry him, not for a while anyway. I want to be a wicked widow for a couple of years to find out what it's like.

Your friend Pat is a big man in the Chicago church now. He looked terrible at his father's funeral in February. Haggard, tired, anxious.

I'll keep you informed on the psychiatrist.

Love,
El

"Did you ever think of marrying, Kev? I mean, have the woman in mind and see it as something you might very well do?"

Joe Herlihy, Marty's older brother, shivered in the raw March wind at Mount Olivet Cemetery. We had just committed to the earth the mortal remains of Annie Prindeville, born in County Galway, Ireland, sixty years before. Her son, Tom, his eyes red and his face bitter, pulled the ritual from the hand of the parish priest and read the graveside prayers, imposing the Church's final blessing on his mother. Tom's wife—Sister Mary Dolores, that was—held his hand fiercely and shouted the responses in loud defiance. The rest of us joined in, realizing more or less that we were participating in an act of rebellion. Even Joe Herlihy, vice-chancellor and a member of the Cardinal's staff, said the prayers.

"Since ordination, you mean?" I said to the vice-chancellor. "Hell, no, Joe, I've been too busy."

Joe shook his head. "I mean ever, Kevin. Is there a woman somewhere who might have been your wife?"

I wondered if Joe, driven almost to distraction by our lunatic

Cardinal, was thinking of leaving the priesthood. We began to walk back to the cars, through the gravestones and around the snow drifts that still dotted the harsh brown turf of the cemetery.

"There was one such," I said in a rare moment of candor, as the frozen turf crunched under my feet.

"Did you ever wonder what it would be like?"

I didn't want to pursue the subject. "Pure hell for her, I fear. My sister, Mary Ann, says I would have made a bad catch."

"The Pope is issuing an encyclical on celibacy this spring—one on social action first, which will be liberal, and then one on celibacy, which holds the line. Pat says the issue is dead as far as Paul VI is concerned."

"You don't need your boss's Roman sources to figure that out," I snapped, as we climbed down from the little knoll at the edge of the graves, sloshed around in a drift, and came to Joe's car. "It's easy to be liberal on things outside the organization and conservative inside. Takes no courage at all."

"What do you think, Kev? Your background ought to give you a sound opinion." He opened the door on the passenger side of his black Pontiac.

"Why must I have an opinion? I don't know what I think about it." I got into the car and slammed the door irritably.

Joe started the engine and waited patiently for the cars ahead of us to work their way out to 111th Street. The sky was gray. Weather forecasts predicted more snow. I was sorry I'd been curt with him. He had a lot to put up with: a crazy cardinal, plus Pat, five years his junior, promoted over his head to become Chancellor. Not to mention a diocese coming apart at the seams.

Moreover, Joe had saved me from Daniel Cardinal O'Neil two years ago. After Meyer's death, and before the arrival of the Archbishop of Newark as his replacement, I was transferred out of St. Praxides and assigned to the university itself. Joe insisted on the transfer, arguing that I could do weekend work at St. Praxides and would be in a safer position if the new Cardinal didn't like scholars. I was angry at Joe and called him some pretty vile names. After O'Neil had been in town for a few months, I apologized. Poor Leo Mark Rafferty was abruptly retired by the Cardinal, who went around town with a list of old pastors to do in, thus destroying any of the power centers that might have opposed him.

Leo died three months later, never quite having recovered from the Archbishop's statement, "Monsignor, you're getting senile." A cheerful thing to hear from your ecclesiastical superior on the Sunday afternoon before Christmas. The new pastor, sensing that the Archbishop might come gunning for me, told me that he could dispense with my weekend services. After eight and a half years my beloved St. Praxides had been snatched away and I was an exile scholar living in the basement of the Newman Club, cut off from the people I had become a priest in order to serve. Some of the St. Prax kids, now becoming young adults, kept showing up, though. They were all the parish I had.

With nothing much to do besides my research, I turned to popular psychological-religious writing. My first book, aptly called *Self-Deception*, was a huge success. I'd found a new vocation that brought money, acclaim, a national audience, and animosity from my fellow clergy.

"You certainly were right about O'Neil," said Joe, turning on 111th Street at last. "The man is a psycho."

"Antisocial personality, technically, Joe." I was giving what was by now a familiar lecture. "Cannot establish relationships of trust with other persons; does not care about others' feelings, doesn't even know that they have them; cannot distinguish between truth and falsehood; does not keep his promises; has no principles; can be the most charming and personable man imaginable, when he wants to be."

"You don't know the half of it," Joe said glumly. "He's also financially incompetent despite his reputation as a brilliant wheeler-dealer; he's left his other dioceses one step ahead of the bailiff, and he's spending us into bankruptcy."

"How? He's not building new schools or parishes."

"Bad investments. And bribes to Rome. If I could only tell you . . ." His voice trailed off. Then, "And the people he has around him—Pat excepted—are either greedy or dumb or both."

"Worse than I thought," I commented, wondering why Joe was telling me.

"And you don't know about the drinking or the woman," he added glumly as he turned toward the Dan Ryan Expressway.

"Woman!" I was incredulous. "Psychopaths don't have women."

"He does. Her name is Margaret Johnson. They've been together for twenty-five years. She's been in every diocese where he's been. Claims to be a cousin, but there's no real blood relationship. He owns a real-estate business with her son. She's got an apartment over on the drive. They talk on the phone every day. He's with her almost every night." He stopped the car in front of a drugstore on Western Avenue.

"All night?" I wondered if Joe was losing his grip.

"No. He comes home about eleven—drunk to the gills. I was on the second floor of the Cardinal's mansion a few weeks ago. There were women's clothes in the bedroom across from his."

I tried to digest it. "I can't imagine him . . ."

Joe's shoulders slumped even lower. "I don't know if they have sex. He's so crazy, you can't tell. He's been able to keep this going for twenty-five years, and only a few people know. I tell you, Kevin, the man is diabolically shrewd. And yet he's so goddamn dumb. I'm sure there's money being stolen from right under his eyes. Smart enough to keep Margaret a secret and so dumb that they're stealing a fortune on him." I did not want to know who "they" were. "If it wasn't for Pat, we'd all go crazy. You don't know what bishops are like, Kevin."

With painful effort Joe disciplined his emotions and put the car back into gear. "I'd call them a bunch of old women, except that's not fair to old women. They're a collection of effeminate, prissy complainers without any guts. O'Neil is only the worst of a bad lot."

"Meyer wasn't like that," I said.

"No, he wasn't." Joe sighed wearily. "He was as straight and sensitive a human being as anyone I've known. Shit, Kev, I know I'm exaggerating. My problem is that all I've seen lately are the products of hormoneless cronyism."

"If O'Neil keeps this Johnson woman, he must have *some* kind of hormones."

Joe shook his head. "Kevin, if I thought he was really enough of a man to lay her, I wouldn't hate the goddamn bastard as much as I do."

"The best thing you can do is get out of that office. Pat can take care of the Cardinal without your help."

"Funny thing," said Joe. "Pat is the only one who can keep him in line. I wonder sometimes about Pat. He says that the boss is a great churchman. Does he really mean it, Kev? You know him better than anyone."

"Hell, yes," I said. "When he's saying it. That doesn't mean a year from now he won't be saying the opposite with equally honest conviction."

"Pat sure is good with the priests who resign, though," Joe defended his boss. "You know that Pat is totally committed to celibacy, yet he treats them like gentlemen. They all swear that if there were more superiors like him, they wouldn't be leaving."

"I bet," I said, not caring whether I sounded sarcastic.

Back in my rooms, I savored the irony of Patrick Donahue as the great believer in celibacy.

The previous February, on a crisp evening, I had been tramping through the snow in the hills above the lake, trying vainly to puzzle out some meaning in what was happening to the Church and to me. There was a light on in the Cunningham home. Mo was supposed to have been in Rome. She had come to Chicago only twice since the end of the Council, during August and at Christmas. I saw her at my family's house on both trips—looking as lovely as ever.

If Mo was in Rome, who was using her house?

I walked to the side of the house and looked through a small opening in the shade. Maureen and Pat were naked on the white rug in front of a blazing fireplace. The scene before me looked beautiful and sweet and tender. I left quickly.

The next morning I was angry at them for the chance they were taking. I was even angrier at myself for having let Pat deceive me so blatantly in Rome.

April 15, 1967

Dear Mo,

Herb insists that we get married. For the good of the children, he says. He wants a family and I'm a ready-made family. I've enjoyed being a mistress for a few months. He says I'd get tired of it.

I certainly haven't tired of sex. I'm more of a sensualist than I can believe. I want to know and do everything.

It will be nice having a husband again, I suppose. I can quit work and go back to school. The kids will have a father. I won't have to worry about sending them to college.

Oh, damn, Mo, I'm marrying Herb because I'm so wild crazy in love with him that it tears me apart to think about him, and

I'm sick lonely without him. I want him next to me in bed all night, every night.

There, you have the real truth. Beneath the sensualist and beneath the clinician you have Ellen, the teenage romantic, hopelessly in love when she's old enough to know better.

We're going to see Monsignor Pat about a church. Herb says Catholicism is important to me and we may as well settle it now. I think he's wrong. I also think we can't get married in church because he's been married before. I guess I didn't tell you that, did I?

Got to run now.

Love,
El

The Newman Club housekeeper yelled down the stairs that there was a young woman to see me. There was innuendo in her voice.

The rear view of my guest, who stood looking out the window, explained the housekeeper's disapproval. Her trim, solid thighs, emerging from a miniskirt, were enough to make the tongue of even the most discreet rectory housekeeper wag.

"Good afternoon," I said formally.

She turned away from the window. "Good afternoon, Father." There was a call to battle in her intonation of the title.

My water sprite was slender and lovely again, and now unarguably sexy. Also spoiling for a fight.

"You're wearing your hair differently," I said, my heart pounding.

For just a moment there was a chance that her anger would dissolve in laughter. Then her lips tightened in a straight line.

"You can tell the family I won't need this year's check. I'm getting married."

"Congratulations."

"Save it until you hear the details. I'm marrying a divorced Jewish psychiatrist."

"If you love him, Ellen, I'm sure he's a good man. Can we sit down and talk?"

She sat on a hardback chair. "He wants to marry me in the Church. I don't care either way. I want you to see him."

"Why?" I asked softly.

"He knows your work. I want him to meet one priest who isn't a complete fool." Her fingers were moving nervously.

"Why does that make any difference, if you don't care about the Church anymore?"

She took a deep breath, searched for an answer, then twisted her mouth in a sad smile. "Kevin still wins the arguments."

"Only when the opposition contradicts itself," I said. "I'll be happy to talk to . . ."

"Herbert Strauss," she said.

"A well-known name. I'd be happy to take Dr. Strauss to lunch at the Faculty Club. It might make things easier if I knew what, if anything, I was supposed to accomplish."

She gestured in despair. "We saw Pat. He says we can't get married in church unless Herb becomes a Catholic. It . . . it just doesn't seem fair."

"Whoever said 'fair'?" I countered, wishing I could make all the hurt go away forever. "I suppose Pat said that the Church claims no jurisdiction over the doctor's first marriage?"

Her shoulders sagged. "Herb went to Israel when he was seventeen and lived in a kibbutz for two years. When he got out of the Israeli Army, or intelligence, or whatever it was, he married a girl he'd known for three weeks. They were divorced in a year. Herb was twenty."

"I surmise that Pat was very affable and eager to help, and

would have charmed the birds out of the trees. But he's still our Chancellor; the Church still has its laws."

She nodded sadly. "You're a psychologist. Was that a marriage?"

"I'm not a canon lawyer or the Chancellor."

"Oh," she said unhappily. "Pat was so smooth and gushy. I hated him. Phony man-to-man with Herb. Can't I do anything, Kevin? He's such a gentle, refined man. You don't have to see him if you don't want to."

"I want to meet him very much, Ellen. I hope he doesn't judge our heritage by me any more than he does by Patrick."

"I'm afraid I'm the criterion," she said sadly.

Daniel Cardinal O'Neil burst into the room like a cyclone coming in off the plains. He threw a copy of *Self-Deception* on the table with such force that the statue of the Sacred Heart was rattled and the picture of Pius XII on the red-fabric wall shook.

"You write too much, Kevin," he announced, as though the matter were settled.

The word was out that he tried to intimidate you in the first charge. The proper strategy was to stand your ground. Sometimes it was hard, because he was an outrageously intimidating man.

"Two books in two years isn't too much," I replied.

"Who gave you permission to write at all? What about censorship? Where does the money go? Who pays you? What's your canonical status? Do you still hear confessions? What kind of a priest are you?"

"As to the last," I said, "a poor one, like most priests. The answers to the other questions are in my files. Cardinal Meyer gave me permission to write. He also said that I did not need censorship."

"I know those things," he said abruptly. "I can't leave you in this work forever. You'll lose touch with the people."

"My colleagues at the research institute are people, Your Eminence," I said evenly. "So are the young people I work with and the university students."

"Not *real* people!" he exclaimed, playing with his pectoral cross. "You've got to work with real people, Father, to be a good priest."

"Yes, Your Eminence."

"What do they pay you at that research thing of yours?" he demanded, slapping the table with his fist. "We can't have some priests getting rich while other priests do the work."

"They pay me the standard salary for a research associate at my level."

"And how much is that?" he demanded.

"You can find the rates in a number of academic publications, Cardinal," I replied calmly. "As to what my exact income is, I should think the question is pertinent only to me, God, and the Internal Revenue Service. Quite candidly, it is none of your damn business!"

The cyclone seemed to die down. Finally he said, "Well, I expect you deserve what they pay you, and you do produce fine work. A man like you can be a real prize to a bishop. I can tell other bishops that one of my men is so good that a great secular university wants him on its staff. All I ask is that you do us proud."

He went on for almost an hour, fishing for information about the love life of the Newman Club chaplain (nonexistent, I was sure), telling improbable stories, and filling me with so much whiskey that I walked for an hour before daring to drive home.

I never heard from Pat about the confrontation. A couple of months later I stopped receiving mail from the chancery. My name had been pulled off the diocesan mailing list at the Cardinal's instruction, an apologetic Joe Herlihy told me. Joe left the priesthood before 1967 was over, much to the sorrow and pain of his younger brother, Marty, who was still protecting St. Praxides.

May 10

Dear Mo,

Well, we are going to be married in church after all. Guess who arranged it? Wrong, not the Chancellor, but our old mutual friend the Rev. Kevin James Saresfield Brennan—whom my lover thinks is one of God's great gifts to humanity.

I won't explain the boring canonical details. Pat messed it up. I went to see Kevin and had a screaming match with him, as I usually do. Well, at least I screamed. He was very gentle. Then he spoke with Herb and found the loophole. Something to do with Herb's wife being a Jew who became a Catholic for a few years as a teenager.

Herb came back from his lunch with Kevin completely dazzled. It never occurred to me that men would like that son of a bitch too. Herb's trying to sort us out. And he hasn't even met you yet. He doesn't know he's marrying an entire Irish neighborhood, not just an Irish family.

Wait till he meets the Colonel!

Forgive me for babbling.

Love,
EL

Monsignor Patrick Donahue officiated at the wedding of Herbert Strauss and Ellen Curran. Ellen was dazzling in a pale-blue dress that Mary Ann whispered was a Chanel and worth at least a thousand dollars. At last, Ellen could now indulge her taste in clothes.

Ellen was angry at me because I let Pat do the honors. She barely said a word to me at the church or at the banquet. Radiant for everyone else, sullen for the hard-eyed gallowglass.

"An interesting ceremony, your mass," Herb said to me as I walked with them from the banquet hall of the Drake to the lobby. "Very similar to our Jewish service."

"To which you never go," said his new wife, pretending I did not exist.

"Same heritage, actually," I said. "Both are part of the religious culture of the Second Temple era. An anthropologist from Mars would think they were the same religion—which they are. The unfortunate split after the fall of Jerusalem is temporary, even after a couple of thousand bloody years."

Herb's intense brown eyes opened wide in fascination. "What an intriguing perspective. We must talk about it."

"Not on your wedding night, darling." His wife took his hand with firm authority. I was awarded an amused, forgiving smile. "You two intellectuals get into one of your talks and we'll miss the plane to Ireland."

"I'll take good care of her for you," said Herb, warmly shaking hands with me.

⁂

She called at three A.M., Chicago time, from Shannon Airport. "I'm sorry to wake you up, Kevin," she said hurriedly when the overseas operator finally got us connected. "And I'm sorry for being a bitch to you at the wedding, and I'm sorry for all the evil, angry things I've ever said to you. I love you."

"Nothing to be sorry about, Ellen," I mumbled groggily. "Have a great honeymoon."

The next morning, after my second pot of tea, I decided that it was not the most brilliant possible response.

I suffered some bad moments when the Six-Day War erupted. They were in Jerusalem, according to their itinerary, when the guns started to blaze away and the bombs started to fall. As far as I could remember the New City, their hotel was near the Mandelbaum Gate. It took five of the six days for them to get word to us that they had not been harmed.

CHAPTER FOURTEEN

1968

The Monsignor's handsome face was haggard; his eyes were bright. He stretched out his arms, furling his purple cloak in the night breeze. He extended his hands in supplication.

"Please go home!" His voice boomed over the public-address system. He adjusted the lapel mike that was pinned to his red-buttoned cassock. "You have made known your grief and your anger. Now go home before there is any more violence. The memory of Dr. King is not honored by senseless looting. Go home before anyone is hurt."

He moved away from the blue and white police cars toward the mob of young blacks, many with rocks in their hands. The policemen followed behind him at a distance, guns drawn. The street was littered with broken glass. A fire truck pulled up next to the curb. Smoke was pouring from the wreckage of a storefront. Floodlights moved up and down the street.

"You all remember me. I played basketball here with you a few years ago. Please go home before anyone gets seriously hurt."

A young black, his face twisted with hatred, threw a rock, not at the Monsignor but at a policeman behind him. There was a volley of shots. Several black youths tumbled toward the ground. The others broke and ran. The Monsignor swayed momentarily and then slowly collapsed. The purple on his cassock was now mixed with a deep red.

The announcer's voice came in over the sounds of the sirens and the gunshots. "You have just seen a filmed report of the shooting of Monsignor Patrick Donahue, Chancellor of the Archdiocese of Chicago, who was wounded earlier this evening while trying to end the riots that have erupted on the South Side. The riots are in protest of the assassination yesterday of Dr. Martin Luther King, Jr. Monsignor Donahue returned to the neighborhood in which he served as a parish priest only a few years ago. A spokesman at Mercy Hospital said that Monsignor Donahue's wound is not critical. Cardinal O'Neil rushed to Mercy Hospital to be at the side of his Chancellor as soon as he heard of the shooting." There was footage of Dan O'Neil going into the hospital. His concern about his Chancellor did not prevent him from smiling and waving to the television cameras. "It is rumored that Mayor Daley has asked President Johnson to send the 101st Airborne Division to Chicago to maintain order. They will come too late for Monsignor Donahue, the third-highest-ranking priest in the archdiocese, who was accidentally shot from behind by a Chicago policeman."

I turned off the television set. It was a foolish, crazy, brave gesture. The kids with the rocks were not the ones with whom Pat had played basketball ten years ago. They probably didn't recognize him. To get caught between the kids' rocks and the cops' guns was asking for trouble. They'd never find the bullet that had creased his shoulder; probably the officer who fired the gun didn't even know that his stray bullet had knocked down the Chancellor of the archdiocese. A black churchman might have been able to do something. A white man in purple robes. . . .

But who was I to criticize? Misplaced or not, his courage was a response to the riot. I was content to sit in my basement, watch the show on television, and wait for the arrival of the 101st Airborne.

If Rome planned to make Pat a bishop, they'd better do it soon. Daniel Cardinal O'Neil could not stand seeing any of his priests getting attention from the press. Monsignor Patrick Donahue was now a media hero. His fall from grace with the Cardinal was certain.

⁂

Maureen and Ellen were in Pat's hospital room when I got there the morning after the shooting. He was resting comfortably, protesting that it was no big deal, asserting that his shoulder would feel fine when the elephant got off it, and ridiculing his stupidity for causing all the trouble. It was a very impressive performance. The television folks would have loved it. I wasn't sure about the Cardinal.

"Great of you to come, Kevin," he said for maybe the fifth time. "The Cardinal just left."

"He seemed to think that he was the one who was shot," said Maureen angrily.

"Maureen," Pat reproved her sternly, "he was worried about me." Pat looked remarkably fit and relaxed for a man who had had a brush with death. Grudgingly, I admired him.

"He was concerned that you might wear yourself out talking to the press," said Ellen. "Said he'd be happy to take care of them for you. Very kind and considerate man."

I permitted myself to take a closer look at Mrs. Herbert Strauss. My first impression had been correct. It wasn't just her smart gray wraparound dress that made her look gorgeous. Ellen was obviously happy.

"Write a story about him for school," said Maureen with a laugh. "Can you believe it, Kevin? Ellen is back in school, studying for a degree in creative writing."

"Well, Ellen, just don't write anything negative about the Cardinal," Pat pleaded, now looking disconsolate and tired.

"I won't, darling." She kissed him on the forehead. "And now I think I'd better take these terrible, anticlerical people out of here and let you sleep. Do stay in the hospital till they release you. Don't listen to His Eminence about how much he needs you at the Chancery." She turned to us, very much like a head nurse, and ordered, "Out!"

We went quietly.

"Come see us sometime," Ellen said, parting from Maureen and me to find her car.

"Sure," I said. But there was no reason to see Ellen Foley Curran Strauss. She was off my worry list.

Maureen was still on the worry list, though. We took a walk along the lakefront, just north of Navy Pier. Mo had her trench-coat collar turned up against the damp mists drifting in off the lake. The towers of Northwestern Medical School and the Hancock Center faded in and out of view in the fog. The elegant Mies van der Rohe glass blocks towered haughtily over their Victorian neighbors.

"You should be glad that evil man prevented you from getting on the birth-control commission," she said, shivering either from the fog or from the thought of Cardinal O'Neil, whom she'd met for the first time at Pat's bedside.

"I thought their report was first-rate," I said. "They gave Paul VI a way out if he wants it."

"That sanctimonious faggot," she spat out bitterly.

"Even for me that's too much, Mo," I protested. The rush hour traffic was roaring by us on the Lake Shore Drive.

"I'm sorry," she said contritely. "You know I don't give a hoot about the Curia. I keep track of it only for Pat."

"When you're not painting," I said.

We turned the curve at the foot of Oak Street and looked

down the long, mist-flaked, golden canyon of Michigan Avenue's "Magnificent Mile."

"I do some of that, too," she said.

We walked silently for several minutes, drawing close to Oak Street Beach. Maureen now came back to Chicago every couple of months. She had been at O'Hare, waiting for a delayed flight to Rome, when she heard the news of the shooting. She rushed back to Mercy and somehow managed to see Pat before the Cardinal did.

"You know about us, don't you, Kevin?" she said quietly, taking me by surprise.

Our footsteps were echoing in the underpass beneath the drive. "Yes, Mo, I know."

"What do you think of us?" she asked, much as she would ask what I thought of her new trench coat.

"I hope you don't get caught," I said lamely.

She laughed. "Oh, Kevin, you are such a darling; always worrying about your friends. Right or wrong, we're still your friends. Okay, after you hope we don't get caught, *then* what do you think?"

"I don't think it's good for either of you. He's not going to leave the priesthood."

"Of course he's not leaving," she said impatiently. "I want to be his mistress, not his wife. He doesn't need a wife, and I don't need a husband."

"What happens when he becomes a bishop?" I said. "He's on the list, you know."

"Sure I know it. I live in Rome, remember?" Her heels were beating a tattoo on Michigan Avenue as she increased her pace. "He'll probably try to leave me then. I won't let him. He can't survive without me, Kev. He'll make a wonderful bishop so long as I'm around to tell him what to do and give him some warm nights in bed. I've found my challenge, you see. I imagine it's not exactly the challenge you had in mind."

"He won't be the first bishop—" I began.

"Celibacy may be fine for someone like you," she said, pushing her hands into her coat pockets. "It won't work for Pat, as we both well know. That's no reason why he should not be a priest . . . or a bishop." After a moment of silence, she asked, "Are you going to turn us in?"

"It's pretty late in the day for me to think about that, isn't it?"

"You never understood Pat." She shook her scarf-covered head as though she were a teacher trying to instruct a reluctant student. "You're good to him, but there's always part of you sitting up there on the Colonel's judicial chair, evaluating, categorizing, forming an opinion, and then passing sentence on Pat. You don't see how generous or how devout or how serious he is. You don't see what the priesthood means to him. You don't see how he loves the Church and the Blessed Mother. You don't see how patient or kind or sensitive he is."

"I guess not," I said, wondering whether they talked about the Blessed Mother in bed.

"I know all his faults," she raced on. "I know them better than you do. I can also look at the good things to which you've blinded yourself, Kevin. I see a wonderful man who is going to do wonderful things for the Church. Just give him a chance."

"Now who's doing the rebounding?" I asked bitterly. Maureen began to sob quietly. I put my arms around her and held her for a moment. "I think what you're doing is foolish and dangerous and wrong, and I still love you," I said.

She laid her head against my Aran Islands sweater and rested it there. "He is a fine man," she said, pleading. "If you knew him as I do, Kevin, you'd love him as much as I do."

❋

The little girl brought him a bouquet of wild flowers she had picked in the park. She was a beautiful, delicate little thing with shining eyes and a smiling face. "I love you," she said shyly.

"I love you too, Sheila," Pat said, stroking her hair. She needed a father. What did his own daughter look like? A couple of years younger . . .

"Why don't you come more often? I miss you when you're not at our house." She climbed onto his lap. Maureen said that the child was transformed when he was around.

"I have to travel a lot, Sheila," he said. "I'd like to be with you more."

"I don't have a daddy," she said, her eyes filling. "Other girls do, but I don't."

"God's the daddy for all of us." He held her tight.

"Will you come and stay with us and be my daddy all the time?" She put her small hand on his face.

There were tears in his eyes. "I'd like that very much, Sheila. Maybe someday I'll do that."

Satisfied, she ran off to play on the swings.

The little girl's haunted eyes were still in his mind that night while he was making love to her mother and when he caressed her gently to sleep. It would be good to be with her and her daughter for the rest of his life. Everything else was straw.

❋

Sunday morning, after mass, I was standing in back of the Newman Center at the university. The new chaplain decided that he didn't much care about the Cardinal and had asked me to come up out of my cave. I was by now a pariah in the archdiocese. I wrote too many books, made too much money, was not part of the parish structure, and was known to be anathema to the Cardinal. The new chaplain needed another Sunday preacher.

"As long as they don't find out downtown what I'm doing, to hell with them," he said. He was an early convert to the concept of a dispersed diocese. In a few years everyone would be thinking the same way.

A pretty young woman came out of the chapel and rather shyly approached me. She looked to be in her early twenties, with short, curly blond hair, thin shoulders underneath her cloth coat, and a clear complexion glowing in the chill spring sunlight. Then I recognized her. "Monica Kelly! Back in town?"

She wasn't sure whether she should hug me or not, and decided she should. "Back from journalism school. Got an apartment near the university and a job at the *Tribune*."

"A long, long time, Monica. I didn't recognize you at first. You're even more beautiful than I thought you would be."

She blushed, muttered something about blarney and then, "I've got a whiff of a story I'd like to ask you about," she said shyly.

"Do you want to go inside?" I asked.

She shook her head, blond curls flying. "No, Father, it's not all that complicated. I know you're a friend of Monsignor Donahue. I wonder if you've heard anything about the financial scandal in the diocese."

"I haven't heard anything, Monica," I said guardedly. "What have you heard?"

"I know that the Cardinal lost four million dollars last year from the funds of the National Conference of Catholic Bishops. Bad investments. He's the treasurer, you know. I also know that the man who handles the Church's investment portfolio at the Illinois National Bank is going to be indicted next week. I know the Internal Revenue Service is investigating some of the Chancery staff. I know that Monsignor Donahue has been having anxious conversations with the Church's legal council. What do you make of it all, Father?"

I chose my words very carefully. "I don't know anything about it, Monica. You *might* be on to something—but be careful. There are some nasty people involved in the money end of things at the Chancery office."

"From Cardinal O'Neil on down," she said sweetly. "By the way, Father," she said as she turned to go, "great sermon!"

⁂

The week after Bobby Kennedy was assassinated, I was in dazed, mourning Washington, hunting down a grant for more research on the subject of emotional well-being. I had dinner with a highly placed member of the National Conference of Catholic Bishops who was interested in the implications of my work for parish renewal.

"You ought to write your next book on local religious community," he said over coffee.

"A good idea, Bishop," I said, and then took a leap in the dark. "Maybe my royalties could go to bail out the diocese after O'Neil runs it into bankruptcy."

"What do you know about that?" the Bishop said, picking up his coffee.

"Four million down in bad commercial papers. IRS investigations. Indictments of an associate. Press still silent because they're afraid." Then, as a throwaway, I added, "Mafia involvement."

The Bishop spit out his coffee. "In the Middle Ages they'd have burned you as a witch," he said, trying to regain his composure.

"Pat Donahue clean?" I asked.

"Who knows?" he said, frowning. "Probably. It's all confused and uncertain. O'Neil has been in Chicago only a few years. Rome doesn't want to send a visitator to look at the books as yet."

"They knew he made a mess out of every other diocese. Why should they think this is any different?" I demanded.

My friend shook his head. "This is much worse, not merely because Chicago is bigger but because for the first time it goes beyond mere incompetence. The Justice Department told us that there was a possible violation of the Securities Exchange Act in the commercial-paper affair. They didn't go ahead, because no one wants to drag a cardinal before the court and because it may have been an innocent mistake. O'Neil isn't a crook—not exactly, anyway. Some of the people around him are certainly corrupt. The investment man, for instance, has bilked people of millions. No reason to assume he's made an exception of the Church. Right now everyone is afraid to touch it."

I ordered an Irish Mist for the two of us. Clean or not, Pat was on the fringe of big trouble.

On the way back to Chicago I decided I'd not tell Monica Kelly anything. She might be the one to bring O'Neil down. She might also bring down Pat and get hurt badly in the process herself. I was sure O'Neil would do himself in eventually, just as Leonard Kaspar had done.

They rushed out of the warm water and sprawled on their big blanket. As far as they could see in either direction, the wide beach was deserted. He felt rested for the first time since he had been shot. Riding the surf gave him a sense of healthy contentment, like a man being rehabilitated after a long war. If only the blazing Mediterranean

sun, the purple waters, and the comforting sand could be the only realities—they and the topless woman breathing heavily on the blanket next to him.

He shifted, rolling over on his stomach so that he would not see her breasts. Maureen thought he was able to compartmentalize his life, making love to her and still playing the role of bishop-to-be without guilt. If only it were true. Since it wasn't, now was the time to tell her that their lives had to change. Though shame and humiliation gnawed at him, he said, "We've got to stop, Maureen. I've got to get my life together. I can't be a bishop and live this way. I can't go on being a hypocrite." His voice broke.

She was silent, chin on her chest, feet pushing the sand relentlessly.

"I love you, and I will always love you," he said. "I'm not ashamed of our love. I'm ashamed of my own hypocrisy."

"You're not the only hypocrite in the Church," she said softly. "Anyway, the Church is going to change, probably when we're too old for it to matter. Why should we wait?"

"It's not going to change, surely not for bishops. If you want"—he fell back on an old argument—"I'll decline the bishopric, resign from the priesthood, and begin a new life."

"Don't be stupid," she said impatiently. "You wouldn't be happy in middle-class domesticity, and neither would I."

"Then we've got to go back to Rome now, and I must be chaste again," he said grimly. "I know I can do it this time."

"No, you can't," she said, and her hands began to explore his body.

"Stop, please, Maureen, stop," he begged, pushing her away. "This is the end. I mean it."

He stood up and walked purposefully back toward the dirt road and their tiny Fiat. He waited a long time until she joined him.

⁂

On July 25 the birth-control encyclical was issued. My family was at the lake. I was water-skiing with my brother Mike and his new bride, Kathy, a brunette fashion model with an IQ approaching a hundred sixty. When we got back to the house on the hill, the rest of the Brennan family—Mom, Dad, Joe, Mary Ann, and her husband—were all sitting grimly around the front porch.

"NBC wants you to make a comment. Film crew on the way," said the Colonel, looking more upset than I'd seen him since he came home from the war.

"Don't worry about me," I said. "I've got nothing to lose."

I read the text of the encyclical. It was worse than I'd expected. The Pope had not responded to the majority report but had merely dismissed their arguments.

That night, Pat Donahue and I were aired back to back on Channel 5 on tape. Calm and cool, Pat read a statement in the name of the Cardinal. "We welcome the decision of the Holy Father, which will put to rest the considerable unease of many people in the archdiocese over this problem. We are sure that all the Catholic laity will respond enthusiastically to the Pope's decision and that in the fullness of the mature reflection of their conscience they will make the proper decisions on this difficult and delicate matter."

"What does that mean?" said Kathy.

"It doesn't mean anything at all," I said impatiently. "O'Neil left for Alaska when he heard the encyclical was appearing. Pat is left holding the bag."

"It means something, Kevin," said my father. "Pat is tossing the issue into the laps of the conscience of the laity."

"Because he knows as well as anyone else that the laity are going to make up their own minds."

"If enough chanceries react that way," Mary Ann said, her

eyes as cold and shrewd as the ones I often saw in my mirror, "won't priests get the signal that they can do whatever they want?"

"They're going to do that anyway," I said. "At least in Chicago they're not going to be hassled."

Then I was on the network news telling a troubled Catholic reporter that the encyclical would be ignored.

"Most priests and lay people have made up their minds," I was saying. "They will not change them. I'm not saying this is the proper response. Only that this is the likely response."

"You think that they will disobey the Pope?" the reporter persisted.

"It is not likely that they will obey him." I'd avoided the word "disobey."

"Then they will leave the Church, will they not?" he said, pushing me.

"A few will. Not many," I replied.

"But, Father Brennan," said the reporter, "some people are saying that Catholics will leave the Church and others are saying that they will obey the Pope."

"And I'm saying both statements are wrong. The Catholic people will neither leave the Church nor accept the letter of the encyclical, however much they may admire its spirit. I do not think priests or bishops will try to enforce it. I don't see how they *can* enforce it unless they put spies in every Catholic bedroom in the country."

My mother gasped in astonishment. Everyone else laughed.

"Then you think that . . . uh . . . *Humanae Vitae* will have no impact on the Church."

"On the contrary," I said, "it will be a disaster. Many people will feel that the Pope did not listen to their problems and that he betrayed them. Priests and nuns are going to leave in ever-increasing numbers. I do not wish to dispute the integrity of the decision. I am saying that it will exact a terrible cost."

Herb Strauss was on the phone almost at once.

"Kevin, you should be a television personality all the time. Brilliant! Many Catholics will be liberated by what you said."

"Only confirmed in their own convictions," I said.

"Who was that?" asked the Colonel when I returned.

"Herb Strauss."

"Which reminds me," said the Colonel. "You wouldn't mind if we sell him the land by the old swimming hole, would you? He wants to build a house up here for Ellen and the kids. Your mother and I figure that we shouldn't hoard all the land on the hill."

"And the money will help us build a bigger house in Florida," Mom added.

"Buy half the state of Florida," Steve added.

They wanted Ellen for a neighbor. I didn't want anyone to buy my magic pond. On the other hand, Ellen was the logical choice if it were to be sold.

I threw up my hands. "Why the hell should I care if you want to let Jews into the neighborhood?"

August 10

Dearest Ellen,

You are such a priceless friend. All these years you've been telling me the truth and I've been lying to you . . . or at least deceiving you. Or maybe I haven't. Maybe you guessed about my affair with Pat.

It was one more case of Old Mo trying to straighten out a weak man. Then I got trapped. There was so much in it for me, physically and psychologically, that I stopped thinking about how crazy it was. Then he ended it. Now that he's a bishop he wants to be chaste. That's not unreasonable, is it? I was furious with him, which shows how messed up I was.

It's over now and I feel as if I've recovered from a long illness. I'm a new woman. I'm painting up a storm and dating a young widower from the embassy.

I think I helped Pat. I can't really be sure. Maybe I was kidding myself all along. I pray that he can make it by himself as a bishop. He means well. Only he's weak, like me. And he's dumb . . . no, that's not true. He's very smart, street smart and brain smart. The trouble is that he's got his life cut up into little cells that don't communicate with one another. So he does dumb things.

Well, it's over, and I can live again.

Be good to Herb and please don't confuse me and Pat with you and Kevin. Different altogether.

Bless you,
Mo

The day the Apostolic Delegation announced that Patrick H. Donahue had been appointed titular Bishop of Heliopolis and auxiliary to Daniel Cardinal O'Neil, Archbishop of Chicago, I was in Mercy Hospital visiting what was left of Monica Kelly. Her face was swollen and bruised. Her jaw was wired together. Her nose and cheekbones were broken. The young resident, a dark, handsome man, told me she had been raped repeatedly and that her breasts had been lacerated with a sharp instrument. There were more than forty cigarette burns on her body. Her front teeth were broken off. She stared at me with dull, blank eyes.

"What are her chances, Doctor?" I asked when we stepped out in the corridor.

"We can put her back together again," he replied. "She won't look all that different from before. But I don't know what we can do about the psychic harm. She was a virgin, you know, Father. An innocent child. At best, it will be a long way back."

It was a professional job. Only the Mob did that sort of thing, and they did it only when someone was getting too close to something serious. Monica Kelly was not all that important, only a young woman who once told me I'd preached a nice sermon. She was also a victim of the crookedness that infiltrated the Archdiocese of Chicago. I vowed that I would get those responsible—even if it meant doing in the titular Bishop of Heliopolis, the youngest bishop in America.

Pat was consecrated a bishop by Cardinal O'Neil, Archbishop Martinelli, and the apostolic delegate in early September. Maureen did not fly in from Rome, and I did not feel that I belonged at the celebration. Herb and Ellen, according to Mary Ann, sat quite close to the speakers' table.

One Chicago laywoman, well over sixty, interviewed by a television reporter, observed proudly, "He's a fine boy. I've known his mother all my life. Mark my words, he'll be cardinal someday."

I smiled grimly over that one. Cardinal O'Neil would not be amused at all.

The massive exodus from the Church, as predicted by liberal Catholic journals in the wake of *Humanae Vitae,* did not occur. Catholics made an important discovery: you can ignore the Pope, and life goes right on.

"And this, Bishop, is our second-grade class. Most of the girls are seven years old. Say hello to the new Bishop, girls." The old nun's dry fingers snapped a signal.

The children curtsied respectfully. The sisters still taught them that. There were still a few things unchanged in the world.

"One of the children will speak for the others," said the lay teacher. Not enough religious to go around, not even in a convent school.

A pretty little blond girl came to the front of the class. The Bishop felt as though an iron ring were clamping shut his heart.

The little girl curtsied. "Good morning, Bishop," she said in a faint but steady voice. "My name is Patricia Carrey. All of the second-graders welcome you to our school. We thank you very much for the wonderful things you've done for our people. We hope God helps you to be a fine Bishop. We will pray for you." She hesitated, took a deep breath, then remembered. "Will you pray for us? And now will you give us your e-e-episcopal blessing, please?" She sighed with relief and knelt in front of him.

The rest of the class knelt, too. He struggled to find his voice. "Thank you very much, Patricia. Thank you all, second-graders. I'm sure that God will listen to your prayers for me much more than he listens to my prayers for you. God loves you very much . . . and . . . and so do I. Now—" he paused, felt the room whirl around him, and then doggedly went on. "Now, may the blessing of Almighty God, Father, Son, and Holy Spirit, descend upon you and remain with you always."

He kissed the top of Patricia Carrey's head.

Later, in his room in the cathedral rectory, the Bishop wept bitterly.

BOOK IV

The Seventies

CHAPTER FIFTEEN

1970

"I wish he had come back the next year, Father." Harry Willewski shook his head, now covered with short, thick gray hair. "I always wanted to beat the shit out of that guy." He rubbed the top of his bare desk regretfully. "Jesuit never even got to the playoffs that year, damn it."

"And Quigley didn't play varsity then," I said gently, not wanting to disturb Harry's nostalgia for the days when neither of us was getting close to forty. Harry's office in the Federal Building was all steel and glass, a southeast corner befitting the first assistant United States attorney for the Northern District of Illinois. The furniture was the same steel gray as Harry's hair. From the floor-to-ceiling windows one could see the south end of the Loop, Grant Park, and the lake in the distance. Harry's round face was even rounder, his massive body going slowly to fat, the fate of athletes whose jobs eat into their exercise time as they struggle with the multiple crises of midlife.

"How the hell do you keep in such good shape?" he said, playing with a North Korean bayonet turned letter opener, delaying the question that had brought me to his office. On one of the shelves behind him was the picture of a pretty woman and a flock of kids.

"Handball, karate, and genes," I said. "You see any extra weight on the Colonel?"

"The less I see of that man the better," he said, and laughed, not altogether humorously. "I want to throw in the towel every time he walks into a courtroom."

The air-conditioning didn't work very well, and the summer sun was turning Harry's office into a greenhouse. I had an appointment on Michigan Avenue in an hour. I didn't want to be late.

"What's up, Harry?"

"I owe you a lunch at the Lawyers Club," he said, starting slowly. "Hate to have you come in this way. And, incidentally, Father, I appreciate your not wearing the Roman collar."

"The name is still Kevin," I said, shifting in my uncompromising steel chair. "And let's have it, Harry."

"Your friend Donahue is up to his purple buttons in slippery financial dealings. I don't mean the unwise investments, the securities violation, or any of those things. There's something strange going on at the Chancery. Too many lay people who work there have too much money. The Mob is in it—one of the fringe groups that the dons tolerate. We've got enough hints to launch an income-tax probe against two of them, and that's going to start a chain reaction. Your friend is the comptroller as well as the Vicar-General. He signs the checks. Either he's part of an embezzlement scheme or he's letting them get away with it. If this thing ever gets off the ground, he could end up doing time in Lexington, bishop or not."

The Federal Building seemed to dip and whirl around me. I hoped the steel chair was tied firmly to the floor. "The Cardinal—he's not very bright."

"Not very bright!" he shouted. "O'Neil sells land for half a million that the next week goes for three quarters of a million.

Not very bright? He's a flaming lunatic. And that money is part of my salary and the salary of everyone who throws in a picture of Mr. Lincoln every Sunday." He groped for his professional cool. "Sorry, Father," he said.

"It's still Kevin, and I don't blame you for getting angry. All the Cardinal does is ship money off to Rome—thousand-dollar mass stipends, and the like, for his cronies. Half-million-dollar gifts to the Pope. He's not an ordinary embezzler, too, is he?"

"We don't think so," he said, and sighed heavily. "Mind you, we're afraid to touch it. Who the hell wants to bring a cardinal and an auxiliary bishop before a grand jury? We just know that Mr. and Mrs. J. Bernard O'Keefe, *née* Sally McCormack, have a lot of money and are seen frequently with an up-and-coming outfit punk named Dom 'the Dummy' Corso. O'Keefe is the coordinator of services at the Chancery, and Sally's the Cardinal's personal secretary. They both own Cadillacs, live on Lake Shore Drive, go to Cortina for ski vacations, and wear clothes that would cost me a year's salary. They're not paying their bills out of their salaries."

J. Bernard O'Keefe was a handsome, broad-shouldered man whose tanned face suggested careful sunlamp treatment. His wife, a statuesque platinum blonde, caused more than a few clerical heads to turn when she walked through the thickly carpeted Chancery corridors. Both of them were sleazy second-raters, fugitives from the world of business. As my father said of J. Bernard, "He's the kind of Holy Name Society president who if he was a plumbing contractor would give the local parish an estimate two times higher than anyone else and expect to get the contract on the basis of his good looks and friendship with the pastor."

"J. Bernard O'Keefe," I said to Harry, "is a vampire."

"And Dom 'the Dummy' makes J. Bernard look like a vegetarian." Harry was playing with his damn bayonet again.

"He's the one who messed up Monica Kelly," I said with sudden insight.

Harry regarded me with surprise. "Yeah, he did it. She was getting close. Not too close, but Dom likes to mess up women. We can't pin it on him. After the election in November we're going after O'Keefe and his wife, regardless of the Church. Tell your friend Donahue to get rid of them before then or we'll have to go after him, too." He slammed the handle of the bayonet against his desk.

"So you want me to act as an unofficial messenger between the United States attorney for the Northern District and the Vicar-General of the Archdiocese of Chicago?"

He leaned back in his chair. "That's the academic in you, Father. The Colonel would never make it that explicit."

"Do me a favor," I said, getting out of my chair. "Get Dom Corso."

"Still play for keeps, don't you, Kevin?" He shook hands warmly.

"To win, Harry, as you may remember." I turned to the door.

"What's the girl to you?" he asked curiously. "And how's she doing?"

"She liked one of my sermons. These days that's enough. And she's not doing very well. All right physically, I guess; still messed up psychologically. May be that way for the rest of her life, though the *Trib* has her doing rewrite stuff now."

Harry shook hands again. "Do me a favor and have Donahue take us off the hook. I'll take care of the Dummy for you. A deal?"

"A deal," I said.

I was depressed. Clerical reviewers tore my books apart, mostly through personal attacks on me, though the secular reviewers thought they were fine. I wrote books, attracted attention, had a nonpastoral job, made money, and hence was an outcast. If I gave up all those things, I could be humble again and happy.

I considered the possibility, since the university power elite had made up its mind to deny me tenure. Their position was that only a priest who withdrew completely from priestly activities and priestly authority could be a good social scientist. As a high-level administrator put it, "You don't have to leave the priesthood, of course, Mr. Brennan. That's no affair of ours. We simply need to know that it won't interfere. If we can have some proof of that, I'm sure most of the objections will be withdrawn."

The same administrator told one of my shocked colleagues in social psychology, "A priest can no more be an objective scholar in psychology than can a card-carrying Communist, and for the same reason: his convictions will dictate his findings."

My stubbornness kept me where I was. I'd be damned if I'd give either the university or the Cardinal the satisfaction of driving me away. Then, to add to my problems, I had a run-in with Georgina Carrey, come back from my past to haunt me.

It shook me badly. It happened at the time of the Kent State tragedy. The research institute, which I now headed, kept right on going, though with some fear on our part that the angry kids might blow it up.

I was sitting in my office, watching a televised mass meeting at Chicago Circle. Father Rick Flannery, a disciple of the Berrigans, was talking—a tall, lean man, looking like the leader of a group of medieval flagellants.

"It is time to tear this rotten society apart," he shouted. "This is the revolution we've all been waiting for. We're going to go forth from this rally and bring America to its knees. We will make bombs, find guns; we will burn, trash, and destroy. We will become the Lord's great winnowing fan, sweeping through this city and purifying it of sin and corruption. We will bring

Chicago and America before God's judgment seat. We will paralyze the corrupt capitalism of this sinful country. We will set free the poor and the miserable of the world. Down with America! Up with the poor! Long live the Democratic Republic of Vietnam! All power to the people!"

One of my colleagues was watching television with me. "Almost think he was a Protestant," he said.

Back on the black-and-white screen was the worn, handsome face of the Most Reverend Patrick H. Donahue, auxiliary Bishop of Chicago. They couldn't have a peace march or demonstration these days without Pat's showing up in full robes, a change of style, surely, from the scraggly sweatshirt of Rick Flannery.

Pat waited patiently for the young people to quiet down, his imposing face and figure demanding silence and finally getting it.

"My dear young friends," he began slowly, "the war in Vietnam, whatever it was supposed to have been, is a tragic mistake. The bombing is evil and immoral. The killing of students exercising their constitutional right of assembly is a crime that cries to heaven. Your protests represent the American political tradition at its finest. I am proud to be with you today to lend my personal support to your protest. You will end the war in Vietnam. You will turn America around. You will revive the American soul. You will begin a new era in American history." Every sentence was being interrupted by thunderous applause. "We will only end the war when we gain control of Congress. We must elect peace candidates in November all over the country. Our protest here today is not merely a cry of outrage against the terrible things that have been done in the name of our great American heritage. We are going forth from here absolutely committed to sending a majority of peace candidates to Congress in November. We shall overcome!"

At this, they began to sing the hymn. Rick Flannery embraced the Bishop as though the two of them had said the same thing. Some of the smarter professional peace types looked unhappy.

The newspapers gave Bishop Donahue unstinting praise for diffusing the threat of the mass meeting. Actually, the kids would have gone back to their homework anyway.

Late in the afternoon, my secretary told me that a Mrs. Carrey was on the line. I'd been half expecting to hear from Georgina now that John was dead.

"You saw him on TV?" she said bitterly.

"I did," I responded, feeling guilty that I had not gone to John's funeral. His massive heart attack had come without warning, leaving Georgina one of the richest women in Chicago.

"I'm going to get him this time," she said so softly I could hardly hear her. "Now that John's dead, I have nothing to lose."

"That's up to you," I replied. I wanted to get rid of her and return to my typewriter. Georgina was into right-wing politics, and, as best as I could gather from her statements to the press, she advocated atomic bombing of Hanoi *and* Peking.

"I'm also going to destroy that friend of yours with whom he's been sleeping," she said even more softly.

"What friend?" I said, wondering if she had used private detectives to watch Pat.

Her voice became a screech. "You know which one! You'd better come to my apartment this evening, or I'll call the Apostolic Delegation tomorrow morning. I've got proof."

The maid let me into the fifteenth-story cooperative overlooking the lake, informed me that Mrs. Carrey would be with me shortly, and then let herself out the door. Inlaid floors, Oriental rugs, a couple of Jackson Pollock originals, and one mobile that had to be a Calder. Georgina had acquired taste as well as money.

There was a bar at the side of the parlor. I mixed myself a very large Jameson's on the rocks and drained it in three gulps as I watched the traffic speed by beneath me in the fading sunlight. Thunderclouds were rolling down the lake. In the back of the apartment I heard the sound of running water—someone taking a shower, perhaps. For the first time since she called, I wondered if the subject might be something other than Pat Donahue. I poured myself another Jameson's.

I kept waiting. The third Jameson's was my worst mistake—even worse than agreeing to see her. I was halfway through it when she appeared, smelling like a fresh spring garden, a purple towel tied at her waist. My brain reeled, more from the Jameson's than from her chest, though heaven knows that was splendid, too.

She was an artfully prepared picture. Her hair, now subtle silver, was long, partially covering her large, firm breasts, which quivered as she walked. She was thinner, paler, and, despite the years, much more attractive than she had been when I first met her. So, the revenge was going to be a spectacular seduction, I thought.

"Good evening, Father Brennan," she said. "I knew you'd come." She stood over me.

I drained the Jameson's. "You look good, Gina," I said, pretending to appraise her carefully while my blood surged toward the boiling point, fury contending with desire. Then the inevitable image of Ellen. "Remarkable what they can do with cosmetic surgery these days."

"You're not going to put me off that easily this time," she said. "Either you make love to me or your friends are going to be all over the *Sun-Times* the day after tomorrow." She walked over to the bar, splashed some gin into a crystal tumbler, and swayed provocatively back toward me.

The weariness and depression of the years cut away at my defenses. "You're a cheap old whore, Gina," I said, "and a pathetic one at that. I don't give a damn what you do to Donahue. If you want to mess up Patsy's life, that's your problem. I'm going home."

I got up to leave, still not sure whether I could make it. I eased my way toward the door, praying I wouldn't fall on my face. I had to get out quickly, before I could change my mind.

My booze-liberated tongue fired a parting shot from the door. "Mind you, Gina, surgery or not, your tits really look good for someone your age."

⁂

At noon the next day, when my hangover began to lift, my secretary told me a young man was waiting in my office.

"Tommy Varco," he said, extending his hand. "Remember, we met at Mercy?"

"Monica's resident?" I shook hands warmly. Monica still came to Sunday mass, pale, quiet, and fretful. No cheery comments about my sermons. Rather, she avoided me whenever she could.

"I need a favor," he said simply.

"I know the word," I admitted, putting my feet up on the desk like a ward pol. "Hey, are you the plastic surgeon? That's a fine job you did on Monica. She looks great."

He beamed. "Glad you like it. I'm proud of the outcome. She looks as sweet as ever." Then the joy vanished from his face. "Well, as sweet as her pictures looked. I didn't know her before."

"Mm," I said, being "nondirective" until he got to the point.

"As you can imagine, I fell in love with her," he said sheepishly.

"Thoroughly intelligent reaction," I said. "Does she respond?"

"More or less." He sighed. "She likes me, but the trauma . . .

She . . . well, she thinks she's ruined for a man. In a way she's right, but not in the way she thinks. If she doesn't come out of her depression, she never will be able to marry. That's where the favor comes in." His eyes were intensely bright. He was a young man hopelessly in love. "There's a psychiatrist who's the best in the Midwest on these problems. He's got a huge backlog of patients. I've heard you know him, and, well, Monica really worships you, and I thought—"

"Herb Strauss?" I asked.

I picked up the phone and dialed a number from the wheel on my desk. Tommy looked like an Italian version of Herb—darker hair, lighter skin, wiry athlete's build, broader shoulders.

"Herb? Kevin. I need a favor. A woman named Monica Kelly, roughed up badly by the Outfit. Great. A Dr. Varco will be in touch."

Tommy Varco's eyebrows were as high as the steeple on the University Chapel. "Thanks, Father," he mumbled. "Monica isn't sure she wants to see another shrink. Some of the ones at the hospital were a little rough on her. When she finds out he's a friend of yours, she'll trust him."

I felt a little less depressed that night.

May 7

Dear Ellen,

I'm going to give it to you straight. You've got to stop acting like an ass and settle up with the Church. The faith didn't give Tim his embolism, it didn't make your mother a bitch and your father a weakling, it didn't even saddle you with four kids before you were thirty. You know a lot more psychology than I do, so you know that all our problems are inside ourselves. If your life was a mess, you chose to make it a mess; if you've straightened most of it out, you chose to straighten it out. I don't give a damn about you and the Church, except you need it and want it so much and you know you do.

None of us can really ever get away from the Church. It was too much a part of our life when we were growing up. Maybe we don't do all the things it says we should do, but we still count on it when we need it.

Forgive me, El, for shouting at you: I thought I gave it up long ago. Your last letter made me so mad. You don't have to torment yourself about religion of all things. Leave Kevin out of it. He's just a distraction.

Anyway, I'm praying to the Madonna every night. The locals here say she always hears your prayers when you pray for someone else. So I give you fair notice: you've got an Italian madonna closing in on you.

Love to Herb and the kids.

Mo

Patrick Henry Donahue was in his sparsely furnished room in the cathedral rectory. He wore an obviously tailor-made collarless white shirt with French cuffs. He had lost weight and seemed hollow and worn, his eyes listless. I congratulated him on his fine talk at the Circle rally. His eyes lighted only briefly. Then I told him about Willewski's message. He turned the color of his shirt.

"As God is my witness, Kevin," he began, his voice quivering, "it's not my fault. It's going on all over the country. They all act as though it were their money to do with as they please. Hospitals, old people's homes—millions and millions down the drain, and no one knows. They think because they're bishops and priests they can lie and steal, and we have to cover for them to protect the Church. I admit I've tried to cover up, but I've not used a cent for myself."

"I know you haven't," I replied, putting my feet on his expensive ottoman. "You *have* signed a lot of checks, however. That's enough to make the government suspicious. How much do you know?"

There was perspiration on his face, despite the noisy air-conditioning. His hands were trembling. He needed a drink, though it was only eleven in the morning.

"I know there's something going on. Bernard and Sally are running the office these days. Thc Cardinal ignores me." He shook his head in dismay. "They're living far above their salaries. I think they play the horses. I have no evidence. There's no way I can get evidence. I don't know what to do. I've prayed for guidance."

Can't you do anything right without Maureen to call the shots for you? I thought to myself. "The Colonel says they're probably kiting checks. Someone at the bank is part of the ring. Do you write checks for petty cash? Do you see them when they come back?"

"I'm the comptroller, still. Dan . . . uh, the Cardinal, doesn't fire people, just takes away their power. I still sign them, but Sally doesn't give me the canceled checks when they come back."

"The next time you sign a petty-cash check, call me. Stall O'Keefe before you give it to him so you can get a Xerox. The first thing the next morning, we'll go to the bank. The president is a friend of the Colonel. We can get the canceled check quietly so they don't know anything's up. We make copies of it. Then we put the canceled check back into the archdiocese's file at the bank. We've got the evidence, and they won't know."

He shook his head dismally. "What do I do with the evidence? The Cardinal won't listen to anything against Sally or Bernard."

"Go to the delegate. Have him send a visitator," I said sternly.

What had happened to the confident speaker at the rally? More compartmentalization of his life.

"I can't do that, Kev. The Cardinal would know the next day. The delegate would never accept the evidence. He'd be furious. Would you go?"

Another rebound. Mo had been right. I still got my kicks out of rebounds. "Sure, I'll go. And then on to Rome, if necessary. Would Martinelli—"

He held up his hands in horror. "Oh, no. Tonio is very close to the Cardinal. You would have to see Benelli. He's the undersecretary of state."

"I've heard of Benelli," I said impatiently.

The next Friday afternoon Pat called me at four-thirty. "I'm at a phone booth, Kev. I don't know whether Sally listens in on my calls. I signed a fifty-dollar petty-cash check this afternoon. Bernard was very angry at me, but I delayed long enough to get a copy made. I hope you know what you're doing. I think . . . I think the Mob is involved."

"Damn right they're involved," I said.

The Colonel, thank God, had not yet left for the weekend. He would talk to the bank president and call me back. In two minutes he was on the phone.

"You and Pat have an appointment with Mr. Murphy at my office at ten. You've got the keys, so be there early. I'm going to have some of my friends . . . see that Pat gets discreet twenty-four-hour protection. If you don't mind, I'll inform Harry Willewski."

The next morning an ashen Cornelius Murphy compared his copy of a draft for five thousand dollars with Pat's copy for fifty.

"It's carelessly done," he muttered in dismay. "They must have been doing it for a long time to be so confident of themselves.

I'm sure some of our personnel are involved. Bishop, this must run into hundreds of thousands . . ."

"More like millions!" I exclaimed.

"What are you going to do, Bishop?" Murphy asked nervously. "Should we begin an investigation immediately?"

"I don't think so, Mr. Murphy," Pat said. "Make some discreet inquiries, but be cautious. We've got to be very careful at our end to make sure we have all the evidence we need. Give me"—he looked at me for approval—"a week or so."

I nodded.

"Very well, Bishop," Cornelius Murphy said grimly. "We'll get to the bottom of this; mark my words."

I thought to myself, As long as we don't end up at the bottom of the lake, wearing concrete gym shoes.

CHAPTER SIXTEEN

1970

Archbishop Raffaelo Crespi was not interested. He kept me cooling my heels in the waiting room of the Apostolic Delegation for more than an hour, an old ecclesiastical trick for putting you in your place. From the outside, the Delegation looks like many of the other buildings on Embassy Row. Inside, it looks like an oversize rectory or convent, with the same papal pictures, the same expensive but ugly rugs, and the same mismatched and uncomfortable furniture.

Finally Crespi appeared, his habitual scowl even deeper than usual. He ignored my proffered hand. "I do not normally see priests who are not in good standing with their own cardinals," he said unpleasantly.

Crespi, a short, fat man, viewed the Washington assignment as a reward for a career of loyal service and an opportunity to go home to Rome and his red hat with a tidy fortune for himself and his family. The delegate received gifts on the appointment of new bishops and also at the time of their installation, if he was present. Crespi managed to be present for almost all of them.

His squat figure, dark skin, and low forehead made me think of the stereotype of a Mob hit man. Idly, I wondered if he were a relative of Dom the Dummy.

I told my story. He did not bother to hide his skepticism. I gave him copies of the checks. He hardly glanced at them. I presented the letters from Con Murphy and Harry Willewski. He refused to look at them.

"Archbishop," I said, "if you don't believe me, you can pick up the phone and call either Mr. Murphy or Mr. Willewski."

"Why should I do that?" he shouted. "It's all absurd. Who is Murphy? Who is Willewski? The Cardinal has not spoken to me about this. Why should I take a discredited priest like you seriously? Why should I believe this ridiculous fable? You are wasting my time."

He rose to dismiss me.

"In less than a month, Archbishop, the United States attorney is going to begin an investigation. Cardinal O'Neil and Bishop Donahue will be subpoenaed to appear before the grand jury. Bishop Donahue may well be indicted. I promise you that the Pope himself will know that you refused even to make a simple phone call to confirm my story."

Crespi hesitated. He saw his red hat hanging in the balance. He looked at me with cunning in his tiny eyes. Was I insane? Probably.

"You are a suspended priest," he began, his lip curling in contempt.

I pulled out my file. "I am not, Archbishop. Here is my file. You may inspect it."

He waved it away. "You would hide the documents of suspension. I will report this conversation to Rome. They may wish to act on it. I myself refuse to take you seriously. Now you must excuse me." He turned and strode out of the room.

He had found the solution. Kick the buck upstairs. Then he couldn't be blamed if anything went wrong. His red hat was safe.

A driving rain was washing Massachusetts Avenue when I emerged from the Delegation. My suit was soaked before I stopped a cab. Crespi would surely call O'Neil, who would doubtless blab to O'Keefe. Before sunset, Dom the Dummy would know. Pat's life might be in danger. I chafed nervously as my taxi crawled toward the Statler through the rain and the rush-hour Washington traffic.

Still soaking wet, I made my first call as soon as I got to my room.

"Bastard," the Colonel said, most uncharacteristically. "What are you going to do?"

"No choice. I've got a reservation out of Dulles in three hours. I'll be in Rome tomorrow morning."

"Will they see you?"

"I'll call Mo. I'm sure she can fix it." I wasn't sure at all, but it was the only card. "Can you increase the guard on Pat? And Monica Kelly, too? The Dummy may want to amuse himself again."

"All right," said the Colonel. "I'm worried about the O'Keefes, though. If they think they're cornered, God knows what they might do."

"They've lived dangerously for a long time," I said. "Maybe they think they're invulnerable."

"I hope so," said the Colonel doubtfully.

I placed the call to Rome and peeled off my wet clothes. I was in the shower when the phone rang.

"Hello." Mo sounded sleepy and confused.

"I've got to see Giovanni Benelli tomorrow afternoon. It's a matter of life and death. Tell him I said that, and that there are millions of dollars at stake."

"Kevin?" she said groggily. "Is that you, Kevin?"

"Still getting my kicks with rebounds, Mo." A pool of water

was gathering at the foot of the phone table. "Benelli, tomorrow afternoon. I'll be on TWA flight 890."

"It's easier to get a personal audience with the Pope than with Benelli," she said.

"If anyone can swing it, you can, Mo."

"I'll try," she said. "Will you stay with me, or should I get a hotel reservation?"

"I'll stay with you," I said without hesitation. What the hell—she wasn't *my* mistress. "Can you meet me at the airport?"

"Why not?" she said. "Be careful, Kevin."

⁂

My heart stopped thumping when the mobile lounge at Dulles lumbered out to the 747.

On the plane going over I met John Mikolitis, a kid from 67th and California who had been on the second string of our city-championship team. Unlike Willewski, John was trim and fit, a rawboned, balding blond.

"I work at the embassy in Rome," he said. "I was home for my grandmother's funeral. Marvelous woman, escaped from the Cossacks by running across the border when she was sixteen."

"Harder to run these days, I guess." I sipped at an after-dinner drink.

"Yeah," said John, leaning easily against the vacant seat in front of me.

"What do you do at the embassy?" I asked, to make conversation.

A slight tenseness in his round jaw. "I work for the government."

"One of those," I said.

"You object?"

"Not I," I replied.

"Pat might." The jaw was even stiffer.

"Depends on whom he was talking to. He could talk for or against the Company with equal vehemence. That's the word, isn't it? 'Company'?"

"In some novels."

I filed the information. Who knows when you'd need a contact in the CIA residence on the Via Veneto.

At precisely eight-thirty the next evening I was shown into the large office of Archbishop Giovanni Benelli, technically the undersecretary of state and, in fact, the chief of staff of Pope Paul VI. Mo dropped me in the cobblestone courtyard at eight, earning me an extra-special salute from the tall, handsome Swiss guard. A series of ushers conducted me from anteroom to anteroom. Benelli offended the Vatican style by working through the siesta hour. He offended it even more by working into the night. I suspect he offended it most of all by his passion for punctuality, an unheard-of compulsion in the Curia.

Benelli's walnut desk was as clean as Harry Willewski's. There were no decorations on the wall. The chair to which I was wordlessly waved was more comfortable than Harry's government issue. Giovanni Benelli's head was almost entirely bald, his brown eyes luminous and intelligent, his posture as tense as a coiled spring. His hands, folded in front of him on the table, seemed curiously passive in comparison to the rest of his body, which radiated enormous energy. Giovanni Benelli was an explosive charge ready to go off.

"Let me see your documentation, Father," he said without preliminaries. "Monsignor Crespi thought you might come to Rome."

I stood up and tossed them on his desk with, I fear, very little ceremony. "Xeroxes of the checks, the letter from Harry Willewski, the letter from Cornelius Murphy, and my official file, without any notification of suspension." I hoped I sounded as tough as I felt.

"What do you think of Monsignor Crespi?" he said in the same tone of voice I had used.

"Monsignor Crespi is a fool. Two phone calls and he could have saved me this trip, you another appointment, and the Church potential embarrassment. There may also be a life or two at stake."

Benelli looked at me intently for a moment and then turned to the documents. He examined the Xeroxes of the checks very carefully, read and reread both letters, and then glanced through my file.

"So," he said, "the great Meyer was fond of you."

"Never could figure out why," I said.

"Unlikes attract, perhaps," he muttered as he looked again at the checks. "Bah! Clumsy forgeries. Fools, fools."

"Which fools are you referring to, Your Excellency?"

Then I was favored with the famous Benelli smile—wide, contagious, utterly disarming. "In this case, Father, everyone but you and me."

Rebound tipped again.

He rearranged the material in a neat little pile. "Do you think we are unaware of Chicago?" he asked. "Do you think we do not know about your Cardinal? Do you think we don't realize our mistake?" He fired the questions as if from an automatic weapon. "Do you know that the fool once tried to give me a thousand-dollar stipend to say a single low mass? Do I look like the kind of man who would accept that kind of bribe? Do you think we do not know how your mayor had to hide the drunken-driving arrest? Do you think we know nothing?"

"I don't know what you know, Archbishop. In any case, O'Neil wasn't your mistake."

The fingers of his hands tapped the desk slowly. "You must understand, Father, that His Holiness was terribly hurt when he was sent by Pius XII to Milan. He is most reluctant to do the same thing to anyone else. In my case"—again the smile—"that is excellent, or many men in the Curia would conspire to send me much farther than Milan." The hands made a quick gesture and returned to their position. Very small hands.

"In the meantime," I said bluntly, "millions of dollars are stolen, lives are ruined, and Chicago is turned into an ecclesiastical wasteland, all because of the Pope's sensitivity for the Cardinal's feelings. He worries about a psychopath and ignores the rest of us."

Instead of blowing up, as I expected he would, Benelli flicked open my file.

"Ah, as I thought, you are a psychologist. So that is your diagnosis. Mine, too, I must say. . . . Well, Father, what are we to do about this problem of money? That must be dealt with first."

"First of all, appoint Bishop Donahue as visitator for finances. Give him the power to bring in an accounting firm and start an investigation. Let him clean house in the administrative end of the Chancery. Let him fire the O'Keefes. Don't make his appointment public. Something is bound to leak out. It can be made to appear that the irregularities were caught quickly by Bishop Donahue's alertness. Don't let the Cardinal get his hands on the money again."

Benelli nodded thoughtfully. "Would you suggest that these instructions be made clear in detail to Monsignor Donahue in the brief that is sent him?"

"As clear as possible, and they ought to go out tomorrow."

His high forehead furrowed. "I will do what I can, Father.

Tell me, is there a company in Chicago that will audit and administer the finances?"

"Arthur Anderson," I said. "The best there is."

"Good," he said, standing up. The hands now went under his red sash. "Return at the same time tomorrow night, Father. I make no promises. I will do what I can."

He walked toward the door with me. Then the famous smile, for the third time. He shook hands with me.

"We are grateful, Father," he said simply.

I declined dinner with Mo at Tre Scalini and instead returned to her apartment. Sheila was asleep. Earlier in the day I had tried to hug her, but she was cool and distant, a lone, unhappy little girl.

"Something wrong with Sheila?" I had asked casually.

"She misses Pat." Mo would not look at me. "He has a wonderful way with children. I think she blames me for losing him."

I sipped espresso and ate cake while I told Mo the story from beginning to end. She listened silently, her usually expressive face as immobile as Ellen's used to be.

"Benelli will handle it," she said confidently when I was finished. "He's even smart enough to know that you've got to give Pat detailed instructions." She shook her head. "At least Pat sees through O'Neil at last. What do you think they'll do?"

"My guess is that they'll give O'Neil a harmless job here, bring in someone else as archbishop when Pat's got the worst of the mess straightened out, and then, after a few months of transition, give Pat a good but small diocese. After that, the sky's the limit, I think."

Mo had replaced her summer dress with a thin—and quite

chaste—white robe. She held the collar together at the neck with fingers that seemed much too thin.

"That would be the sensible thing to do. You can never be sure in this town, though." She tightened her fingers on the robe, as though she feared to tempt me with the sight of her throat. "What do you think of him now, Kev?"

"I wouldn't want Giovanni Benelli as an enemy," I said, going after another piece of cake.

She smiled wanly. "I meant Pat."

There was only one light on in her elegant parlor, casting subtle shadows over the chairs and table. Our silhouettes looked like classical figures on the wall. The street noises of the nearby Piazza Farnese seemed many miles away.

I rubbed my hand across my forehead. "After all these years, I don't know what to say. I know I'm too harsh on him, and I have to watch everything I say because I'm so conditioned to be cynical about him. He's been a good auxiliary and VG under difficult circumstances. He's spoken out more bravely than most on public issues. He's holding the Church in Chicago together. He's courageous in this financial mess, when his life may well be at stake."

"But . . ." She released her grip on the robe. It was a very lovely neck.

I shrugged and poured my fourth cup of tea. "But nothing."

"You think he's shallow and unpredictable and maybe even a bit of a conscienceless person, just like O'Neil, don't you?" She sounded like the Colonel examining a witness. "You think there's something missing in his personality, especially because he's never been very good at celibacy?"

"There's something missing in everyone's personality," I said, "mine included. There must be an inner core of something good about Pat. I've always wanted to help him. And you love him."

She reached for a Kleenex and began to weep quietly. "I know I'm well rid of him, yet I miss him terribly."

I decided that it was time to tell her about Ellen's new "environmentally sound" house at the lake and to ask discreet questions about her painting, of which she was still doing very little.

When I went to my room to go to bed, she kissed me good night, affectionately. "You're wonderful, Kevin," she said softly.

"I take such praise wherever I can get it," I said, returning her kiss.

I locked the door to my room when I stripped for a shower. Then I felt ashamed of myself and unlocked it.

⁂

The next night Benelli was standing when I entered his office, just as the clock of St. Peter's chimed eight-thirty. He handed me a large, unsealed envelope.

"You may read it if you wish, Father," he said expansively, his hands still in the sash. "It contains everything you asked for."

I sealed the envelope, which was addressed to Monsignor Patrick Donahue. "Not necessary, Eccellenza. I trust you."

A very big grin this time. "Should you ever want to work here—" he began.

"We'd shout at each other every day, Eccellenza," I replied.

We both laughed.

"How much money, Father?" he asked, serious again.

"As a guess, between three and four million," I said. "Presumably Pat will keep you informed. There may come a time when you decide that you don't want to know the exact figure."

He nodded sadly. "As to the other matter, Father, I will do what I can. Again, I make no promises." He sighed expressively. "The Cardinal has given gifts to many people, many highly placed people."

"I know you will do your best, Eccellenza," I said. And meant it.

⁂

Pat acted quickly. The O'Keefes were fired on Friday; Arthur Anderson's accountants discreetly appeared the following Monday morning. The Colonel unobtrusively installed himself at a desk in the Chancery. Harry Willewski paid a visit to Pat and later called me and said, "The son of a bitch turned into a good guy. He's doing this thing right."

"Any indictments?" I asked.

Harry hesitated. "I really couldn't say, Kevin." Then, "Oh, hell, you've a right to know. We don't want to indict them. It would do more harm than good. Anyway, they're going to slip again, and somebody—another jurisdiction, maybe—will get them."

Harry meant that his boss knew that an indictment involving those who worked for the Church would be an enormous political liability.

Dom the Dummy wasn't satisfied, however.

Pat called me just before the Labor Day weekend. "Did you see the papers?" he asked, his voice hushed.

"I've been busy trying to catch up on the jet lag and my work. What's happened?"

"Sally O'Keefe was beaten and raped and slashed last night. They made Bernard watch. My God, Kevin, what have we done?" He sounded stricken.

"We haven't done anything," I said, "but I'm going to do something."

I called the Colonel and told him what I was going to do.

"You're playing God, Champ," he said.

"If the government of the United States and the State of Illinois can't protect people, then do we have a choice?"

Another pause. "You're right, Kevin. I wouldn't have the courage to do it; I'm too civilized, I guess. That isn't an insult, Champ. Sometimes a little bit of uncivilization is necessary."

"Furthermore," I argued, "he might want to try for a repeat on Monica. We all owe her something for blowing the first whistle."

"You're right, Champ," he said slowly. "I'll have them double the guard on her for the next couple of days."

I sat looking out the window of the research institute for a long time. The campus was deserted. The building was almost empty. I should head for the lake and the last dregs of my wrecked vacation. I knew I wouldn't. I wrestled with my thoughts a little more, decided that, either way, I was playing God, and that my first obligation was to protect those I cared about.

Though I'd called before coming over, Monica opened the door of her apartment on Fifty-third Street very tentatively, the chain latch left on. She looked wary and tired. When she saw it was me, she brightened. There was a trace of the innocent smile I'd seen on the face of a High Club sophomore so long ago.

"I'm sorry, Father," she said apologetically, clutching her robe at her neck, just as Maureen had. "Tommy had me out late last night, and since I had the day off, I thought I'd catch up on my sleep."

The facial reconstruction was perfect. A paper-thin white line here and there somehow made her even more attractive. "Tommy seems to take a lot of interest in his patient," I said lightly.

"Tommy's my Pygmalion. He's remade my face and my body and fallen in love with his own work."

"You read too damn much if you think that," I said. "And where's the tea for the priest?"

She came back in a few minutes with tea and chocolate-chip cookies.

"I must thank you for Dr. Strauss, Father. Now that I know I'm going to make it, everything's different."

There would be a wedding by Christmas. I was damn well going to be there as officiant. I told her about the story. She could have it if she wanted it. I also laid down my conditions. She listened thoughtfully and nodded.

"It ought to be told, Father, and I'm the one to do it. Okay, I'll call my editor." She was back in a moment. "He said go. I promise you it will appear that the theft was found quickly through the alert work of Bishop Donahue."

The story appeared in the Sunday papers. Dom Corso was named explicitly as the torturer of Sally O'Keefe. The O'Keefes' losses in horseracing were alluded to, as well as their discharge from the Chancery by the Vicar-General, Monsignor Patrick Donahue. It was broadly hinted that the O'Keefes were victims of Corso's "juice" racket. There was no comment from Bishop Donahue. A Chancery source (Kevin Brennan, to tell the truth) explained that Bishop Donahue, learning of the involvement of the O'Keefes with gamblers, had no choice but to terminate their employment.

The Cardinal was not mentioned; nor was there a hint that the O'Keefes were part of a ring of embezzlers. Monica did not report the firings from the bank, because I did not tell her about them.

In the end, O'Neil adamantly refused to accept a transfer to Rome, but Pat was sent to Benton Harbor, Michigan, as bishop of that city. The Arthur Anderson men stayed in the Chancery, and no more money was stolen there. The Cardinal, however, kept selling property at bargain prices and sending thousand-dollar mass stipends to Rome.

⁂

On Thursday, the housekeeper told me there was a visitor in the office.

"I said to myself, I'll just show up and sit there till he sees me," Ellen said with a dubious grin.

She was attractively pregnant in a maroon maternity dress.

"I suspect congratulations would be well received," I said.

"It's so different this time." She sat primly on a chair in my office, a novice still, if a pregnant novice. "I didn't have time to know whether I wanted the other kids or not, poor dears. This little fellow"—she patted her belly—"we've wanted for a couple of years, and he just wouldn't cooperate. Serves me right, I guess."

"I'd say that he's very lucky. Irish-Jewish genes are hard to beat."

She reached into a hand-tooled-leather attaché case and took out a thin book. She offered it to me hesitantly. "Peace offering."

The book was entitled *Nutmeg,* and was written by Ellen Foley.

"Herb said it was an Irish book and I ought to use my Irish name," she explained.

It appeared to be a collection of comic essays about family life.

"Congratulations," I said.

"Look at the dedication, Kevin."

" 'For all the Brennans,' " I read out loud. There was a sting in the back of my eyes.

"Advance sales are over fifteen thousand," she said complacently. She was pleased as punch with herself. "And I'm setting up a scholarship fund for seminarians in honor of the Colonel."

She hesitated, her gray eyes now clouded with worry. "Will he mind?"

I leaned back in my chair. "Mind? Does a polar bear mind snow?"

There was an awkward pause between us. So this was why Ellen wanted to see me—to give me a book and tell me about the way she would repay our gift.

"I want to go to confession, Kevin," she said, now very serious.

"I'll get a priest," I said, moving toward the doorway. "Just go into the chapel and—"

"You don't understand. I want to go to confession to you." She knelt on the floor in front of me. I wasn't going to be given much of a choice.

"Bless me, Father, for I have sinned," she began. "It's been . . . Oh, Kevin . . . It's been almost ten years . . . I'm scared!" She took my hand.

"I'm kind of scared, too," I said.

"I suppose the worst thing I've done besides staying away for so long is . . . well, I committed fornication with Herb many times before we were married. I seduced him as coldly and as calculatingly as I could." Her head was bowed now so I couldn't see her face. "He didn't have a chance. I liked doing it, Kevin, partly because I enjoyed defying the Church."

"Wait a minute," I said. "I don't think you believed it was very wrong then, and I don't think you believe it is wrong even now."

Her hand relaxed. "I was so confused and angry. Would you let me get away with saying I was confused and angry and did things I'm ashamed of?" She still wouldn't look at me.

"So long as you don't include landing Herb in the things you're ashamed of."

She giggled. Then, turning serious, "I spend too much on

clothes. I'm terribly vain. I get impatient with the kids, and I snap at Herb. I'm sorry for that every night when I say my prayers."

"You say prayers every night?"

She finally looked at me, eyes enormous with surprise. "Of course I do. I can't go to sleep without telling God good night. Even when I'm mad at him."

Fornication, seduction, impatience with kids, and telling God good night. Doubtless she told God good night even when she jumped into her sinful bed with Herb.

"I'm still waiting for the real sin, the only sin," I said.

She tilted her head. "I've told everything."

"You haven't told the one important thing. You were mad at God and mad at the Church and pretended for a long time you could get away from both."

"I don't want to talk about it," she said.

"Then no absolution," I said firmly.

She tugged her hand to free it. I wasn't going to let it go. "Don't you have an ounce of compassion in that ice-cold soul of yours?"

"If you want compassion, Ellen, go to your husband or have him recommend a psychiatrist who will listen sympathetically. If you want absolution, don't play games."

She stopped tugging. We were quiet for a long time.

"That's the only one that does matter, isn't it?" she said. "All right, Kevin, I'll say it, and you'll have to mop up the tears on this hard floor of yours. I blamed the Church and God for things that were inside me and my family. I focused on all the ugly things and forgot about Father Conroy and Sister Caroline and first Communion and May crownings and High Club dances and midnight mass and all those wonderful things that I love so much. I gave them all up because I was angry. I blamed the Church for Tim's death. I loved him so much. I couldn't save him, and I thought the Church should have saved him. Even when I was doing it, I knew I was wrong and that someday I'd be kneeling on the floor before you and pleading to be let back in."

"And now you have done it," I said, feeling a huge burden lift away and go spiraling off into space. "And the damn-fool Church says, 'Ellen Foley Curran Strauss, we really didn't notice you were gone, because we never let you go.' "

She put her head against my knee and wept. Then she gathered herself together and said, "So Ellen's worst sin was against Ellen. . . . For these and all the sins of my life I am heartily sorry and ask pardon of God and penance and absolution of you, Father. Is that the way we say it, Kevin? I feel so dreadfully out of it."

"It will do," I said, relaxing. "And the penance is going to be a big one. Say the Lord's Prayer for the men in your life—your father, Tim, Herb, your sons, Pat, and me."

"Only one 'Our Father'?" she said in surprise.

"I don't think God needs to hear it twice to know what prayer it is," I said, and then uttered the words of absolution—or of reconciliation, as we must now call them. I permitted my hand to rest on her blond head for a moment before I helped her up.

"Will you baptize my baby?" she asked.

"I will," I said.

"And will you come have dinner with us often?"

"I will," I said again, though I wasn't so sure about how often. "I want to know your children better."

Ellen sparkled with maternal pride. "Oh, Kevin, I'm so proud of them all."

"Fine parents."

There was a quiet moment—not anxious, just quiet—while we both thought of Tim.

"Thank you," she said brightly.

At the door, she spun around abruptly. "I don't want to leave without apologizing to you, Kevin." Her eyes were wide and anxious. "You must forgive me for the terrible bitch I've been to you." A single magic sentence wiping out a decade of anger.

"I really think you're entitled to a dispensation that permits you to be angry at me anytime you want. I'll forgive you, Ellen, as I hope you have forgiven me."

CHAPTER SEVENTEEN

1970–1971

December 27

Dear Mo,

You'll never guess what new mother, carrying her infant son and surrounded by her four other children, walked down the aisle of St. Luke's at midnight Mass to receive Communion for the first time in ten years? With her Jewish husband beaming proudly, as though he had won a convert?

Now I'm reconciled to both the Church and Kevin, neither one of which seems prepared to admit that I was ever unreconciled. It was as if I'd received Communion the day before yesterday.

I do love Kevin most dearly and am no longer angry with him. He is still terrified of me, though I think he'll relax with me only when I've offered to sleep with him and he's had a chance to say no.

Anyway, it's going to be a very happy New Year for me. I'm starting on a new book. I owe you for much of my happiness. Is there any way I can help to make your New Year happy? Please give me a chance if there is.

I've got two sick kids—too much Christmas—so excuse the short letter.

Love,
ELLEN

P.S. If Kevin said yes, I wonder what I'd do.

As I flew back from Christmas vacation with my folks, in Arizona, I was not in a happy mood; nor was I particularly cheered by the presence of the two young Jesuits who were sitting next to me wearing clericals, an unusual phenomenon for Jesuits in this day and age. They were both from the West Coast province and were graduate students in psychology, one at Harvard and the other at Yale. I was still wearing my vacation sport clothes, and they didn't bother to ask my name or my work, so filled were they with the importance of their mission to update the Church. It developed that they were both behaviorists, hard-core disciples of B. F. Skinner.

"You see," one of them informed me in a tone appropriate for a freshman introductory course, "the Church has become irrelevant because all its positive reinforcement is scheduled for the next life and all its negative reinforcement is scheduled in this life. We're promised joy only after death."

"Precisely," said the other. "Only when we introduce more positive reinforcements in *this* world and forget about what comes *after* will people listen to us again."

"I see," I said, pretending that I was a layman. "What happens to your . . . schedule of positive and negative reinforcements after the . . . uh, Resurrection?"

They both laughed smugly. "We think that kind of reinforcement is irrelevant," said the Yalie. "The Resurrection myth is outmoded. Obviously, it stands for the kind of psychological rebirth that takes place when the proper mixture of positive and negative sanctions produces satisfying behavior as a replacement for unsatisfying behavior. We can do without the afterlife now."

"No heaven? No Resurrection?" I asked.

"Of course not," said the Harvard man. "Most people don't believe it, anyway."

"How come Catholic psychologists haven't said this before?" I asked. "This fellow Brennan—"

The Yalie interrupted me. "He ought not to be taken seriously; he has no reputation in the profession."

"He's hardly a priest," said the other. "He's not very interested in the Church, just in piling up money."

"And he's very hard to work with, has virtually no close friends."

"Oh," I said.

The flight went on, as did their lecture. I was only too happy to leave the plane at Chicago. They stayed on for the flight to Boston.

Before leaving, I tried for a bit of minor revenge. "It's been good to talk to you, Fathers. I'm so interested in what you had to say. I think I'll drop a note to your provincial congratulating him on providing education for such thoughtful and progressive young men. I'm sure he'll be interested in all the fine things you had to say."

Instead of being frightened, they were delighted.

The war raged on in Vietnam. The Colts beat the Cowboys in the Super Bowl. It was disclosed that we had invaded Laos and Cambodia. The violence grew worse in Northern Ireland. And I sat morosely in my cave, realizing that the Church was a whore and would break my heart every time I tried to love it. My mother's hair had turned as white as the Colonel's, and a few snowflakes had begun to appear in my own.

In the midst of all this gloom, Maureen, lovely as always, visited me in my basement office at the Catholic Center, where the new chaplain let me receive visitors.

"It's an enormous favor I have to ask, Kevin," she said, crossing her legs and lighting a cigarette. "I'd like you to keep an eye on Sheila for me while I'm away." I tried not to look at her legs or wonder how long it took her to put on all her makeup.

"Your folks took care of us Brennan kids during the war, Mo. I'm glad to keep an eye on Sheila. But even if I weren't, we'd owe you that, at least."

She wrinkled her nose. "Exactly what the Colonel said. You two are cut from the same cloth. Anyway, Sheila needs to be in America and away from me. I'll be coming back often to get ready for my exhibitions. I don't think she'll miss me all that much." A frown momentarily crossed her face. "And I'll feel better if I know you're watching. . . ." Her voice trailed off.

"I suppose I ought to be discreet and not ask—but have you seen Pat?"

She reached for her purse, and then thought better of chain-smoking in my presence.

"No, I haven't. He's busy, I'm sure, in his diocese, and I'm busy with my new life. That's over, Kevin. I'm a big girl now, and I've got a man on the line who doesn't need mothering."

"Sloane? The Protestant?"

"From a bishop's bed to a WASP's." She laughed. "I always was unpredictable."

"And wonderful," I added, envying Sloane Adams, of the Foreign Service.

She kissed me and was off into the gloomy winter mists. I kept my fingers crossed.

There was never a shortage of favors to be granted. In March it was an old friend from my seminary days, Casey Zenkowski, rotund, bald, and merry.

"Hey, Kevin," he said, "you look like hell, all skinny and hollow."

"Too much exercise," I said.

"Bah!" He lit one of his cigars and admired it. "Real Havana." He puffed the cigar contentedly. Casey was a pastor of a Polish parish turned mostly Hispanic. He said three masses each Sunday, preaching at one in Polish, one in Spanish, and one in English.

"How are the others?"

"What others, Kevin? All that's left is me and Nick, now that you've imposed exile on yourself. And Nick is tired. He takes things like papal encyclicals more seriously than we do. Lately he's been crying about how bad the Church is and how terrible it is that the Church can send us someone like O'Neil."

"We shouldn't let them have that kind of power over us, Casey," I said.

"Right. So you'll have dinner with Nick soon, and cheer him up?"

"Sure, Casey. And thanks for telling me."

I filed Casey's request for future action.

The next request for a favor was well disguised. It came from Patrick Donahue.

He called me from Benton Harbor and proposed in his velvet-charm voice a sail in his new boat, the *St. Brendan,* on a Thursday in late May. I was not particularly fond of sailing, but the warmth and friendliness of his invitation was irresistible.

The *St. Brendan* was a thirty-foot Tartan that Pat handled like a toy in a bathtub, even though we were in four-foot waves and a twenty-mile northeasterly breeze. We left the gasoline-smelling marina in New Buffalo—on the edge of his diocese—and eased down the channel toward the open lake. I held the tiller while Pat, trim and fit in white sailing shorts, scampered about, hoisting the various sails and shouting nautical commands that I barely understood.

"I keep the *St. Brendan* inside the diocese," he said, breathing hard as he sat next to me and gently pried the tiller from my inexpert hands. "I don't want to pretend that I don't have it. I work hard all week long, and I won't hide from either my priests or my people that I need an occasional afternoon on the lake for relaxation."

"You certainly look good," I said, huddling inside my windbreaker. Warm May sun or not, I didn't see how Pat could stand the bare chest, but I had to admit he looked the typical healthy, self-disciplined young athlete.

"Getting away from Chicago was the best thing that ever happened to me," he said. "It took away a lot of the pressure. Lord knows I don't have much free time in Benton Harbor, and I've got my spiritual thing in order again. I pray every day. I'm doing my damndest. . . ."

His voice trailed off. I knew that if I looked at his blue eyes, I would see the dots of fear again.

"I'm sure you are," I said. "I think the worst is behind you, Pat."

"I certainly hope so," he said fervently. "It was hard at first. Now it's easier."

"I've never seen you so happy. You seem to have found your role—bishop, and captain of your own ship."

He laughed. "I think I get into trouble with women when the pressures and responsibilities become overwhelming. Benton Harbor is just the right amount of challenge. Any more and I'd . . . I'd be back to the same old thing."

We came about and began racing toward the shore. My stomach had not quite made up its mind whether to be sick.

"You wouldn't accept promotion?" I asked.

"Absolutely not, not even to Grand Rapids or Detroit, much less to Chicago. I know they like what I'm doing here, and that I'm supposed to be tabbed for bigger things, but I'll turn them down flat. Even if my life lasts forty more years, I intend to die as Bishop of Benton Harbor."

"I'm sure it's a wise decision, Pat."

He gripped my arm. "You told me once I should stay at Martyrs. You were right. Every time I move up, I get in trouble. I can't go back to Martyrs, but I can stop the climb right here. And I'm going to."

I knew he meant what he said. I wasn't sure he would mean it tomorrow, though.

Cream-puff clouds floated over us, and the blue-green, white-foamed waters slipped by us as the *St. Brendan* deftly rode the waves. The wind and the sun bathed us in reassuring peace. Before the trip was over I peeled off my jacket and shirt and was scampering around, enthusiastically hauling the ropes—or "sheets," as I was told to call them. When we finally glided back into the harbor, Pat and I were sitting next to each other in the stern, breathing hard, relaxed, happy, and, briefly, close friends again.

"Kevin," Pat said, his forehead creasing in a deep frown, "I need another favor."

"I've never said no," I responded.

"It's not very big this time." He laughed mirthlessly. "Strike that. It's very big to me, though it won't take much effort on your part."

"Shoot."

"It's Patsy. I worry about her." His voice was strained. "John Carrey took good care of her, as far as I could tell. I don't think Gina gives a damn. She's going to marry Arnold Tansey, and Arnold gets along well with John Junior. Anyway, Patsy will be odd person out." He gently guided the *St. Brendan* toward her slip, putting the auxiliary motor into reverse at precisely the proper moment. "I don't worry about the money end of it. There's no shortage of that. But there could be a shortage of human affection. Patsy's in school with Mo's kid, Sheila, a really sweet child. And I hear the two of them hang around with Ellen's oldest, Caroline. You're close to Sheila and Caroline, I know, so it shouldn't be hard for you to keep an eye on her."

"You love the child."

The boat nudged the pier and then stopped, like a bird returned to its nest. "She's all I have now. You know how angry my family is about my going to Benton Harbor. They blame me for Mom's death, as though I could have turned down the appointment and stayed in Chicago. Who else is there for me to love but Patsy?" He tossed a line around the mooring pin. "Will you, Kevin?"

July 1

Dear El,

Just a note to say I'll be in the States for a few days. I have to make some arrangements for my first exhibition. I'll spend a weekend with the exhibitor in Michiana and then come up to the lake for the week of August 7th. I do want to see Sheila. Her letters are great. You and the Brennans and the McNeils have been so good to her. I thought I'd be able to spend the whole summer at the lake. It would be nice to be with everyone again, kind of return to our youth. But I must get the paintings ready for the exhibition. Also, damn it, I wanted to spend more time with Sloane. It's a very warm, comfortable sort of relationship, nothing spectacular. He's not capable of being spectacular. He's not weak, though, and he's more than passable in bed. He wants to get married, being more of a family person than I. Summer has been a time to know him better. I think I might just be ready to go along with what he wants.

See you soon.
Mo

July 15

Dear Mo,

Everyone is ecstatic to hear you're coming. We have a guest house behind our place where you and Sheila can stay and get to know each other again. She's fine, relaxing and laughing a lot.

I'm sorry you're not here this week. Kevin is at the Brennans' looking more lean and lonely than ever. Caroline and her crowd have developed a crush on him and sit at the side of the Brennans' swimming pool every day, soaking up his wisdom as if it's a sun tan. He's very good with them, knows how to adjust to each one's problems, even a sweet little waif named Patsy Carrey. It's been a wonderful experience for the kids and has restored Kevin's confidence that he's a good priest. It won't last once he gets back to that damn hole in the ground in which he lives (a form of self-punishment that is so obvious I can't see why he doesn't know it).

Oh, yes, marry Sloane. We won't even hear discussion of any other alternatives.

Love you, see you soon.
El

Maureen walked along the shaded road of Michiana feeling quite pleased with herself. Sheila was happy at school. The owner of the gallery was delighted with the plans for her exhibit next year, as was the woman's husband, whose wholesale grocery business, Maureen suspected, picked up the deficit at the gallery. Best of all, a car full of teenage boys had whistled at her. That, for a woman approaching forty, she told herself, was worth a week in a spa. She was glad she had lost weight, and looked sexy in a T-shirt and shorts.

She thought of Sloane. When she went back to Rome, he would want to marry her. Maybe it was time.

She reached the road at the foot of the dunes. The lake sparkled in the noonday sun, lazy swells creeping up to the beach. Why hadn't her grandfather and old Jeremiah Brennan bought property here instead of in Wisconsin?

A large black Ford went by on the lake road, stopped, and then backed up.

"Hi, stranger," said a familiar voice.

"Pat!" Her world whirled around her. She leaned against the side of the car.

"I've got a boat in New Buffalo. Great day for a sail."

"I'd like that," she said, forgetting about anything else in her life.

The boat was barely beyond the breakwater when they were in each other's arms.

CHAPTER EIGHTEEN

1972–1973

Daniel O'Neil did to himself what Rome had been unable to do. One night in the autumn of 1972, just before the reelection of Richard M. Nixon, he drove his Cadillac through the guard rail on Lake Shore Drive, down the embankment, and into the lake. The Cadillac sank like a rock. Monica Kelly called me even before the news was on the radio. "No one is going to say it, Father," said Ms. Kelly—Mrs. Tommy Varco in private life—"but there was an empty bottle of bourbon in the car. The police have stopped him at least half a dozen times this year for drunken driving. Dick Daley covered it up, though he didn't want to."

"Are you going to print it?" I asked, sleepily, wondering if it was real or a dream.

"Are you kidding? In this city? Who do you think will be the next bishop?"

I suggested a name—off the record.

Rome didn't wait long. Within six weeks Bishop Patrick H. Donahue, of Benton Harbor, was appointed seventh Archbishop of Chicago. He was forty-one years old, the youngest archbishop in the country. When I heard the announcement on the morning news, I felt as if I were caught in a blizzard.

⁂

"So we have accomplished much work, have we not?" Tonio stretched his arms over his head, like a man waking from a nap.

"We have," said Pat, piling the papers into a neat stack. "We're ready for the meeting tomorrow. I told you it wouldn't take all afternoon."

"We were fortunate that the principessa *should choose to go to Ischia to benefit from the springs."*

Tonio filled both brandy glasses again. "The peace here at our villa facilitates the work, no? Is that not the word you Americans use? 'Facilitate'?" Tonio was in one of his mocking moods. Pat had never seen him so relaxed and genial. He had even unbuttoned the top button of his cassock.

"Is not the sunset lovely?" Tonio said. "So much peace, so much beauty, so much quiet . . . and of course the warmth of friendship." He raised his brandy glass in salute.

Pat responded with his own raised glass. "I'm worried about some of the appointments in America. A lot of weak bishops who don't seem to understand. . . ."

Tonio sipped his brandy slowly. "Do not worry, caro. *His Eminence said to me just the other day how impressed he is with your understanding of your responsibilities."*

Pat felt his face grow warm with pride. "I appreciate the trust of the Holy See."

Tonio was looking at him with intense, eager eyes.

"You will go far, my good friend," Tonio said. "Being an American, you will not forget those who helped you. We Italians, I fear, do not value loyalty so highly." He rose from his chair and walked over to Pat. "Perhaps I could put some Vivaldi on the phonograph?" His hand was on Pat's arm, digging into his muscle with a grip that was both tender and tenacious.

Pat was confused. "I prefer Cherubini," he said lamely.

"Ah, we have finally begun to civilize you, my American friend." Tonio laughed. "You come to understand the subtle distinctions of our music."

The record player was turned on in the near darkness, and the pulsating music began. Tonio returned, this time putting his arm around Pat. "Surely you will permit me to offer you a cold supper. I have a very old bottle of Po wine we could drink with some sausage and cheese—a real peasant meal. All the servants are gone. It is only you and I." His voice was soft and seductive.

"That's kind of you, Tonio," Pat said, his voice trembling slightly. "But, you see, well, I'd be afraid to drive down to Rome with another half bottle of wine in me."

"It would not be necessary to drive back in the darkness. Surely you could leave in the morning. There will be less traffic on Monday morning than on Sunday night." There was a light, caressing tone in Tonio's words.

Nervously Pat sipped his brandy. "I wish I could, Tonio." He was perspiring despite the cool mountain breeze. "Perhaps another time. I've promised to meet some friends for dinner."

"Of course, caro*." There was scarcely a trace of disappointment in Tonio's voice. He was gracious, charming, as though nothing had happened.*

He won't hold it against me, Pat told himself as he drove down the mountain. To Rome. And into the arms of Maureen.

The winter before Pat had been elevated to Chicago, Maureen Cunningham had sold her luxurious family home at our lake and bought a small house in Beverly Shores, Indiana, just across the state line from Pat's diocese. Mo now commuted from Rome on a more or less regular basis. She had done enough painting to have an exhibition in Chicago, which the critics had greeted with mixed notices. As the *Sun-Times* put it, "Ms. Cunningham has instinct for the colors of Middle Western America, particularly light growing out of darkness. However, she seems to lack the seriousness and, perhaps, the discipline to concentrate sufficiently on what she sees. The result is a collection of works that are always attractive but somehow disappointing. They lead you to suspect that her vision goes much beyond what she shows us."

I read it four times and still didn't know whether it was good or bad. When I talked to Mo at the gallery, she seemed delighted.

"Hey, Kev." She dashed across the gallery to hug me. "The damn liberals like my stuff."

"I thought they were saying you could do much better if you tried to," I said, catching my breath with some difficulty.

"Oh, don't be a creep. Everyone knows I'm shallow. They said I was shallow but nice." Maureen was showing her thirty-eight years, more in the weariness of her face than in the lines of her body.

"Is the exhibition a success?" I asked.

"Hell, no," she said merrily. "I won't make nearly enough money to pay the expenses. Hey, when you going to come down to my place at Beverly Shores?"

I said I would come down during the summer, a promise that I wouldn't keep. We saw little of Mo in those years. The Colonel had "retired," now that Joe was in the firm, and commuted between the lake and Tucson, having dumped all his Florida holdings in exchange for what must have been half the Santa Catalina mountains. Even though he and my mom reveled in their six grandchildren, they seemed content to spend their late sixties more and more quietly enjoying each other. The Colonel's hand trembled slightly now when he reached for a fork. Unlike most people, he didn't try to hide the quiver. "It shook a lot more at Bastogne on Christmas day, 1944, let me tell you," he'd say, and laugh. "And it wasn't the cold, either." I no longer felt sorry about their growing old, and prayed, when I found time to pray, that I would become old as full of grace as they.

A few months after Maureen's exhibition, I was walking to Kroch's on one of those sudden spring days in mid-March that fool us Middle Westerners. "Hello, Father," said a musical voice next to me.

It was Ellen, wearing jeans, a Notre Dame sweatshirt, and a Windbreaker, looking like anything but the mother of five. Her ponytail was fastened by a rubber band, and she had not bothered with makeup. She looked ten years younger than Mo.

"Nice time in Mexico?" I asked.

"Uh-huh," she said thoughtfully. "Herb really needed the time off. You do, too, Kevin." She turned her compassionate gray eyes on me. "Herb wanted to invite you, but, well, I thought you'd feel out of place."

"I don't know," I said, trying to joke. "A *ménage-à-trois* could be fun." I held open the door to the bookstore for her.

"Vulgar beast. What a terrible thing for a priest to say."

"I'm a terrible priest."

"You are not." She patted my arm. "Kevin, are Maureen and Pat having an affair again?"

"What makes you ask?" I focused on the hardbound–best-seller table just inside the door.

"As soon as Herb and I got to our hotel room in Mexico, I went out on the balcony to enjoy my first sight of the ocean and the beach. I heard voices next door. The balconies are protected so you can have privacy. . . . I recognized their voices." The deep breath failed her. She picked up the latest Helen MacInnes book, but held it wrong side up.

"Did you see them later?" I asked, incredulous.

"God, no. I mean, I didn't want Herb to find out. What would he think of the Church? The next day, I talked to a bellman who told me that they had checked out. Mr. and Mrs. Cunningham—and Mr. Cunningham was a tall, handsome man with graying blond hair. It was none of my business, but . . ."

"If the Coast Guard ever catches them screwing in a Lake Michigan storm, it's going to be all of our business."

She returned the book, unopened, to its stack. "Please, God, nothing like that happens."

On the way home I fantasized about romantic Mexican vacations. I was as much in love with Ellen Foley as I had been at the yacht-club dance twenty-four years ago.

⁂

I also loved Patsy Carrey. The eleven-year-old waif affected me as if she were my own daughter. I presented myself dutifully once a week at the door of the convent school to take Sheila and Patsy out for a soda. Sheila was the excuse. My friend Maureen wanted me to look after her daughter. Patsy came along naturally enough as her closest friend. They both were blossoming into lovely young women. Sheila was erratic and unpredictable, sometimes solemn and pious, sometimes displaying her mother's recklessness and verve.

Patsy was always the same—delicate, fragile, incredibly sweet and affectionate. Each week she brought a gift—a poem, a drawing, a passage copied in exquisite lettering from a book. Seeing her had started as a burden, but now it was an eagerly anticipated pleasure. I made no reports to her father and would not do so until I was asked.

In April, with showers alternating with dashing patches of blue, Patsy and I sat huddled over a Formica table in 31 Flavors, sipping on malted milks. Patsy sipped very slowly, trying to make her treat last as long as possible. Sheila had the flu, I was told, and could not come. The sisters took it for granted that Father Brennan would escort either or both of the girls for their weekly treat. I wondered if Georgina knew or cared.

The child looked up at me and smiled a slow, heart-breakingly winsome smile, her long eyelashes fluttering. "May I ask you a few questions, Father?"

Having discussed sex with her and Sheila a few times, I expected that this would be the topic.

"Fire away, Patsy," I said. I debated having a second malt for myself. I could work it all off in a session with Calvin Ohira the next day.

"Do you really love me?" she asked.

"Yes, I really do."

She colored as Pat did when complimented. "Why?"

"Because you are lovable," I responded.

"Any *special* reason?"

"I have a weakness for cute blondes."

"Are you my father?" she asked quietly.

"No, Patsy," I said, feeling a sting behind my eyes. "Why would you think I was?"

"My father wasn't my real father," she said, brushing away some tears with the back of her hand. "I have blue eyes, and both my father and mother have brown eyes. John wasn't my father's son, either. I thought you might be my father, because you love me so much."

The pain in my chest was very like what a heart must feel when it is breaking. "I'm not your father, Patsy," I said lamely. "If I were, I'd be very proud to have a daughter like you."

"May I pretend that you're my father?" she said, the sun of her slow, sweet smile breaking through the gloom.

"No, Patsy, we shouldn't pretend about things like that. Just tell yourself that I love you as much as if I really was your father."

Patrick Donahue came to Chicago like a warm southwest wind at the end of a bitter winter. He appointed the executive committee of the Priest Senate to be his consultors, instituted an elective pastoral council with a representative from every parish in the city, promised strong financial support to all the inner-city parishes, revitalized the Newman Clubs (providing an assistant who forced me out of the Catholic Center and into an apartment), went to the symphony concerts and the Art Institute exhibitions, appeared on television talk programs, met with the editorial boards of the two major newspapers, told all the priests to call him Pat, opened the diocesan books to public accounting, and promised that no more than thirty thousand dollars would be spent without approval of the executive committees of the Senate and the pastoral council. He even played basketball with the kids in the seminary.

By the spring of 1973, with the Watergate scandal burgeoning, he was the toast of the city—the handsome, progressive, charming, democratic Archbishop. He was easily the most popular archbishop in America. Chicago editorial writers hailed him as the kind of leader Americans needed in an era of crisis and disillusionment.

Nick McAuliff resigned from the priesthood that year.

"I'm tired, Kev," he said in my office, his face contorted with pain. "So damned tired. I don't care about the politics or the changes or birth control or any of those things anymore. I'm worn down. I've given all I have to give. There's nothing inside.

I've got to have a little love before I die. I'm so lonely." His voice choked. "She's a wonderful woman, five terrific kids. It's not sex. I don't care much about that. I just need love. She loves me. I can't go on being empty."

"If it's what you're doing, Nick," I said, disguising my feeling of betrayal and desertion, "I'm sure it's the right thing to do. May you have all the happiness you richly deserve."

A month after the marriage, Nick invited me to supper at his house to meet "Lonie." I had a Review Panel meeting in Washington and couldn't come. The tone of his voice told me he thought I was making up the excuse.

Even with the rejuvenation of the Archdiocese of Chicago under the brilliant leadership of Pat Donahue, the American Church continued to slide downhill. Schools were closing; priests and nuns were leaving; those who stayed were confused and uncertain. Seminaries and novitiates were being boarded up. The hierarchy gave up on birth control and began to move toward a new policy on annulments. Despite the appointment of more pastoral men by the new Delegate, the leadership did not recapture much credibility (save for Pat, who was a national hero). Fads and fashions swept through the Church with frenetic speed. Scholarship of the sort I'd become skilled at was treated with open contempt. Attendance at mass was half what it had been, though the large population bulge of young people hid the decline. Financial scandals were surfacing in dioceses and religious orders. New bishops were discovering that their predecessors had spent money recklessly and that state auditors were waiting for them on the day of their installation.

My parents were away much of the time. My brothers and

Mary Ann were busy with their families. The community of young people from St. Prax collapsed. I was lonely.

I stuck it out, writing research reports and books. Occasionally a bishop called me late at night asking for suggestions—secretly, I suspect, for fear of offending Pat.

Kevin Brennan, the inevitable leader of 1948, was a nonperson. Patrick Donahue, who had survived at Kevin Brennan's discretion, was Archbishop of Chicago.

⁂

Pat had been in Chicago six months before I heard from him. "Archbishop's office on the phone," my secretary said anxiously.

"Yes," I said into the phone. "The proper address for the mailing list is the one here at the research institute."

There was a frigid silence at the other end of the line.

"The Archbishop wants to see you this afternoon," said an impersonal and efficient voice.

"I've got a seminar this afternoon." I was spoiling for a fight. "And if Pat Donahue wants to speak to me, he knows my phone number."

"I'll relay your message, Father," she said frostily.

Pat called back in five minutes. "Hi, Kev, what's up?" he began brightly.

"My name on the mailing list is what's up," I said. "I hate missing your weekly words of wisdom."

He laughed as though it were a great joke. "Kev, I don't know where time goes. When I came here, I said I've got to check things out with Kev the first week. I can't tell you how much I appreciate your tact and discretion in staying in the background. A lot of people were watching me closely to see if I play favorites. They know that I couldn't say no to you. Anyway, we can forget about all that now. Do you have a night free in the next couple of weeks to stop by the house for supper?"

We settled on a date.

Pat spent most of his time in the cathedral rectory. He kept the house on North State Parkway as a place for entertaining guests, especially civic personages; for having parties for priests, one every week; and for "private conversations," as he'd explained with a self-deprecating smile at a meeting of the Priest Senate. I guessed I was a "private conversation."

A young priest opened the door on a sumptuous September evening. He was a handsome young man, almost indistinguishable from an earlier Pat, save for brown hair instead of blond.

"Art McGrath, Father," he said respectfully. "It's an honor to meet you. I've read all your books and I wait eagerly for the next one, on Enthusiasm. I bet it replaces Ronald Knox's work as the principal contribution to the field."

Another goddamn smooth-talker. "My name is Kevin, Art"—I shook his hand—"and my approach will not be historical, as Knox's is. I hope to complement his work, not replace it."

"I still want to read it," he said genially.

I was ensconced in the Archbishop's private study on the second floor. He'd be a little late, Art explained, because he had a long conversation with Archbishop Benelli that afternoon that had thrown his schedule off.

In a room down the corridor a pretty young woman was pounding away at a typewriter. Promptly at six, she rose from her desk, came to the private study, looked suspiciously at me, and put a thick folder on the desk. "For His Excellency's eyes only," she said severely.

"Where's the Xerox machine?" I asked, grinning at her.

She gave me a dirty look and flounced out. I wondered if Pat was screwing her.

I waited forty-five minutes, which was at least less time than O'Neil had kept me waiting.

Pat embraced me Roman style, though without the kiss. "Kevin, Kevin. God, it's good to see you. You're looking great. Not an extra pound of fat. Would you like a Jameson's? Special Reserve? Sixteen years old?"

"Pepsi," I said.

He peeled off his red-buttoned cassock, tossed it on a couch, and went to the ornate bar. His martini was a lot drier than it used to be. He seemed to be in condition. His hair was undoubtedly bleached, though I gave him no bad marks for that. The boyishly handsome Archbishop.

"To the future of Chicago!" he said.

We clinked glasses. My hostility melted.

Our dinner was easy and relaxed. He explained his policy decisions and asked my advice about personnel problems, taking notes on what I said. He was especially interested in what kind of empirical research I thought the diocese ought to have. He ate sparingly and took only a few sips from his wineglass.

"What do you think of the new Chicago?" He waved his fork breezily as I plunged into my second helping of roast beef. "Public accountability for funds, merit promotion, democratic decision-making, consultation with the laity, spiritual renewal. Can you name a better post–Vatican Council diocese in the country?"

His glee over the changes in the archdiocese made his boasting seem boyishly harmless.

"Still the honeymoon," I said acidly.

His crestfallen expression pleaded for something more. He wouldn't get it, though—not until I found out what he had in store for his old friend Kevin.

After dinner we were back in his study. He poured me a magnificent port, offered me one of his Cuban cigars, which I declined, and leaned back expansively in his chair. "Well, Kevin, what do you want to do in the new Chicago?"

"Just what I've been doing," I said. "The research I do is important for the Church, and so are my books."

He waved his cigar. "Yes, but hasn't there been some problem with the university over the quality of your research?"

The muscles in my forearms began to tighten. "The research institute is independent of the university, Pat. I have a ten-year contract with them. Some people tried to get me a university appointment and ran into bigotry. That does not affect the research institute."

He frowned thoughtfully. "I'm not an academic, Kev, but I can't imagine bigotry in a university today."

"Then try to imagine it," I said coldly. "Would you like the details?"

Again he waved the cigar. "Oh, no, that won't be necessary."

I sipped the port. "Great port, Pat. Anyway, I've had offers from a half dozen major universities. I like Chicago too much to leave."

"I'm sure you're the best there is in the Church, Kevin; that's why I want you on my staff. Would you take over our Research and Development Office? I've got your notes here, and I'm sure we could scrape together funds to get it going. We're short of money, but there must be lots of foundations in Chicago." He crossed his hands behind his head in contentment. "It will be great to be working together again."

"No," I said softly.

Pat frowned. "Kevin, I wish you'd think about it. We really need you in the diocese."

"I work for myself, Pat," I said. "Five, ten years ago maybe I'd leap at such a job. Now I'm my own boss, I get grants larger than the diocese could imagine, and I do what I want. I'm too old to give any of it up."

"For the Church?" His eyebrows lifted in mild reproof.

"I'll be the judge of what the Church needs from me," I said, my voice rising.

He puffed thoughtfully on his cigar. "I'm your archbishop, Kevin. I have the right to make some input, don't I?"

"Make it," I said, reaching for the port bottle and refilling my glass.

"The problem I face is the unity of the presbyterate. A lot of men resent your independence and, quite frankly, your income. I can't have the great inequality in responsibility and work and . . . pay that a job like yours represents, since it is of dubious use to the Church in a time of an increasing shortage of priests. It is especially difficult because you're known to be a friend of mine. I'm under great pressure, Kevin. . . ."

"Even O'Neil didn't mess with the assignment Meyer gave me," I said.

"Please, Kevin," he said, leaning toward me. "Don't make it difficult for me."

I smiled benignly.

He frowned and rolled the cigar in his fingers. "You don't give me much choice, Kevin. I'm going to have to order you to leave the research institute and come on my staff. I will issue that order in the name of holy obedience."

A chain reaction went off inside me. I remained calm and self-possessed on the outside. Inside I was boiling.

"Do you still screw Maureen?" I asked conversationally.

"What?" He turned pale.

"I don't mean tonight." I smiled genially. "I mean when you're in Rome or she's in Beverly Shores. Does she come here at night? Is she the first woman to be fucked at 1555 North State?

Or if not Maureen, whom do you take to bed? How about that pretty iceberg who types for you and makes your phone calls? Have you gotten into her yet?"

"Kevin . . . how dare you—"

"Shit, Pat, I dare anything." I finished the port and rose from my chair. "I don't want anything from you. Just leave me and my work alone, that's all. Don't bother me and I won't go after you. But try messing with me once more and your entire dossier will be on Benelli's desk quicker than you can say 'red hat.' "

"Dossier?" he said.

"Every single love affair of yours, from Stanley Kokoleck and the waitress in Mundelein on down. All in elaborate detail." It was a lie, an ace up my sleeve. "I'm sure the Holy See would be especially interested in the escapades of Mr. and Mrs. Cunningham in Acapulco. And what about your daughter, Patsy? Wouldn't she like to know her father is an archbishop? Do you ever think about her, Pat?"

"Often." He was slumped in his chair, his face in his hands.

"Remarkable resemblance, Pat. It would make a great story. My friend Monica Kelly doesn't have much affection for you. I don't imagine she'd care about what happened to Patsy." An absolute lie, but he didn't know it.

"You wouldn't, you couldn't . . ." He was now a hollow shell.

I leaned against the door frame. "Well, thanks for the meal . . . and the port."

"It would destroy Maureen." He was pleading.

"Mo knew what she was getting herself into, lover boy. And if she's destroyed, it will be your fault. Leave me alone and the dossier stays in my lawyer's office."

"Lawyer?" He withdrew his hands from a face now tight with terror.

"Sure," I said. "You don't think I'd take any chances, do you? And by the way, Pat, you'd better be the best goddamn archbishop in this country, even after this public-relations honeymoon of yours is over. If you start blowing things, I'll send my dossier on to the authorities just for the pure hell of it."

His pale lips moved as though he were trying to say something.

"See you around, Pat. Give my love to Mo." Then, at the doorway, a final shot. "Just like the old days, huh, Patrick?"

Weeks later, when my conscience finally broke through and told me I was guilty of cruel and vicious overkill, I still didn't feel very guilty.

CHAPTER NINETEEN

1974

In the summer of 1974 Richard Nixon was leaving the presidency, *Chinatown* was the popular movie, Solzhenitsyn came to the United States, the kids were listening to The Who, and the Chicago Cubs didn't win another pennant.

My monograph on mental health got good reviews (save for a few written by priests or ex-priests); I was elected to a professional honor society; I received offers for more lectures than I could accept; a number of bishops were ignoring the informal interdict that existed in Chicago and were requesting my consulting services; an occasional young priest showed up at my doorstep despite the ban on me. The worst, I told myself, was over.

I saw enough of Ellen to know that she was happy. Patsy, Sheila, and I were together often. Sheila was more relaxed and cheerful than she had been, though her piety was as severe as ever. Caroline Curran was unbearably beautiful and serenely unaffected by the attention it brought her.

Life went on, vigorously, irresistibly. Yes, the worst was over, I thought.

In fact, the worst was yet to come.

June 10

Dear Ellen,

Sorry I've been so tardy in responding. There won't be an exhibition this year; that's final now, I'm afraid. I haven't done enough work and my heart hasn't been in what I have done. It's been a bad winter here, and I'm not feeling as well as I should. I'll be in Chicago several weeks this summer, most of them at Beverly Shores, though I will cheerfully accept your invitation to spend some time with Sheila at your guest house again. My child is almost a stranger to me now, though I think a happier stranger than she used to be. I failed her, I'm sure, and feel guilty about it. It's done though, and that's that. You and the Brennans and the Sisters at the school seem to have made up for a lot of my mistakes. All I can do is pray for her, which I do every night.

Sometimes I feel sick at my own piety. But despite all the evil things I've done, I do believe.

I'm also putting on weight again. I'm going on a diet tomorrow. I'll be a svelte aging matron the next time you see me, or you won't see me.

The affair with Sloane goes on. I don't have the heart to send him away. Yet I won't give up my freedom to be tied to anyone. I also find his lovemaking dull. I'm occasionally dating a certain Alfredo DeLucca. Maybe you've heard Kevin talk about him. He's part of one of the old Church families here. A very interesting and sexy man.

See you soon. Love to Herb and the kids.

Mo

Fredo DeLucca was hurting her, deliberately, skillfully, precisely. She reveled in the experience of pain and pleasure, enjoying the sharp stab of agony that repeatedly leapt through her body. The pain was inflicted carefully. Not enough to do any damage, not enough to be unbearable.

Amused by her reactions, he chuckled softly. Then her pain crossed the threshold of tolerability. She screamed. Fredo chuckled again. He kept her suspended over the valley of suffering and joy, moved her gently back and forth from one side of the valley to the other. And then, as she pleaded for mercy, he inflicted quick, excruciating torture, followed instantly by sublime ecstasy.

It was an experience she wanted again.

After checking with Marty Herlihy for the "best spiritual director in the archdiocese," I was ushered into the solemn and stately presence of Sister Mary Carmel. She listened quietly to my description of the responsibility I had assumed for Sheila.

"Yes, Father," she said when I was finished. "And no."

"Oh?"

She smiled with a nunlike sweetness that I thought had gone out of fashion. "Yes, you're doing exactly what is right for the child, and no, I will not replace you as her director. Why should I? You have the psychological skills, the sympathy, and the child's confidence. I don't propose to let you escape from the charge which God has thrust upon you. Should you need advice on specific problems, you may call me."

"You're right, I guess, Sister. Thanks for the wisdom." I rose to leave.

"Father." She seemed to hesitate.

"Sit down, please," she said in a tone only mothers superior could command. "You did not resent what I just said?" She tapped the desk thoughtfully. "You are a famous psychology expert and I am a nun without academic credentials."

"I could give you a list of Jesuits who would disagree with that." I rose again in an effort to escape from those probing eyes.

She dismissed the Jebs with a faintly imperious wave of her elegant hand. "Do sit down, Father. I won't bite you."

I sat. "Yes, Sister," I said meekly.

"I am the mother superior, Father, though we do not use the title anymore. Nonetheless, or perhaps for that very reason, I will be candid. I will not be a spiritual director for a child who, having you, does not need me. I will, however, act as *your* spiritual director since you, having no one, *do* need me." I gulped. "It is your option, of course," she said, dismissing any obligation with a wave of the same hand that dismissed Jesuit psychologists. "You will doubtless wish to think about it for a time."

"No, Sister," I said. "And yes."

She arched her eyebrows. "Touché!"

I stood up again, and this time managed to make it to the door. Academic credentials or not, Sister Mary Carmel was perfectly capable of digging sharply enough into a man's psyche to get at the truth, as I was soon to learn.

⁂

I didn't need any spiritual direction to deal with Patsy.

We were sitting in the ice-cream parlor for our last soda of the season. Maureen was in town, so Sheila was not with us.

With my permission, Patsy was holding my hand. She was glowing with happiness. Caroline Curran provided Patsy with an occasional date; the boys liked her and treated her with respect.

"It's been a very important year in my life, Kevin," she said, her even white teeth flashing in a smile that was a carbon copy of her father's. "I've grown up a lot. I know that I'm a good person. I can cope with Mom and Arnold's indifference. I understand how much they've suffered. I can be me."

It was the pseudo-seriousness and the pseudo-insight of the very young. Patsy was fine china that would break easily and, I feared, often. Yet the present moment of self-satisfaction was not to be denied her.

"I'll see you at the lake soon."

Her clear complexion colored. "Oh, sure. Mom and Arnold are just as happy as I am when I go to your parents' house to be with Annie McNeil. She's so much like you, Kevin."

"Even more like her mother," I said.

"All the Brennans are wonderful," she said, melting my heart and causing it to do a couple of disorderly tailspins.

"Annie is part McNeil," I said, to keep the record straight.

Sheila walked briskly down the pier in New Buffalo. Her mother had not been at the house in Beverly Shores when the taxi deposited Sheila there. A note said she'd gone for a sail in the Archbishop's boat. Sheila wasn't sure that an archbishop ought to have a boat, even an archbishop like Archbishop Donahue, who worked so hard and was such a nice man.

She thought about it and decided that such a holy priest as the Archbishop must know what he was doing. If it was all right for him to ride in the boat, then it was all right for her to ride, too. Her mother didn't exactly say that she was welcome on the ride. She didn't say she wasn't, either. Sheila changed into a swimsuit and put on a T-shirt and shorts and asked the boy next door if he would give her a ride to the marina.

He seemed pleased, and asked her to go to the movies with him on Saturday. When he dropped her at the end of the pier, she gave him her best smile and said she'd love to go.

Sheila lived in a world of mists and fog, of confusion and moods, of nameless fears and inarticulate hopes, of deep piety and vague, though powerful, longings. Her time in America had not changed her world. It did make her more confident of her ability to survive in it.

She searched for some time, unable to find the St. Brendan. *She was afraid that she had missed out on the ride. Then she saw the gold letters on the stern of a boat one rank down. She ran back to the base of the marina and out on the next pier. Breathlessly, she jumped into the boat and pushed open the cabin door.*

Every detail of the picture was burned instantly into her mind, never to be erased. Her mother was wearing white jeans and was naked to the waist. She was leaning back against the dining table, supporting herself with both hands. Her face was twisted in a contorted mask of pain and pleasure. Her long, dark hair fell on her shoulders like soot on snow. The Archbishop, completely naked, was bent over her breasts, sucking as though he were an infant taking nourishment. One of his hands held the breast that was nursing him while the other hand fondled the other breast. Sheila realized that she had never seen her mother's nipples before.

Then she began to scream hysterically.

In time, the screaming stopped and there was darkness.

"You feel yourself cut off from other priests?" said Sister Mary Carmel, adroitly looking at her watch. "You feel you're the object of clerical envy? You are sure that you are not the victim of what in another you would call paranoia?"

"I don't know how important it is. Not very important, I suppose." I was sorry I'd told her about the bulletin in Ellen's parish.

"How can it be unimportant?" she persisted, her voice firm and demanding. "A pastor who proudly boasts he hasn't read your work nonetheless denounces you as an enemy of the Church, attributing to you teachings you have never written, attitudes you do not have, and motivations that he could not possibly know even if they do operate in your personality. Of course you are hurt by his dishonest attack. Why do you think insensitivity to the attacks of envious persons is a virtue? Why are you afraid that people will say you have a thin skin, especially since you do?"

"Maybe I *am* paranoid."

"Oh, I rather doubt it, Father," she said airily. "I merely raised the question. The reaction, I'm sure, is common. You will receive little support from your fellow clerics. All the more reason that we must find some way to build a support community for you. A sensitive, lonely, and loving man such as you should not be left alone."

It was the first of many times that I would feel as though Sister Mary Carmel had stripped off my clothes.

Ellen paused over her journal and then began to write slowly and carefully.

> I stumbled into a confrontation with Maureen today. It may have damaged our friendship beyond repair. I am writing this account because Herb is not here to talk to and I want to get it all out in the open. I am sure I bungled it. I'm sure, too, that while I was trying to be helpful I was also very angry, and the anger got in the way, maybe destroying the helpfulness.
>
> Appropriately enough, we were swimming nude in the pool, both defenseless in the most primal sense. Mo was shocked when the kids and I peeled off our swimsuits before jumping in the water. I flattered myself that while she'd been the "fast" teenager, she now had a false modesty and I had a valid modesty.
>
> "I'm too fat to be doing this," she said in embarrassment as she stripped.
>
> "Nonsense." I grinned. "You're a perfect nude model."
>
> "Rubens," she said as she dived into the water, "is out of fashion."
>
> Nevertheless she enjoyed the frolic as much as the rest of us.

Then I chased the kids—Caroline, Annie, Sheila, and Patsy—up to the house.

"We old women need time to talk," I said.

"Lot of loveliness there," said Mo a bit sadly, watching the girls walk toward the house.

I agreed.

We were hanging on to the side of the pool, shoulder to shoulder, breathing heavily from our exertions.

"We'll miss Sheila," I said. "She's become quite the lively self-possessed young woman."

Mo would not look at me. "It's been good for her. But if she wants to finish up in Ireland, that's her business, I guess."

"We were surprised," I said.

"She tell you why?" Mo asked, glaring at me suspiciously.

"No," I said. "I didn't ask. Mary Ann didn't, either."

Mo leaned her head against the tile of the pool. "She caught Pat and me horsing around on his boat. Became hysterical. We had to take her to the hospital in Michigan City. Took a couple of days to bring her out of it. She told me I was a filthy whore. She won't talk to me in private. She's going to Ireland because she doesn't want to be near either of us."

I closed my eyes and hung on to the edge of the pool for dear life.

"Go on, say it. Tell me what a disgusting tart I am and what a terrible mother."

As I write these words I begin to comprehend that if I'd said something like that there would have been no quarrel. Poor Mo needed punishment and instead she got sympathy.

"I won't say it because I don't think it. I love you too much, Mo."

"I'm not worth loving. I don't care. And, God damn it, don't patronize me."

"Don't hate yourself," I pleaded.

She said nothing.

"Forgive me if I sound like I'm preaching a sermon," I said, starting my sermon. "The only thing that worries me is you. Sheila will grow up; Pat will always have the Church. What happens to you? You're a beautiful woman with half your life ahead of you. When you're not with Pat, you paint, you're happy, you have other friendships. You don't help him and he hurts you." I tried to put my arm around her shoulder.

She shook off my arm and moved down the pool, as though to distance herself from me. "A lot you know about it." Her voice was subdued, hurt.

"I don't know anything except that you're hurting and I don't want you to hurt."

"You've got Kevin and I've got Pat. What's the difference?" she shouted.

Like all friends, Mo knew the weak links in a friend's armor. "I don't fuck him," I said.

"You would if you could."

"Sure, I would," I said. "But I don't." And then I got angry. "I don't sleep with him, I don't let my love for him interfere with my family and my marriage, I don't let it stop my writing, and I don't make him sick with self-loathing and guilt."

"That's only because he has no balls." She glared at me, her face wrenched with emotion. "If he went after you, you'd do anything he wanted."

"You're wrong, Mo," I said solemnly. "Not because I'm any better than you but because I've been lucky enough to have other loves in my life. You can find other loves, too."

It was, in retrospect, too late by then. Once I'd permitted her to talk about our crazy foursome we were locked into a fight from which we could not break out.

I should have kept my mouth shut. I think.

"If I want any advice from you, I'll ask for it. You don't know anything about men." She pulled herself out of the pool and covered her body with a robe. "Go fuck yourself. You'll never get a good fuck from a man."

She stormed up to the house, clutching the robe with her hands while its long white skirt flowed behind her like the wings of an angry angel.

We were reasonably civilized at supper with the Brennans. Then she went in silence to the guest house.

We must live with our mistakes, Kevin once said, sometimes not even knowing for sure whether they are mistakes.

The sky was gray and threatening as I drove up to our summer home, the kind of day that our downstate classmates used to call "twister weather." My sister-in-law Kathy rushed down the steps, her face red from weeping.

"Patsy's in the hospital." She struggled for words. "She's badly hurt. A hit-and-run driver ran into her and Caroline and Sheila this morning. Mike and Herb are there. All the others, too. They want you . . . for . . . the last rites." She was sobbing again.

I turned on the ignition. "The other two?" I asked, in a daze.

"Sheila has a broken arm; Caroline's got a lot of cuts and bruises."

The little Catholic hospital in Genoa, Wisconsin, looked too small to house such tragedy. I rushed through the door. The young woman at the information desk said "Three-twelve" before I could ask. I dashed up the stairs and down the corridor.

They were saying the rosary when I came in, Ellen leading it. The room was filled with nuns, the Currans, and all the Brennan adults except Kathy. Herb and Mike stood at the head of the bed. On the other side were a young priest and an equally young intern. Mike shook his head. The soft, prayerful murmurs filled the room with a kind of solemn peacefulness.

In the center of it all was a tiny, smudged face surrounded by a halo of disheveled yellow hair. Her eyes were closed.

The young priest slipped around to me. "I'm sorry, Father. I've already given her the last anointing. They weren't sure. . . ."

I gripped his arm. "It's all right, Father. You did exactly what you should have done."

The rosary continued. Patsy opened her eyes, looked around the room nervously, and then shut her eyes again.

The Colonel whispered in my ear, "Internal injuries. Hit-and-run driver. They were out walking on the road, on the shoulder, as they should have been. Driver was either drunk or high, drove off the road and hit them, then back on. Probably a stolen car. Caroline got the license number."

My eyes found Caroline. She was on her knees next to the priest, her face expressionless, her lips moving automatically in prayer.

I slipped out of the room and called the Chancery-office number of the Archbishop's secretary. "Kevin Brennan, Art. Tell the boss it's a matter of life and death."

"Archbishop Donahue," said a cool, formal voice a moment later.

"Patsy's dying," I said bluntly. "Hit-and-run driver. She's in a hospital in Genoa City."

"Oh, God, no!" he shouted. Then there was a long pause while he fought for control of his emotions. "I'll say a special prayer for her at mass, Kevin."

"You don't seem to understand, Pat. She's dying. She'll be dead in a few hours. Don't you want to come—"

He hung up on me, though not before I heard a tormented sob.

I went back to the room. Patsy was trying to sit up, her delicate face twisted in fear. "I don't want to die," she said weakly. "Please, don't let me die."

The peaceful monotone of the rosary ceased. I searched for something to say.

Caroline beat me to it. She sat on the side of the bed and put her arm around her friend.

"Don't be afraid, Patsy," she said tenderly. "It's going to be all right. We're here with you, and we'll take care of you until Jesus and Mary come to bring you home. I'm very angry at them. We love you as much as they do, and they shouldn't be taking you away from us. I guess they figure they need someone like you around to get things ready for the rest of us characters when our time comes. You'd better prepare a great house for me . . . a big lawn with all kinds of neat boys singing songs in my praise all day long."

Patsy smiled, leaned her head against Caroline's shoulder, and relaxed peacefully against her pillow.

"Kevin," said the dying girl. "Are you here, Kevin?"

"Yes, Patsy, I'm here." It did not sound like my voice at all.

"May I hold your hand until Jesus takes it? He's my real father."

Mike signaled me that it was only a matter of moments.

The young priest handed me the ritual.

"In the name of God the almighty Father who created you,
In the name of Jesus Christ, Son of the living God, who
suffered for you,
In the name of the Holy Spirit who was poured out upon
you,

Go forth, faithful Christian.
May you live in peace this day,
may your home be with God in Zion,
with Mary the Virgin Mother of God,
with Joseph, and all the angels and saints.

"My sister in faith,
I entrust you to God who created you.
May you return to the one
who formed you from the dust of this earth.
May Mary, the angels, and all the saints
come to meet you as you go forth from this life.
May Christ who was crucified for you
bring you freedom and peace.
May Christ, the Son of God, who died for you take you
into his Kingdom.
May Christ, the Good Shepherd,
give you a place within his flock.
May he forgive your sins
and keep you among his people.
May you see your Redeemer face to face
and enjoy the sight of God forever."

Just as I finished the prayer, Patsy extended her arms as though she were embracing someone. "Oh, yes, I'm ready now," she said in a voice that was filled with sweetness and love.

Then she died.

Art McGrath parked the Cadillac with the big "100" on the license plate in the driveway at the back of the hospital.

"Go in and check, Art?" Pat said in a strained voice.

In a few moments the young priest returned. "Everyone's gone. The body is in the hospital's morgue, in the basement, waiting for the undertaker. Sister understands that you've promised her family to give her your apostolic blessing, even if . . . if there's no sign of life."

Pat, his face distorted with grief, got out of the car. "I suppose this goes against your theology, Art. Mine, too, I guess. Yet it's a symbol, and it means a lot to her parents."

Art shrugged.

They took a few steps through the glaring sunlight and then entered the cool, dark back corridor of the hospital. An elderly nun in old-fashioned habit kissed Pat's ring. "My prayers for all who knew her," she said.

"Thank you, Sister. Thank you very much." Pat whispered his reply as though he were in church.

The nun led them down the steps, into a dim corridor, and then through a door she opened with one of the many keys on a ring tied to her cincture. They entered the room, and she turned on the lights. The room was white—walls, floor, tables, two chairs. There was more glare than the sunlight provided outside. Against one of the walls there was a bank of cabinets, like files. Art felt his stomach turn over. He had never been in a morgue before. Clean, smelling of antiseptic, at once denying and affirming death.

The nun opened one of the cabinets with yet another key and slid back the shelf inside. Inside a plastic bag, like the kind in which office equipment is covered, there was a lovely wax doll. Gently the sister unzipped the top of the bag, revealing a pretty face with blond hair, the rest of her young body covered by a freshly pressed sheet. She looked like a statue, almost alive and yet an infinity of miles from life. The nun made the sign of the cross as she folded back the plastic.

Pat choked a sob. Art looked at him uneasily. This whole crazy trip was utterly unlike Patrick Donahue. He reached out his hand mechanically. Art gave him a pocket stole and a ritual.

Pat said the prayers in a dull Latin monotone, barely giving Art and the sister the cues for responding their amens. Then he imparted the final apostolic blessing, switching to English, as though the dead girl could hear. "And by the power given to me by the Holy See, I impart to you a full remission of all your sins and a plenary indulgence. In the name of the Father and the Son and the Holy Spirit. Amen."

Art didn't particularly believe in plenary indulgences, and he suspected Pat didn't, either. Yet, for a moment, he imagined he could visualize the child entering heaven on angels' wings. She certainly looked like an angel. Sweet, innocent face, somehow familiar.

Pat paused a moment. "All right, Sister," he said softly. "Thank you very much."

The nun made the sign of the cross again, unfolded the bag, quickly zipped it shut, closed the cabinet, and locked it.

The Archbishop sat in the back seat of the car on the trip to Chicago, tears streaming down his cheeks. Suddenly Art knew why the young girl's face was familiar.

He whistled softly to himself and felt intense sorrow for Patrick Donahue. Funny, he'd always suspected that the man went in the opposite direction. Perhaps there was something beneath that sleek façade after all.

⁂

Arnold Tansey called my father that night to say that he and Georgina held us personally responsible for the tragedy, and that we would be hearing from his lawyers—an empty threat, of course. He also warned us to stay away from the wake and the funeral.

I wanted to go anyway. I was overruled by everyone else. We had our own funeral mass on the front porch of the family house. I have no memory of what I said in the sermon.

Pat, as a close friend of the Tanseys', said their mass. All around the diocese, priests marveled at the reports of how deeply moved he was. Wept through half the sermon, they said. Proved he had a heart, after all.

CHAPTER TWENTY

1975

"This has been the year in which women have become a more serious problem for you than your Archbishop." Sister Mary Carmel folded her hands beneath her brown scapular as she always did when she scored a point against me. "I wonder if a skilled psychologist like you has been able to find a pattern in such events?"

In her old-fashioned brown and white habit Sister Carmel might have been thirty-five or she might have been fifty. Her smooth, alabaster face and thick expressive eyebrows gave no hint.

I shifted nervously in my familiar chair, which was as old as the monastery building—pre-Fire if not pre–Civil War. "Sun spots?" I said hopefully.

She sighed impatiently. "I will lay out two possibilities for you, Father. It may be that you are getting old and hence less capable of dealing with women by your usual methods of protecting or charming or dominating them, or it may be that you have been sufficiently purified by your sufferings so that you are now able to enter mature relationships with women. They perceive this new vulnerability and react accordingly, each in her own way."

"What sufferings?"

"The turning point," she went on patiently, "was when Ellen became a person in her own right. She offered you adult friendship. You are not able to accept it; nor are you prepared to reject it. So you hesitate. The only saving grace the Lord has vouchsafed you is your liking for women."

"Of course I like women. Celibate or not, I'm a heterosexual."

Again the dismissing wave of her hand. "That is precisely the point. You have kept women at a distance during your life because of the need to protect your priestly vocation. Presumably you now see that in your case that vocation is protected by God's grace."

⁂

Sister Rogeria showed up in my office one hot August day, claiming that she was doing a master's paper on the psychology of religion. She wanted to interview me for suggestions about the direction in which she should go. It was the first of many lies from the plain young woman with a dagger face and disorderly brown hair.

Most of Sister Rogeria's questions did not deal with either psychology or religion. She wanted to know about my work habits, my lifestyle, my attitudes toward the "Third World," my feelings about homosexuality, my beliefs about the role of women in the Church. I grew impatient with her as she laboriously wrote down the verbatim answers to each of my questions. However, I endured her for three and a half hours, since helping priests and nuns was, I thought, part of what little vocation Pat Donahue had left me.

Just before I left for Rome on a long-planned Vatican research project in late September, the first of Sister Rogeria's articles appeared in the *National Catholic Reporter.* The headline was "Rich Priest Professor Ridicules Third World, Defends Colonialism." It described my alleged wealth (actually underestimated because she didn't know about the stock from the Colonel). It cited my comment that the Third World was mostly a collection of military dictatorships and that the ordinary people in the Third World countries were better off when British and French governments protected them from intertribal genocide. I'd said a lot of other things, too, none of them quite so spectacular. Sister Rogeria was not interested in a comparison between Tanzania and Kenya or in a careful economic analysis of various Third World countries.

Pat sent me a clipping of the article with his personal card—name printed in red, of course—and a note: "I wish you would not say such things, Kevin. It embarrasses the entire Diocese."

I left for Rome without replying to him. Sister Rogeria had fired her gun, I thought, and that was that. I didn't know that she had a whole arsenal.

The first evening in Rome I ate supper with my friend Monsignor Adolpho at Roberto's, around the corner from the Vatican on the Borgo Pio. As we sipped our Campari and soda, Adolpho silently handed me the latest issue of the *National Catholic Reporter.* "Priest-Psychologist Hits Gays," announced the headline. In the article Sister Rogeria reported that even though the American Psychiatric Association had voted to remove homosexuality from its list of mental illnesses, a priest who "claimed to be a psychologist" had described gays and lesbians as suffering from a "serious disorder." She left out all the qualifications, all the insistence on the human rights of homosexuals, all the distinctions about pastoral and personal response, and concentrated only on my remark that homosexual liaisons lack many of the characteristics that reinforce the "durability of heterosexual unions." To refute me, she quoted many "distinguished" Catholic psychologists who said that gay unions were as good as heterosexual unions. Most of the people she quoted were therapists with masters' degrees in counseling and guidance.

"So," said Adolpho, "the Holy Office will be pleased to find that you agree with them."

"I'm afraid I'll get another note from my Archbishop, pleading with me not to embarrass him," I said ruefully. "It's going to keep on. I suspect she's got a lot more arrows in her quiver."

Adolpho gestured expressively with his huge, peasant's hands. "Do not worry about your Archbishop. Already they know here he is a lightweight."

Roberto's was filling up, the dining room sticky from the warm night air. The diners, all in some form of clerical dress, ranging from the cassock to a Protestant-like gray suit, seemed to be engaged in conspiratorial conversation.

I felt constrained to defend Pat.

"He's done a spectacular job of putting the pieces back together," I argued. "The priests and the people love him. And since when do you have to be a heavyweight to be an archbishop in America?"

Adolpho laughed. "I have no influence"—a patent falsehood—"I just listen. Now, tell me your plans."

I explained that I was conducting a psychological study of the papal election. He was immediately fascinated.

"Ah, my friend, the papacy is so much. Just last Sunday, at the end of one of those interminable canonizations with which we amuse the crowds during this holy year, the poor Pope, after he finished mass, hobbled around the front of the altar and for just a moment smiled and waved to the people. They went wild with joy. They don't read his encyclicals; they don't like his hand-wringing; they're put off by his refusal to retire at seventy-five as other bishops must. Yet when he smiles and waves, he is for a brief moment the incarnation of Catholic Christianity. That is what the papacy means. He has tried hard, my friend—all those trips, the struggle against the conservatives in the Curia, protecting the Council. You will say that he has alienated the liberals who would have gladly supported him. I agree, but you do not know what disaster he has avoided."

"Like the birth-control encyclical?" I started to wolf down my fettuccine.

"You Americans are the only ones who worry about that," he said. "Here they see the huge crowds who have come to Rome for the holy-year pilgrimages and they say, 'See, the Holy Father was right. The people listened to him!' "

"Do they look at the birth rate in the Catholic countries?" I argued. "Do they realize how many of the pilgrims are carrying the pill in their purses when they shout 'Long live the Pope'? Do they know that their credibility on sexuality has gone down the drain? Do they know what's happening to vocations?"

Adolpho held up his hand again. "Some do, Kevin, and some don't. They are still stirred by the faith of the pilgrims. Self-deception? Of course, but you do not understand Rome if you think that a short-term crisis worries them. They will tell you that it is a shame that the Church is dying in the North Atlantic world, but that Eastern Europe and the Third World are the future."

"They can write off the West that easily?" I said, in dismay.

"From within the walls of the Vatican"—he gestured down the Borgo with his wineglass—"Chicago is only a small and new city. They take the long view, which means centuries. It is," he smiled ruefully, "a marvelous excuse for not coming back to your office after siesta."

"And the election?"

"No one talks about it. The Synod of Bishops last year brought many of the cardinal electors to Rome. The Pope is not well, yet there was not a mention of a conclave. It would be indecent to speak of it while the Pope is still alive, would it not?" He grinned amiably.

"How will they find out who the candidates are?"

He threw up his hands. "They will read about it in *Time* magazine, where else?"

"And the Curia will dominate the election?" I asked glumly.

"You must understand, Kevin"—he pushed aside his half-finished fettuccine—"the Curia has many advantages. The cardinals will be summoned from all over the world, perhaps without any warning. They will be pulled away from their business. They will be weary from jet travel. Perhaps it will be very hot here. They will not know the procedures or the issues or the candidates. The Curia will know how things are done. They will choose the ones who preach at the novena of masses for the repose of the Pope. They will know where the bathrooms are. They will control the procedures." He folded his massive arms and leaned on the table.

"So they'll dictate the outcome?" I said, close to despair.

"I will tell you a big secret, Father Kevin Brennan," he said in a solemn whisper. "They are disorganized, faction-ridden, politically inept. They control the Church because they are the only ones here. Whenever the *stranieri*—the foreigners—come to town, they beat the Curia." He waved his fork around at the dining room. "When it is a struggle between poor politicians and terrible politicians, who will win?"

"A few Chicago Irishmen could go a long way," I said.

"Like Patrick Cardinal Donahue, perhaps?"

❋

Maureen was already in her room when I returned to her apartment. Our greeting at the airport was perfunctory. She knew about my threats to Pat, and had been cool toward me the few times we'd seen each other since then.

I took a shower and went to bed, leaving the window open to catch some of the pleasant night breezes. Rain was supposed to sweep in from the southwest the next morning. Rome smelled more acrid than it had during the Council, but was less noisy because most of the Vespas had been replaced by tiny Fiats.

The rains came earlier than had been predicted. Lightning, thunder, driving torrents of water, swept into the city. I awoke to hear Mo closing the window of my bedroom.

"Can't let everything get soaked," she said sleepily.

"Of course not."

She sat on the edge of the bed. "Can we talk, Kev?"

"When couldn't we, Mo?" I was as much on guard against my own emotions as I was against hers. "I don't have a dossier, if you were wondering."

"The damn fool," she said. "I don't know what got into him. Just because a handful of priests were bitching about you."

"You know better than that, Mo," I said, wishing I'd stuffed pajamas into my flight bag.

"All right." She sounded impatient with me. "He's got some hang-ups about you, just as you do about him. It was still foolish to think he could order you around. But you didn't have to be that cruel. I bet you enjoyed every second of it."

"I didn't start the fight," I said defensively.

"You sure finished it, though, didn't you?" She was furious

with me. "Do you know he wanted to resign after that night? I spent two hours on the long-distance phone telling him he was crazy. He's got this thing about going into a monastery and doing penance for the rest of his life."

"Might not be a bad idea," I said, wishing I could see her face.

"Like hell! He's a good archbishop, isn't he? The best in the country, isn't he?"

"Because you tell him what to do." I was angry, too.

"What does that matter? Pat needs help, and you won't give it to him." She pounded the bed.

"He should not be an archbishop," I insisted.

"Who should? You? You can't forgive him for surpassing you. That's your trouble, you miserable son of a bitch."

"At least I don't need to hop in and out of bed with every woman I see. Anyway, don't worry, I'm not going to blow the whistle on you two. I didn't mean the threat, as I'm sure you realized right away. He's too stupid to see that I'd never do it."

She was sobbing, as though in great pain. "I love him so much, Kev. Every time he tries to end it, I let him go; then he comes back. I can't live with him and I can't live without him. I'm destroying him, too. Oh, God, I don't know what to do. I can't sleep at night worrying about it."

I pulled her head to my chest and stroked her long, black hair. "It will work out somehow, Mo."

"No, it won't," she said with conviction. "We're both damned. I wish I could squeeze some happiness out of the few years we have left."

I began to caress the velvet skin on her back, enjoying the softness of her body through the thin nightgown.

"You're not going to hell, Mo," I said. "Neither is Pat. It will work out. Give it time. It will be all right."

She relaxed in my arms, now supple and quiet. "You should get yourself a husband," I said clumsily.

"Who would want a used-up old woman?" she said.

"You're neither used up nor old, and you know that," I said, taking a very deep breath.

Soon she was sleeping quietly in my arms. I arranged her on the bed and covered her with the sheet.

"Great lover, Brennan," I told myself. "You get a beautiful woman in bed with you after four decades of fantasizing and you put her to sleep."

I retaliated by going to sleep myself.

When I got back from Rome, I found that Sister Rogeria was still blazing away. She had combed the reviews of my technical books as well as the popular ones and woven a catena of quotations out of context into a damning indictment of my professional competence. "Priest 'Expert' Hit by Critics," said the headline. Then there came a slanted version of my battle with the university. "Reveal Incompetence Reason for Tenure Decision on Priest 'Expert.' "

The Colonel phoned from Tucson. "She's just gone over the line," he said. "We'll slap a libel suit on her. Professional incompetence is an actionable charge."

"Might not be worth it, Dad," I said mildly.

He gasped. "Champ, I'm the one that's getting old, not you. Don't you want to win?"

"I may be getting a sympathy vote on this one," I said, thinking of that possibility for the first time.

"She's going to send her booklet on you to all the bishops and pastors in the country."

"Where's she getting the money?" I sniffed a conspiracy and began to share the Colonel's lust for battle.

"Your old friend Georgina Carrey, now Georgina Tansey," he said promptly. He still knew all the inside dope, even from the shadow of Mount Lennon.

⁂

Ellen thought the Archbishop's easy chair was like an enormous bathtub: once you sank into it, you'd practically have to climb out. She was lonely, tired, and more than a little drunk. She did not want to have to climb out of it.

"This is a nice house, Pat," she said, swallowing more cognac. "But despite the size and all the chimneys, it doesn't seem very comfortable."

"I think Archbishop Feehan built it more for show than for living. It's Mercy Sisters land, you know. Feehan's sister was a Mercy nun. They apparently bought the land so that he could build the house on it. O'Neil tried to sell the land for a skyscraper condo and discovered he didn't own it. The sisters told him he could go ahead and sell it, but they wanted the money." He laughed. "So it's still here, a historical landmark and a damn uncomfortable and inconvenient one at that. Terribly expensive to heat and cool."

For all its plush carpets and expensive antique furniture, its oak panels and fabric wall covering, the "Cardinal's Mansion" hardly seemed worth the effort. The tour of the mansion was an anticlimax, even after the dull Orchestra Board dinner that she had attended earlier in the evening. She had gone alone because Herb was out of town, and had been delighted to find Pat sitting beside her at dinner.

"What are the payoffs, Patrick?" she asked, her tongue thick with Scotch, wine, and now cognac. "I don't think it's the expensive suits, or the fancy license plate, or the first-class airplane tickets."

He nodded in understanding. "Some of them like the power, the ability to force others to do their will. Others like the acclaim, the title 'Your Eminence' or 'Your Excellency,' the look of respect, even subservience in the eyes of others. I saw what that led to in Dan O'Neil, and I don't want it. I'm human, as you well know, so I don't dislike *all* the things that go with the office. But if that were all, I'd resign in five minutes. You and Kevin may not believe it, but it's true."

"I believe it," she said solemnly. "Maybe those things attracted you once, but something else keeps you living in this awful Victorian barn now."

He nodded his head in silent agreement.

"What?" she persisted, finishing her cognac and resolving that she would not drink another drop.

He made a wry face. "I'm a damn good archbishop, Ellen. One of the best in the country. You couldn't find a more democratic, responsible, progressive diocese anywhere in the world. We've cleaned up the mess O'Neil made, and we're moving ahead. "He hesitated for a moment and shook his head as though to clear it. "I'm happy with my accomplishments. Isn't that enough?"

"More than enough," she said.

He filled her cognac glass and walked back to the couch, his body tense.

She should leave. The conversation, late at night, in the dim light of the opulently uncomfortable study, was becoming a surrealistic dream.

"I should be going home now, Patrick."

"Okay," he said. "I'll get your coat."

He left the room and came back in a moment, her evening wrap in his hand. She stood up unsteadily. She imagined his blue eyes had a hard gleam in them as he held her coat for her.

As she turned to push her arms into her coat, he grabbed her by her shoulders and spun her around. His lips came down hard on hers. Alcohol and fright paralyzed her. "No," she pleaded.

At first she tried to fight him. He was strong, and she was small, weak, and drunk. Her resistance seemed only to amuse him and to increase the cruel light in his eyes. He hates women, she thought as she drifted deeper into the nightmare.

He was more skillful now than he had been the night in the state park. Holding her immobile with one strong arm, he undressed her leisurely, playfully. Exhausted and beaten, she sank toward the bottom of the nightmare.

He carried her over to the couch and renewed his explorations. She was ready for him, more than ready. Her sighs were turning into moans of pleasure. Dear God, I don't want to. . . .

He continued to play with her, pushing her to the brink of pleasure and then pulling her back.

Then he stopped.

He staggered away from the couch, collapsed on his knees by his desk, and sobbed. He pounded his head against the cushion on his desk chair like a man in epileptic frenzy.

Instantly she was sober, a nurse again. Her sexual hungers disappeared. Covering herself with her slip, she rushed into the corridor, found a bathroom, and came back with an armful of wet towels. She knelt next to the ranting Archbishop and wrapped a towel around his face.

"It's all right, Patrick," she said soothingly. "It's all right."

Slowly his shoulders stopped shaking and his sobs diminished. Then, like a balloon losing its air, he collapsed. She helped him back to the couch. His face was that of a dead man.

She sat in the chair nearest him, still huddling behind her slip.

"If you're going to have a fit," he said hoarsely, "it's a good idea to have it with a psychiatric nurse around." His laugh soared toward hysteria again.

"Stop it, Patrick!" she barked.

He buried his head in his hands. "Ellen, I adore you. I've al-

ways adored you. I didn't want to do that. This terrible thing happens inside of me. I didn't want to do it."

"I know that, Patrick," she said reassuringly, though her heart was still thumping madly. "If you wanted to do it, you would have finished."

"I'm kinky. Always have been, I guess. When I'm away from Mo, and when things are bad here . . ." His head remained buried in his strong hands.

"You need help, Patrick," she said calmly, as though it were perfectly normal to be sitting nearly naked in an archbishop's house discussing his emotional problems.

He sobbed again, not hysterically but deeply, sadly. "I'm so ashamed. You and Maureen and Kevin are more important to me than anybody I know. Yet I mess up Maureen's life, I alienate Kevin, and then I try to rape you. I don't want to hurt any of you. I love you all."

"Especially Kevin," she said in a burst of understanding.

He looked up at her. "You know that, too, do you? Especially Kevin. You won't tell him?"

"Of course I won't tell him."

"I'm probably more of a homosexual than anything else. There's no anger or hatred then, only peace. Strange, that's the first time I've ever spoken the word about myself."

"That's too simple, Patrick. Your relationship with Maureen gives the lie to that explanation."

He stood up shakily, like a man recovering from a long illness. "Kinky, anyway."

"A good prospect for therapy. You'd get it sorted out quickly, Pat. You've got to do it. It's been bothering you for all your life."

He laughed weakly. "An archbishop in therapy. You're kidding, El. It would never work." He paused, then said, "Don't worry. You're as safe now as you would be in a convent."

Only after he left the room did she realize she ought to dress. As she put on her clothes, she almost persuaded herself it had all been a dream.

He came back into the room and suggested he drive her home.

"Forgive me," he pleaded as he opened the door for her and they went outside.

"Of course, Patrick, of course." She hoped it sounded sincere. "Promise me you'll think about getting help?"

"All right," he said. "I'll think about it very seriously indeed."

In the dim glow of the streetlight his handsome face was wasted, haggard.

She knew he would not seek help. Ever.

CHAPTER TWENTY-ONE

1977

Patrick Henry Donahue was raised to the sacred crimson within a week of my twentieth anniversary in the priesthood.

I'd fought to the edge of my depression and gloom. My books were selling better than ever; my group of young people from the St. Praxides days, most of them now in their thirties, had revived itself. I was finding myself a niche in the American Church—on the outer fringes, indeed, but a place where contentment might be possible. Yet I could not take the final steps out of the fog. Pat's appointment to the Sacred College, for which I ought to have been prepared, drove me back into the thick mists.

"The Church is on the upswing," I said to Sister Mary Carmel. "People are going back to church. They've found that they can be enthusiastic Catholics and ignore the Church's teachings. My sister and brothers are dedicated lay persons whose consciences are untroubled by birth control."

Sister Carmel permitted herself a smile. "And God has managed all of this without your assistance and despite your predictions. How inconsiderate of him!"

I was dejected, battered, and lonely. I didn't need her harassment.

"You are upset now because your classmate has been made a cardinal," she continued. "You acknowledge that he's one of the best archbishops in America. What offends you and depresses you is the thought that you are in part responsible for his success. You must decide at each new promotion whether you are going to bear the burden of that responsibility any longer."

"He's a *papier-maché* man, Sister, a walking inkblot. You saw him at the Call to Action meeting in Detroit. He repeated every liberal cliché in the books. Then he went to the bishops' meeting, helped to torpedo the recommendations of the conference, and got a red hat for a reward."

She sighed her most exasperated sigh. "Is he the first churchman to be politically skillful? Is he the first archbishop to find celibacy impossible? Is he the first *papier-maché* cardinal? You will never denounce him, Father. You will keep tipping back rebounds to him, as you put it, for the rest of your life, if necessary. You must, however, give up this ridiculous conceit that if you were not around to save him, the Almighty would not find another instrument for using Patrick Donahue as an agent in His Plan. You indulge yourself overmuch in assuming responsibility for designs which are the Almighty's and not your own."

"He's going to get caught," I said gloomily.

"I daresay." Her hands were under the scapular again. "And, Good Father, the Church will survive, as will God's love for you."

I had supper that evening at the Chicago Club with Herb and Ellen. His hair was now completely gray. Ellen permitted certain flecks of the same color in her soft, blond hair because she knew that it made her even more hauntingly lovely. At forty-three my water sprite radiated mature, satisfied sexuality the way a golden mum radiates joy in the face of the inevitability of winter.

"Darling Kevin"—her smile was slower now and more captivating—"would I be risking interdict if I asked why you have rediscovered the good doctor and myself?" The waiter brought the poached salmon she had ordered. There were only a couple of tables occupied in the solemn and august dining room. The men at the tables had not taken their eyes off Ellen since she had come into the room.

"We thought at first," said Herb, tasting the claret cautiously, "that you were worried about Caroline. Yet who could have a more poised and lovely eighteen-year-old daughter, even if she is going to Notre Dame, God help us all?"

"So we have a mystery." Ellen's gray eyes consumed me just as they had done in the Sugar Bowl at the lake when we were kids. "Why is Kevin worried about us? It isn't Caroline; it isn't any of the other kids. Does he think we're having trouble in our marriage?"

"You think I see you because I'm feeling responsible for you?"

Ellen put down her fork. "Once a month, regular as clockwork, for the last five months. Suddenly, without warning, Kevin Brennan is a fixture in our lives." She put her hand on mine. "When Kevin Brennan becomes a fixture in anyone's life, he's worried about them, or feels responsible for them, or is trying to help them. We appreciate and enjoy the help; we just want to know what it's for."

"I see you every month because Sister Mary Carmel said I ought to." My face was as hot as the June sunlight. "She thinks it's good for my spiritual life to have you as friends."

Ellen looked suspicious and a bit angry. *"Who,"* she demanded imperiously, "is Sister Mary Carmel?"

"My . . . well, I guess 'spiritual director' would be the right label." I plunged into my beef Wellington. "She's lovely"—good, that will make Ellen even more jealous—"and profoundly concerned about my spiritual welfare. She prescribed more interaction—my word, God knows—with close friends."

"She knows about me . . . us?" Ellen was still dubious, but the corners of her mouth were turning toward a grin.

"She knows how much you and Herb mean to me. She says I have to spend more time with people. I hope it doesn't sound as if I'm using you."

"For the love of God!" said Herb in a rare outburst of near profanity.

Ellen was laughing. "Kevin's got a woman spiritual director. How absolutely marvelous. Darling, you must tell us all about her. Does she make you say your prayers every night? Do you keep a record of your worst faults? Does she give you absolution? Is she *really* pretty?"

"Ellen," said Herb in mild reproof.

"Kevin knows that I'm laughing so I won't cry." She looked at me with misty eyes. "I'm so glad that you . . . I don't want to say 'that you've found help' . . ." She smiled brightly. "I'm glad you found someone who has enough sense to make you see us every month. Would you like to try for every two weeks?"

I wanted to escape. "Don't know. I'll have to ask. She says virtuous habits are acquired slowly."

"Just *how* pretty is she?" Ellen said.

"Absolutely gorgeous," I said. "Tall, slender, willowy, jet-black hair, the kind of figure that never has to worry about calories and is immune to the temptations of such worldly things as chocolate."

Mrs. Strauss sniffed disdainfully and ordered chocolate mousse for dessert. They both wanted to meet Sister Mary Carmel.

No way.

⁂

Pat was a superb lover now, more demanding than Sloane, more gentle than Fredo. His preliminary caresses were tender and sensitive. He prepared her slowly and leisurely, awaking every cell in her body, delaying their union until she was witless with desire. Now his strength served to heal and cherish her, and his demands were more for her satisfaction than for his.

"Thank you so much, Pat," she breathed, covering herself with her slip in the surge of modesty that often followed their lovemaking. "I've felt so terrible about Sheila. I needed to be loved."

His fingertips stroked her face. "Poor Sheila has to live her own life," he said gently, "just as we have to live ours. In Dublin she's trying to find her independence. She'll be back." He pried the slip out of her hands, wanting to enjoy all of her. She told herself again she had to lose weight and exercise more.

"You're a very sensitive and tender man," she said.

"If I am, the reason is that you taught me how to be both," he whispered softly, his lined face taking on that sad look that meant he was beginning to think once again about the terrible contradiction that tore at his life. "You've taught me to be everything that is good in me. It's not much, God knows, but I owe it all to you." He began to disengage himself from their embrace.

They would not make love again, not this afternoon. She felt cheated. She lay on the couch naked. As he dressed, she willed that the image of her body would burn itself into his memory so that he would come back again before he left Rome.

"I'm surprised that Kevin and the Strausses didn't come for the consistory," she said.

"I'm not," he said, slipping the small, cardinal-red cloth under his collar.

She regretted that she'd brought up that subject, of all subjects. "Still not good between you and Kev?" she said sadly.

He put on his black coat; it fit his broad shoulders perfectly. "How can it be good between us? He has the power of life and death over me. For all I know, even now there's a letter on Villot or Caprio's desk denouncing me. I've got to live every minute knowing that Kevin can wipe out my career with a flick of his finger." His shoulders tensed with constrained rage.

"He'll never do anything of the sort, Pat. He hasn't so far, has he? He wouldn't have threatened you if you hadn't backed him into a corner. Can't you make peace with him?"

He came and sat next to her on the couch. "I know that, Mo," he whispered gently as his fingers stroked her cheek. "It was absolutely stupid of me. Kevin is the best friend I've ever had besides you. I can't help being mad at him, yet it breaks my heart that he's not here celebrating with me. It really is as much his victory as mine."

She could teach him what to say and what to do and how to make love. She could never give him depth, just as she never could take away from Kevin the excess of depth with which he was cursed. If only somehow the two of them could be averaged.

"This is something you've wanted ever since you went to Quigley, isn't it?" she asked gently.

Pat frowned. "I thought I saw it in my vision of the Blessed Mother. I never thought it would happen, though. Maybe I'd be better off if it didn't happen. You thought that long ago, didn't you?"

He stood above her.

"I might have been wrong." She touched his arm.

"Regardless of whether it's good or bad for me, it's happened. I suppose I should be delighted. Yet it doesn't seem really to make

much difference. I wish Kevin were here—though heaven knows a red hat wouldn't impress him in the slightest." He seemed reluctant to go. "I've decided that I'm going to retire on my twenty-fifth anniversary," he said thoughtfully, his mind and imagination far away. "I'll have done the work I came to Chicago to do. It will be time to try something else. I'll be the first one to show that you don't have to be a cardinal for the rest of your life."

"What will you do then?" she said, guiding his hand to her breast. He did not resist. "I don't know," he said, fondling her, still thinking of something else.

He looked at his watch. "Damn, it's later than I thought. I promised Tonio and Fredo I would have a drink with them before the reception tonight at the Italian embassy to the Vatican. Isn't it wonderful that Tonio and I have been elevated at the same time?"

She let go of his hand, giving him up to his other world. For Tonio Martinelli she was never any competition.

She thought of all the other women who must have loved cardinals down through the centuries. Some of them had surely made love to their cardinal lovers in the very palazzo where her body and Pat's had so marvelously intertwined half an hour before.

She and Pat were part of the wrong century. In another age they could have loved openly. Now they had to pretend. What if he found out that she was sleeping with Alfredo DeLucca? Would he understand? He was so much more superb a lover than the depraved Fredo, who could succeed only when he was harsh and cruel. Yet, increasingly, she needed someone harsh and cruel, someone who would inflict pain that would override the deeper pain that was always within her.

It was a hot afternoon. A pleasant lethargy flowed through her body. How good it was to sleep naked on a couch in an old palace in Rome, listening to the distant sound of laughing children . . . and to dream that you were a tragic heroine from the past.

⁂

The Synod of Bishops in the fall of 1977 was the nadir of Pope Paul VI's regime. Representatives of bishops of the world came to Rome to talk about the education of the young. Even the most dense knew that the Church had no credibility with young people because of its stand on sexual morality and, in particular, because of its seemingly hypocritical insistence on a birth-control position that its laity rejected, its clergy refused to enforce, and its hierarchy honored only by lip service. Yet no one dared mention the problems of sexual morality and sexual credibility, for fear of offending the aged Pope. Nor was there any discussion of a possible conclave, even though the Pope was visibly slipping every month.

"Are they blind?" I demanded of Father Carter as we sat in his office, deep in the Vatican, watching workers tend the carefully cultivated autumn flowers in the garden. "How long do they think this man is going to last?"

Carter, a Los Angeles Jesuit who would have much preferred watching the Rams on an October Sunday afternoon, waved his slender artist's hands. "It's a funny thing. There was more talk about a conclave at the Synod three years ago. No one thought he would last this long. Now people are saying that he's as sharp as ever."

"Do you believe that?" I asked.

"I believe that he's sharp for about four hours every day."

I felt sadness for Paul VI, a well-meaning man whose dreams of an orderly change in the Church had been shattered. He was clinging to life as we all did—a few short years for the best of us and the worst of us.

"And the conclave?"

"Nothing has changed, except now Benelli is in Florence and a cardinal," Carter said.

"A favorite?" I asked. He would make a very tough pope.

"I doubt it," said Carter, rising to walk to his small window. "No, Benelli has made too many enemies here. My guess, though, is that Benelli will play king-maker for some noncurial Italian, maybe Ursi, of Naples, or Luciani, of Venice."

"Isn't Ursi a bit . . . unstable?" I pretended to watch the gardeners but watched Carter all the more intently.

"Gets crazier by the day." Carter shook his head, more interested still in the Vatican gardens, which was an immediate problem, whereas the conclave, by his estimate, was at least a year away.

"Your friend Pat is cutting a wide path here. The only American cardinal with any flair. He could be an important man in the conclave. He's got the moves." Reluctantly he returned to his desk and slumped to his chair, his ascetic face thoughtful.

"What about a foreigner?" I asked him at the door.

"I don't see it," he said, shaking hands. "Not enough votes ready to break the tradition. They'd have to find an acceptable Italian. Not likely."

"Who's worth watching?" I persisted.

"If someone gives you long odds, bet on Wojtyla, the man from Cracow," he said slowly. "Very long odds."

"A Polish pope?" I said, with all the prejudice of the Chicago Irish. "Don't be silly."

⁂

"God, it was nice to see you and the Strausses again," said Maureen, expertly dodging a Fiat driven by a lunatic. "I was afraid they were mad at me. I didn't answer Ellen's letters or call you when I was home last time. I guess you know why, don't you, Kev? I'm glad they don't hate me."

"I gather that you and Ellen had an argument about Pat," I said cautiously. "She told me none of the details."

"It's all over, anyway." Her eyes were fixed grimly on the

autostrada. "Pat ended it last summer. I can't blame him. It's the right thing to do."

Ended it *again*, I thought.

"He told Ellen and Herb about Sheila's marriage. It gave Ellen the excuse to call you, though she would have found one," I said.

"She's always loved me." Maureen lit a cigarette from the lighter on the dashboard. "I was unspeakable to her."

"Forgiveness is a good thing," I said piously. "Reconciliation is better."

"So you're going to be reconciled to Pat?" she said, pouncing on me. "He needs your help, Kevin."

"I doubt it," I said. "Did he tell you that?"

She angled the car into the loading zone at the international terminal. "No. I don't see him. We've both got it out of our system."

I'll believe that when I see it, I thought. I leaned across the front of the car and kissed her cheek with affection.

"That was nice," she said. "How come all the attention?"

"Don't ask for explanations," I said, opening the door of the car.

"Next time, would you stop in Dublin and see Sheila?" Her handsome face looked pathetically old for a moment. "She's so young to be married."

"Sure I will."

I put down my flight bag and kissed her again, this time not worrying about the boundaries of passion. We clung to each other as we had nearly three decades before on New Year's Eve in Florida.

"I won't ask why, Kevin," she said, breaking away. "I know why, and thanks."

As the plane for home soared out over the glittering blue of the Mediterranean, quickly breaking through the Roman smog, I thought of Mo's glittering blue eyes.

Sister Mary Carmel would approve.

He walked the cobblestone streets slowly and reluctantly, a piece of lead filing being drawn powerlessly toward a magnet. The Piazza Farnese was deserted, not a trace of the open-air market that kept it throbbing during the day. He paused at the head of the tiny, winding street that led to Maureen's palazzo. *Poor woman. Her eighteen-year-old daughter already married to a man in Dublin, Maureen informed only after the wedding. Poor, dear, fragile woman. He listened sadly to the echo of his footsteps.*

It was not pity that was drawing him toward her bedroom. It was finished again last summer when she came to Chicago. He resisted her invitations to Beverly Shores, though at the last minute he had almost succumbed. A call from the Apostolic Delegation and a hasty plane flight to Washington saved him. He came to Rome confident that the temptation resisted last summer could be resisted again. For three weeks he had been successful, throwing himself into the work of the Synod, losing himself in the very discreet background politics in preparation for a conclave that he believed was still a long way off.

He walked slowly down the street and stopped at the door of her palazzo. *This section of Rome always smelled faintly of human excrement—a smell probably hundreds of years old. Her affair with Fredo, delicately hinted at by Tonio, made it easier. Was he in there now? Not likely. Fredo didn't spend the night with his women. He looked at his watch. One-thirty. No, she was probably alone. He found the key in his pocket. He knew when he had put the key in his pocket earlier in the afternoon that he was going to come here.*

He was tense, tied up in cruel knots. He would punish Maureen for being a temptress and for being unfaithful to him. One last wild, vicious fuck and he would be done with her forever.

He turned on the lights of her bedroom. She opened her eyes and watched him move toward her bed. He wanted to beat her, savage her, leave her a bloody mess. She deserved to be raped without mercy. His hands clenched and unclenched rapidly. He was breathing heavily. Is Fredo better in bed than I am?

He touched her throat gently. He moved his fingers across her face. She relaxed in response to his tenderness. She needed to be healed. He would heal, not destroy.

CHAPTER TWENTY-TWO

1978

I watched the Cardinal Archbishop as I preached the homily at my parents' funeral mass. His anguished face reflected as much loss as I felt.

"We must look on death not as the beginning of a voyage but the end of one, not as the start of a mysterious and dangerous journey across an unknown ocean but an arrival at a safe harbor. It is not a dubious farewell we bid to those we love as they are embarking on a dubious pilgrimage; it is rather a homecoming, a celebration of victory rather than an admission of defeat.

"There is sorrow in our hearts this morning, and that is as it should be. We have come to say good-bye, a temporary good-bye, indeed, but still a good-bye. Yet we know that we will meet the Colonel and his Lady again when they are present at our own homecoming, a homecoming, need I say, which the Colonel will have arranged with his usual quiet, behind-the-scenes efficiency.

"He once told me that after Cassino, everything else was pure bonus. We are glad for the bonus that kept him and Mom with us for more than thirty years since then." My voice cracked. There were some tears in the first row—Mary Ann, Mike, Joe, Steve, Kathy, Helen, the nine grandchildren. Not too many tears, though. The Brennans grieved privately. "We know that they would have been happy to go together." A helicopter had crashed into their house at night. Quick, perhaps painless. "And we believe that they will arrange our homecomings together—with Mom having the last word, as Irish mothers always do." Now there were some smiles. "So there is grief this morning, more grief than we Brennans are able to show. But there is also hope, unquenchable hope, indeed the laughing hope with which we Irish always defy death just as the Colonel did at Cassino. We say not good-bye to James and Mary Brennan, but as Catholic Christians, with our implacable hope, we say, simply, 'See you around.' "

Pat was crying openly. So was Ellen. So, I was sure, was Maureen. I ended the sermon and went on with the mass as quickly as I could.

The Colonel would have loved it.

We buried them in the cemetery behind the new church at the lake. The Cardinal and I gave the final absolution together.

Afterward I slipped away from the family and went down to the Sugar Bowl. Herb, Ellen, and Mo were already there, as if we had some pact to return. Save for us and the waitress, the place was empty. It still smelled of stale milk.

"Do you remember," said Ellen, "the first night—"

"You were as mouthy a little kid then as now," I said.

"The jukebox played 'It Might as Well Be Spring,' " said Mo, dabbing at her eyes.

"And everyone said you looked like Jeanne Crain," I added.

Herb watched us, his gentle eyes moving from face to face, fascinated and, I think, awed by the Irish response to death.

"And you treated me like I was a third-grader," Ellen said, her voice shaking.

"A pretty smart third-grader, with an appetite for chocolate malteds and fingers that jumped away quickly when they were touched."

"Let's all order one," said Maureen. "Miss, may we have four malted milks? See, Kevin, you don't do the ordering for all of us anymore."

"Don't I? Make it six," I said to the waitress, as I noticed the Cardinal and Art McGrath come in.

Pat hesitated as though he wanted to run, then squared his shoulders and joined us. So did McGrath. Today I would not think harsh thoughts.

We were good for two or three more rounds of nostalgia. Then it was time to go. Pat, Art, and I were the last to leave.

"It's not the end, Kevin," Pat said, gripping my hand.

"No, Patrick, it's not."

For a moment we were close in our sense of loss. Then we went our separate ways.

March 1

Dear Mo,

It's settled. Herb and I are going to Ireland in September. It is also settled that Kevin is coming with us, though he is in such a daze that I don't think he realizes he's agreed. Then we'll come down to Rome to see you. Herb has a weekend in Munich and we're going to spend time in Florence (s'cuse me, *Firenze*) before we go home.

Ria is sixteen tomorrow, the spitting image of me except around the eyes; and in very short order Caroline is going to stop being a teenager, though she's capable even now of five-minute interludes when she acts as if she's thirty.

Time passes.

I'm worried about Kevin. We all suffer when parents die. He was so close to his. His life is so lonely, partly by his choice. I don't know how he stands it. Herb thinks he's close to the breaking point. It's as though he has nothing left to live for. Half the time he doesn't hear what you say.

He loves the damned Church but it hurts him. He keeps on loving it and it keeps on hurting him. It always will. Why can't he see that we are the Church—every bit as much as the miserable idiots who run it and make him suffer?

Scratch "miserable idiots" and write "fragile human beings." I'm so filled with charity I make myself sick.

If I love him and you love him and our children love him (and does Ria ever have a teenage crush on him!) and his family loves him, then why does he let himself be hurt by the Cardinal and the Pope and the stupid, envious priests who bait him?

Let "stupid, envious priests" stand. My charity has its limits.

Herb says that Kevin is entering a period that ought to be his most creative time. We're both afraid that he'll shrivel up like a dried-out grapefruit.

Do I sound like a romantic novelist when I say that despite my worry about him, I think Kevin's sufferings have somehow *purified* him? The old arrogance and ruthlessness are still there. He is occasionally as fiercely competitive as he ever was. Yet, particularly with the kids, he is almost terrifyingly gentle, strange as that sounds. Herb thinks that might be the first sign of a breakdown.

He's still mourning for Patsy, too.

Dying to see you.

Love,
ELLEN

We were sitting around the Strauss swimming pool having drinks when we were interrupted by the arrival of the Cardinal Archbishop of Chicago and his faithful aide, Art McGrath, both in full clerical garb, complete, in Pat's case, with red socks.

"Herb! Ellen!" Pat said heartily. "Art and I were driving from Milwaukee and I thought I'd show him the old stomping grounds. Beautiful house you have here, Herb! Blends right in with the trees. And Ellen, you've saved the old swimming hole. Congratulations. Wonderful! Kevin, this is an unlooked-for surprise. Now, introduce me to all the kids."

A superbly staged entry. Our democratic, hearty Cardinal.

"Kevin, I hear you're doing a book on the next papal election. You'll have to wait awhile to finish it, I'm afraid. I saw the Pope before he went to Castel Gandolfo. For a man his age, he's remarkably chipper."

Not a word I would use to describe Giovanni Montini, even in the best of health.

Despite the heat, the Cardinal and Art kept their collars on and protested that they would have only one quick drink.

"We were talking about celibacy before you came," said Ellen solemnly. "Do you think there's going to be a change, Pat?"

He swished his Scotch thoughtfully. "We're going to tough it out, El; the resurgence of spirituality in recent years indicates that people are going to want more emphasis on the eschatological dimensions of Catholicism. A celibate priesthood is nothing, if not an eschatological symbol, don't you think, Herb? I'm sure we'll weather this crisis just as we have the others."

"The problem may not be celibacy, for all we know," said Art McGrath, watching me curiously. "Maybe we're not encouraging people to vocations anymore because we have lost faith in ourselves. You've written on this, haven't you, Kevin?"

So he wasn't altogether a stooge. "Yes," I said hesitantly, "but I'm not convinced that priests are all that inhuman. Some of us, anyway."

Ellen slipped a matching robe over her swimsuit. "What *is* the point in celibacy, Kevin?" she said with that innocent smile I'd learned to fear.

"Maybe we ought to make it optional." I knew as soon as I started to talk that I was going to be outrageous. "Yet I'd hate to see us lose it. The world, Catholic and otherwise, needs the witness of a few people who are living proof that you can intensely and passionately love members of the opposite sex without having to jump into bed with them."

Ellen bit her lips as though she were trying to suppress a smile. Herb's eyes lit up. The youngsters froze in place, suddenly interested in the debate. In the distance a phone rang.

"Trouble with having someone like Kevin in the diocese," said Art McGrath, "is that he says things like that. Stops the conversation dead." He munched blissfully on a potato chip.

Brendan Curran came running from the house. "CBS News on the phone, Father," he said urgently.

After I took the call, I went back down the walk, through the trees, and rejoined the others. The conversation had changed to the architecture of the Strausses' summer home. I signaled to Pat that I wanted to talk to him.

"The Pope had a heart attack at Castel Gandolfo," I said. "CBS says that he is not expected to live."

"I'd better be moving," he muttered. "Oh, God, Kevin, we ought to be ready, but we're not. We've got to keep in touch in Rome, Kevin." He shook hands warmly.

"I know it's selfish of me," said Ellen, "with the dear man not even in the ground—but will this interfere with our trip to Ireland with you in September?"

I couldn't recall that I'd agreed to any such trip.

"Ellen," Herb said mildly. "Kevin has other things on his mind."

"I'm sorry, Kevin, I'm just selfish."

She looked worried. I didn't have the time to ask what was on her mind.

⁂

Art McGrath gave Pat's coupon to the clerk at the counter in the Ambassador Lounge. "Four-thirty-four to Rome," he said. "The Cardinal is leaving for the conclave."

The young woman was flustered. "Yes, of course, Father. We're saving a seat for him, most comfortable one in first class. There will be no one in the row with him, so he'll have complete privacy."

Then she saw Pat. "We have a private room available just around the corner, Your Eminence. You can relax there until boarding time. If you don't mind, I'll need to see your passport."

Art produced the passport.

Pat had aged in the last twenty-four hours. He was always a puzzle to his secretary. Art did not think the responsibility of electing a pope would weigh so heavily on him. He'd have guessed Pat would take it all as a lark. Instead, he was dead serious, even grim.

"We'll pray for the guidance of the Holy Spirit." The young woman smiled nervously.

"Thank you very much," Pat said automatically, then forced his legendary smile. "We'll need it."

⁂

Jordan Bonfonte, the Rome bureau chief of *Time,* put his portable radio in his pocket. At first the smoke seemed white, then black, and then, for forty-five minutes, gray.

We began to stroll away, joining the rest of the disappointed crowd in the fading daylight. "Thank God it wasn't white," Bonfonte said with relief. "I'd have only twelve hours to do a cover story."

Then lights went on behind the curtains on the windows leading to the balcony of St. Peter's. *"Attenzione,"* said the ominous voice on the public-address system.

The crowd shrieked with joy. We rushed back through the barricades to the foot of the obelisk. The doors swung open. Floodlights focused on the balcony. Felici. Well, *he* didn't win.

"Annuntio vobis gaudium magnum. Habemus papam!" We have a new pope! He was clearly very pleased with himself. *"Albinum Cardinalem Sanctae Romanae Ecclesiae Luciani!"*

Jordan disappeared to dash off his story. I picked my way through the cheering crowds, past the forbidding palace of the holy office and down the Via Aurelia to the Michelangelo. Somehow a letdown. Only four votes to choose a virtual unknown from Northern Italy. We would look pretty foolish to the rest of the world.

At my hotel, I watched the new Pope, who had taken the name John Paul, on the small television set. A magnificent smile—dazzling, happy, radiant. A smiling, joyous Pope. Maybe a good idea.

Sabatini's again. This time a splendid September evening with a cloudless sky and a light breeze that drove off the inevitable Trastevere smell. Father Carter, charmed as anyone would be by the twin blond heads of Ellen Strauss and Monica Varco, told fascinating stories about this ancient district "across the Tiber," a picaresque place even in the time of the Caesars. He didn't miss the story of Alfredo Ottaviani's evil eye.

"I can't believe people in the Vatican would take that seriously," Monica said. "They really don't, do they?"

Carter relished it. "I get a creepy feeling every time he looks at me." The silverware glittered; the wineglasses sparkled; the white tablecloths glowed; the waiters were especially attentive; the wine flowed.

"How's your book on the papal election, Kevin?" Carter finally turned to the subject that had brought me back to Rome.

"Almost finished. It's not all that much of a story. A one-day conclave in which an Italian pope is elected almost by acclamation. What kind of a pope has he been?"

Carter stirred his espresso thoughtfully. "He's learning the job very quickly for an outsider. I hear that yesterday Casaroli went to him with six decisions about Eastern Europe, and he made five of them on the spot. It would have taken Paul VI five months. Casaroli is telling people that they're all the right decisions, too."

"Why don't they use him more on television?" said Monica. "We saw him at the audience yesterday and he held everyone in the palm of his hand. He even had Father Brennan smiling."

Our chance meeting with Monica and Tom Varco in the lobby of their hotel in Rome had disconcerted her. Herb's warm invitation that they join us at dinner gave her her confidence back. If her former therapist didn't mind, why should she?

Carter laughed. "The Vatican doesn't even have color-videotape capability."

"So get it." She waved her hand as though it were a minor problem. "You've got the hottest television property in the world. Syndicate the Pope!"

Everyone laughed. The Pope a hot property, indeed!

I went to sleep immediately when we got back to the hotel, and dreamed of Herb and Ellen, confusing them with my parents. Sister Carmel appeared in a bikini to tell me about "God's holy will"; then there was a helicopter crash and the ring of sirens. Sister Carmel was laughing diabolically. "God's holy will!" she shouted.

I climbed up out of my sleep. The siren was still sounding. No, it was the phone.

"Pronto," I mumbled.

"Carter, Kevin. Sorry to disturb you. Vatican Radio just announced that the Pope is dead. Magee found his body this morning. He must have died last night. Tucci is saying the Mass of the Resurrection on the radio now. When we were talking last night about him being a hot property, his body must have already been growing cold."

I began to worry again. We were in trouble. The last compromise Italian was gone.

CHAPTER TWENTY-THREE

1978

Patrick Cardinal Donahue shook too much parmesan cheese on his *spaghetti alla bolognese.*

"God, Kevin, how long has it been since we've had lunch together?"

"Ages," I said noncommittally. I took some secret comfort from the fact that my Cardinal Archbishop was showing his years. Compared to the other cardinals, he was still young and handsome, but his hair was streaked with gray and his face was beginning to bloat.

"What do you think is going to happen day after tomorrow?" he asked expansively, refilling my glass with *vino da casa.* The Cardinal Archbishop was taking a dissident priest to lunch on the Borgo Pio, but there was no cause to spend a lot of money. Nor would we go to one of the places where the press might encounter us—Marcello's or Roberto's, close to the walls of the Vatican.

"The papers are all predicting Siri will be the next pope," I said. "I don't believe that. Siri doesn't have the votes. He's a stalking horse for someone else." I nibbled on a bread stick.

Pat liberally spread butter on a thick crust of Roman bread. A muscle in his neck was throbbing. He was in trouble again and wanted me to get him out of it. I suspected as much when he proposed lunch.

"Fredo DeLucca set it up," he said.

He washed the crust down with a huge swallow of wine. He would get to his problem in his own time.

"And doubtless his cousin, the Archbishop of Perugia, is mixed up in it, too," I said.

"Right." He waved his fork before he plunged it into his pasta. "They and their friends want to keep the papacy in Italy. If it comes to it, they might even like to see Antonio himself." He was warming to his subject. "Benelli isn't thought to be too old at fifty-seven. Antonio is five years younger."

A homosexual pope at fifty-two, I thought to myself. "They must be mad," I said derisively.

"Not necessarily, Kevin." He waved his fork again. "This is a very different kind of conclave from the last one. People are afraid. They want someone who will keep the Church from falling apart, someone who is tough on Communism, someone who will bring an end to all the flabbiness since the Council. Antonio and his friends could live with Siri, of course, or even with Felici. But they would like to have it for themselves."

It was time to bring the charade to an end. I leaned forward, fixed my eyes on his, and gave him the scenario. "The first morning Benelli and Siri will cancel each other out. That afternoon they try for a compromise-type Italian. But there's no Luciani. The next day, they—you—elect one of the *stranieri*."

Pat listened intently, not touching his food. He nodded. "Can't fool a West Side Irishman, can you, Kev? Sure, that's what's going to happen, but not without the American votes. That's where I come in." He took a very long draft of wine. "Most of my American colleagues will go along with Siri the first morning. If I clue them to Colombo in the afternoon, he may win it. Even if I don't clue them that way, they still might do it. I only get important at the end of the first day, when chaos sets in."

"What do you think the *Sun-Times* and *Tribune* headlines will look like if you guys elect Colombo, a seventy-six-year-old, to succeed a sixty-five-year-old who died in a month?"

Pat dismissed the headlines with an imperious wave of his hand. "He's probably going to get the American votes anyway. He's a good man. Antonio would settle for him as a last-ditch savior of the Italian papacy."

"Who the hell is Antonio? What makes him so important?"

Pat turned pale, took a deep breath, and said softly, "He's the man who is blackmailing me."

I drained my goblet.

Pat rushed on. "You know that DeLucca was Maureen's lover some of the time. Before the August conclave he gave some terrorists the key to her apartment. They rigged hidden cameras in the bedroom, and when we were, uh . . . they got pictures. They didn't use them in August, because they saw that Luciani was going to be elected and thought they could manipulate him."

"Who are *they*?" I demanded, trying to keep my rage in check. I couldn't believe it—pictures of a cardinal in bed!

"Oh, I don't know. DeLucca, Antonio, some of their friends, a few monarchists and extreme right-wing capitalists, some bankers who want to get Marcinkus out of the Vatican bank so they can use it. Then there's a right-wing terrorist group—the Slaves of St. Anthony of Padua. Those kind of people."

"You've seen the pictures?" I asked. Classy blackmail would be better than sleazy blackmail.

He nodded miserably, all the verve gone. "Fredo showed them to me. They gave an American newspaper—a big one—the story and promised them the pictures. The reporter came to me asking for confirmation or denial. I told him the whole thing was ridiculous. Threw him out of the Villa Stritch. Worst anti-Catholic bastard I've ever seen. Then I got a phone call from Antonio saying he was shocked to hear about the calumnies that were being spread about me. His cousin Fredo would tell me how to stop them. I had lunch with Fredo—right here—on Wednesday. He showed me the pictures and assured me that there was nothing to worry about. The American paper would never get them, because he had been able to buy them from the terrorists. I could have them after the conclave, when he would be able to get all of them. Antonio called me later in the afternoon, didn't mention the pictures, gave me my orders for the conclave—nicely phrased, of course, but orders just the same." He wiped the corner of his mouth with a napkin.

"Is the newspaper a scandal sheet?" He shook his head no. "Then they won't do a thing without documentation. They won't print the pictures, but they'll do the story and the pictures will get leaked so a scandal sheet can use them. You've been had, Pat. I don't suppose you know where the pictures and the film are."

He pushed his clenched fists together. "As a matter of fact, I do. A young priest on Antonio's staff owes me some . . . uh, 'favors' is, I guess, the word we'd use. The pictures are at Fredo's villa in Forio. That's a fishing village on the far side of Ischia, in the Bay of Naples." He hesitated. "Will you get them for me, Kevin?" The little-hurt-boy look was in his eyes. One last rebound?

"If I don't?"

"Then I'll have to play it by ear." His voice was soft, his face torn in agony. "I've thought about killing myself, though if I haven't done it before now, I probably won't do it. God in heaven, Kev. . . ." He was crying now, the brisk front having crumbled. "I didn't become a priest for all this to happen. I just wanted to save my soul. The Blessed Mother promised me that I would. That's why I gave up a family. I never wanted anything else." His voice faded. "Maybe I've deceived myself all along."

"How can I communicate with you once you're inside and the voting begins?" I said.

"That's easy," he replied, brisk and businesslike again. "Rent a red Lancia Gamma. At three times—eight-thirty in the morning, five-thirty in the afternoon, and ten at night—I'll look out from the Apostolic Palace over the piazza. If the car is parked in front of the Congregation of Bishops building and its lights blink precisely on the hour—three times—I'll know you destroyed the pictures."

I weighed the situation carefully. Obviously he had mapped the whole thing out in his mind. I'd been tipping rebounds for Patrick Donahue all my life. He took it for granted. In trouble? Call Kevin, let him bail you out.

"No," I said crisply.

"Kevin, please!" He extended his hands in supplication.

I slipped out of my chair. "Why should I bother? Suppose I risk my life and get those pictures back. Will you stop screwing Mo as well as screwing up her life? Will you vote for anything but your own career once you get inside? Will you put me back on the mailing list? Sink or swim on your own, Eminenza. It's high time."

I walked off toward Hadrian's tomb, even though my hotel was in the opposite direction.

Two hours later I returned to my room at the Michelangelo.

I called the Villa Stritch. I must have awakened Pat from his siesta.

"Eight-thirty, five-thirty, and ten?"

"Right," he said, thoroughly awake now.

"I'll see what we can do."

"I'll be forever grateful, Kevin. When it's all over, I'll resign. I promise."

"Just put my name back on the mailing list."

⁂

I caught a cab up to the Rome Hilton. Mrs. Strauss was not in her room. Her husband had already left for his meeting in Munich. I tried the swimming pool. She was slashing furiously through the water, propelling her body as though it were racing calories from the pasta. When she saw me, she bounded out, wrapped a towel around her shoulders, and ran over to me. My throat constricted at the sight of her, a reaction as disconcerting as it had been thirty years before.

"Why so glum, Kevin?"

"I'm afraid I'm going to have to cancel our date tonight."

She huddled under the towel, shivering in the deceptive October sunlight. "All right," she said solemnly. "What's worrying you?"

I told her.

"How ugly. How cheap and ugly. I'll make the reservations in Ischia and book the car. Red Lancia. Expensive taste, our Cardinal. *Two* hotel rooms, so don't worry. You check with your CIA friend over at the embassy, the one you met on the plane, and get some of his toys, safe-blowing things and the like. We can't leave till tomorrow, anyway. I'll call Herb at his meeting in Munich and tell him you and I are going away for a weekend and that he should trust my virtue, not yours. No need to worry him about all the details. We'll have to do some shopping—black sweaters and slacks." She paused thoughtfully. "Soft-soled shoes."

"You're crazy if you think I'm going to let you—"

"Try to stop me." The tilt of her jaw told me that no disagreement would be tolerated.

"You have a husband and children. You can't risk your life."

"Kevin Brennan"—her lips were a thin, hard line; her bare shoulders firm and unmovable—"you can argue with me all afternoon and all day tomorrow. I'm still coming. I'll do the worrying about my husband and children. When I tell him—afterward—Herb will be proud of me. So will the kids. Anyway, no one is going to get hurt."

I argued for half the afternoon; then I gave in. We Irish males are genetically programmed to give in when we see that tilt of the jaw.

I saw Mikolitis at the embassy and collected a remarkable number of toys, some of which Calvin Ohira had demonstrated one day when he opened a padlocked room in his basement. I was constrained to show them to my co-conspirator, who watched with the wide eyes of a child being told about witches and dragons.

She did not like the .38 very much. Neither did I. I doubted that I could ever fire it at a human being.

I tried again the next afternoon to talk her out of her lunacy as the ferry moved out into the Bay of Naples. She just laughed at me as her blond hair danced in the fresh sea breeze.

Ischia was a volcanic block barely discernible in the distant haze, larger than Capri and farther out in the bay. Reading from the guidebook, Ellen informed me that Forio was an old fishing village with an artists' colony on the far side of the island. The Santa Catarina was our hotel, a lovely little place, I was assured. There was also a thermal spring to which many foreigners came because of its famous "recuperative powers."

Ellen glanced about the ferry. Most of the cars were

Mercedes-Benzes. The occupants were mostly elderly German businessmen and their firm-bodied young mistresses.

"Hmm . . . I bet I know what the springs are supposed to recuperate," Ellen said. She frowned as she remembered why we were on the ferry. "What will they do to Pat if they find out?"

"*They* won't do anything if it doesn't become public. Pat is not the only cardinal in history with a woman in his life. Hell, his predecessor had a blonde living in his house with him, traveled around the world with her, owned a house in Florida with her, and was arrested by the Chicago police for drunken driving with her. Yet Rome never acted on him."

"Are all the cardinals that way?" she asked softly.

"No." I kept my eyes averted from hers. "Most are chaste these days, some of them because they're neuters, others because they're committed celibates, like me."

⁂

The melody of the Veni Creator Spiritus echoed and reechoed in Pat Donahue's brain. For the few moments of the procession he felt exalted and proud—a garbage man's son voting for a pope, for the second time. The Holy Spirit would be working through him. Then came the dramatic Exeunt Omnes from Monsignor Noè, and after considerable shuffling and hesitating, Cardinal Villot, the camerlengo, *or "acting Pope," closed the door, and the key turned in the lock.*

The conclave had begun again.

He was patient during the long, tedious oath-taking in the Sistine Chapel. The elderly men, who had been appointed to the highest positions in the Church, swore the most solemn of oaths, under the pain of the most terrible excommunication, that they would not reveal what happened in the conclave and would not politick for the election of themselves or their friends. The chapel was stuffy and hot; the cardinals were restless and uneasy in their scarlet cassocks and cappas. Cardinal Wojtyla, of Cracow, sitting next to Pat, was reading a philosophical journal, something Marxist, judging by its title.

Pat leaned over to Wojtyla and said in English, "Bringing Marx into the conclave, Eminence? Shame on you!"

The broad-shouldered, handsome man looked around with mock furtiveness and grinned. "My conscience is clear."

Pat watched one old man after another swear on the Bible at the front of the chapel. If he concentrated on the ceremonies, he was able to forget for a few moments his own peril. Blackmail seemed unreal in this historic old chapel, already beginning to smell of heavy robes and masculine bodies. The scandal would rock the world. He would resign, go to a monastery—New Melleray, maybe—and live the rest of his life in penance.

Wojtyla nudged him. It was his turn to take the oath. He walked wearily up to the altar. He was the youngest elector, and he felt as if he were the oldest.

After supper Marcel Flambeau approached him in the narrow, corridor leading to the makeshift refectory. "I will be direct," said the handsome old Luxembourger. "We think that by lunch tomorrow Cardinal Benelli will be near victory."

Was Flambeau speaking of wishes or certainties? Pat decided it was the former. He shook his head negatively. "His Eminence can never get seventy-six votes."

A spasm of disappointment touched Flambeau's usually immobile features. He nodded silently and walked slowly down the corridor. Pat turned and climbed the steep staircase to the attic of the palace. The luck of the draw had given him a tiny room with high-barred windows. In the distance were the hills looming darkly against the night sky; closer in, the Janiculum, where he had gone to college and dreamed of someday voting in a conclave.

He sank his head into his hands and groaned. He was imprisoned, not only in the dark, hot room with its uncomfortable bed and hard plastic chair but in chains that had bound him since he was a child. He wanted to sob in outrage and agony, but no tears would come. Dejectedly he looked at his watch. Even Kevin could not have got the pictures yet. Still, he walked over to the windows. The ledge was at eye level. Standing on tiptoe, he could look down at the piazza. Almost empty. A few sightseers, some security guards, perhaps a few reporters. A steady stream of traffic coming up the Via delle Conciliazione. There was a red car in front of the Congregation of Bishops, next to the souvenir shops. His heart surged with hope, but the car moved beyond the Bernini columns without blinking its lights. It was not a Lancia.

He waited for a quarter of an hour. The late-night traffic dwindled. He sighed.

There would be no visitors tonight. The cardinals would wait for the signals on the first two ballots to begin the discussions that somehow did not seem to violate their solemn oaths. The last time there had been a knock at the door at this late hour it had been Flambeau, making certain that the Americans would support Luciani.

Poor Benelli, the abrupt, gifted little man with the magic smile, had been a much better politician for his friend than he was for himself. Votes would be wasted for him. A touch of guilt stabbed at Patrick Donahue. "Gianni" was responsible more than anyone else for his promotion to Chicago. He was letting him down. Loyalty demanded a better showing for Benelli.

He thought for the first time in several days of Maureen and felt sorry, though not for her. Mo would survive; she always would. He was sorry for the happy family they might have had together if he had listened to Kevin in 1949 and gone to Notre Dame. How many priests before him, even how many cardinals, wished they could live their lives over?

He groaned again and began to unbutton his sweat-soaked cassock. He could stall through the first day. Then he would have to decide. The issue would probably be clear. Would he vote for his conscience and let his life and career be destroyed, or would he vote the way Tonio ordered, and survive still another day?

⁂

The ferry port at Ischia was shrouded in dusk when we arrived, and Forio was dark by the time we had picked our way around the island on the narrow two-lane road. The tiny village seemed to be mostly hill and sand. The Santa Catarina was clean and neat and very crowded with handsome Teutons who didn't need the recuperative springs.

"The October weather probably attracts them even though the season is over," Ellen said as we waited in line to check in.

Then we encountered a problem. There was a reservation for Mr. Brennan, none for Mrs. Strauss. A twin bedroom was available, if the *signore* and the *signora* . . . The clerk's smile was partly leer and partly plea. Ellen's face was deathly pale, and her eyes were tightly closed.

Of course we would be *molto contento* with the arrangement, I told the clerk, hiding my discomfort beneath an urbane smile.

"I didn't, Kevin," she pleaded as the elevator wheezed to the second floor. "I really didn't."

The room was spacious, with white walls and a large red throw rug. The beds, a sufficient distance apart, were covered with comforters. I tipped the porter and thanked him.

Our window looked out on the sea, a vast blackness at the foot of the hill. Ellen, in blouse and jeans, stood like Lot's wife, frozen in the middle of the room. "I didn't," she repeated.

"I know you didn't," I snapped. "Anyway, I'm going out on a scouting expedition."

The village was strung out over the lower streets of the hill beneath the hotel. Most of the homes seemed occupied, windows open, light streaming into the night. A light ocean breeze with faint smell of salt and fish was caressing the hillside. Romantic October in the romantic Bay of Naples.

In half an hour I was calmed down and back in the hotel television room with Ellen, watching the news replay showing the cardinals marching into the conclave, proceeding from the Pauline to the Sistine Chapel. "There he is," Ellen whispered as Patrick passed the camera, singing lustily and looking as though he had not a care in the world.

Then there was a shot of Villot closing the door and a cut to the face of an Italian newscaster.

"What did you learn?" asked Ellen, who had changed to a sleeveless black dress.

"Signor DeLucca is still at his villa. It is expected that he will go to Rome tomorrow, but no one is sure. Signor DeLucca is a very private man. However, his servants went up to Rome yesterday and it is not thought—"

"So," said Ellen, "why aren't we eating supper?"

Later, as we ordered supper in the low-ceilinged, spacious dining room, I said to Ellen, "We are not as outclassed as you might at first think." I was calming down. Of course it was the hotel's mistake.

"Who's outclassed?" she demanded. "This dress cost—"

"It's a pickup conspiracy, like the pickup ball teams we used to put together on the spur of the moment back in the neighborhood. Fredo DeLucca has connections with some ambitious ecclesiastics who have pushed a little bit beyond what the other curialists would do; some shady, quasi-neo-fascist businessmen who want to get clout with the Vatican bank, probably for smuggling money out of Italy; and a feather-brained right-wing terrorist group that doesn't belong in the same league with the Red Brigades. He has probably brokered the whole business, figuring on collecting money from everyone involved. Maybe they have something on some other cardinals, too, though I bet they get all their dirt from DeLucca. I think they're dangerous, but mostly because they're dumb."

"We'll beat them," she said with serene confidence. "Trust me."

"I'm going to have to," I said.

After supper we sat in the sun parlor of the hotel, listening to the waves pound against the beach and sipping our coffee. I declined brandy. My desire for Ellen, dormant during our ride from Rome, was imperious again. Brandy would weaken my defenses. She was profoundly amused by the awkwardness of our situation. I was frightened. Her simple black dress, purportedly not sexy, made her all the more attractive—a middle-aged matron with a girlish figure, teasing eyes, and a fey twinkle.

She sipped her cognac and favored me with a smile. "There's always been this electricity between us, hasn't there, Kevin? Ever since that night when we were in the back seat of your car . . . the day you got so angry because Pat lost a silly baseball game?"

"Let's go for a walk down to the beach before I try to answer that one."

We picked our way down the stairs and stepped on to the still-warm sand. Holding on to my arm with first one hand and then the other, Ellen took off her shoes. "Now, about that game when Pat wouldn't destroy the catcher . . ."

My face was warm and I tried not to look at her. "I remember the little kid in the ponytail pretty well. I lied to my mother about her the next morning."

"Oh?" said Ellen.

"My mother said you'd developed a cute little figure, and I said I hadn't noticed."

She laughed. "The electricity has never gone away, has it? Will it ever go away, Kevin?"

I felt as weak as if I'd run a couple of miles. "No, Ellen, it will never go away."

"Not even at death?"

I took a very deep breath. "If my faith means anything to me, it means that the electricity between us survives death, just as the sun survives the night."

"Let's suppose that this . . . we'll keep on calling it 'electricity' . . . gets out of hand and we make love tonight. What then?"

"I guess it means that we'd stay out of the same bedroom in the future, especially when we're trying to wire papal elections. I'm not going to give up the Church, and you're certainly not going to leave Herb."

"Our commitments would remain unchanged?"

"We're too deeply into them ever to change, Ellen. You know that."

"So there is not all that much to be afraid of, is there? I mean, not really?"

"No," I said, hoping my voice didn't sound as unsteady to her as it did to me. "The worst wouldn't be all that bad."

"I will make love with you tonight, Kevin, if you want."

"Thanks," I said slowly, "but no thanks."

Her relief was as palpable as the starry sky above the ocean. "Why not?"

"Oh, hell, Ellen, a whole lot of reasons. Mostly because I think it would probably destroy the electricity, and that's too important in my life to give up." I took her chin in my hand and tilted it up so I could see her expression in the starlight. "And, damn you, woman, if you don't stop smiling like a mother who is proud of her son for giving the right answer at the end of a lecture, I'll take you up into our room and dunk your gorgeous head under bathtub water for a half hour."

As we rode up to the second floor in the slow-moving, creaky elevator, she asked, with a saucy motion of her head, "Ever spend a night in a room with a woman before?"

"With Mo once," I said, seeing a chance to regain partial control. "Same bed, in fact."

"You expect me to believe that? . . . What did you do?"

"I didn't do anything. She fell asleep."

"Well, *I* certainly wouldn't fall asleep."

"You might," I replied, bowing her out of the elevator.

Later I was in my twin bed, securely covered by a sheet and a light blanket. A small bed lamp lit Ellen's side of the room.

The shower stopped, and Ellen emerged from the bathroom in a more or less modest sleep shirt. I passed another test.

"Your legs are pretty enough for a middle-aged woman, Ellen," I said, feigning sleepiness.

"Hmnf," she said indignantly, turning off the light before she slipped into bed.

"Good night, Kevin."

"Good night."

"It would never have worked, you know," she said. "You would have turned into a hard-drinking, cardiac-prone Irish lawyer, and I would have become a fat, neurotic, frustrated suburban bitch. We would never talk about it, but we would both know in our hearts that we made a terrible mistake."

"Maybe."

"No 'maybe' about it. If you didn't have your Church and I didn't have my Herb, we'd never be able to love each other as much as we do. God's been good to us."

"I guess," I said, suspecting that she was right.

⁂

The Curial Italians swaggered up to the altar to cast their votes with arrogant self-confidence. "Triumphalists," muttered Cardinal Patrick Donahue to the Prince Archbishop of Cracow. The latter rolled his frosty blue eyes and continued to plow through his book of Marxist philosophy. What was he thinking? Pat wondered. Supporting Benelli, he had been told, but then what? What would he think of me if he knew?

The Archbishop of Genoa, Giuseppe Siri, came back to his seat slowly. Siri was neither a conspirator nor a dissembler. More honest than most of his allies, he was an old man who said openly what he thought. What had he said in that foolish interview leaked just before the conclave? He didn't know what "collegiality" meant, the magic word that had stood for freedom and democracy all around the Catholic world. Suppose that interview came out on schedule while we were in here. My God, would the press have a field day. And I've just voted for him . . .

His stomach wrenched in self-disgust and he bent over in sharp pain; next to him, Wojtyla raised an eyebrow in concern.

"Italian breakfast, Eminenza?" he whispered.

The votes were announced and tallied. Forty-six votes for Siri—twenty more than on the first ballot, in August. Martinelli was beaming; he seemed to nod at Pat from across the aisle.

I'm responsible for maybe half of those extra twenty votes, Pat told himself, and felt the pain in his stomach again. God, Maureen, I do love you, despite it all.

Wojtyla received five votes. "Five more votes than I received, Eminenza," Pat said, "and I hope you have an EKG with you."

The Pole reached into the folder on the table in front of him and pulled out a sheet of paper. Without comment he passed the sheet to Pat. It was an EKG—one indicating a very strong and steady heart.

The second ballot moved more quickly. This time, Flambeau was smiling. He was justified. Siri fell back; Benelli gained. Not enough, though, not enough, Pat told himself. Sorry, Gianni, I wish I could vote for you.

On the way to lunch he heard an American cardinal commiserating with Siri. The haughty, aristocratic old man replied, in Italian, "It is language, Your Eminence. You need to know many languages to be Pope. I am too old to learn them."

Pat Donahue sat down across from Marcel Flambeau in the modern-art gallery of the Vatican Museum, which had been turned into a conclave refectory. He remembered bringing Maureen here shortly after Paul VI had opened it. That was just before . . .

He buttered a piece of bread. "The plot thickens, Monsieur le Cardinal," *he said to Flambeau.*

"For you, Cardinal," replied Flambeau, his eyes twinkling, "it has always been thick."

⁂

Forio was one of the most beautiful places in the world. No wonder the rich Germans tried to stay young here. Ellen and I were on the farthest point of a sand spit, beneath a great rock. The sand was a finger jutting out into the bay; the rock was an oversize fingernail. Behind us the village shone in the golden sunlight like an expensively designed movie set. The houses clustering on the side of the hill were painted pink and yellow and blue, matching the fishing boats that rested on the sand or floated lightly in the tiny inlet. Patches of haze drifted across the spit, and then were chased away by a quick draft of wind.

I watched DeLucca's villa with a tiny, powerful binocular, courtesy of the CIA. Ellen lay facedown on the sand.

Finally I saw the unmistakable profile of Alfredo DeLucca coming down the stairs, leading to the driveway.

"He's coming," I whispered, though there was no one near enough to hear us.

"Great," she said sleepily from the sand. " 'Bout time."

"He's about fifty yards away," I said, now standing up and looking over a low outcropping of the rock, "with a portable radio. Setting up for a bask in the sun and ready for the news, just in case someone is elected this morning."

"Let me see," said Ellen, struggling out of the sand. "Well, he's not that bad-looking, if you like the type. I think Signor DeLucca ought to meet a pretty American widow woman."

"You can't—"

"Don't be a prude, Kevin." She patted my cheek. "You hold these rings." She wrenched them from her fingers and put on her short white robe, left it open, and walked off on the sand, swaying provocatively.

The Siri supporters staged a wild shouting session in the courtyard after lunch. They were angry over the victory that had been snatched away from them. Pat Donahue watched from a window. There was still no way out of his own trap. He might just as well have been down there with men he despised. He was one of them. More despicable than the others.

He would have to make his decision by tonight. He walked slowly back to his room.

He sat at his desk, trying to think. A discreet knock at his door. Before he could say anything, Martinelli's sleek hair and pointed features. "Colombo," he said, and was gone. Sighing, Pat Donahue buttoned up his crimson cassock. There were three Americans to visit before the voting started. They would tell the others.

Colombo, a seventy-six-year-old man who had already resigned his own city, was to be Bishop of Rome. Did Antonio think he could control Colombo, or was it a last gamble to keep out the stranieri?

Until now, his treason had been only to a man who could not be elected and in favor of another man who could not be elected. But now he was betraying the Church.

Ellen walked back across the beach and knelt next to me. "I don't think he's all that handsome." It was the teenage voice I heard from behind a malted milk a long time ago. "I don't know what women see in him. His line is very obvious. Anyway, I have an assignation with him at six o'clock to watch the conclave smoke and have a 'small dinner.' His servants have left and he, himself"—she drew the words out slowly for all their dramatic effect—"must leave for Rome at nine tonight. And, Kevin, don't worry about what's left of my virtue. The dear at the embassy gave you that small tasteless pill you can put into almost anything and make a man—or a woman, if that's what you have in mind—go to sleep in sixty seconds and wake up half an hour later, not remembering anything that happened. I can hold any man off for sixty seconds. Now, go back to the hotel and bribe them to describe me as 'La Signora Brown' if anyone calls."

I should never have told her about the pill. The tilt of her chin told me it was useless to argue.

CHAPTER TWENTY-FOUR

1978

The afternoon had been dramatic—and then terrifying. Benelli did not gain on the third ballot. The Siri votes slipped. The wild horse of the conclave was running without a rider. Then a dramatic surge of votes toward Colombo on the final ballot of the day. The old man would almost certainly be elected tomorrow. Antonio Martinelli seemed satisfied. Wojtyla frowned at the ten votes he had received. There was no amusement in the frosty eyes now.

Then, at supper, Colombo had insisted in a loud and determined voice that he would not accept. His fellow Italians, seated around him at the table as though to isolate him from contamination, tried to quiet him down. The genial old man indulged in a rare display of temper. The Church needed a younger man; he would not accept. Antonio's smile disappeared.

I watched the *fumata* at the end of the first day on the television set in the hotel in Ischia. A huge crowd packed the *piazza* and the Conciliazione halfway to the Tiber. A great moon slowly emerged behind the Castel Sant'Angelo and climbed above the river. Searchlights played on the dome of St. Peter's and the walls of the Apostolic Palace. Even on the small screen I could sense the electricity of the crowd. The Italian commentator babbled on, unnecessarily trying to increase the tension. Pictures of Benelli, Siri, Pappalardo, were flashed repeatedly on the screen.

Finally, the smoke, and wild cheers from the crowd. *"Bianco, bianco!"* screamed the announcers. Then the white turned gray, and then black.

"Nothing works right in this country," said an American businessman.

"Good theater, lousy union," I countered.

The commentator regained control long enough to report that the smoke now seemed to be *"Nero! Nero!"* Some of the crowd were beginning to depart. The others in the television room slipped away. Then the commentator said that Radio Vaticana had announced that the smoke was black. I walked out onto the patio to eat a desultory dinner and wait for the return of my Mata Hari.

Ellen had left, arrayed in a black and white wraparound dress whose appeal was not exactly understated. She had her bottle of pills and a compact with a tiny radio. If she opened the top of the compact, the monitor I was carrying in my pocket would beep and I would come running with my .38.

The evening crept on and I heard neither beep nor bell-like laughter. The full enormity of our folly was closing in on me. I didn't need the threat of loss to tell me how much I loved Ellen.

I walked out into the street. No one in sight. Ischia closes down early on Sunday night. At ten o'clock I'd go after her, no matter what.

I went into the lobby and watched the clock move with maddening slowness. The moment the hour chimed, I turned toward the staircase landing. Halfway to the steps I heard the click of heels on the lobby floor—the determined click of feet moving rapidly.

"My Lord, Kevin, not here in the lobby," she protested as I embraced her.

Leaning against the wall of the patio, to which we had fled lest the concierge hear us, she closed her eyes. Her face was pale and tense. "I don't think I'm intended for this career, after all. I'm just a simple housewife from Cook County." She opened her eyes. "Oh, don't look that way, Kevin. My chastity is no more damaged than it was; he's a very evil man, though. I can't see what Mo . . ." She shook her head. "Anyway, he's leaving at eleven o'clock and there's a wall safe in his room. I managed to get a key to the house so you won't need any of those fancy tools. Kevin, let's get away from this dreadful place as fast as we can."

⁂

Elegant as always, his cassock unmarked by perspiration, his hair neatly combed, Cardinal Antonio Martinelli relaxed on the plastic chair. "So," he said grimly. "Tomorrow will be the day of the foreigner. They are going to play their Polish card. Well, I think we can stop that. He will never win without the Americans." He eyed Patrick Donahue speculatively.

The pain in Pat's stomach was now intense. He sat uneasily on his hard bed. "I don't know that I can hold them, Tonio. You know how many Poles we have in the United States." He was sitting on the bed, whose single spring and thin mattress provided even less comfort than the old beds at Mundelein.

"They must be held," Martinelli snapped, his eyes flashing. "The Church must be protected from its enemies. Tell them that he was married and had a child. That he is much softer on Communism than Wyszynski. You yourself saw him reading a Communist jour-

nal in the chapel. Tell them that he is involved in modern philosophy and writes erotic poetry." He raced on, his pointed face glowing with fervor. "All of that is true, by the way."

"Have you ever tried to tell John Krol anything, especially about another Pole?"

The Archbishop of Philadelphia was dismissed with a delicate wave of the hand. "Krol we will lose; you must prevent him from influencing the others."

"That's easier said than done. Wojtyla is known and admired in America."

Antonio stood up. "The Church must be protected from Communism. Do not let the Americans vote for him, caro mio. *It would be bad for the Church."*

There was no red Lancia at ten o'clock. Shaken, unnerved, Patrick Cardinal Donahue sat at the table next to his bed, head in hands. One more chance. He would wait until eight-thirty in the morning. If there was no signal from Kevin, then he would have to block the election of Karol Wojtyla.

❦

"We must catch the midnight ferry," I said, pulling a black sweater over my head. "Allow three hours to Rome—three and a half, counting the ferry ride—another hour for delays. We'll be there at four-thirty. Plenty of time. If we have to wait until the two-o'clock ferry, we'll get tied up in rush-hour traffic."

Ellen crammed her dress and her slip into the suitcase. She reached for her black cashmere sweater.

"You're staring, Father Kevin," she said, pulling the sweater down over her shoulders.

"My eyes are caught by the disarming grace/Of Titania in black and magic lace."

"Good God," she said, and laughed. "Thirty years between

Romantic couplets and you choose a time when we're playing CIA." She touched my cheek gently, the way I had touched her fingers at the Sugar Bowl. "Come on, let's get out of here. Someone has to be sensible."

I checked us out of the hotel. We carried our bags down the back stairs of the hotel, loaded all but the tiny black bag from the embassy into the trunk of the Lancia, and drove slowly toward the first level of the village. The mist was thick, almost impenetrable. And it was very cold.

"What if the mist stops the ferry?" asked Ellen.

"We'll worry about that when it happens."

It was a steep climb up the wet cobblestone streets to the top of the hill. The mist had turned into a fine rain. We went past DeLucca's villa in the darkness, and had to come back to find it.

"This is it, I'm sure," said Ellen. "The pink house with the lion on the door. His car is gone."

We crept around to the back and scaled the wall, she with more agility than I. We climbed up the back steps, slipping on the wet wooden staircase. Ellen lost her footing, stumbled, and began to fall. I grabbed her.

"Thanks, Kevin," she whispered, her voice trembling.

I began fiddling with the key to DeLucca's door. "Damn, are you sure you took the right key, Ellen?" I demanded.

"Of course I am," she replied haughtily. "Do you want me—"

"Sssh. You'll wake up the dead with that voice. Ah . . . it's open."

We crept into DeLucca's office, an expensively furnished room with light wood furniture and pastel drapes. I closed the door and we were in total darkness. "The safe is to your left, Kevin," said Ellen, "behind that painting."

A tiny beam of light moved to the darkness, probed the wall, came upon a buxom peasant girl, and stopped.

I took the minute flashlight from her trembling fingers and focused it on the wall. I lifted off the picture. Just as Ellen promised—a safe. Then we heard the cars.

Not one but two, stopping just outside the villa, their headlight beams shining on the garden walls behind us.

We were frozen, unable to react.

Ellen broke the spell. "There's a closet on the other side of the office, things stored in it. Give me the light, Kevin. There it is. We'll hide there. . . . Be careful. Don't trip."

I replaced the painting, kicked a chair, and bumped noisily against a desk before I found my way into the alcove after Ellen. There was just barely room for the two of us. The door clicked as it locked us in. Footsteps on the stairs. How many machine-gun-toting terrorists?

The door opened and a light went on, its rays creeping in around the edges of the door. Ellen's fingers dug into my arm. There was a crack through which I could see a large section of the room. It was DeLucca and two others, a man and a woman.

Fredo was angry. "It was stupid of you to come. You should not be seen together. There was a woman here today who I thought might be a spy, but she was too stupid."

The figure behind me went stiff with rage.

"My editor cannot approve any more payments unless I see the merchandise." I recognized the voice. So that's why they were speaking English. I was shocked that such an important American publication would be cooperating in a blackmail game. "Investigative reporting" covers a multitude of sins, I reminded myself.

The third person was a young girl, a classic Roman

beauty—tall, thin, handsome; long, straight hair; high, small breasts pressing against a sweater much like Ellen's. Her eyes and jaw were hard.

DeLucca spun the knob on his safe. He took a thick envelope from the safe and passed it to the reporter. "Here, look at them and tell your editor that either I have the bank draft by tomorrow evening or I will send them to someone else."

"Very nice." I couldn't see the American's face, but his laugh went with a leer.

"Do you want to see them?" DeLucca asked the girl.

"Unnecessary," she replied tersely. "We know he is a degenerate."

"Excellent," said DeLucca, turning to the reporter. "Now, if you would be so good as to leave. You must be on the twelve-o'clock ferry. I will be forced to take the two-o'clock, as I must be seen at the Vatican Salla Stampa tomorrow morning."

My heart sank. That would put us on the four-o'clock ferry, three hours to Rome, three and a half with the ferry ride . . . an hour to spare.

The American left without saying good-bye. A few minutes later we heard his car growl into life, skid on the driveway, and slip away into the night. My legs were already cramped from standing, and we might have a long wait. DeLucca put the envelope back into the safe, spun the lock, and hung the painting over it.

"A glass of wine, *signorina*?"

She made an indifferent sound.

"You are very lovely, my dear," he said. "It is a shame for such a lovely woman to waste herself on politics. There are so many better things you might do with yourself."

The girl told him he was a degenerate pig.

DeLucca laughed. "It is a shame to let such a body go to

waste. Soon you will certainly be dead or rotting in some prison."

Only then did the girl seem to realize her danger. She told him what the Servants of St. Anthony would do to his genitals if he touched her.

He was amused. "Oh, I think not, *cara mia.* Doubtless your fellow terrorists treasure the purity of their young women, but I am too useful a contact to be harmed. Your champions of the faith need a few like me to do the things that they cannot do."

The girl was sitting in a chair near his desk. We heard her making a rush for the door. DeLucca beat her to it and turned the lock.

"Consider your position, *cara.* I am stronger than you. No one can hear your screams. Your colleagues will do nothing to harm me. Would it not be wiser to cooperate and enjoy my attentions? In any case, your resistance will only add to my pleasure."

The girl ran across the room toward our closet. DeLucca reached out and grabbed her arm, just as she got close to the door.

Ellen's fingers dug into my arms. We had no way of getting out of the locked closet.

DeLucca mocked the girl's screams and struggles while he tormented her. When she gave up the fight, no longer able to resist, he did things to her body that made her cry in pain. Then, judging from his comments, he discovered that she was a virgin, and settled down to enjoy the pleasure of ravaging an innocent.

"So, *cara mia,*" he said as they left, "cry now. You will get over it, and for the little time you live you will remember with pleasure what your Uncle Fredo taught you." His tenderness was half serious, half sarcastic.

It isn't as easy to shoot a lock off a door as it seems on television shows, especially when you're trying to muffle the sound with a heavy sweater. I had to blast a hole in the door and then put my hand through it to open the door from the outside.

"Let's get the pictures and get out of here." I put two tiny capsules on the safe, hooked them to a small box, and flipped a switch. There was a muffled noise, and the door fell off the safe. DeLucca was an amateur. The people who made the explosive were pros.

I gave a silent Ellen the light while I went to the safe. There was an enormous stack of envelopes. DeLucca was in the business. I took the top one, opened it, slid out part of the first picture, and shoved it back in. God, poor Maureen! I squeezed the envelope open to make sure that the negatives were there.

Ellen handed me a metal wastebasket she found on the floor. I dumped all the remaining envelopes in the basket. Ellen held the light on the basket as I poured a liquid over it. The contents seemed to evaporate, like a puddle in hot sunlight. In less than a minute there were only a few drops of the fluid in the bottom of the bucket. A number of other souls were freed from purgatory along with Patrick Cardinal Donahue. Now, if we could drive back to Rome in time, he could go on with his responsibility of electing the next pope.

We went down the front steps of the DeLucca villa out into the mists. A few steps across the slippery street we encountered two young men with switchblades. They were dressed like middle-class Italian college students—dark suits, conservative ties. Unlike their left-wing counterparts, the Slaves of St. Anthony were not carefully trained or disciplined. They were wild romantics out of a Verdi opera. They were also very shaky.

They motioned to us, and we obediently followed them across the sand pit and down the beach. They had a knife at Ellen's windpipe, and I was not inclined to argue with them. They took our watches and wallets but didn't seem really interested in them.

We stopped near the massive rock. The mists swirled around us—almost a fog. One of the terrorists stood by me, his knife poised. The other spun Ellen around, twisted her arm behind her, and cut her sweater from top to bottom. So, that's what they wanted.

"Our woman has been raped. Now your woman will be raped. Then you both will be tried by a sacred court," announced the taller of the two, a thin-faced adolescent with an ugly scar across his cheek.

"We didn't rape your woman," I protested. "One of your own allies did it."

He paused. "Nonetheless, if it were not for your degenerate cardinal friend, this would not have happened."

"St. Anthony wouldn't approve," I said.

"Like St. Anthony, we are defenders of Christian civilization."

I was tired of arguing with a madman. I heard Calvin Ohira's instructions as though he were standing next to me. With one quick chop of my hand, I broke the wrist of the scar-faced punk who was pointing the knife at me. He screamed and dropped the blade.

His friend hesitated, startled by the sound in the darkness. I saw his neck clearly outlined against the stars. My hand swept toward him in a fast, swinging motion. It hit with hard, brutal precision. I heard the sound of escaping breath as he fell to the sand.

I returned to my screaming guard, who had somehow found his knife and was coming for me. This time I hit him on the jaw. As he joined his unconscious friend on the sand, I was on top of him, fully intending to break every bone in his body. Ellen pulled me off. "Don't kill him, Kevin. Please don't."

If I knew what they were going to do two days later, I would have killed them both gladly. Instead I retrieved our watches and wallets, and we hurried back to the village and jumped into our red Lancia. We would be lucky to catch the four-o'clock ferry.

It was five when we reached the *autostrada* for Rome. The ferry had inched across the choppy bay as though it were not sure where the shore was. The extra half hour seemed like half an eternity. Ellen cried herself to sleep in the car while I tried vainly to solve the puzzle of how the two crazies knew so quickly that their virgin had been violated.

We were two thirds of the way to Rome when, just at dawn, we ran into a police roadblock. They were checking every car. It took a half hour. Two uniformed *carabiniere* looked at our passports and waved us on. I asked in Italian the reason for the search.

The lieutenant shrugged his shoulders. A horrible murder, a well-known man mutilated and killed.

"Who?" I asked.

The cop hesitated; then, since we were Americans, he decided there was no reason not to tell us.

The famous journalist Alfredo DeLucca.

Ellen was able to hold back her hysteria until we'd left the roadblock. Gradually, I soothed and calmed her.

We got off the *autostrada* at the Via Aurelia exit. It was ten minutes after eight. Twenty minutes to get to San Pietro. Roman rush-hour traffic.

⁂

The Archbishop of Chicago peered out the window of his room. Eight-twenty-nine, and no red Lancia. No way to communicate for the rest of the day. Why didn't he think of setting up a noon rendezvous time? No matter. He hoped nothing had happened to Kevin.

Maybe nothing would happen today. Maybe it would deadlock. Maybe before the evening fumata *he would look out the window and see the red car. But between now and then, he would try to beat a man who might make a superb pope.*

He did not notice when the numbers on his digital watch passed eight-thirty. It was twenty to nine when he looked again. No red Lancia. He sighed, buttoned his cassock, slid his cappa magna *on his broad shoulders, and left his room.*

⁂

It took us thirty-five minutes from the Via Aurelia turnoff to the Piazza San Pietro. They were already back in the Sistine Chapel. The piazza was alive with the Monday-morning tourist trade. Only the barricades, the large numbers of multiuniformed security forces, and the television platforms suggested that it was a morning different from any other first day of the week in the Eternal City. We were supposed to be there at eight-thirty. We arrived at eight-forty-five. I'd finally missed a rebound.

A weary, streaky-faced Ellen and I ate a late breakfast at the curb in front of the Hotel Columbus, halfway down the Conciliazione. We read the morning papers, walked over to the Salla Stampa to gossip with Micky Wilson, the brilliant "old Roman hand" from *Time,* and waited for the *fumata.*

When it finally came, at eleven-fifteen, it was unquestionably black. The public-address system confirmed that. They'd finally got the smoke to work right, and at the same time some genius had discovered the PA system. Some things in Italy and in the Church would never change.

There was nothing to do until evening. I told Ellen to go to the Hilton, get some sleep, and wait for Herb. I trudged by the gate of the Holy Office, along the Via Aurelia, and into the Michelangelo. I slept as though I had taken one of Ellen's pills.

The Prince Archbishop of Cracow was supposed to get fifteen or sixteen votes in the first test of the "mathematics of the spirit." He got twenty-one, at least five more than expected. John Krol was grinning like the cat who swallowed the canary. Antonio Martinelli was staring at Pat as cold as death. Karol Wojtyla had listened, thunderstruck, as his name was called out time after time. When the tally was announced, he sank his head into his massive hands.

Those that want it don't get it, and those that don't want it get it. Pat hummed a Polish song he had learned at St. Wenceslaus in Chicago. The Prince Archbishop looked at him. This time there were tears in his eyes.

I gave the signal—the three flashes—at exactly five-thirty. Deep down, I knew it was too late, but we had to play out the scenario. Then I found a parking spot around the corner, just off the piazza of the Holy Office, and joined Ellen and Herb at the barricades. The sky was turning dark; the searchlights were already on. The crowd looked smaller than the night before, though it was still early.

Ellen was wearing a gray skirt and jacket, Herb a brown business suit. Both looked somber, troubled. Maureen was with them, equally somber.

"Alfredo?" I said to her.

"I've done my crying, Kev," she replied. "We ended it in August. He was a terrible man. I . . . I must have sunk pretty low. Anyway, I'm sorry that he's dead. Such a terrible death. No one deserves. . . ."

The piazza filled up by six o'clock. The crowd grew quiet as the hand clock moved toward six-fifteen. "How much longer?" asked Ellen nervously.

"Any minute," I said, finding it hard to breathe and hard to talk.

At six-thirteen the smoke began, clear, unmistakably white smoke pouring out of the tin chimney, swirling up in the searchlight beams and losing itself in the hugeness of the night. The crowd went wild. This time there was no doubt: for the second time in three months, we had a new pope.

Who would he be? Benelli? Siri? Willebrands, of Holland? Someone nobody had dreamed of? My chest was tight. God, if it were Siri, how would we dare go home?

The crowd was festive, as though they were enjoying the suspense. The Swiss Guard trooped in—the only professionals in the Church, as far as I was concerned—then a noisy Italian army band, legitimately present because the piazza is part of Italy, even though the dome is in Vatican City.

At six-forty-three the lights went on behind the doors. Someone came out to set up the mikes. The curtains rolled back. Then the door swung open on the balcony, slowly, majestically. The cross-bearer and the acolytes came out—just like the old days in the seminary, save for the red robes. Then Pericle Felici. Thank God it wasn't he.

"Annuntio vobis gaudium magnum," he began, and was interrupted by a tumultuous roar. My heart was in my throat, a tight knot in my gut. . . .

"Habemus papam."

Another burst of cheering. Pericle didn't sound very happy.

He spun off more Latin.

"Carolum . . ." Absolute silence. Charles. Charles who?

"Who? Who?" Ellen was screaming.

"Sanctae Romanae Ecclesiae Cardinalem . . ." A final pause for the last ounce of dramatic effect.

"Wojtyla!"

"Qui sibi imposuit nomen Johannis Pauli." Felici glanced briefly at the crowd and retreated quickly into the comforting protection of San Pietro.

No one seemed to move. The crowd was stunned silent.

"Charles who?" said Ellen.

I was laughing. History had made . . . a Polish joke on the world.

An Italian poked me. *"Padre. È papa nero?"*

"No," I said. It wasn't a black pope.

"È papa asiatico?" I tried to stop laughing, but I couldn't.

"Non è papa asiatico," I managed to get out.

"Ma quale papa?" he persisted.

"È papa polacco!" I exploded.

He pounded his head in a characteristic Italian gesture that usually indicates the world is about to come to an end. *"Magari!" Un papa polacco!"*

"What does it mean, Kevin? What does it mean?" Ellen was tugging at my sleeve.

"It means that for the first time in his life, our friend the Cardinal Archbishop seems to have tipped in a rebound without my help."

I dragged them over to the Vatican press office. I wanted to see the Pope's face on the television screen. Jimmy Roache, the American press coordinator, was already passing out biographies.

"How many languages?" I asked. "Italian?"

"And eight or nine others!" said Jimmy.

"He's got to talk to them," I said. "Tradition or not, they're surprised and hurt out there."

Jimmy shrugged. "He's the kind that might."

On the television screen we saw the doors open onto the balcony again. A big, broad-shouldered man with a somber face appeared. The Italian reporters exclaimed angrily that they didn't like him.

"Doesn't look like a pope," Herb whispered in my ear.

Wojtyla greeted the crowd, in Italian, "Praise be Jesus Christ."

A lot of people in the crowd responded, "Now and forever."

He had a deep, powerful voice and a strong presence up there.

"May Jesus Christ be praised. Dearest brothers and sisters, we are still all grieved after the death of the most beloved Pope John Paul the First. And now the most reverend cardinals have called a new Bishop of Rome. They have called him from a distant country, distant but always so close for the communion in the Christian faith and tradition.

"I was afraid to receive this nomination, but I did it in the spirit of obedience to our Lord and in the total confidence in his mother, the most holy Madonna.

"Even if I cannot explain myself well in your—our—Italian language, if I make a mistake, you will correct me.

"And so I present myself to you all to confess our common faith, our hope, our confidence in the mother of Christ and of the Church, and also—and also to start anew on that road, the road of history and of the Church, to start with the help of God and with the help of men."

The cheers were deafening.

"He'd do well in the neighborhood," I said to Ellen. "He

knows all the political moves. He owns these people already. Listen to them cheer."

Then everyone was crying—Maureen, Ellen, Herb, and, across the room, Kevin Star, of the San Francisco *Examiner.*

"What are you crying for?" I asked Herb through my own tears.

"Your goddamn Church," he shouted, "is a virgin and whore. As old as sin and as young as a flower bud. That's the kind of woman I like!"

Ellen clung to him. "Herbert . . . what a terrible, awful, wonderful thing to say."

"At least she's alive," I said.

"God damn it, she's alive." He was stroking the head nestled on his arm.

Just then I'd settle for Ellen as a symbol of the Church.

Maureen dragged us back to her apartment for champagne. "Remember the first time?" She grinned at me as she gave me her glass, her eyes sad and tired. Would they always be that way?

"Another time of new beginnings," I said, toasting her.

She turned away quickly.

Her neighbors poured in with their own sparkling wine. The Italians were as happy to be liberated from the massive weight of tradition as we were.

Then it was time to get back to the Michelangelo. There was work to do tomorrow. I heard Ellen and Maureen planning a shopping expedition.

I agreed reluctantly to join them for lunch at the L'Eau Vite.

As I was leaving, Maureen held my hand. "Do you think I could really pretend it was January 1, 1949?"

"If you want." I held the hand tightly.

"I'm not too ugly to find a husband somewhere?"

"Are you serious?"

"I'd like to be." She looked forlorn.

"Pat?"

"I don't know. Let's talk about it again before you go back. Sloane's still lonesome, I think."

CHAPTER TWENTY-FIVE

1978

The Ristorante L'Eau Vite was cool, elegant, classical. Inside, one left behind the narrow, grimy streets, dirty walls, unsmiling pedestrians, tattered wall posters, and the sickish gasoline smell of modern Rome. The atmosphere of the place belonged to another century, an era gone or an age yet to come.

At two-thirty, while we were still lingering over dessert and cognac, customers and staff rose to sing—in the language of one's choice—the Lourdes Hymn. Maureen, Ellen, and I sang it lustily, in happy memory of our grammar-school days when we all prayed to our Lady of Lourdes for miracles—such as a passing mark on an English test, an invitation to an important party, or a victory in a close game. Herb looked intrigued, as he often did when his wife's religious faith impinged on his life. Always respectful, he rose with the rest of us. He hummed the last stanza of the irresistible melody.

We were basking in the warmth of Wojtyla's triumph, a sun rising brilliantly above the fog and haze.

"It will be interesting to see what Cardinal Pat has to say," Herb said. He drained his cognac as if it were a tumbler of water. "Too bad he couldn't join us for lunch."

"He'll tell us that the Pope is an old friend and that his election is a turning point in Catholic history," said Maureen. "Do you want me to give his whole speech? Pat works on his public image these days, even with his friends."

The lightning flash of anger passed as quickly as it had come, and the harsh lines on her face relaxed. I saw again in my mind the spasm of relief on Cardinal Patrick Donahue's face at the press conference when I had given him the thumbs-up sign, my last rebound for the son of a bitch.

The serenity of L'Eau Vite disappeared in the glare of the autumn sunlight and the noise of traffic as soon as we walked out the door.

"My car is across the street," said Maureen quickly. "See you tonight."

I excused myself with a plea that I had to check the Vatican press office. Ellen and Herb would have the cab back to the Hilton to themselves.

I glanced at Maureen walking across the tiny Piazza San Eustacho, her trim legs moving briskly beneath the tight skirt. Lovely legs, I thought. Not for the first time such human appendages had affected a papal election. Above her, the stag's head that stood in the place of the usual cross on the top of San Eustacho reminded me that Rome had seen many beautiful women during its years of paganism and Christianity.

As I turned back to Herb and Ellen, I saw out of the corner of my eye a man get out of a car a few yards away with a submachine gun in his hand. It was one of the thugs from Ischia, the one with the long scar on his face.

"Our women are raped!" he shouted in English. "Your women die!"

After that, all was frame-by-frame slow motion. Blood

spurting out of Maureen's legs as she crumpled to the street, the sound of popping firecrackers, the gunman turning and pointing the weapon at us. Foolishly, I tried to shield Herb and Ellen. The man raised his gun; firecrackers popped again.

The gun tilted forward out of his hand. Splotches of red appeared across his chest and he slumped to the ground, falling over his weapon. The driver tried to start the car. Yet another popping sound and the machine swerved across the narrow street into the wall of L'Eau Vite.

The slow motion ended and I heard other sounds—people screaming, cars screeching behind us, sirens in the distance. I dashed across the tiny piazza to the motionless figure twisted in a crimson pool, thinking irrelevantly that I was the last one to see her beautiful legs before they were torn apart. I knelt beside her and cuddled her head in my arms. She opened her weary, weary eyes.

"I'm going to hell, Kevin," she said in the same matter-of-fact voice with which she had said, a few moments ago, that she was going to her car. "I'm an evil, shallow woman, and I'm going to hell." A tear formed in each eye and slipped slowly down her face. Her eyes closed.

"No, you're not," I said. "God loves you, Maureen. You're not shallow and you're not wicked. *Sono sacerdote,*" I mumbled in bad Italian to the white-helmeted cop with the automatic weapon in his hand. *"Lui e medico."* I pointed at Herb, conscious for the first time that he was behind me trying to stop the flow of blood from Maureen's thighs. He looked at me, shrugged his shoulders, and went back to his frantic work.

Maureen opened her eyes again. I became aware of how tightly I was holding her limp body. "Does he really love me?"

"Pat?" I said uncertainly.

The old grin. "No, silly, God. I've tried . . . I usually make a mess of things . . . but I try . . . at least sometimes." She winced with pain.

Ellen knelt beside me, her face twisted in terror and grief. "God loves you so much, Mo, that he never lets go of you."

I said, "Just like he never let go of Jesus. Hold on to his hand and he won't let go of you."

She nodded. I was holding one hand, Ellen the other. God was getting a lot of help.

"Oh, my God, I'm heartily sorry . . ." She stumbled through the old act of contrition, not strictly required anymore, but a help still. "Tell Sheila I love her."

"*Ego te absolvo . . .*" I began in Latin, shook my head angrily at the lapse, and went back into English. "I absolve you of your sins in the name of the Father and of the Son and of the Holy Spirit."

Maureen sighed as though she had touched God's extended hand. I glanced at Ellen. Her eyes were shining. Behind her a police ambulance stopped and white-garbed medics materialized all around us.

"Tell them the whole story, Kevin." Maureen's voice was momentarily strong again. "They'll find out someday about Pat and me. Write the story down somewhere. It isn't as bad as they think. We tried. Promise me you'll write it all down. . . ." Her hand was very tight on mine.

"Padre, per favore," pleaded one of the medics trying to disentangle us. "I promise," I said to her, and she released me.

We were in a small waiting room at the Gemelli Clinic just around the corner from where Maureen's life was slipping away—Herb, Pat, Ellen, and I. The very handsome, very smart commandante of the *carabiniere* with whom I had just finished talking said that the assassins were members of the Slaves of St. Anthony of Padua, that we were lucky to be alive, that one of the terrorists was dead, the other had already provided interesting information about the rest of the terrorist group, and that it was apparently a random act of violence. He cocked an eye at me when he said "apparently." I did not react.

My Cardinal Archbishop sat slumped in one of the wooden chairs, his head hanging on his chest. "Best clinic in Rome," he said dully. "Deskur is here."

"Who?"

"Wojtyla's closest friend in Rome. Social Communications Office. Had a stroke just before he went into the conclave. Not expected to live." Pat's words were mechanical.

"Did you tell anyone you were coming to lunch at L'Eau Vite?"

"Actually I did." He paid little attention to the question. "I mentioned it to a friend at the secretariat. Then I got hung up on a call from Chicago."

A corridor door swung open. A big man in a white cassock swept by. He saw the red trim on Pat's cassock and stopped abruptly.

With tremendous effort, Pat came alive. *"Santità?"* he began, then lapsed into English. "A woman we've known all our lives was shot this morning by terrorists." His voice choked, and then, recovering his cool, he introduced each of us.

The Pope had an approving smile for Ellen, whose hand he held longer than any other pope of this century would; a courteous handshake for Herb, who, thank God, didn't try to establish that he was only a fringe observer of Catholics; and a frosty twinkle for me.

He extended his huge hands in front of his chest. "May I bless the woman?"

"Si, Santità," said a nun who had materialized from nowhere. *"Per favore."*

Pat looked at me desperately. "Would you go . . . Father . . . I . . ."

I was in business again.

So the Pope, the busy little nun, and I went into Maureen's room. She opened her tired eyes just as he blessed her, grinned a weak grin, and extended her hand. The Pope took it gently, his face showing as much pain as I felt.

Maureen began softly to pray. "Remember, O most gracious Virgin Mary"—the Pope and I joined her in St. Bernard's old prayer, he in heavily accented English, I in a voice hoarse with grief—"that never was it known that anyone who fled to Thy protection, implored Thy help, or sought Thy assistance was left unaided. Inspired by this confidence, O Virgin of Virgins, my Mother, I fly unto Thee, to Thee do I come, before Thee I stand, sinful and sorrowful. O Mother of the word incarnate, despise not my petitions and my needs but in Thy mercy hear and answer me. Amen."

Maureen closed her eyes and smiled.

John Paul's eyes were deep in sorrow as he said good-bye. He took my hand, almost tenderly. The man knew what suffering was from the inside.

Half an hour later, we all stood around Maureen's bed. The last moments were near. Pat had entered the death room reluctantly. Ellen began the rosary, since neither priest seemed to think of it.

Maureen Cunningham Haggarty slipped out of life much more quietly than she had lived. One moment she was breathing; the next moment she was not.

"Dona ei pacem," I said. "Peace at last, Cousin Mo."

Herb led Ellen gently from the room. They would have to meet Sheila at the airport.

The Cardinal and I stood in silence, looking down at the dead body of a woman we both loved.

After a long while, Pat turned to me. "I did it all for you, Kevin," he said. He was calm, almost philosophical. "I did everything in my life to please you, and you never once said a kind word to me, ever. I played basketball for you; I went to the seminary for you; I became a priest for you; I saved the diocese for you; I voted for the Pope for you; and you never gave a damn. You're still what you always were, the rich bastard who patronizes everyone and loves no one."

I said nothing.

Pat went on, almost as if he were in a reverie. "You're the leader and the writer and the intellectual, the priest everyone admires. I can be a cardinal, and I'm still the garbage man's son to you. You watch me and criticize me and judge me. You don't care about me; you don't love me; you don't give a fuck whether I love you or not. You've ruined my love; you've taken everything away from me. Now Maureen is gone, and I don't care whether I live or die."

His voice had become choked, his face twisted in grief.

"Maybe you're right, Pat," I said. "I haven't been the kind of friend you've wanted. I—"

"I loved you more than all the others," he said. He knelt beside the bed, sobbing quietly.

I went out of the room, turning only for a final glance at Maureen's peaceful madonna face.

EPILOGUE

1981

I helped Ellen climb out of the pond.

"Old lady can't quite make it by herself anymore," she smiled. "Not when there's a strong arm around, anyway."

"Gracious Titania, like good red wine . . ."

"Stop it, silly." She brushed her lips against mine before she slipped a shirt, matching the green of her swimsuit, over her head. The quick touch of lips was familiar now, but still surprising.

"Titania," I said, "is an imp, a female Puck, a woman leprechaun—"

"Be quiet," she said, "and enjoy the sunshine."

The sun was blazing hot in the sky above the trees. We sat at the edge of the pond, our feet dangling in the water. The old magic would never quite return. It was now just a pool for swimming in before supper with Ellen and Herb.

"How does Pat like his new job in Rome?" she asked cautiously.

"Art McGrath says he loves it." I pulled my towel more tightly around my shoulders despite the heat.

"Was he really kicked upstairs? Do they know about him and Mo?"

"As to the first, it depends on whom you talk to. The position of head of the congregation that reviews canonizations may seem downwardly mobile, but he *is* the only American in the Curia."

"And the second?"

"You saw the newspaper stories. The *carabiniere* raided a cell of the Slaves of St. Anthony; four young men killed, one young woman in a mental clinic. Martinelli is conspicuous in his absence from Rome. Officially, no one knows the reason for Maureen's murder. That doesn't mean that Wojtyla doesn't have some guesses."

There was a silence between us, the only sound the buzzing of the flies.

"You didn't let him down." She put her arm around me and leaned her head on my shoulder. "You're not responsible for any of our lives. Patrick, Maureen, and God knows I—we all made our own decisions. We lived our own lives. Mourn, Kevin, but don't brood."

"What if I hadn't been so damned responsible? What if I had left all of you alone—"

I was cut short by delighted laughter. "Oh, my God, Kevin. I'd be the fat woman in the circus if you'd left me alone." She gracefully extricated herself from our embrace but continued to hold my hand.

In her joyous laughter we were both young again; our lives were beginning; they stretched out ahead of us like the mysterious forest beyond the pond.

"Laughter, like love," she said, as if reading my mind, "is stronger than death. You know that, Kevin. You preach it. Why don't you practice it? Why don't you let all of us love you?"

The setting sun turned the clouds lingering over the Wisconsin treetops pink, then gold.

Part of me had died with Maureen in that room in the Gemelli Clinic. Another part was being born here by my spirit-haunted pond.

Pain . . . chaos . . . rebirth . . . death . . . laughter . . . resurrection. Love stronger than death. A woman wrote that line at the end of the Song of Solomon.

Maureen, Patsy, Mom, the Colonel, Cardinal Meyer . . . all stronger than death. Ellen, who would go down into the valley of darkness laughing.

"You *will* let me love you?" A hint of anxiety in the grin.

"Do I have any choice?"

"None whatever. You never did."

All the pictures blurred together in the colors of the setting sun. I'd have to straighten things out with Pat somehow.

"Let's go have supper," I said, breaking the almost religious mood. "I'm starved."

"Typical Irish male," she sighed, as I helped her to her feet. "I'll be expecting an adequate couplet by tomorrow morning."

"For you, Titania," I said, shoving her in the direction of the house, "nothing will ever be adequate."

As we walked back to the house and supper with the Strausses and the Brennans and the Currans and the McNeils, I could hear in the back of my head—in Latin, so God could understand—the De Profundis, the psalm for the dead. I was asking God to give peace and light to James and Mary Brennan, to Timothy Curran, to Maureen Cunningham, and to Patsy Carrey.

Out of the depths I cry to you, O Lord;
    Lord, hear my voice!
Let your ears be attentive
    to my voice in supplication.

If you, O Lord, mark iniquities,
Lord, who can stand?
But with you is forgiveness,
that you may be revered.

I trust in the Lord,
my soul trusts in his word.
My soul waits for the Lord
more than sentinels wait for the dawn.
More than sentinels wait for the dawn,
Let Israel wait for the Lord.

For with the Lord is kindness
and with him is plenteous redemption;
And he will redeem Israel
from all their iniquities.